IRISH

Jack Renouf Series Book 4

JOHN F HANLEY

AUTHOR'S FOREWORD

Irish Lass is the fourth in the Jack Renouf series and follows immediately on from the third, **Diamonds For The Wolf**, which ended in June 1941. While this is a stand-alone adventure and it is not necessary for you to have read any of the first three novels, you might find these brief outlines of interest.

Jack Renouf and his immediate friends are all 18 years old when this series begins. They should be completing their education or learning trades and planning their futures. Instead they have to develop new and dangerous skills, most of which are only of use during a war. Inevitably, once put into practise, these could destroy what remains of their youthful innocence and impact severely on their humanity.

AGAINST THE TIDE (1939) is set on the island of Jersey ten miles from France and 100 from England. The narrative voice is Jack Renouf's. A farmer's son, he is eighteen and in his final term at Victoria College. He is a talented actor and a very competitive swimmer, on the brink of selection for England at the Helsinki Olympics. He has gained a place at Wadham College, Oxford to read English but his father would prefer him to do something useful. Jack is as stubborn as his father but doesn't understand why he is so angry with him all the time. Unexpected events take their relationship to breaking point as Jack and his friends attempt to disrupt a German funded plot to defeat the embargo on industrial diamonds imposed by the Democracies.

THE LAST BOAT (1940) opens in the middle of the greatest naval disaster in British history when the Luftwaffe bombs and sinks the hastily converted Cunard liner, HMT *Lancastria*. In the ten minutes of bombing and strafing, over 5,000 troops and civilians are blown apart by the high explosive bombs. These losses represent more than one third of all members of the British Expeditionary Force killed in the nine months of war so far. The news is so shocking that Churchill suppresses it and the report into the loss will remain sealed until 2040.

But this is only a beginning for Jack, Saul, Miko, and Lt Commander Brewster who survive the attack and must fight their way back to Jersey through the German advance. During this journey they encounter a cargo so important that only Miko, the refugee physicist, really understands what might happen should it be intercepted by the Nazis.

DIAMONDS FOR THE WOLF (1940) having escaped from Jersey just after the German invasion, Jack is on leave from commando training in Scotland and staying with his friend Saul in London. They are instructed by Saul's boss, Lt Commander Ian Fleming, Deputy Director Naval Intelligence, to attend a party at the Soviet Embassy in London. Fleming, who later wrote the James Bond series, has devised a plan, *Operation Ruthless,* to pinch a German code book to help Alan Turing decipher intercepted radio signals at GCHQ. This involves crashing a captured German Heinkel bomber in the English Channel and the ditched crew overpowering a Kriegsmarine vessel. He needs at least one German speaker, one pilot and three commandos. He also has another important task which will involve inserting Jack into Jersey to compile a report on its German defences. What could possibly go wrong?

If you enjoy these stories I would be most grateful if you could spare the time to post a short review on Amazon.

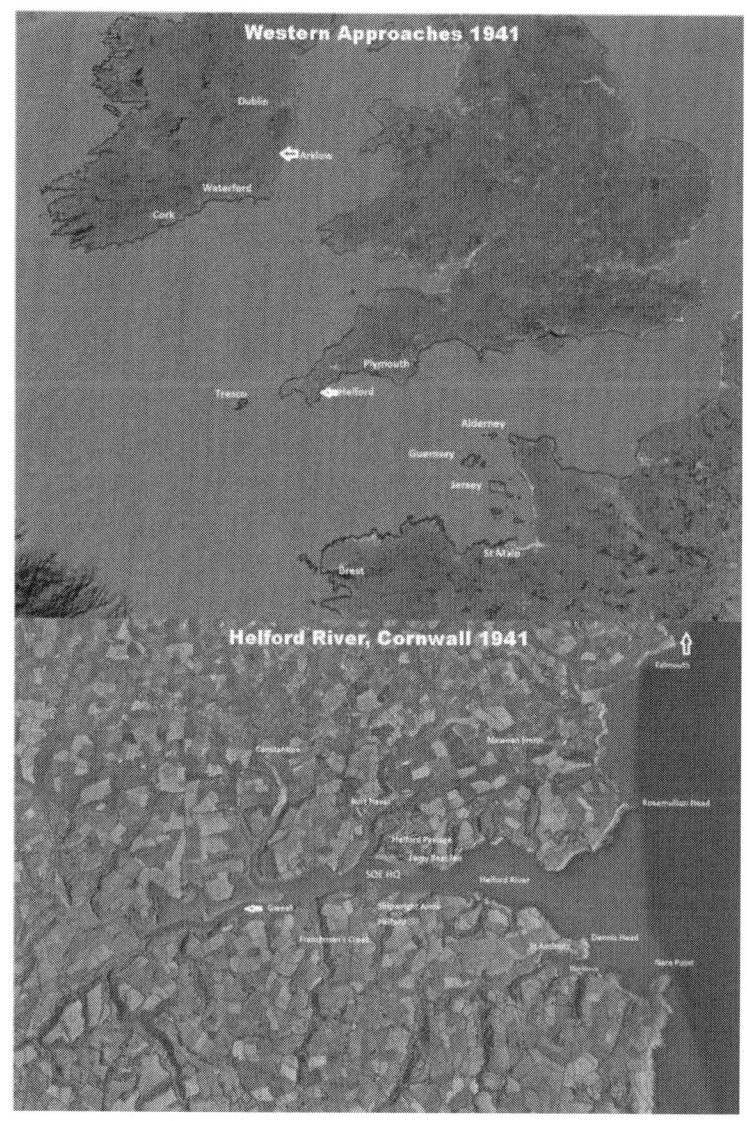

<u>25 July 1940, National Archives of Ireland</u>.

The IRA says that:

"Nazi Germany is the guardian and energising force of European policy...and a protector of national freedom".

"if...German forces should land in Ireland, they will land...as friends and liberators of the Irish people".

<u>From the IRA's War News, 23 Nov 1940</u>.

"Oh; here's to Adolph Hitler;

Who made the Britons squeal;

Sure before the fight is ended;

They will dance an Irish reel."

CHAPTER 1

Friday 11th July 1941 21:30 - Southern Ireland

What do a German Jew, a South African Jew, and two Jerseymen have in common — apart from sitting stunned in a battered Morris Eight saloon nose down in an Irish ditch? We all spoke English which was a start but cursing is a reflexive emotional action so German competed with French. Afrikaans was too embarrassed to speak as its owner had been driving the car. Willie, the German, was in the front passenger seat so had to push the rearward opening door up to extricate himself. I was sitting behind Willie and my door opened forward so it was easier. Joe unwound his six foot four inch frame and struggled out before yanking Saul's door open. He hauled him out, lifted him high enough to clear the ditch, and dropped him onto the wet road.

We were dressed in civilian clothes and masquerading as sailors but, not for the first time, I wondered how convincing we looked. Joe was extra-large in every area, from his massive head, cauliflower ears, distorted nose, lantern jaw, and a mouth large enough to accommodate two doughnuts at a time. At nearly seven feet, his wingspan exceeded his height by eight inches which though ideal for defending a water polo goal, made him look rather odd. His hands and feet were huge which was an added bonus for swimming. His party trick was to hoist a galvanised bucket of seawater over his head and walk it for over a hundred yards in deep water. His hair was black and cut short but he still retained the side parting his mother had favoured when he was a child. Though hooded by eyebrows reshaped through playing rugby, his eyes were a deep and piercing blue and his smile infectious. He had plenty of experience in motor boats but had never been on a schooner. I could only award him three out ten for his appearance as a sailor used to frigging in the rigging.

Willie had sailed over 1,000 miles on a schooner and, though not as agile as a real deckhand, was competent enough but he looked like a caricature of a Nazi soldier. Normally bald, he'd let his hair grow during his recent deployment in Syria. Now it was cropped and revealing blonde shoots. Without Joe as a comparison, he looked immense and powerful. Four years in the French Foreign Legion had reduced his body fat to virtually zero and his muscles, tuned by intense swimming training in his youth, gave him a sleek appearance. In better times, he could have replaced Johnny Weissmuller as Tarzan in a Hollywood film. His pronounced cheekbones and mischievous eyes acted as a magnet for women. I'd score him only four out of ten.

Saul looked like the academic he was. Five foot nine inches and about eleven stone, wringing wet, he hated swimming. He had extensive experience in motor boats and navigation but zero under sail. His posture was somewhere between slouched and horizontal and he moved with the energy of a hibernating tortoise yet I'd detected some change in the last six weeks. He was tight lipped about where he'd been before we joined up for this latest of Fleming's wild schemes but I had an inkling that he might have been forced into some physical activity. His ginger hair was much shorter than usual and his face seemed thinner though it was still as pale and freckled as ever. His golden eyes were his stand out feature and he prided himself on his self-taught charm. I'd known him now for nearly eight years but hadn't seen anything in that time which made me believe he looked anything like a sailor.

This left me. I'd been accused of lacking self-awareness which I didn't think was a bad thing. Growing up on a farm, I knew I had acquired considerable physical strength, particularly in my shoulders and arms. My hands roughened by working on engines, although smaller than Joe's, were also very strong and my feet were larger than they should have been for someone only five foot eleven inches tall. Like Joe, I had a large wingspan and like Willie, broad shoulders and muscles developed through swimming. We'd both trained for the Olympics and he'd been selected for the German team in 1936 until a rival exposed his Jewish parentage and he was dismissed. I'd trained for the 1940 Tokyo Games though, after the Japanese were stripped of them because of their behaviour in China, they'd been moved to Helsinki. I'd achieved a qualifying time for the British team in the 100 metres freestyle but Hitler had put paid to that. I'd also sailed over 1,000 miles on a schooner and was more agile if not as strong as Willie. My hair was growing again and curls were re-emerging, which would please my mother. So, on balance, I was probably the most likely to pass as a sailor to untrained eyes.

We'd made good time from Arklow and had just passed Gorey which reminded me of home in Jersey, as the medieval Castle of Mont Orgueil in Gorey was only a mile or so from our farm. Originally built to dissuade the French from invading the island, it was now part of the German fortifications to keep out the British. The Irish didn't need castles for that task as they had declared themselves a neutral country. I'd some experience of neutral Portugal and Spain, both run on the whim of dictators. Eire had achieved independence through force but it was still a democracy. The countryside was more open than Jersey's and lined with a mixture of sycamore and oak trees though the whole island would fit in between Gorey and Camolin.

Saul found his voice but, as he was the only one who spoke Afrikaans, addressed us in perfectly accented English and said, 'Don't blame me, you buggers. The road's wet and the sun blinded me as I rounded—'

'You seem to enjoy encounters with trunks, don't you?' I asked him.

'That was an elephant and I wasn't driving at the time —'

Willie was examining the telegraph pole which lay on its side blocking the road. He glared at Saul and spoke in his precise English. '*Petseleh*, you drive like an elephant. Why you let him, Jack?' He brushed the grass and mud from his jacket as he advanced on Saul who, for once, didn't flinch.

'You don't like driving on the left so you refused, remember? And Joe is too bloody big to get behind the wheel. As for Jack, he just wanted to daydream about that Irish colleen he was fawning over in Arklow. What was her name?'

'Erin.' Joe answered. 'Really, Jack, haven't you got enough woman trouble already without looking for more?'

'Oh shut up the lot of you. Let's see if we can get the car out of the ditch.'

Willie laughed, 'It will take a recovery vehicle with a winch or a tractor with chains to do that.'

He was right. Even Joe would struggle. As an eighteen year old, he'd towered over all of his friends and now, after two years of Army training, he was even larger and could find employment as a circus strong man when he wasn't carrying full fighting kit, a Bren gun, spare barrel, bipod, Lee Enfield rifle, several magazines for both, and half a dozen mortar rounds for his squad.

But we weren't here to fight.

In fact, Fleming had forbidden us to get into any trouble. 'It's a neutral country.' He'd drawled. 'They might hate the English but they need us for trade and employment. Of course, there's the Irish Republican Army which has declared war on the British Empire but they're really a bunch of gangsters masquerading as terrorists and no real threat. Yes, we know they're in contact with the Germans but Hitler has his plate full in the East right now. However, I would advise that you steer clear of them as they can be pretty uncivilised.'

Wise advice but coming from a man who'd so often thrown us into the deep end of his crazy schemes, not particularly helpful. However, this one appeared relatively straightforward though, as usual, he had omitted to give us the full story. Even Saul wasn't sure why he wanted us to charter an Irish schooner and sail it back to Cornwall to join the Helford Flotilla in the base he'd helped set up to insert Special Operations Executive agents into France. It was our fault, I suppose. When Willie and I had returned from Portugal on the schooner *Cymric,* the captain, Dermot McConnell, had suggested that his owner might be open to some lucrative charter work — off the books of course. Fleming had dismissed the idea at the time and sent us to France instead. But now he wanted that schooner — probably hoping he could pass it off as a neutral, in one of S.O.E.'s sabotage trips to France. Not ours to reason why, though another of his schemes seemed to be in tatters as we were over fifty miles short of our destination where McConnell would be waiting for us. Instead, we were stranded on this deserted road as the sun set over the hills to our right. Camolin was the nearest town, six miles away, though the Dublin and South Eastern Railway ran almost parallel to the road about half a mile to our left.

The four of us were in the service of the King — even Willie, who was German and on detachment from the French Foreign Legion. Saul and I were sub-lieutenants in the Royal Navy Volunteer Reserve and wore the wavy green Special Branch stripe under the single gold one. Joe was a corporal in the Hampshire Regiment but based in Helford as part of the Flotilla where he had responsibility for a whole armoury of British and foreign weapons. However, Lt Commander Ian Fleming, Deputy Director of Naval Intelligence, who'd appropriated our services for himself, had insisted that we carry out this mission unarmed. Willie and I had pocket knives, Joe had his fists, and Saul would have to rely on his wits and his tongue.

I'd salvaged a torch from the car and asked Joe and

Willie to hop down into the ditch and lift the front of the Morris so that I could inspect the damage. Relegating Saul to the role of lookout, I crawled under the chassis and shone the torch over the underpinnings while the other two grunted impatiently above me. The light confirmed what I'd suspected — the track, drop arm, and axle beam rods were bent. Given a hoist and the right tools, I might be able to repair it. I wriggled out and shook my head.

'Joe, just pop back along the road will you. Wave down any vehicles and warn them. Saul, retrieve our gear from the car. Willie and I will scout the area.' Fleming had put me in charge again even though Saul had six month's seniority over me. Willie was vastly more experienced and more capable in all military matters apart from underwater wrestling and sniping, but he'd refused to become an officer. As far as I knew, his father was still a colonel in the Wehrmacht so perhaps that was one of the reasons as he'd disowned his son and Polish wife when the Gestapo had discovered that she was three-quarter Jewish. That was enough for Willie to be identified as *Mischling zweiten Grades* under the Nuremberg Laws and he'd been stripped of his Reich citizenship. Shortly after, he'd fled the country and joined the French Foreign Legion. His mother had disappeared and he feared the worst for her. If a father and son reunion ever occurred, I suspected that Willie would emerge as an orphan.

Neither Joe nor I had any Jewish blood but, much to Saul's amusement, I'd identified as a Jew since playing *Shylock* in a school play. I also had a daughter who was a quarter Jewish – one of the several parts of my relationship complications that concerned Joe.

I was musing about that when Willie called me over to the bank where several lengths of scots pine, fashioned into telegraph poles, had been stacked. It appeared that the one in the road had fallen or been pushed from the top of the pile. There were footprints all around the stack but we couldn't spot any other sign of human activity though I sensed we were being watched from the tree line. We gathered around the pole and I called out for Joe to come back and help us move it. That should be easy enough.

'We passed a road a few hundred yards back with a sign mentioning quarry traffic. If there is one, it should have a workshop. It's much closer than Camolin. They should have a telephone. Shall we clear the road and hike up there?' Saul asked.

'Sounds like a plan but can you manage to walk that far or do you want Willie and Joe to carry you?' I teased him. His addiction to cigarettes and dislike of exercise marked him out in the new world of fit young men called upon to undo the serious errors of politicians whose love of a peaceful life had so blinded them to reality.

Saul threw a few Yiddish words at me, which made Willie laugh and then three of us, whose muscles weren't just in our mouths, set about moving the former tree trunk.

Our invisible watchers must have been waiting for us to grab the pole so that our hands were occupied.

The first voice, thick with a Southern Irish accent echoed from the woods. 'Ands on yer 'eads!'

That didn't sound too friendly but Saul surprised me by responding in German.

I caught the gist of it but kept quiet, as although fluent in French and now competent in Russian, I'd never made much effort to learn the language of the enemy. Joe was limited to English with a heavy Jersey accent and a smattering of gutter French. Willie had at least six European languages plus Yiddish and Hebrew and he had that commanding tone of a real German. I almost stood to attention as he barked out something.

The response was immediate but from a different direction. 'Shut yer gob, ye maggot, or I'll shut it for yer.'

Another voice — this time from the other side of the road beyond the ditch. 'On yer knees and 'ands on de groun' wha we can see 'em.'

Willie spoke in broken English with a strong German accent this time. 'What want you with us?'

'Ye German?' Another voice.

'Ya – you speak?' Willie asked.

I launched into some French, which must have baffled them, as there was silence for a moment followed by a sharp crack as a bullet pinged off the Morris then ricocheted over our heads.

Communication skills exhausted, we stood up and put our hands on our "eads". I'd counted three voices and the shot had been fired from another direction so we were surrounded. They were almost certainly IRA so Saul's German pretense might be the best course of action for the moment.

Gradually they revealed themselves. Two with Lee Enfield rifles, two more with Mauser K.98 rifles, one with an MP-40 machine pistol and three with what looked like Webley revolvers. This mix would be an ammunition nightmare for their quartermaster. They were young, late teens perhaps; some were wearing woollen jackets similar to ours, two were in overalls, and two more were in shorts and jumpers.

Saul broke the deadlock by speaking in English with a strong Afrikaans accent. 'We do not understand you. Can you speak English?'

An older man wearing a trilby and a shabby three-piece suit, approached from the trees. About five foot seven with a heavily pockmarked face barely disguised by a few days growth of grey stubble, he grinned then answered. 'We hate the fuckers but of course we speak their benighted language — only some of us have a brogue which you might find difficult. If I speak slowly can you understand me?' He was trying to sound like one of Fleming's aristocratic chums.

Progress of a sort, so I responded in a strong French accent. 'Merci, monsieur, who are you?'

'No, you caffler, we ask the questions so don't vex me. If you are Germans, what the feck are doing parking your old banger in the shuck?'

'The what?'

'Ditch, you bollix! Now answer my feckin' question.'

Was this a random ambush – highway robbery per-haps or had they been tipped off about us? We had agreed with the schooner owner's representatives that, if challenged by the IRA, we would say that we were chartering a vessel but for the Reich and not the hated British so I responded in French accented English. 'Someone rolled a telegraph pole into the road and, rather than attack it with the bumper, our driver chose to kiss the...shuck instead so thank you, but yes we do represent the Reich. May we take our hands down and be civilised? We are your friends.'

He snorted. 'That remains to be seen – you could be British spies. We need to talk properly but not here.' He issued some commands in what was probably Gallic and his band of ambushers closed up on us.

One at a time, we were called forward to be frisked while covered by seven guns carefully arranged to avoid any danger to themselves. While the odds were not in our favour, even without Saul's help, I was confident that we could have disarmed three of them but the risk was too great. One at a time, we had our hands tied behind our backs with twisted wire – this gang had some experience in this business. Flying head-butts and savage kicks apart we were effectively neutralised and at their mercy.

Once he was satisfied, their leader told us to walk in single file back along the road. Two hurried ahead and covered us with their rifles while two more kept behind and to the side — out of the line of fire. The remainder finished our task and rolled the pole off the road.

As Saul had noted, there was a turn-off with a signpost with details about a quarry and we were guided uphill in the gathering dusk until we arrived at an unmanned gateway. We were ushered inside the complex, into a large concrete storehouse and made to sit cross-legged on a dusty floor dimly lit by oil lamps swinging from the girders above.

During the walk, I'd spotted a shed with a couple of trucks parked outside and what seemed to be a maintenance garage inside, complete with a hoist. Dotted about were quarry vehicles, which would have sufficient power and traction to extract our Morris. Now, if we could only find a way to sweet talk our way out of our restraints, we might be able to continue our journey.

CHAPTER 2

Predictably, Fleming had soon lost interest in the mission as it lacked the adventure and action he so desired for himself and left him little vicarious pleasure to extract. He'd passed our briefing over to one of his aides, Grady, a lanky, pompous RN lieutenant with an irritating false laugh, who didn't have much time for wavy navy hostilities-only officers like Saul and myself. He was thorough though, and had taken us through the risks and precautions we would need to take. The principle danger was interception by the Gardaí, which would lead to embarrassment and temporary internment. The secondary risk was the one we were facing now – capture by the IRA.

In the first case, carrying German documentation would have resulted in more than diplomatic embarrassment; especially since the Luftwaffe had bombed Dublin six weeks previously with nearly 100 casualties and 300 properties seriously damaged. An unfortunate accident or a deliberate warning to the Irish to maintain neutrality? Grady said that the jury was still out though the Germans claimed that the devious British had misdirected the Luftwaffe's navigational beams to cause the incident. Whatever the cause, it had strained diplomatic relations between Berlin and Dublin and internment for German spies could now be a very long-term affair. On this basis, we were denied any documentation and would have to rely on our cover story and adjust it to fit the circumstances.

Those had now changed and our best hope was to

pretend to be German agents and convince our captors that we were here to assist them in their declared aim of defeating the British Empire. It was clear from Grady's briefing that, although the Germans had been working with the IRA, they had not found them a particularly trustworthy or effective organisation — rather, one in decline and suffering from delusions of power. The previous August, Sean Russell, the IRA's chief of staff, had died from "natural causes" aboard the German submarine *U-65* during a mission from Wilhelmshaven to Galway. His body had been buried at sea and since then there had been little contact between the Germans and their erstwhile allies. However, Eduard Hempel, the German ambassador, working out of the legation in Dublin had been sending reports to Berlin by telegraph and shortwave radio. Our intelligence services had intercepted these though we weren't told how and MI6 provided regular updates to Naval Intelligence and S.O.E. about German activities in Ireland.

None of that was much help to us now as the IRA's leader returned carrying a Lee Enfield rifle with a fixed 18-inch bayonet. 'Now, gentlemen, let us have a frank discussion. We have some experience in these matters and we have the sole use of this facility until Monday morning, if necessary.' He pointed the rifle to a steel beam above us from which hung chains and a pulley system. 'We haven't had the pleasure of holding a conversation with any British soldiers yet but we've tested this apparatus on some traitors from our own country.'

One of the overall-clad youngsters grabbed the dangling chains and worked the contraption along the beam towards us until it was nearly touching Saul. He didn't recoil which seemed to annoy the leader who reached forward and prodded him with the bayonet.

Saul didn't react but just looked up at him placidly, and asked, 'what's your name?'

'Never mind my feckin' name. I want to know yours – and the real one at that!'

'Well, you only had to ask. There's no need for violence. I'm Saul Marcks, a member of the *Afrikaner Broederbond*, and I hate the British Empire just as much as you do, sir.'

'So that might explain your use of German. But what the feck are you doing in Ireland?'

'Carrying out orders, just like yourself. We're here to collect a ship – a schooner — to run under neutral colours and disrupt that bastard Churchill's incursions into France.'

That was music to the Irishman's ears as he smiled and advanced towards Willie. 'You spoke German as well. What's your feckin' story?'

'*Oberleutnant* Wilhelm Von Gersdoff, of the Abwehr, but you can call me Willie if you prefer.'

'I think I'd prefer it if I had you hanging upside down from that chain and Shaun here teaching you some manners with this bayonet. Why, I believe, he amused himself for nearly two hours with the last bastard who took the piss. Isn't that right, Shaun?'

'Nearly four 'ours it wus before de shoite bled oyt, Mr O'Farrell.'

'And did you learn anything of value?' asked Saul

O'Farrell laughed. 'Not after the first twenty minutes – the rest was for amusement!' He prodded me next. 'You're not German are you?'

'No, I'm Breton and have no love for the English. My name is Jacques Renouf and I'm working for *le Régime de Vichy* as is my friend, Joseph Buesnal, who is something of an expert in German weaponry.'

That was a stab in the dark but I'd seen one of the youngsters fiddling with his MP-40 machine pistol and wondered how good their training had been. Joe was indeed an expert. Perhaps O'Farrell might welcome some help. We knew the IRA had received some shipments of guns and ammunition landed via submarine – making those work effectively wasn't easy without comprehensive training.

Willie picked up my cue. 'Tell me, Mr O'Farrell, is there anything we can do to help you? Do you have any German equipment which needs servicing for example?'

But O'Farrell wasn't completely daft. 'I'm still not convinced you aren't British spies. You don't have any papers and how did you get here?'

Willie answered. 'I'm sure you can understand why we aren't carrying identification as we were more likely to be picked up by the Gardaí than yourselves. I understand that we Germans aren't so popular after those Luftwaffe *dummkopfs* bombed Dublin last month. We did have something better than documents though – 1,000 punts worth of gold coins. We gave that as a deposit for the schooner. It was meant to be ready for us in Arklow but it was moved to Waterford for final fitting out. We were loaned that car to get there and collect it.'

Sometimes the truth is better than an elaborate lie.

'Who took the deposit?' O'Farrell asked

'The deal was arranged in Brest with a schooner captain on his way back from Portugal. He's waiting for us in Waterford—'

'Name?'

'Brendan MacKenna. He's a charming man – hates the British but...'

'But what?'

'Not sure he has any love for you Republicans either.'

'Fecked if I care.' He clicked his heels together in a parody of a German. 'Patrick Desmond O'Farrell, commanding officer, 2nd Active Service Unit, North Wexford Brigade, 3rd Eastern Division, *Óglaigh na hÉireann* — that's Irish Republican Army to you heathens — shits on all snitches, squealers, and English arse-lickers. It won't be long now before our friends and allies help us unite Ireland and the Brits and filthy Jews are just a rusting stain on history. Then we'll take rats like MacKenna and make them choke on those words.' He beckoned one of the youngsters over to him. 'Get some paper and a pen then write this down – in feckin' English and capital letters so that I can read it.' He smiled, revealing brown teeth then prodded Willie again. 'You still haven't told me who you met in Arklow and how you got there.'

'Well, it's a long story but we didn't swim or parachute in. I can't tell you any more than that.'

'So, you came by submarine – that's not such a feckin' secret is it? But whose palm did you cross with the gold?'

'I think his name was Foley – we met in The Marlborough Hall on St Mary's Road. He was acting for the owner's agent but I don't know either of their names. Our contact was MacKenna and we expected to meet him in Arklow – not have to drive all the bloody way to Waterford—'

'Where in Waterford?'

'The Munster Bar — on the Mall.'

He nodded. 'I know it well. Now, you just sit there comfortably while I make some phone calls.'

Saul called out, 'while you're doing that, I'm dying for a piss. Can you take me outside or something...?'

'Feck — Shaun can cut it off for you if you like. OK, two of you take the poxy coppernob outside – give him a clatter if he tries any shenanigans.'

Saul was hauled to his feet and the wire removed before being pushed towards the entrance. If it had been Willie, Joe or me then there might have been a chance of overpowering the two guards but O'Farrell's assessment was correct. There was little to fear from Saul other than an ear bashing. I tried to speak to Willie in French but was told to shut up by one of the other kids.

Willie's story was close enough to the truth though he'd invented the names. O'Farrell might find someone in Waterford or Arklow to ask questions but that would take time and that was our friend in these circumstances. I glanced up at the chains and imagined Shaun playing gleefully with a swinging human shackled upside down by his ankles until he was just a corpse.

CHAPTER 3

It's amazing how time flies when you're sitting cross-legged on a cold floor with rusty wire biting into wrists trapped behind your back. I didn't waste it though and rehearsed several possible moves – all of which seemed to end in abject failure. There was a glimmer of hope when Saul was dragged back clutching a table. Another bespectacled and grossly overweight man shuffled in with some papers in his hands. O'Farrell followed carrying a cup which, from the smell, was full of good coffee. Oh the joys of neutrality. Two more youngsters appeared carrying three chairs between them and placed these under one of the overhead lamps. Saul was pushed on to one of them and the table placed in front of him. O'Farrell sat down alongside just out of reach of our feet while his fat companion placed paper and pen on the table.

He handed a booklet to O'Farrell who waved it at us. 'Do you know what this is?'

Before I could provide an inappropriate response, Willie spoke, "*Anleitung für die Bedienung und Verwendung des M.G.34*". It's an idiot's guide — the field manual for the MG-34 machine gun.'

'Give the shite hawk a banana. It is indeed and it's in feckin' German and of no feckin' use. After this Afrikaan shoite has finished writing down your story, he's going to translate it for us.'

'How many MG-34s do you have?' Willie asked.

'Jaysus! None of your feckin' business—'

'But you want us to show you how to use them?'

'Not you – Frankenstein can do it.' He pointed to Joe. 'You say he's an expert.'

Two of the kids pointed their Lee Enfield rifles at Joe and worked the bolts to chamber a round in each. Another slipped behind him and cut the wire with a pair of pliers. A new youth appeared carrying what looked like a brand new MG-34 — a squad light machine gun — with a much higher rate of fire and muzzle velocity than our Bren gun. This example was complete with sling and bipod. It was a complex beast, expensive to produce but really effective in action until it jammed. The manual would provide all the information they needed to operate and maintain it if Saul translated it accurately. Unfortunately, unlike the rest of us, he wouldn't have the knowledge or experience to sabotage the instructions effectively.

Before the youth handed him the gun I spoke up. 'If you'd been able to read the manual you would realise that you can't field strip a machine gun on a dusty floor. You'll need some clean sacking or a mat.'

O'Farrell snapped his fingers and someone scurried off and returned with a rug which he placed in front of Joe who was now kneeling in anticipation. He was about to show off like a magician which should draw the attention of everyone. Of course, they wouldn't provide any live ammunition for the machine-gun but this could be our only chance. There were now two Lee-Enfields with bullets up the spout pointing at Joe, two heavy Webley revolvers out of effective range for untrained fingers, two Mauser K.98s, which would take precious seconds to load and an MP-40 sub machine gun which I suspected was for show rather than action. I didn't think there was anyone behind us so the odds weren't as bad as they'd been earlier. During Joe's demonstration I planned to ease myself up into a loose crouch, ostensibly to get a better view but ready to spring up if the opportunity presented itself. Everything would depend on Saul. Could my oldest friend who'd studiously avoided our school's cadet force and never shown any interest in weapon handling, whom I had protected from bullies, and had never wanted to learn how to fight, seize the moment and give Willie and me a chance? Apart from English, the only other language Saul, Willie, and I had in common was Russian. I rehearsed the words I'd need, turned to watch Joe begin his show — then a new idea struck me.

'Commander O'Farrell, how long do you think it will take Joseph to strip and reassemble the MG?' I asked.

He looked at his fat companion who shrugged and muttered something.

'My quartermaster says the feckin' thing is jammed so it's going to take him five minutes at least.' O'Farrell laughed. 'It he does it in less, you can all have a cup of coffee before we beat the shoite out of you!'

'And if he does it in less than one minute and dry fires it afterwards, how about something to eat as well?'

He snorted. 'Fack away. You want jam on your egg?' The gang laughed. 'I tell you what, yer chancer, as you seem as sharp as a beach ball, if he doesn't do it in under one minute, I'm gonna wrap that chain around your ankles, hoist you up and Shaun can tickle your arse with his bayonet.'

'I thought you Irish were more shrewd with your betting. Don't you prefer to fix the race before it starts?'

'Jaysus, you're a mentaller. Are you suggesting that we break his fingers first and blindfold him? Don't be so feckin' stupid!'

I knew that there were twenty separate movements to the disassembly, so forty in all, then the dry firing. I needed them totally focused. 'Breaking his fingers would indeed be stupid but I bet you coffee, food, and our freedom that he can do it all blindfolded and in well under a minute!'

O'Farrell conferred with his fat friend again. 'Fine, have it your way. If he succeeds then we'll consider your requests. If he fails then, after this Afrikaan pisspot has translated the manual, I'll knee cap the ginger bastard. Sound fair to you?'

I had to sound less confident, so hesitated and grimaced before replying. 'Do you have a second hand on your watch?'

O'Farrell smirked. 'Of course, but it looks like you're brickin' it already.'

'OK, let's increase the bet. If he does it, you'll help us repair the car and escort us to Waterford—'

'And if he doesn't?'

'I'll tell you where to find the rest of the gold coins.'

'Jaysus, Mary, and Joseph. You're as useless as tits on a bull. Now you've told me there's gold, we'll all have our own bets on how long it will take Shaun to scrape that little piece of information out of you with his bayonet.'

I glared at him. '*Merde*, it will be a lot longer than Joseph takes with the gun.'

He held out his wrist and tapped the watch. 'We'll see so—'

I interrupted. 'When it gets to twelve o'clock call out and he'll start. Thirty seconds later he'll be finished!'

All the Irishmen hooted.

I knew Joe wouldn't be able to achieve that time but I hoped he, Saul, and Willie would be counting in their heads.

The kid with the machine gun placed it in on the rug. Joe put his hands on it then someone produced a canvas hood and pulled it over his massive head.

O'Farrell looked at me and grinned. 'Five...four...three...two...one...begin!'

After seven seconds Joe had removed the sling, bipod, and butt and was extracting the driving spring. Six moves later he had removed the bolt and had the long barrel in his hand and the count in my head had reached twenty-seven.

I called out, ' *sbit' oruzhiye*, Saul!' then sprang forwards and kicked O'Farrell in the nuts. Willie took out two of the kids and Joe used the barrel to smash Shaun and his helper to the ground. He whipped off the hood and was setting about the two with revolvers as Willie demolished the one with the K.98 and I head-butted the one with the MP-40. I whirled round to help Saul but was amazed to see that the two guarding him were on the floor and he was smashing the fat man in his enormous belly with the butt of a Lee-Enfield. He didn't even seem to be panting after his exertions. Who was this new Saul? He'd need to explain what he'd done with the old one!

'Forty seconds,' called out Joe as he pointed at the casualties. 'I'm not sure we can reassemble this lot though!'

He used the pliers to cut the wires round our wrists while Saul collected all the weapons. Our action had taken all of ten seconds. Joe had deliberately slowed down stripping the machine gun so that he had the long barrel in his hand when we reached thirty seconds. We all knew his record for the party trick of fieldstripping and reassembling a MG-34 blindfolded was forty seconds — fortunately, the bogtrotters hadn't believed me.

It took rather longer to clean up and hobble the remnants of the Irish Republican Army. Willie retrieved his knife and took O'Farrell away for a chat. Normally, his "chats" were relatively quiet but this one was particularly noisy and, when he returned with the Irish commander, we weren't surprised to find the evil bastard's socks were stuffed in his mouth.

Thus, acting on "information received"', we found the remaining weapons, ammunition and explosives in the concrete store the quarrymen had been "persuaded" to lease to their terrorist protectors. Joe checked all the weapons. With some care and proper maintenance, all six MG-34s would be serviceable, as would the ten MP-40s. The rifles were robust enough to survive the handling of these incompetent nitwits and fortunately they hadn't tried to activate the stick grenades. There were several 500 gr 'Westfalit' demolition charges and two crates full of 325 gr sticks of 'Dynamit' with another 100 or so Nr 8 detonators. Enough to start a small war if they'd had the expertise to use them.

We had that knowledge and experience so decided to put those explosives to good use. Tempting though it was, we decided to leave the German weapons behind. We kept four of the Webleys along with a supply of .455 hollow point rounds — real man stoppers which had been banned by the Hague Convention— and bundled all the other weaponry and grenades back into the store. Explosions are quite frequent occurrences in quarries and accidents do happen. This was going to be a spectacular one. The quarry staff wouldn't return until Monday. Whomever O'Farrell had telephoned, might turn up sooner but there was nothing we could do about that now. If they did arrive before we left we were confident that the IRA would suffer even more reductions in their ranks.

This left the problem of the Morris and O'Farrell's now in-Active Service Unit. I didn't really want to spend the rest of the night repairing the car but we couldn't leave it in the ditch, so Joe and Willie took a caterpillar-tracked quarry vehicle and some chains then retrieved it and dumped it in the garage. That would be a puzzle for the workers. There was a serviceable Ford flatbed truck we could use for the rest of our journey.

We had to make a decision about this pathetic gang. They'd not been prepared to show us any mercy and had tortured and killed some of their own people on this site. Willie persuaded O'Farrell to boast about other successes they had enjoyed. On his admission, the total of deaths was in excess of twenty. He also confessed to more than a dozen knee-cappings and numerous savage beatings including several administered to mothers and sisters of those suspected of not being sufficiently anti-British.

We had been briefed that the Irish government despised the IRA and had executed several for their crimes in Ireland. In reality, they were little more than thieves and gangsters driven by a perverted ideology, so delusional it had elevated Hitler to an iconic status. Willie, as usual, had a robust approach and wanted to execute the lot of them by placing them with the weapons and blowing them all up together. Joe felt that they didn't deserve any mercy. Saul was more ambivalent and thought that it was the Irish State's problem and that we should wash our hands of it. We'd decommissioned them – that was enough. I tended to agree with him but we needed to leave a message without compromising our own friends who were letting us lease the schooner. That meant we couldn't leave the Morris in the garage. I had to either fix it or dispose of it where it couldn't be found. Reluctantly, I set to work and, with Willie's help, just after midnight, it was roadworthy again. Steering would be a problem and the track rods were not entirely straight so it wasn't going to be a smooth ride. We now needed to get a message to McConnell that we'd had an accident and been delayed. He certainly wouldn't be waiting in the Munster, as we were due to meet him some distance away in Campile.

At some point we'd need to make an anonymous call to the Gardaí and tell them where to find our "terrorists" but these needed a lesson before we left them. Willie was disappointed that I'd decided to be lenient and he reminded me that we weren't going to beat the Nazis by playing by the rules. He had a point. We'd both killed several times before without our consciences being too troubled, and often in a premeditated and callous manner, though those particular creatures had been beyond all hope of redemption for their inhumane cruelty.

This was different. Most of these were teenagers following orders and probably terrified of the consequences if they didn't. Shaun was different — he'd boasted about his sadism and was clearly a psychopath. O'Farrell was also beyond redemption. Dead men tell no tales and we were going to be stuck in Ireland for another couple of days at least. We'd told O'Farrell too much about our plans and he might try to buy some favours with the Gardaí by giving them chapter and verse which would put us, McConnell, and the owners in Arklow, in jeopardy. Perhaps Willie was right.

Joe, who didn't usually get involved in discussions, put it simply. 'If the bastard had found out we were British what would he have done with us?'

Saul was even more direct. 'If he'd known that two of us were Jews, how long would he have allowed Shaun to play with us before we *"shuffled off this mortal coil"* bleeding and screaming?'

'I understand but these silly kids don't really, do they?'

'O'Farrell and the fat man are the real problem – they know too much. Be honest, Jack, they sealed their own death warrant when they captured us. You know what we would have done if they'd been Nazis don't you?' Willie patted my shoulder. 'There's only one solution for them. Spare the kids if you must, but make an example of that little sadist — preferably with his own bayonet.'

I sighed then nodded my assent and he and Joe dragged O'Farrell and his quartermaster off to the concrete store so they could commune with their weapons and munitions. Saul and I secured the kids to the walls of the storeroom by wiring their ankles and wrists. During this grisly activity we spoke in either German or French to reinforce that we weren't British. I ignored their squealing by imagining what it must have been like when they were watching and enjoying Shaun using his bayonet to butcher a living human. Finally, we wrapped the chains around Shaun's legs and used the pulley to hoist him upside down until he was swinging five feet off the ground. Saul approached with the K.98 and prodded him gently but he screamed and begged until I could bear it no longer so I ripped the socks off one of the other kids and stuffed them in his mouth.

Ironic applause signalled Willie's return. He inspected my handiwork then pulled Shaun's head close so that he could whisper in his ear. It had been bright red as the blood pooled in it but Willie's words must have reversed the effect of gravity as the colour disappeared from his face. As it did from the others when Willie whipped out his knife, ripped the shirt from Shaun's body then carved the Swastika into his chest.

Two years previously, the most violence I had witnessed had been in a water polo match against the old enemy, Guernsey, during the annual Inter-insular. Since then, I'd witnessed horrors which should have made eighteen year old Jack Renouf vomit his heart up and prevent him from ever sleeping again. But, such is total war, I'd become so desensitised that I embraced dreamless sleep with enthusiasm.

As a parting gesture, mainly for the benefit of the youngsters who would have to retell their story many times to the authorities and friends, Willie gave a speech in German. He told them how much the Reich valued their assistance but that kidnapping and threatening to torture and kill those entrusted to carry out the Fuhrer's historic mission was unacceptable and needed to be punished. Saul translated this for them before we clicked our heels together, raised our right arms, and shouted, 'Heil Hitler!'

I used the telephone and called the emergency number we'd been given to contact McConnell. The call was answered by a woman with a rich Irish lilt to her voice. It was well after midnight but I could hear the raucous sounds of a party in the background. McConnell wasn't available at the moment but she promised to deliver a message. She seemed amused by my call and sounded more than a little tipsy. I asked if McConnell was with her. She found that even more amusing and told me to come straight over and she'd retrieve him for me. I asked her where she was. 'Horswood House' was the response which was the address we'd been given. I'd worked out that at an average speed of 30 mph we could reach there in about two hours — telephone poles and elephants permitting. So I told her that we'd be there about two a.m. and asked whether we should rest up somewhere first. She feigned horror and insisted that we make haste before all the booze ran out. I promised I would do my best to bring four thirsty men there as quickly as I could then asked for her name.

'Molly,' she said 'What's yours?'

'Jack,' I replied.

She hiccupped and told me how much she was looking forward to meeting me in person then hung up. That lifted my spirits but I decided to keep the party as a surprise from the others just in case we were further delayed.

As we left, Willie cut the telephone lines into the building then shinned up the nearest pole to sever those as well. A few minutes after the Morris had rattled and shuddered down the quarry road, the weapons store erupted behind us vapourising O'Farrell, the fat man, their delusional dreams, and all the Nazi gifts inside.

CHAPTER 4

Leaving witnesses behind was a risk especially as they would remember the details of the car including its registration number so I asked Saul to remind me to get a message to our contacts in Arklow and alert them. Perhaps they could report the car's theft to the Gardaí. My shoulders were shaking with the effort of holding the steering wheel as I hadn't been able to straighten the track rod or the drop arm completely and every bump or undulation in the road caused considerable vibration. While I'd had it on the hoist, I'd checked the brake linings and suspension. The car had led a hard life but had been well maintained though the hydraulic shock absorbers were sealed units and couldn't be serviced — only replaced. I'd also cleaned the plugs, checked the timing, and adjusted the flow through the S.U. carburettor. She should last for another fifty miles at least but the engine wasn't happy as the tappets kept up a raucous chorus of complaint.

Talking was difficult but I asked Willie to tell us what more he'd extracted from O'Farrell, especially how he'd discovered us in the first place. We'd lied about the submarine of course and had actually been rowed in during nautical twilight from *Daisy May*, the only one of Helford Flotilla's Cornish fishing boats which wasn't disguised as a Frenchie, and landed at Arklow Head. We hadn't been spotted until after our meeting when we'd picked up the Morris and stopped for a meal and a drink in The Olde Ship on Main Street. One of O'Farrell's informants worked in the pub and was suspicious, especially as we looked foreign but spoke in odd English accents and were studying a map. He listened in while serving us and learned that we were talking about following the railway line and driving through Enniscorthy to New Ross. He made a note of our car then called O'Farrell which had given him time to set up an ambush. Hopefully, the kids who might have listened to our story would either forget it or dismiss it as a tissue of lies. For their own health I hoped they would be so traumatised they'd forget everything.

We had arranged to rendezvous with *Daisy May* the following day at 18:00, twenty nautical miles south of Hook Head at 51° 47' north and 06° 58' west. The schooner needed a full crew of ten though only four would transfer from the fishing boat for the nearly 200 nautical mile haul to Helford. We'd expected to be sailing from Arklow to the meeting point, which, under auxiliary power and the few sails four of us could manage, would have taken at least eight hours. From the mouth of the River Barrow it shouldn't take more than three. If we failed to turn up on time, *Daisy May* would circle around for an hour then return to that spot every twelve hours for two further days before scuttling back to Helford and giving Fleming the news that another of his plans had sunk without trace.

Under prodding from Willie, Saul revealed the mystery of his transformation from wastrel to warrior. While Rachel and I had been on our twelve-week RNVR course at the Royal Naval College in Greenwich and taking Russian lessons at night, he'd been having painful lessons in unarmed combat culminating in two weeks at the Achnacarry Special Training Centre where he'd been tutored in the dark arts of silent killing. Joe, Willie, and I had all endured life in that forbidding academy and our old instructor in close combat, Bill Fairbairn, seemingly remembered us, was surprised to hear we were still alive, and sent his regards.

In unison, we recited his training mantra: 'Get tough, get down in the gutter, and win at all costs... I teach what is called Gutter Fighting. There's no fair play, no rules except one: kill or be killed.'

'Happy days,' said Willie.

'Bugger that – bloody nightmare. How could you enjoy that torture?' was Saul's response.

'Worked for you...and fortunately, saved us didn't it?' I said which ended that discussion.

One of the other joys of operating in a neutral country was the availability of fresh food though we understood that hunger and poverty were rife in the large towns and cities of Eire. Even under German occupation, I felt sure that my parents wouldn't starve on our farm in Jersey. Another blessing was the lack of blackout. The Lucas electrics on the Morris barely provided enough illumination on full beam but it was a lot easier than navigating on an English road in the complete dark. And dark it was, as, unlike Portugal and Spain, Ireland enjoyed refreshing rain, seemingly every hour. We splashed through puddles unnoticed until it was too late to steer around them as I struggled to see through the greasy patterns produced by the arthritic windscreen wipers. However, we reached the large town of Enniscorthy in forty minutes without incident though Joe declared that he wasn't going to risk sleeping while I was at the wheel. By 1.30 a.m. we had traversed Clonroche and were heading for New Ross and the River Barrow which separated County Kilkenny from County Wexford. It was a mere ten miles further to Campile and Horswood House.

The wheels had suffered more than my arms and, just after passed Rathgaroge, we had our first puncture. I'd expected this and made sure there was the correct pressure in the spare and it was no problem — other than having to wake up Willie to help change the wheel. With Joe on board we didn't need a jack either. Skirting New Ross, I set course for Campile but the steering was becoming nigh impossible as the rod was oscillating so much that I hit a pot hole and we kissed good bye to another tyre. Game over. Even Joe couldn't carry the car another seven miles. We pushed the poor old Morris off the road and into a copse of trees near a signpost for Knockmullin.

The rain had taken a break and I could detect a faint moon glow through the scudding clouds. It was nearly 3 a.m. now and I was glad I hadn't mentioned the party. Seven miles without much kit to carry shouldn't take more than an hour if we didn't get lost. According to our briefing, sunrise would be at 05:15 local time so if the moon disappeared again we could expect nautical twilight by 03:30 followed by civil twilight by 04:00. We might have missed the party but we should be in time for breakfast.

Saul was of the opinion it would have been better if we'd borrowed a boat from New Ross and rowed down river to Campile. In fact he suggested we walk back there, which was less than three miles, and do just that.

Joe picked him up in a fireman's lift, hoisted him onto his shoulder, and then started walking down the road while Willie and I took in in turns to slap his wriggling arse.

CHAPTER 5

It was easier than most route marches we'd experienced though we had to double back on ourselves a couple of times in the maze of lanes. After a couple of miles we stumbled across a water pump outside the Church of Saint Mary and Saint Brigid near Ballykelly and slaked our thirsts. Joe had discarded Saul who, despite his new prowess at unarmed combat, still lacked the fitness of the rest of us. He pulled out a cigarette to refresh his lungs but no one could help him with a light.

The moon assisted us and we made good progress without needing to use our only torch until we found another pump near Horswood. We were close now and took a final rest in the growing twilight before tackling the final miles to the River Campile. We took our time trying to get a feel for our surroundings until we reached a stone bridge over a meandering stream. In the distance, across acres of grassland glistening with morning dew, we could see a large house and collection of outbuildings. A winding driveway snaked towards it from the road. As we paused, the sun rose from behind us and illuminated the eastern façade of Horswood House revealing an imposing rectangular shape.
It was a massive detached pile – three stories above ground and, as we walked along the driveway, we could see its southern aspect held at least six rooms on each level with three windows on the eastern side as well. As the sun rose higher I could see more farm buildings scattered around it. This was almost certainly an old stately home split up into a series of tenanted farms.

McConnell seemed to have interesting connections.

Saul grabbed my arm. 'Listen.'

I'm no horseman but I recognised the pounding of hooves before an Irish wolfhound careered around the western corner of the house chased by a lone rider on a black stallion. The hound seemed undeterred by our unexpected presence and bounded on. The horse, which looked like an Arabian, had more attuned senses than its rider and whinnied and tossed its head in alarm. The woman reined in and stared in our direction then squeezed the horse's flanks with her boots and cantered towards us. The puzzled hound followed more cautiously.

Willie gave an appreciative whistle as the rider pulled up and gazed down at us. She was a vision of copper hair and green eyes which now probed us carefully.

'I'm Molly,' she said. 'Which one of you is Jack?'

In unison, Willie and Saul called out, 'I am.'

Before I could contradict them, Joe whispered in my ear. 'Careful, you've got enough woman trouble already.'

She dismounted, strode up to Willie and examined his face. 'It's not you.' She turned to Saul who walked forward arms wide, obviously hoping for a welcome hug. 'Not you either.' She smiled up at Joe then shook her head. 'Which leaves you.' She held out a gloved hand to me and smiled. Her freckled face was flushed from the ride and her smile emphasised her sculpted cheekbones. Her lips were red with lipstick, some of which had smeared across her teeth, and her emerald eyes were flecked with gold — but there was something disconcerting about them, something hidden. I shook her cold hand firmly. 'Uncle Dermot has told me all about you and Big Willie...' she launched into a stream of German and Saul and Willie doubled over with laughter.

'What did she say?' I demanded.

Saul spluttered. 'I'll tell you later but, believe me, it was a very accurate description.'

She smiled at my puzzled expression. 'I didn't mean to be rude but I'd heard you didn't understand German so I thought I'd check.'

Joe piped up. 'I don't understand the bastard language either but, a pound to a blood orange, I could make a good guess.'

I was desperately trying to recall what I might have told "Uncle" Dermot about my private life during our voyage on *Cymric* the previous year. I couldn't recall anything so it must have been loose-mouthed Willie. Of course, he knew everything about Rachel, Caroline, and Masha. He liked Rachel but didn't have any time for the other two. Joe was in love and blissfully happy with Leading Wren Dorothy Collins who was also based in Helford. Saul had yet to find anyone though I knew he was extremely fond of Rachel. Willie had determined not to get involved with any women until the war was over.

Molly patted her horse fondly. 'Sorry, Simba, that's it for the moment.' She turned towards the house. 'Come on, follow me. Breakfast will be served soon and Uncle Dermot has some business to discuss with you.'

The wolfhound sniffed my leg then pissed over my boots before trotting off behind Simba. I hung back with Joe while Saul and Willie walked with Molly, chatting to her in German.

Joe patted my shoulder. 'You know, I've often envied you and wondered what it must feel like to attract the pretty girls...but it's a mixed blessing isn't it?'

'Too bloody true — like receiving unwanted affection from dogs.'

CHAPTER 6

The house was as grand internally as it was imposing from the outside though it could hardly be described as beautiful. Its rendered stone walls and rusticated coins gave it a somewhat grim appearance and reminded me of Guernsey's grey granite which was so much less attractive than Jersey's welcoming pink. Molly ushered us into a large dining room just off the central hallway, pulled a sash, which I assumed rang a bell below stairs, and then excused herself, as she had to attend to Simba. She instructed the hound, who was appropriately named Attila, to sit. He looked at me balefully before obeying and slumping to the floor.

Minutes later, a pretty young girl hurried in then skidded to a halt, staring open-mouthed at the four brutish looking men standing awkwardly in the middle of the room. As usual, Saul was the first off the mark and asked her name.

'Caitlín, sir. What are your names?' She asked in a soft yet almost sensuous brogue.

Saul introduced himself with what he thought was a charming flourish which made her blush and edge back towards the door.

'Would youse like tea or coffee?'

'Three of us would love a cup of tea but one of us is not so civilised,' he pointed at Willie. 'You can bring him a mug of black coffee.'

She shuffled further backwards. 'Sorry for the delay but breakfast will be served soon.'

She paused in the doorway and sniffed.' There's a bathroom at the end of the 'all on the lef' if any of youse want ter freshen up,' muttered something else to herself then fled.

After taking her polite hint, we returned to find three bone china teacups and a teapot on a silver tray with the usual array of spoons, sugar, and cold milk on the mahogany sideboard. A ceramic mug with "Camp Coffee Is Still The Best" stamped on it sat by itself on a coaster. Willie snorted his disgust and looked around for a suitable receptacle into which to empty it.

There were several flower displays in the room but he choose a large Aspidistra. Commonly known as the cast iron plant, I doubted it could digest the dubious liquid; a mixture of water, sugar, coffee essence and chicory without the only ingredient I suspected Willie craved — caffeine.

He was dribbling it carefully into the large pot when a voice, which could carry into a schooner's upper crosstrees in a full gale, made him freeze. 'Desist immediately. Do not murder that plant.' Dermot McConnell, looking even more bearlike than the last time we'd met, strode across the room. His face split into an enormous grin as he grabbed Willie and embraced him with a man hug. The mug fell from Willie's grasp onto the parquet floor and shattered.

The big Irishman left Willie to clear up the mess then shook my hand while thumping my back with his other massive paw. He'd met Saul, hadn't been impressed then, and merely nodded to him now. He stood back and examined Joe. 'Now, who's this brute – there's some

Celtic blood in there, to be sure!'

I introduced them and watched while they tested each other's handshakes and backslapping. My money was on Joe but he backed off first.

McConnell told us to sit down then called out for Caitlín to bring more teacups and some proper coffee. 'Now, boys, it's good to see you but we have some problems. The Colonel and his wife will be down soon to join us. He hates the Nazis. I'm sure he'll tell you his war stories if he has the chance but he has to be careful. This country is less neutral than the Germans would like but we don't want to compromise him. His son is in England training with his regiment, the 5th Enniskillen Dragoons, and young men from Eire crossing the border to join the hated British can be social suicide for their parents. However, you can be sure he'll give us his full support but there are informers everywhere especially —'

'IRA, perhaps?' I asked.

He shook his head. 'Aren't too many of them this side of Dublin – the bastards operate mainly in the border area — in their inimitable way, kidnapping, protection racketeering, robbery, you know the usual cowardly terrorist behaviour. They've even threatened to kill anyone north of the border whose names they read in the press as having donated to the Spitfire Fund—'

Willie interrupted. 'So, who are these informers?'

'The usual ragtag bunch — the envious, the greedy, socialists, Nazi sympathisers but principally those who are still living in the past and hate the English with a passion—'

'Would we be better off speaking German then?' Saul asked.

'Not since the end of last month when the bastards bombed Dublin and killed and injured so many civilians.' He paused and lowered his voice. 'My niece, Molly, woke me up to tell me you were here. She's been looking forward to meeting you especially after I told her about your activities in Portugal. I think she believes that the only good German is a dead one—'

'She's a fluent German speaker though her accent is more academic than natural. Why the hatred?' Willie asked.

McConnell sighed. 'One reason is that a close friend of hers was...' he stopped speaking and looked towards the doorway.

'It's alright, Uncle, you can tell them.' She sat down next to me and reached for the teapot in the silence. 'No, perhaps you're right. It's my story. I hope they'll understand. I sensed when I met Jack that, despite what his friends may say, he's quite a sensitive soul.'

And so she told us of a young Irish girl, convent educated, who had gained a place at Trinity College in Dublin to read medicine and continue her study of the German language. Of how she was allocated to a room in a hall of residence and paired with another girl, Shona. She was from a poor part of the city, had won a scholarship to read mathematics, and relieved the burden on her family in their overcrowded house by choosing to be a weekly boarder. Their friendship had developed even though they were from vastly different backgrounds. Through Shona, she had met Eamon, an engineering student. They had fallen in love and she'd feared telling her parents. How, on the night of Friday 30th May, Shona had returned home to their tenement house near the Newcomen Bridge, and had died with her father, mother, three sisters, and two young brothers when a high explosive bomb, aimed by German airmen, had fallen on them. She had heard the news and hurried to North Strand Village, found it cordoned off, and had searched for Eamon who lived in the adjacent Seville Place. She'd dug with the rescue teams until her hands bled to pull the injured out of the rubble. How she'd found Eamon unconscious, broken, in many parts, pulse fluttering, barely breathing. How she'd forced her way into the ambulance, sat by his bedside for three days holding his unresponsive hand until, on Wednesday 4th June, as the dawn crept in, his eyes had opened briefly. He'd squeezed her hand briefly before the light faded from his eyes and her heart.

We listened in silence. Tears pricked my eyes and I let them flow. She reached out and held my hand. 'So that's why I hate the Germans and why Uncle Dermot has agreed to ask if I can help you sail the schooner to England so that I can fight the bastards myself.'

'Darling, you can't do that.' The voice was pure upper class English and we all stood up as a tall, robust featured woman with auburn hair pinned into a bun, strode into the room, reached out, and touched Molly's shoulder. 'Uncle Dermot has told us of your crazy plan but it's impossible. You have a career, you can be a doctor, save lives not destroy them. You can't do this.'

Molly let my hand go and took the woman's instead.

'I'm sorry, Mother, but I can and I will and neither you nor Daddy can stop me.'

I could but I glanced at Willie and Saul. They both nodded imperceptibly. We needed German speakers and German haters. Rachel was in France helping to organise a resistance. Our daughter was in England being cared for by friends. Masha, my Russian indiscretion, was somewhere in Europe probably hiding from the Gestapo. Caroline was still in German Occupied Jersey with her Nazi sympathising father, safe perhaps, but in permanent fear of her half-brother, one of Himmler's minions, and the very embodiment of Aryan malice.

I didn't speak though, as I'd sensed another presence in the room. The voice was authoritative yet kindly. 'My love, of course we can stop her, lock her up if necessary but what would that achieve? She's made her decision. If we hadn't known before, we know now that this is total war. Civilians are dying without raising a finger against the enemy. We could hide in caves until this is all over but what then? What if the Nazis defeat the Russians and come for us? Who's going to save us? Neutrality will count for nothing. You're English, she's half-English and I fought against the bastards in the last war so being Irish won't help me and it won't help cousin Dermot either especially if he goes ahead with this latest scheme.'

He offered his hand and I shook it. 'I sense that these young men are not going to turn down her offer. These are desperate times and strong-willed women like our daughter with medical and linguistic skills and fire in their bellies are needed. I know you shed tears for our son when he went off to fight, as I'm sure you did for me but I came back and so will he. The only thing I will ask of Jack, here, is that he promises that he will do everything in his power to ensure that she is well prepared and trained. He can do no more than that.'

Unfortunately, I had very little real power or influence. At present, I was a very tiny cog in Fleming's increasingly private war machine but her father wasn't asking for guarantees and I could make that promise, so I did.

Caitlín bustled in. 'Mrs O'Connor wants ter know if yer are al' ready for your breakfasts now.'

We demolished the spread with relish, constrained only by the need not to embarrass our hosts by wolfing it all down too rapidly. There were definite benefits in living on a farm in a neutral country. I doubted we'd breakfast as well again for some time. Molly seemed happy enough to chat with me though I sensed that Willie would like to give her another opportunity to practise her German. In the past, Saul had conspired with Caroline, who also spoke fluent German, to share their opinions, generally unflattering, about me in writing and conversation.

I asked Molly about her friends who'd been at the party when we spoke on the telephone the previous evening and she confessed that, apart from her parents and uncle who'd been indulging themselves drinking toasts in the dining room, she'd been alone with a gramophone, the wireless, and a bottle of Jameson's whiskey that was older than her. Trying to clear her head had been the main reason she'd been out so early riding Simba, her brother Arthur's horse. They were very close and he loved that horse though, now that his regiment had become fully mechanised, he'd arranged for Simba to be returned to Ireland. Not an easy feat but McConnell had organised it. Though he was only distantly related to her father, he'd always been referred to as Uncle Dermot

Her mother, who held the courtesy title of The Honourable Constance Farnham, had more pedigree than Simba and had met Molly's father in the Punjab when he was posted there from Cork in 1912 with 1st Battalion of the Leinster Regiment. Constance's father, although from the lowest rank of the English peerage, was General, the Baron Woodhall, and adjutant of the Governor General's Bodyguard. A significant part of his duties was liaising with the Leinsters who were the garrison regiment and this involved many social occasions to which her mother was invited. Neither the Baron nor his wife, Lady Victoria, had been too keen on his daughter mixing with a bunch of "bog-trotters" and were scandalised when she started a relationship with a lowly captain, but she'd ignored both of them. Therefore, Molly supposed that some of her headstrong wilfulness must be inherited along with the hereditary title of "The Honourable" as, along with her brother and mother; they were the only living relations of her grandparents and thus the hereditary peerage. I thought that Fleming, snob that he was, would love that and looked forward to introducing them.

Because of "Uncle" Dermot's loose lips, she already knew as much as she needed to about me so I didn't interrupt her. At one point she stopped, took my hand again, and made me promise that, having got her sad story off her chest, I would ensure that it wasn't mentioned again. I promised and said I would ask the others to keep it to themselves but warned her that, should we get back to England in one piece and the authorities wanted to recruit her, she would have to be prepared for the most intrusive questions.

I do find it easy to talk to women, especially attractive ones — Saul would call it a weakness — he preferred to charm them with witticisms but wasn't a good listener. He claimed that I lacked self-awareness and that my empathy was contrived and opportunistic. Perhaps he was right but then he did have ginger hair.

After breakfast Colonel Farnham and his wife left us and, while Shona cleared the table, we followed "Uncle" Dermot to a drawing room on the other side of the entrance hall. We'd discussed how much we should tell McConnell before we arrived and agreed that we would tell him the truth but, with Molly in the room, that was impossible. I explained that we'd been delayed because of a crash caused by Saul's inattention and then we'd suffered two punctures. That was factual after all. Perhaps, when the moment was right and Molly out of earshot, I'd tell him the rest. He confirmed that his original plan had been to hand over the schooner then return to Arklow in the car which had been loaned to us. However, because of Molly and a growing desire of his own to take a more active role he'd decided, that if we'd accept him, he'd help us sail the ship to Cornwall and offer his services to the British. He had no other immediate family to worry about and confessed that the Dublin bombing, along with other "accidental" Luftwaffe attacks, had hardened his resolve. I'd removed the number plates from the car and the rotor arm from the distributor and now suggested that it might be best to leave it where it was for the moment. He said he would let the schooner's owner know and explain what had happened to the car.

It was only about 300 yards along a footpath to the mouth of the stream which flowed past the house into the Campile River. According to McConnell it was mid-tide at present so the river was navigable down to where it met the River Barrow and only a short trip across to Cheek Point where the schooner was moored. The estate's boundaries ran all the way along the river and there was a large boat house in good repair though the tidal nature of the river restricted use to less than eight hours a day this time of the year. The clinker built boat was about eighteen feet long and in excellent condition and the Johnson 26 hp. outboard motor started first time. McConnell steered us out into the stream which wasn't running much deeper than five feet at that point. We motored under the railway bridge and out into the centre of the river. Molly informed us it was no more than three miles and we were soon hugging the shore and heading west then north to take advantage, as she explained, of the tidal flow before swinging south to approach Cheek Point. As we neared I could spot the twin masts of a schooner almost hidden against a row of tall trees.

McConnell pointed. 'That's the Strand. She's moored up there while we complete the rigging.'

As we drew nearer Saul seemed agitated. 'She looks a bit tired to me, captain.'

'She's no spring chicken that's for sure but she's sound as a bell. She'll be seventy-four years old next month.'

'You have to be joking!' Saul looked fit to burst and the nearer we got the more I realised that he had a point.

'That's a hulk, Mr McConnell, not a seagoing schooner. What are you playing at?'

'Don't insult the *DI*, she's a legend. Used to be called

the *Sarah Anne* and she's sailed the seven seas.'

'Bloody looks like it as well.' Saul was livid. 'We can't use that. We were promised a seaworthy schooner which could pass as a neutral trader not a fucking museum piece!'

'Steady lad. It's bad luck to curse a ship!'

Molly couldn't contain herself any longer. She burst out laughing. 'Now, just look at your faces. Can't you feel when your legs are being pulled?'

'Very funny, but we don't have time for larking about. Where's the real ship?' Saul demanded.

McConnell tried to keep the laughter out of his voice. 'Not far away but we have to board the *DI* anyway. We bought her for salvage and there's some rigging we still need. Patience now.' He cut the engine and drifted alongside.

Molly sprung up, grabbed the cargo netting dangling from the hulk's flank then vaulted the gunnels and disappeared over the side. 'Come on, lads, I need some help. Don't let a poor weak lass do all the work!'

Willie shot off and joined her leaving Saul with a dilemma. He was still red faced from McConnell's joke and it must have looked a difficult leap from our little boat which was dwarfed by the *DI*'s rotting hull and rocking now from the wash we'd generated on our arrival. I nodded at Joe and we grabbed a leg each and hoisted him onto the netting then shoved him over the side. He treated us to a series of Afrikaans curses then disappeared.

Minutes later, we had a collection of tackle and rigging lines tangled around our legs. Our three scavengers lowered a large sack full of metal bits then clambered aboard. McConnell cast off, reversed away, and headed east along the shore. I suppose, if we'd looked more closely from the other side of the river we would have spotted the three masts and rigging only partly obscured by the buildings on the quay. He'd had a good laugh at our expense but, the closer we got, the more impressive this new ship looked. She was called *Irish Lass* and was slightly shorter in length and beam as *Cymric*, but she had a wooden rather than iron hull. She might not be able to carry as much cargo but she looked sleeker and it was speed rather than capacity we would need if I'd read Fleming's intentions correctly. Best of all, she had very large black rectangular patches displaying "EIRE" in yellow letters painted on both sides of her hull.

McConnell read my thoughts. 'Not bad is she but I need your help with the iron topsail. We'll need that as we're a bit short handed.'

'Iron topsail. Is this another of your jokes?' asked Saul.

'He means the auxiliary engine, you dunce! What is it, Mr McConnell?' I asked.

'Twin screw Gardner diesel.' He pointed to the sack, 'should be good for ten knots if you can resurrect it with these spares. And, Jack, please call me Dermot or captain.'

While the rest of them stowed the salvaged gear I dumped the sack onto the deck and descended into the cramped engine space. The Gardner was a bit of an antique but it passed all the initial checks. I thought ten knots was a bit optimistic but first I had to start it. The old beast spluttered then honked and clattered before I felt the drive shafts shudder beneath my feet. I listened carefully but everything seemed to be running smoothly so what was Dermot fussing about? I switched off and returned topsides, opened the sack, grabbed a piece of tarpaulin placed it carefully on the polished deck then emptied it onto its protective cover. There were pieces of pipework, some gaskets, parts of a fuel pump and other items I couldn't identify. Only one thing was certain—these were not spare parts for a Gardner diesel. Was this another of his jokes?

I found him in the cargo hold fiddling with what looked like a manifest. Though inwardly seething at his pointless humour, I started gently. 'What have we got here then?'

'The best Irish beef, thirty tons — that'll probably find its way onto your black market. Twelve tons of pit props for your Welsh miners — on their wages they won't even be able to afford the bones. Oh, and some dairy products from Campile – mainly butter. Do you know that the Luftwaffe dropped four bombs on the Shelburne Co-op and Creamery in Campile last August? They killed three lovely lasses, Mary, Kitty, and Kathleen, all of them in their prime.'

'That couldn't have been deliberate — they must have been lost.'

'What? At two o'clock in the afternoon on a bright summer's day! Lord "Haw Haw", in one of his wireless broadcasts, warned that Ireland would be bombed if it kept providing food to Britain. Apparently the

Germans found crates of butter abandoned at Dunkirk with the name and address of the creamery. They've bombed other places several times since — some accidently perhaps, but Dublin was definitely a warning. We've lost several ships to their submarines as well. So much for neutrality but we're too weak to declare war on the bastards.' He tucked the papers into his jacket. 'Anyway, what did you want?'

'The engine. It's fine. The sack is full of junk—'

'Engine junk though! Enough to fool an inspection do you think?'

'Right, you'd better tell me exactly what's been going on. No jokes and no lies please.'

'OK, we're being watched. I sailed *Irish Lass* down to Waterford with a crew to load up with this cargo which our orders show is to be delivered to Falmouth where we will pick up twenty-five tons of coal and other cargo and take it back to Arklow. That was part of the plan and the price. We faked engine problems and moored here two days ago. Most of the crew returned to Arklow by train apart from Rory and Liam — you probably remember them from our little voyage on *Cymric*—'

I laughed. It would be difficult to forget those two pranksters. 'Where are they now?'

Two figures, covered in white sheets, jumped out and teased me with ghostly noises. 'Gran' soldier yer are lettin' us sneak up on yer,' said Rory.

'How yer gonna club de Nazis if yer canny clap de ghosts?' inquired Liam as they removed their disguises and shook my hand.

It was good to see them again and it was one of their milder pranks. Lucky they'd chosen me rather than Willie to pounce on though. He wasn't as spiritual as I was.

'Where's *Cymric*?' I asked.

'Licking her wounds in Arklow after a little misunderstanding with the fucking Luftwaffe — bastards. She'll be out of action for a while so my crew aren't too happy at the loss of wages.' He sighed. *'C'est la guerre.* These two want to join us if you have no objection.'

'The more the merrier. With the help from *Daisy May* we'll have a full crew.

'Anyway, you're posing as the relief maintenance crew sent to fix the problem. You'll take her out on the engine for a test run then...you know the rest.'

'So, it wasn't just a joke. You approached from the north to deceive the watchers. Who are they?'

'I don't know. Could be agents providing information to the Germans so that they can enforce the food blockade. Could be customs agents looking for undeclared and untaxed cargo. Probably not the IRA though.'

'Could we find them and induce memory loss?'

'Yes, but who's watching the watchers? You remember Portugal? In a neutral country everyone is watching everyone else. Best leave them alone and hope to outwit them.'

'Did you contact Arklow and tell them to report that the Morris had been stolen?'

'Of course.'

'Rory and Liam, why don't you sneak off and see if you can surprise Willie.' I suggested. As they scampered off I took Dermot's arm. 'There's something else you need to know but promise not to tell Molly or those two.'

He agreed so I gave him chapter and verse about our encounter with O'Farrell.

He didn't seem shocked or even surprised. He found the grandiose title O'Farrell had bestowed upon himself amusing though there had been an Eastern Division with nearly four thousand men during the civil war which followed the Anglo Irish Treaty. After their defeat, the IRA active service units had faded away and only a tiny rump of chancers and gangsters was left. Mobsters, like O'Farrell waged their own private wars and prayed for the Nazis to save them from their own government and the hated British. The Gardaí were meant to hunt them down but there was still a lot of sympathy for them in certain areas. 'I shouldn't worry about it — we're getting used to German "messages". I think your boss might even approve.' He laughed and shook his head. 'You really are a ruthless bastard, Jack Renouf. Tell me, would you have killed those dockers in Liverpool if I hadn't stepped in?'

He'd saved Willie and me from a rampaging gang of dockers armed with cargo hooks and other weapons when they mistook us for German agents. The city had been bombed the previous evening with grievous loss of life and they were determined to exact their own extra-judicial revenge. Against nearly 100 angry Scousers, who set their own laws in the docks anyway, we had little chance. We'd drawn pistols and grenades but they were prepared for losses if only they could get their hands on us and gut us slowly.

Dermot had been looking for us as Saul had just turned up to collect us from the *Cymric*. Fortunately, he knew the dockers' leader and intervened with his Irish humour and defused the situation. Would we have killed them? Willie and I had discussed it. We were surrounded and couldn't even dive in to swim away. We agreed that we would have shot to wound and thrown a grenade to a safe distance. If that hadn't stopped them, we would have shot each other rather than be tortured to death by the blood lust of a mob irrational with grief.

I gave him my simple answer. 'No.'

'So, there's hope for your eternal soul, yet. We'd better get back to the house to collect our gear, check the forecast, and then catch the tide.'

CHAPTER 8

Farewells can be excruciating but the Farnhams kept their upper lips extremely stiff even though I could sense their inner turmoil. We shook hands with Molly's parents and even Caitlín and Mrs O'Connor who had come out to wish us a safe journey and press packages of sandwiches on us. Molly seemed to have packed for a world cruise and Saul was quick to offer help with a case which looked like it should have contained a machine gun but was, she assured us, just her violin. Simba whinnied from the stables as we hurried down the path. I turned to look back and wonder if any of us would ever see the grand house again. I yearned to see my own parents and our farm where I'd buried my brother, murdered by the Germans. Unless Fleming had another scheme which required me to sneak on to the island again there was little chance of that in the near future. Without thinking, I grasped Molly's hand and squeezed it.

She pulled it away. 'Don't, please don't.' Her eyes were moist so I apologised, bit my lip, and let her move on. Dermot loaded extra fuel and other provisions onto the boat and we followed the same route as before, approaching the quay at Cheek Point from the north to deceive the secret watchers.

Dermot had called in a favour and got the forecast from the weather station at Roche Point and it wasn't too bad for our purposes. There was a shallow depression spreading north and the barometer had dropped several points in the past few hours. Thundery rain was predicted though visibility was still excellent. The sea was moderate but there was a force five blowing from the north. As our first leg was due south that would be very helpful for our sailing rig. Might get tricky later as we rounded Lands' End and beat up the English Channel though.

By the time we'd stowed everything and prepared *Irish Lass* for sea, the tide was right so we cast off and manoeuvred her out into the Barrow Estuary. Soon we were passing Duncannon to port and making a steady six knots against the flooding tide. At 16:00 Dermot noted in the ship's log that we had left the Hook Head Lighthouse and were entering the Irish Channel. If we could maintain this speed we should reach the rendezvous point well in time for the meeting.

With the extra hands now on board, Dermot suggested we practise some sailing. Willie and I were familiar with schooners but Saul and Joe, while experienced in motor boats, hadn't spent any time clambering up ratlines. Molly was as agile as any seaman and goaded Saul and Joe while rigging the flying jib by herself. After a few miles we dispensed with the engine and gave *Irish Lass* her head under canvas. She was as speedy as I hoped and soon we were bustling along, according to the trailing log, at a steady twelve knots with bursts up to eighteen. With all sails rigged, I suspected she could exceed that by some margin. She'd be even faster if we could careen her and clean the barnacles and other marine growth from her hull. Dermot had a turn at the wheel while we settled into a broad reach before running with the increasing wind.

I was enjoying the sensation and sucking in the sea

air when Saul called down from his perch twenty-five feet up the mainmast. 'Dead astern – looks like a fast vessel heading our way.'

I scrambled over the futtock shrouds and up the ratlines to him, took the binoculars and climbed another twenty-five feet to the mainmast crosstree, I found the bearing and tried to focus through the gaps in the canvas. There was a definite v-shaped curl of water above the horizon and closing fast from the coast. I hailed the quarterdeck, 'well it's not a submarine or another schooner. Captain, does the Irish Navy have any fast patrol boats?'

'Here take the wheel Molly, keep it on that bearing.' Dermot shimmied up alongside me and took the glasses. 'Feckin' hell. It's the MCS in one of those Thorneycroft MTBs you sold them.'

'MCS? What's that?

'Marine and Coastwatching Service – it's what passes for our navy.'

'Is that going to be a problem?'

'Probably — the speed goes to their heads and they love showing off. They've got six of those little buggers now — more than 40 knots but probably not in this sea and bloody great 20 mm cannon as well as torpedoes. Nothing we can do. Just have to wait to see what they want — they might just be passing.'

'How many crew?'

'Two officers and ten men.'

'They ever do any fighting?'

'Not that I've heard of though one of them supposedly helped at Dunkirk.'

We clambered down past Saul and handed him the binoculars.

Willie joined us on the quarterdeck. 'Can't be more than twelve crew – not like on a *schnellboote.* We can handle them. Would Fleming like an MTB for the flotilla?'

Dermot snapped back. 'Don't be stupid. Even if we did take it without loss of life what are you going to do with the survivors? Toss them overboard, take them to England and stick them in prison or send them back so they can tell everyone that *Irish Lass* is working for the British?'

'Ok, so we can't fight them. So what do you suggest?'

'I have the navicert and our manifest is in order. There's no contraband on board apart from your revolvers and we can ditch those over the side. The problem is your lack of ID. I can pretend you're a temporary crew and that you've mislaid your papers but that won't wash.'

'What's the worst case apart from them stuffing a couple of torpedoes into us?' I asked.

'They won't do that. Waste of torpedoes. That cannon could sink us without too much effort. No, if they're not satisfied, they'll escort us back to their base.'

'Where's that?'

'Cobh in Cork.'

'That's the last place we want to go! Has this happened to you before?'

'We've been boarded and searched thoroughly before, especially by your Royal Navy, but our documents have always been in order. The Germans just bomb or strafe if they don't like the look of us despite the EIRE signs or even because of them.'

'They're signalling, ' Saul called out. 'It's Morse. "H.E.A.V.E. T.O."'

Dermot turned to Rory. 'Start reducing sail. I'll let them catch us. I'll see if we have enough of the paper work they really like — you know the crinkly kind with Lady Lavery on them. The buggers prefer the blue, red and purple but I only have the green one-punt ones, though. Shame you used all your gold in Arklow—.'

I interrupted him. 'Belay that. Molly, keep on this heading. Saul get down here we need your mathematical brain.'

He slithered down almost like a real sailor and joined us. 'I've already calculated. From twenty-five feet up there, I could see just over five nautical miles. You were at fifty feet so you could see over seven. Down here the horizon seems only about four miles distant. Our topmast is over 100 feet so they've been able to see that for over twelve miles—'

'Captain, how far are we from the rendezvous point?' I asked.

Dermot checked the chart. 'Between six and seven nautical miles.' He waved the sharp points of the navigation dividers at me. 'If the MCS has had our masts in sight for nearly six miles then so has your fishing boat. But what can they do against an MTB?'

'Plenty! It's not an ordinary boat – we've fitted a Petter Atomic four-cylinder diesel engine with at least 250 BHP — English, not like those Italian *Isotta Fraschini* engines in the MTB. Even fully laden, she's managed 26 knots in a sprint. There's a 20 mm cannon which can be deployed in under a minute and she carries two MG-34 machine guns —'

'And the BOYS anti-tank rifle, don't forget that,' Joe interjected.

Dermot shook his head. 'We don't want to start a war. Wouldn't your *Daisy May* back off?'

'Probably. They'll be surprised. From their height above sea level they won't spot the MTB until its less than four miles away,' Saul answered. 'Wait, let me think. If we increase sail and up our speed to 20 knots and the MTB runs at 40 they'll reach us at the same time —'

'No they won't,' Interrupted Molly, 'don't forget *Daisy May* is travelling towards us. She'll reach us first!'

A girl trumping Saul at maths — how delightful. I struggled not to laugh.

'Only if we alert them,' Willie said.

'Could try raising them on the radio,' Saul proposed, 'though the Irish will probably be monitoring.'

'We could speak in French — that will fox them,' suggested Willie.

I shook my head, 'No, there's a better way. I spotted the flag of St Piran in the locker. We've used that as a distress signal before and Daniel Lagadec is skippering *Daisy May*. He'll recognise it. Who fancies a trip up the topmast?'

'I'll go,' volunteered Molly. I need some exercise.'

'I'll help,' offered Liam. 'She might need a leg up—'

Dermot cut him off. 'No you won't, you dirty bugger I know what you're thinking.' Apart from Molly, we all did. 'You go and set the main topsails. We'll give them a run for their money.'

Dermot retrieved the black flag with its distinctive white cross and handed it to her. She shot off like a kitten up a curtain and, a minute or so later, the Cornish flag was streaming out 110 feet above us. She dropped down to the crosstree and called out that she could see a fishing boat coming towards us about six miles away and it seemed to be increasing speed.

Now we could only wait. If the MTB piled on the speed or the wind dropped, the Irish Navy would be alongside us before *Daisy May* could do anything to help. I was sure that Daniel had been instructed not to start a war with the Irish though, if our pursuer had been German, he would have rushed in with all guns blazing.

While Dermot resumed at the wheel, I took Saul, Willie, and Joe aside and we agreed that we would not be going back to Ireland under arrest. If that meant Eire lost one of its fleet then so be it.

CHAPTER 9

The MTB did increase speed. We could hear the howl of its four petrol engines. Saul estimated that it was at maximum revs and probably exceeding 45 knots. He didn't think it was a speed they could sustain for too long. But, as the laws of physics dictated, it was enough — especially as the gods of the weather hit us with a thundery squall which smacked hard into the sails and deprived us of a few knots.

Dermot called Molly down, sent her into the saloon to dry off, and ordered her to stay there. Willie returned from the hold with our revolvers and handed them out along with several handfuls of ammunition. We secreted them in cubbyholes on the quarterdeck and watched as the MTB overhauled us on our starboard side.

Its captain was holding the rail on his tiny bridge with one hand and screaming at us through a megaphone held in the other as his boat bounced over our wake. 'Heave to immediately or I will fire on you!'

We were riding on a reasonably stable platform and could certainly hit the exposed crew with our revolvers but they were so limited in range that the MTB only had to back off then pepper us with cannon, machine gun, or rifle fire. Not a battle we could survive. Meanwhile, *Daisy May* was closing with us rapidly. If we could keep the MTB at arm's length for another five minutes we had a chance.

Neither the MTB nor *Daisy May* would have seen each

other yet though Daniel would be aware that we were in trouble. Just to emphasise that Saul fired a red maroon high over our masts. This displeased the MCS captain and the cannon barked as a shot splashed into the water less than fifty feet in front of our bows.

Dermot shrugged at me then gave the order to reef the sails. As *Irish Lass* lost way, he grabbed his own megaphone and shouted at the MTB's captain that we were carrying perishable cargo and couldn't afford to lose any time. This seemed to annoy him even more and their port side Lewis machine gun sprayed a burst through our mainsail.

Dermot grabbed a white flag from the locker and waved it dramatically while shouting a variety of curses. Rory, Liam, Willie, and Joe were working like navvies to haul in the sails while Saul managed the wheel but that wasn't enough for the irate captain and he had another short burst fired over our heads.

This pushed Dermot over the edge and he grabbed the wheel then spun the rudder forcing the schooner to come about. I suspected that his real intention was to ram the pesky motor boat but it bounced out of the way and waited for *Irish Lass* to skid across the waves and wallow in its own wake.

The flimsy wooden MTB edged alongside until its bridge was level with our port gunnel. Two of its crew threw grappling hooks while another two secured fenders to their hull. They were better trained in boarding than I'd expected and within seconds their captain was standing on our quarterdeck with three of his crew pointing Thomson sub-machine guns at us. Two more clambered aboard and, using pistols, herded

Willie and Joe up to join us. Rory had disappeared and Liam was struggling to manage our flapping sails.

I still couldn't see *Daisy May* and hoped that Daniel would weigh up the situation before storming in.

The captain of the MTB marched up and shouted in Dermot's face. 'What the feckin' hell do you think you're doing, you gobshite? You're going to answer for this.'

Dermot roared back. 'Who the feck do you think you, are shooting up my ship? You're worse than the feckin' Nazis. Where's your authority for boarding us? What's your feckin' name anyway?'

'O'Leary, Lt Commander in the MCS.' He waved his pistol. 'This is my authority. I'm going to search you for contraband. Now, show me your manifest.'

'Contraband? We're carrying beef, butter and pit props to Falmouth in exchange for coal – there's no contraband,' Dermot bawled at him. I guessed he'd given up on his plan to bribe the officer. 'Follow me and I'll show you.'

'Steady now. I'll give the orders. Murphy, Flynn, and O'Shea, you guard this bunch. Duffy and Boyle, you come with me.'

Dermot pulled the manifest out of his jacket pocket trying to protect it from another rain squall and handed it to me. 'Come with us Jack. You can read it off while I show this eejit what's what.'

That left three young Irish sailors, albeit with sub-machine guns, to keep two highly trained commandoes and Saul under control. Two seconds was all that would be needed before they were chewing on the barrels of their guns but would those still on the MTB start shooting? With their commander on board I doubted it but didn't really want to find out.

Dermot shoved me ahead and I opened the main hatch and descended into the hold. It was light enough with the hatch open but the officer holstered his pistol and pulled out a large torch. Now that we were beam on to the sea the motion below was unpredictable and we all had to use one hand to steady ourselves. I could dispose of Duffy and Boyle and felt sure that the young officer would be no match for Dermot. But this could still end peacefully if our cargo matched the manifest.

And it would have if Dermot hadn't been daft enough to hide fifty cases of Jameson Whiskey under the beef carcases. Stupid sod. Of course there was a massive profit to be made on the English black market but this was contraband and the MCS had us bang to rights. This wouldn't be just a fine. We'd be taken back to port and arrested and I couldn't let that happen. I eyed the two sailors and waited for the next roll of the hull.

Suddenly a ghostly apparition scurried over the pit props screeching insanely. For once, Rory's unique sense of humour was a blessing. I don't know if Duffy and Boyle were more surprised by Rory's antics or mine but it wasn't laughter that felled them. It appeared that O'Leary's nose had collided with Dermot's fist as he was still nursing it when Duffy tried to be brave and discovered that the butt of the machine gun, I'd wrested from his grasp and rammed into his solar plexus, had as much stopping power as a sledgehammer.

I called Rory over and gave him one of the guns then

scrambled up the ladder with the other one to peep out of the hatch. Willie spotted me, nodded to Joe and suddenly half the MTB's crew were *hors de combat*. I clambered over the lip of the hatch and scurried to the gunnels. The crew were manning their weapons and so intent on covering the confusion on our quarterdeck that they'd failed to spot *Daisy May* creeping up behind them.

Our crews were very well trained in hostile boarding and four of them leapt aboard to grab the four manning the cannon and two machine guns before they could swivel them towards the new danger. That left one officer staring helplessly from the bridge and one other seaman probably in the engine room. Saul was ahead of me and jumped down and headed for the WT cabin which housed the MTB's radio.

Minutes later everyone was on *Irish Lass's* quarterdeck including Daniel, the skipper of *Daisy May*. Apart from the second officer, all of the MTB's crew were now secured in the hold where, as far as I was concerned, they could drink all the whiskey. I decided not to make a fuss about it for the moment, as we had to decide what to do with the sailors and their boat.

I was pretty sure that Fleming would not want it for the Helford Flotilla and not just because of the unreliable engines. However, that gave me an idea which I discussed with Saul. I asked Willie to have a quiet word with the second officer in the mess to discover if there'd been any radio communication between the MTB and their base. It didn't take him long and the poor officer, though white faced, was still wearing his socks on his feet when they returned. He claimed that the

MTB's radio was on the blink so they hadn't been able to report anything. I sent Saul to check his story. When he returned he confirmed that a valve had blown and there wasn't a replacement. Now we had a plausible solution.

Daniel had the necessary explosives and fuses and Willie helped him rig the engine room on the MTB. Those Isotta Fraschini Italian engines would be living up to their reputation. Petrol engines were notoriously volatile — especially poorly maintained ones. Fires spread rapidly on wooden boats and those carrying torpedoes and lots of ammunition were just a disaster waiting to happen. We were well out of sight of land, had sent up a red flare so the scene was set. All we needed to do was put the blame on the Germans which gave me another idea so I sent for Molly.

She agreed to tend to the six injured Irish sailors and discover as much as she could about the action from their perspective. Dermot, Saul, and Joe liked my plan though Willie thought I was being soft again. Before we released the MTB, I sent Rory and Liam back to it to retrieve all the crew's personal gear. Saul recovered any documents which looked like they might be useful while Joe scavenged for weapons and ammunition. The cannon was too heavy to move but the Lewis machine guns, rifles and ammunition were hauled aboard *Daisy May* and stowed away. Satisfied that it had no further use, Willie set the fuses and we released it.

We motored away and I had all the sailors brought back on deck to see the fireworks. Dermot showed them their kitbags and explained that they would be allowed to rummage through them and retrieve personal items later and that we would be treating their wounds. They were young Irish lads so when they saw Molly their reaction was as expected though she smiled indulgently at their wolf whistles. It eased the tension before I invited them to line the rail and watch as their boat was blown apart as if it had been hit by a high explosive bomb. I'd seen that before though I doubted any of them had. It had a sobering effect.

O'Leary's busted nose was treated first but, when he was brought back from the mess, Liam shook his head and took him down to the hold. I wasn't surprised. He shouted something to his crew but Willie stepped across to stop him from saying anything else, took over from Liam, and then hustled him down into the hold. He'd probably need another visit to Molly later. None of the others were brought back after Molly's ministrations and were probably enjoying the whiskey I'd arranged.

Willie returned and took me aside while Liam led the remaining five down to the mess with McDonnell, Joe, and Saul. O'Leary had "volunteered" some additional information. He'd been due to return to Cork with his boat, which needed maintenance, when he'd been called into the Harbour Master's office and left alone with a smartly dressed stranger. This individual claimed to be from G2, the Directorate of Military Intelligence; Eire's version of MI5. He told O'Leary that a schooner had just left from Cheek Point and that he should follow and intercept her. There was a suspicion that she might be carrying contraband or worse. He didn't specify what that might be but, even if she had the correct documentation, he was to escort her back to Cobh. A case of the watchers, watching the watchers watch the watchers. Typical behaviour in neutral countries. Willie was sure that O'Leary didn't know any more but had speculated that the "worse" could be German agents. In any event, he claimed he was just following orders.

'Sounds like this G2 were on a fishing expedition and sent someone with a shotgun to catch some mackerel,' I said.

'It's also possible that O'Farrell's little gang has been discovered. I told you dead men tell no tales.'

'Do you think he might be seduced by our plan?'

'Not a chance.'

The four additional crewmen we'd picked up from *Daisy May* — all Bretons — now took over the vessel while Daniel, Willie, and I waited for Molly to join us.

'Well, thanks for that. I've always wanted to play nurse to a bunch of frisky young men. They're fine and very pleased with the whiskey. Their captain's a bit of a fascist though and they don't seem to like him very much. They were surprised that he opened fire on a neutral Irish ship but he's been reckless before. They all seem to be itching for some action though. What surprised me was their physical condition. They all seem undernourished. I'd expect that in the slums of Dublin and Cork but the navy doesn't feed them very well. They resent the fact that Irish produce is sold abroad and hated the thought that this load of beef was going to feed English mouths. I know that many like them have slipped over the border and joined up. I asked them about that and they say it's mainly to get three square meals a day and some pay to send home. The ones I saw certainly aren't republicans and feel their government is being feeble over the German attacks. None of them wanted Eire to declare war though, yet they seem keen to fight. I suppose that's young men for you — too much testosterone and too few rational brain cells — so, I think they might go for your idea.'

In the global scheme, their fate was of little significance. Willie would accuse me of giving in to my conscience. Perhaps he was right as Hamlet said..."*conscience doth make cowards of us all*" but he was unstable and riven with grief at the time. We'd all suffered the "*slings and arrows of outrageous fortune*" and some of us had taken "*arms against a sea of troubles*". I'd studied Shakespeare and had spent two terms at Wadham College in Oxford poring over his works line by line before Hitler had shaken me out of academia. Yes, "*the native hue of resolution*" could be "*sicklied o'er with pale cast of thought.*" After watching helplessly while the Germans had bombed the *Lancastria* off St Nazaire then machine gunned the survivors and tried to set them on fire with incendiaries, I'd resolved not to "*lose the name of action*". I didn't share these thoughts but beckoned them to follow me into the mess.

It was a tight squeeze but once all the Irish lads had the large tot of whiskey in their hands, Dermot asked them to listen. He introduced me as a sub-lieutenant in the Royal Navy.

'Don't worry, lads. I'm not English but I'm fighting against the Nazis. I'm from the island of Jersey which the Germans bombed and occupied just over a year ago. They killed my brother, and my parents and all my relations are now under their heel. Because of my local knowledge, I've been inserted onto the island recently to reconnoitre their defences. It tore my guts out to see what they're doing. They are ruthless and have subjugated my island. I will do everything I can to secure its release from the bastards.' I watched their faces closely and sensed some empathy.

I asked Joe to speak next. 'I'm not good at this speechifying business but I'm a Jerseyman as well. Jack and I grew up together and everything he says is true. I speak English but, as you can hear with a funny accent...' That got a laugh. 'It's not as strange as yours though.' That really amused them. 'We've been under the protection of the English for over 800 years — that doesn't mean we have to like them but they're much better than the French — no offense, Daniel, and who wants to be ruled by the Germans?'

One of the sailors answered. 'O'Leary might — he's a bit of a Nazi.'

This sparked a chorus of approval but now for the decisive test. I'd asked Willie to frighten them first and he did. He roared at them in German. I didn't know what he was saying though Saul looked worried. They seemed stunned but it was from the harsh tone, the arrogant sneering. They now seemed restless, indignant, and more than a little afraid. He stopped barking and spoke softly in perfect English. 'Yes, I'm German but I'm also a Jew and you probably know what that means in Hitler's Reich. My mother has disappeared, probably into a camp for undesirables but I've heard nothing. *Nacht und Nebel* Himmler calls it. Night and fog – where anyone they dislike just disappears. I escaped in 1936 and joined the French Foreign Legion — there were many of us Jews there, German, Italian, Spanish, Russian; virtually every nationality in Europe. I hate the Nazis and will keep killing them until Hitler and his gangsters are all destroyed.'

The mood had changed again. I knew the IRA shared the Nazis' contempt for Jews and suspected that these young men might have an unflattering image of them as money-grabbing feeble aliens but Willie would have shattered that image and now, perhaps, they could see that some of them, at least, were courageous warriors.

I had planned to ask Saul to say a few words but, after Willie, it seemed pointless and might backfire. They now needed to hear from one of their own. Not Dermot, but Molly.

'Hello lads, I've treated some of you and we've shared some banter though Patrick Murphy, I have to say you have a wicked pair of wandering hands.' Murphy blushed as his crewmates laughed at his expense. 'You've heard from these strangers but I'm as Irish as the rest of you. Do you want to know why I'm here? And, before you ask Leading Seaman Boyle, it's not to put life back into your "you know what"!'

She had them in her hand now. 'I'm Molly Farnham. My father is Irish and he fought in the last war with the Leinster Regiment against the Germans and the Turks. He won the Military Cross and the Distinguished Service Order. He retired with the rank of Colonel and was immensely proud of the young Irishmen who fought, were injured, and, in many cases, died for their country and freedom. He loves Eire and will defend its independence with all his might, but he despises the IRA

— especially after they burnt his regiment's barracks in Crinkill to the ground in a cowardly attack in 1922. My brother hates the Germans and he crossed the border, as many of your friends and relations have. He joined the Enniskillen Dragoons, fought in Belgium, and was evacuated at Dunkirk. I know one of your boats helped out there and you probably know of sailors who manned her.

'You will also know about the German bombing of Campile last year which they targeted because they'd discovered butter produced in its creamery on the beaches of Dunkirk!' This caused a stir as that raid, along with many others, had incensed the whole country. 'But I want to tell you why I'm here. I'm a medical student at Trinity College in Dublin — that's right Mr Duffy, I wasn't poking you at random.' She waited until the laughter subsided. 'I had a roommate, Shona and a boyfriend, Eamon who was the same age as many of you. On the night of 31st May, Shona was visiting her family and the Luftwaffe dropped a bomb next to her house. Her father, mother, grandparents and all her brothers and sisters were killed instantly. She clung on to life for another two hours in pain beyond our comprehension then sweet Jesus took her away.' She paused; bit her lip, 'My boyfriend was in a neighbouring street. He was dragged out of the rubble and rushed to St Vincent's Hospital. I sat by the side of his broken body, holding his hand, for three days...' her voice caught as the tears flooded down her cheeks. She choked them back and forced out the next words. 'That's why I'm here, for them, for Ireland and to kill as my Nazis as I can! Are you with me?'

There was no hesitation. They yelled their approval and cheered her.

I let their emotions subside then explained what would happen. 'Daniel here is the skipper of *Daisy May*. He's a Breton and his story is much the same. His village has been occupied, some of his friends killed by the Nazis and he wants to fight back. My friend Saul, was bullied at school because he's a Jew from South Africa. Captain McConnell has been braving the Germans to deliver coal and other essential supplies to Ireland. His own schooner is being repaired after a Luftwaffe attack last month. Many of the crew of *Daisy May* are French. Ironically, we have no English, Welsh or Scottish with us at present though there are several who operate from our base in Cornwall from where we attack the Germans in France on a regular basis.'

I paused. They were all listening intently. 'We'd like you to join us, join the Royal Navy, keep your current ranks, get paid — not a lot, I confess — but enough as all your other needs are looked after. Because we are classed as Special Forces, our rations are very good indeed. But there are great risks and I won't downplay those.'

They were all staring at me, especially the officer who had made Willie's intimate acquaintance. 'The main problem is that, initially, you will all be posted missing and your families will be distraught. However, in a few days, if you decide to join us, the Red Cross will be informed that you were rescued and taken to England where you decided to join the fight against Germany.'

I looked each of them in the eye. 'If you decide not to join us you will be treated well and put in an internment camp until the war is over or Eire joins us. You will be able to write to your families though all mail will be censored. Unfortunately, to preserve the secrecy of our mission you will not be granted leave until circumstances change. The story we will present is that your boat was attacked by a German bomber and you were picked up by Daniel's fishing boat which you will discover is almost as well armed as your own—'

'What about O'Leary?' Murphy asked.

'After the abuse he offered Molly when she was treating him, we've decided that we don't wish to make him any offer and he will be interned for the duration.' This provoked another cheer. 'Are there any other questions?'

There were lots of them of course and I was able to provide reassurance though Molly did turn down Murphy's offer of marriage.

The officer, whose name was O'Connor, asked. "What about Flynn? He's married — does that mean he won't see his wife and daughter again until all this is over?'

Conscious that I was acting without any authority and that everything I'd told them could be overruled anyway, I was prepared to make any promise but Dermot answered for me.

'Listen lads. The reason you're been offered this deal is so that we can preserve the identity of *Irish Lass*. If we can, it means that she can still operate between England and Eire and, if necessary, bring wives and other dependants over to the UK, if they really want. In theory, they're safer in a neutral country but you've all seen or heard that this isn't really the case as the Nazis can't be trusted. If the truth gets out that she's under Royal Navy control then that's no longer possible.'

There was an uncomfortable silence. I hadn't intended to tell them more but I understood Flynn's predicament and spoke softly. 'I have a daughter; she's sixteen months old and her name is Taynia. I smuggled her and her mother Rachel, who's half-Jewish, back from Jersey. But she refuses to marry me. Taynia is being cared for by friends and Rachel has chosen one of the most dangerous roles in this war. She's working behind the lines in Occupied France as an agent helping to build a resistance network.' I swallowed. 'I'm sure I don't need to have to paint the picture of her fate if she is captured by the Gestapo.' I paused, aware that some of them were gasping in horror. 'I tried to stop her but she was adamant. She didn't want our daughter to grow up in a world ruled by tyrants...'

Molly touched my shoulder. 'Thanks Jack. We all understand, don't we?' She looked at them closely and they all nodded. 'Now lads, it's time to decide. I'm going to ask you each for your name rank and number which I will write down. I'll also ask if you are going to join us or choose internment. I'll start with you, Mr Murphy.

He gave her the details and said that it would be a privilege for him to serve and fight the bastards. In turn, they all followed and gave the same pledge so I asked Rory to issue more liquid rations.

Willie whispered in my ear, 'You make a good recruiting sergeant. Let's hope Fleming appreciates your efforts.'

Daniel called *Daisy May* to us and we transferred the Irish sailors, along with all their kit, to her specially designed hold. Our disguised fishing boat would speed on ahead and unload in Helford where the crew would be formally inducted into the service — if the authorities agreed. If they didn't then it would no longer be my problem.

I didn't want O'Leary trying to change their minds so had him gagged and sent on after they'd all settled into *Daisy May's* commodious hold which had been equipped to accommodate up to twenty commandoes. O'Leary would be kept incommunicado in a separate cabin until he could be handed over for "special internment"— something we'd done before for troublesome people. We'd carry on to Falmouth, unload our beef, butter and pit props then take *Irish Lass* up the Helford to Port Navas to await for whatever daft scheme Fleming had designed for her.

CHAPTER 10

From past experience, I knew that customs officers in Cornwall were just as concerned about contraband as their Irish cousins so, much to Dermot's relief, I had Daniel transfer all the cases of whiskey to his boat. I knew they would be put to good use in the Flotilla. I kept half a dozen bottles back for personal use, as I felt sure Dermot would want to celebrate his famous victory. Whether he wanted to or not, I was going to insist the silly bugger drank far more than he really needed.

After re-rigging the schooner and patching the bullet holes in her mainsail, we set off on the original heading. Daniel had agreed to broadcast a fake message in the clear that he'd seen a German bomber attack and destroy an MTB in the Irish Channel but that he hadn't been able to search for survivors, as he'd had to take evasive action to prevent it sinking him as well.

All sails set, we ran before the wind and occasional rainsquall at a steady fifteen knots. I asked Dermot to resume command. Saul could navigate but it made sense to use his experience before I encouraged him to become insensible with the whiskey. He estimated another nine hours before we reached Land's End on the Cornish coast and altered course for Falmouth. As the sun's faint glow disappeared off our starboard side we took advantage of the neutrality convention, lit the schooner from stem to stern, and decorated the masts like a Christmas tree. Lanterns were positioned on our flanks to light up the EIRE sign just in case a trigger-happy U-boat captain spotted us through his periscope.

Rory's secondary role was ship's cook and, though his pranks were sometimes amusing, I recalled that one needed a robust sense of humour to cope with his galley offerings. It was with a sense of relief that those not on duty settled down in the mess at 22:00 to pick the bones out of his Irish stew. We would all need to be at our sailing stations by 03:00 when we were due to transit between the Scilly Isles and the unforgiving rocks of Cornwall's south west coast. According to Dermot, these and the Lizard, which followed, were some of the most dangerous waters in the world to navigate at night especially during the blackout when Longships, Wolf Rock, The Lizard, and St Anthony lighthouses were switched off. Occasionally they were lit dimly for escorted convoys but we were on our own — a blazing beacon of neutrality. Assuming we didn't kiss those protuberances, we still had to deal with unfavourable tides and the swirling menace of the hidden rocks of the Manacles Reef off Coverack. Hundreds of wrecks littered the coast in these treacherous waters. At least we'd have a rich stew to keep us warm if we had to swim for it. Liam had provided musical entertainment for the crew on *Cymric* on the journey from Lisbon to Liverpool though, to my untutored ear, his sawing on the strings of his battered violin had failed to strike a harmonious chord. Now, to aid our digestion, he assaulted the poor instrument with a bow, the hair of which must have been plucked from an almost bald horse. I was clapping along with the others as he fiddled through yet another jig when Molly arrived carrying her violin case.

'I hope you've actually got a machine gun in there — Liam's horse needs putting down,' I shouted.

She sat down, elbowed me aside, and placed the shiny black case on the table. 'Don't be such a Philistine, Jack. You told me that you were once a Shakespeare scholar—'

'That's stretching it,' Saul interrupted, 'he did look good in tights though. But he does love the violin — especially when played by a pretty Russian.'

There were times when I wanted to poke him in the eye and this was another example of one of his misplaced attempts to sabotage my relationship with a girl he fancied for himself. Of course he was referring to Masha who had stunned me at the Russian Embassy with her virtuoso performance of a haunting folk tune. I was no Philistine but I wasn't a connoisseur either — just a soppy romantic far too easily moved by powerful music intensely played — as he was well aware. Caroline, Masha — surely this beautiful Irish lass wasn't going to reduce me to tears as well. I struck the first Shakespearian chord: "' *If music be the food of love, play on; Give me excess of it, that...*'" but my memory failed me leaving clever clogs Saul to continue the verse.

"'*The appetite may sicken, and so die.*

That strain again! It had a dying fall:

O, it came o'er my ear like the sweet south,

That breathes upon a bank of violets,—'

Molly thumped the table, "'*Enough; no more: Tis not so sweet now as it was before.*'" Which demonstrated that, as neither Saul nor I had the slightest musical ability, we should bite our smug lowbrow tongues.

Liam had been listening to our pathetic exchanges and waved his bow in her direction. 'Well, girl, are ye going to play or waste time bantering with these ignorant Sassenachs?

In answer, she extracted a polished violin and richly strung bow, plucked the strings, made some minor adjustments, got up and paraded around the table to stand alongside him. Tucking the rest under her chin, she smiled at me then started to play but it was as far removed from an Irish jig as could be imagined. It was bewitching, almost mystical; ancient in its mystery and far removed from our vicious war. I stared back at her as she swayed gently with the music careless now of the tears pricking my eyes. She held my gaze and nodded softly — a deeper connection now made. We all listened in silence until the end. Liam looked perplexed but Saul applauded enthusiastically — too rowdy by far in the enclosed space still resonating with the notes of her violin.

She lowered her instrument. 'Not quite Shakespeare, Jack. Purcell, a hundred years later: "*If music be the food of love, sing on, sing on, sing on till I am fill'd, am fill'd with Joy*". Not much chance of that at the moment is there?'

'Holy Mary, mother of God! Carry on like that and we'll be abandoning ship!' Liam shook his head, 'You sound like you've found the bees but missed the honey. Follow me now, afore the Divil takes your last shilling — *Swallowtail Jig*!'

He was good, but together they were great. Foot tappingly amazing and we danced around the table to

"*Geese in the Bog*", "*The Irish Washerwoman*" and many others, each announced by Liam until he was over-taken by thirst and we collapsed exhausted but might-ily cheered. He had the last word as he frowned at Molly. 'If ye play mournful scratchings like that again may the lamb of God stir his hoof through the roof of heaven and kick you in the arse down to Hell.'

Irish Lass sailed on, as, unlike our MTB pursuers, we seemed to all have four leaf clovers pinned to our breasts. At 06:15 I was able to record in the ship's log that we'd passed the Manacles and had a visual siting on the tall spire of St Keverne Church. As we transited the mouth of the Helford we were intercepted by a fast patrol boat and boarded. Saul had already estab-lished radio contact with our HQ in Helford and was able to satisfy its commander of our bona-fides. He was a bit snotty, but then the full time RN officers were more than sceptical about our wavy navy and "special branch" credentials. He was disgusted to find *Irish Lass's* registered captain ill in his cabin, especially as the con-fined space reeked of alcohol and vomit. However, he'd received orders and escorted us through the Carrick Roads and into the inner harbour. I didn't count them but there must have been at least 100 ships of various sizes from heavily armed cruisers and minesweepers down to rusty old tramp steamers. Accommodating those and dealing with the unionised workforce, must have been a nightmare for the port authorities — one which was shared with the ships' crews as we were forced to moor alongside two other neutral schooners from Sweden and told to wait our turn. As Willie and I had discovered in Liverpool, it was the dockers who dominated in harbours and seemed to have their own socialist agenda. Now that the Soviet Union was an ally perhaps they would receive instructions from Moscow to be more helpful.

CHAPTER 11

Helford: Sunday 20th July 12:30

We'd escaped from Falmouth after unloading our cargo then taking on board 508 sacks of coal — remarkable only because they weighed fifty kg each and had *Guimarota* stamped on them so were hardly a British product. In addition we loaded nearly ten tons of Algarve oranges in 338 crates as well as another 500 hessian sacks full of Alentejo wheat. Both products' weights were recorded in kilograms. Only Fleming would know why this cargo had been shipped from Lisbon via another Irish schooner and left for *Irish Lass* to load. Saul had calculated that we had over 200,000 oranges in our hold and, after sitting up the creek near Port Navas, at best they would now be in their third week since picking. Soon they wouldn't even be worth trying to turn into juice though there were plenty of cider presses near to hand. They still tasted delicious but if we ate any more we'd have an orange glow to supplement our suntans.

Along with Molly and Dermot, Saul had been summoned to London for a meeting with Fleming while we unloaded the ship again before careening her in the creek and cleaning her hull and twin screws. The Flotilla had increased in size considerably in the past six months and we were able to grab hands from other boats and the HQ schooner to help us as the CO was ever mindful that this clandestine set up was one of Fleming's favourite pet projects. Before reloading, we had our local shipwright construct a secret compartment in the forward hold. Along with storage for weapons in the bulkhead spaces he and his team built six bunks and, to keep everything ship shape and Bristol fashion, the bottom ones had pull out drawers for clothing. My No.5 officer's uniform would be stored in one, as Fleming had insisted that I should wear it if I was on the point of being captured so that I wouldn't be shot as an agent provocateur. As commandos or S.O.E. agents could be cooped up for some time the luxury of a thunder box chamber pot had been installed. We just needed a shower and hot and cold running water and we wouldn't be far short of an interior berth in a luxury liner. Fleming had acquired the latest Canadian built Marconi radio receiver and heavy duty battery pack in case we were isolated. The antennae was shared with the main ship's radio and routed through the bulkhead.

We selected a skipper from one of the other vessels and bet him five pounds that he wouldn't be able to find the compartment. He knew where to look but couldn't discover the mechanism for opening it. The shipwright watched with interest and, pleased with his work, suggested we give our dungeon for crazy people a code name. I asked if he had one in mind and without hesitation he said "Bodmin" which amused the other locals observing our game as this was apparently where those poor souls with mental deficiencies were held in Cornwall much like "St Saviours" was in Jersey. However, once we'd relieved the skipper of his money and let him see inside, he pointed out a rather obvious flaw. If we were expecting agents or commandos to hole up in there for any length of time we'd need proper ventilation. The engine compartment already had two scallop shaped vents protruding up through the main deck to provide passive ventilation as diesels swallowed air at an alarming rate. There was a slight risk but we took a feed pipe off one of these and fed it into the compartment. As long as we didn't run the engine when it was occupied this should be adequate though, if we were being inspected by the enemy, the occupants would need to be very quiet, as any sound would carry up through the pipes to the deck. We also installed an additional voice pipe from the cockpit. One of the naval engineers gave the Gardner a full service which he guaranteed would increase her horsepower by twenty per cent. Unfortunately, perfectionist that he was, he'd polished the outside as well. I'd spent some time trying to disguise his work by smothering it with oil and dust. However, with the clean hull, *Irish Lass* should have been gifted quite a speed boost.

After work, Rory and Liam would join Joe, Willie and me for refreshments in the Ferry Boat Inn. The two Irishmen were disappointed in the tied house's St Austell pale ale which was even weaker than its name implied so Joe had manufactured an excuse to visit Helston and returned with a small cask of the Blue Anchor's Middle ale which had been delighting the Cornish for centuries. I liked it but it was far too sweet for men weaned on Guinness so I had to relieve the stores of some Pussers rum to lift their spirits. As a consequence they became unusually loquacious and I discovered that both had distant relations working in Jersey. As many young Jerseymen had left the island to take the King's shilling in 1940, the authorities had paid the passage for nearly 500 southern Irishmen to help on the farms. We'd rejected such help, as my father didn't trust them or the "conchies" who had also been recruited by the Farmer's Union. Many had found work in local hotels and restaurants but, since July 1940, even though they were neutral and treated well by the occupying Germans, they were just as trapped as the native population.

Earlier, we'd received a message that Saul was returning and Dot had taken the Bedford to pick him up from the recently opened Predannack RAF airfield near Mullion. Middle ale exhausted, I was staring into the insipid depths of my St Austell pint and looking forward to picking his brains and force-feeding him oranges when he waltzed in with Dermot and Molly in tow. Joe excused himself and wandered out with Dot and the two Irishmen retired to the bar leaving Willie, Dermot and myself to interrogate Saul and Molly. I hadn't expected to see her again and her warm smile cheered me up. Their news didn't though.

'He's crazy!'

'No one's disputing that, Jack, but he's the boss. After all, Hitler's a raving lunatic but he's got seventy million following his orders—'

'Yes — all the way to Hell we hope. Fleming can't really expect Molly—'

'Shush, Jack. He's not as bad as you pretend. In fact, he's charming.' She pinched my wrist and smiled at me.

Saul and I groaned in unison and Dermot laughed as he returned with four pints and caught the gist of our conversation.

I looked around but we were alone in the corner booth. 'Let me get this straight. His nibs wants us to take *Irish Lass* to sea on a course for Lisbon, come about off Ushant create false entries in the ship's log, tack up channel, fake an emergency and put into German Occupied Jersey under the neutrality act to effect repairs...' I paused and looked at their faces to see if this was some bad tasting joke. But they sipped their pints calmly. 'Molly is going to charm her way ashore and meet up with this Diarmuid Molony who owns a business—'

'He's Liam's second cousin on his mother's side so it shouldn't be too difficult,' Dermot said. 'There might be a small problem with the next step though Fleming seemed to think it would be a piece of cake.'

'Piece of shit, more like! Doesn't he realise that the Germans will search *Irish Lass* thoroughly. She's miles off course. They're bound to interrogate us—'

'Not you though, so we might escape without killing any of them—'

'Yes, I'm to be unconscious and bandaged up with only 200,000 oranges to throw at my enemies—'

'Relax, Jack.' Molly placed her hand on my arm. 'Liam's cousin will buy the cargo. The Germans will be delighted with the fruit and wheat. The coal will be most welcome as well. Don't you see it could be the start of a regular arrangement?'

'I can understand the food but why would the Germans want twenty-five tons of coal in July?'

'Joe would be amused by that silly question,' Saul laughed.

'Why?'

'Surely you remember he worked for the Gas Company.'

'So?'

'If you hadn't slept through our chemistry classes you'd remember that town gas is produced by heating coal in a furnace, trapping the gases, cooling them, removing the tar and other liquids then passing the remaining mix through a purifier and storing the result in a gas holder.' He gave me the look our old chemistry teacher had perfected for the class dunce. 'That giant cylinder in Gas Place isn't there for decoration. It's called town gas and, guess what, it supplies the heating and lighting for St Helier where most of the population live. If you want a more detailed explanation ask Joe next time you see him.'

There are times when I understood why he'd been bullied at school. Perhaps they were right. The black market economy would trump all and there would be Germans only too willing to take a slice of the profits. Molony probably had a business arrangement with the garrison quartermaster and *Reichsmarks* would be useful in Portugal. 'OK, that part of the plan might work but this nonsense about me pretending to be Irish and Molly taking me to the hospital for treatment is ridiculous. What if I'm recognised?'

Dermot laughed again. 'We'll make sure even your own mother won't recognise you. It's amazing what blood and bandages can hide.'

'Yeah — my blood! What if—'

Saul interrupted. 'I can see you're coming around to the idea. You're probably only worried that I won't be there to hold your hand.'

'That's the only scintilla of hope in this doomed enterprise—'

'Away with you. Stop blathering and come with me so that I can teach you how to be an Irishman.' Molly pulled me up and manoeuvred me out of the pub and onto the beach. Perhaps there was something for me in this plan after all.

She said that she wanted to swim in private and asked me to borrow a boat and take her to somewhere quiet. She suggested that I bring some liquid refreshment and perhaps a bite to eat. She also warned me that she wasn't a strong swimmer and that I had to be prepared to rescue her if she got into difficulties. I thought she'd got that the wrong way round, as I was the one likely to get into difficulties, though not in the water. From past experience, I also knew that my efforts at rescue would be pretty feeble.

Within minutes, I'd changed into my maroon Bukta trunks, scrounged some lunch, which didn't include oranges, liberated a flagon of home brewed cider from the officers' mess, and secured a dinghy with outboard to the end of the jetty. The tide was rising and it was getting hotter by the minute so we might not need the two blankets I'd packed unless we wanted to be really private in the shade of some bushes while she taught me how to be an Irishman. In slightly less time than it would have taken me to row to Falmouth and back, she returned wearing an aquamarine Jantzen swimming costume which actually took my breath away.

Saul had purchased it for her from the Army and Navy Stores in London after their meeting with Fleming. He'd probably seen it as an investment but I suspected he would receive precious little return on it. He was a generous soul and we waved graciously to him as he spotted us chugging away. The water was probably about sixty degrees on this side but I knew that around the little harbour at Gillan, across the creek from St Anthony, it would be at least three degrees warmer. The grassy mound the locals called the Herra, with its sunken yet smooth crevices, was also the perfect spot for a private conversation. Hot July or not, it was still chilly as we motored out to the mouth of the Helford past The Gew and around Dennis Head. I noticed the goose bumps on her pale freckled skin but she refused the blanket I offered. The sea was mirror calm and, apart from the murmur of the silenced Seagull engine, the only sound was a soft swish as the bow cleaved the water. Molly sat alongside me on the stern thwart and I let her steer the dinghy. Perhaps it was the preternatural silence but we hardly spoke and then only in hushed whispers.

After a very brief and disappointing swim during which she skilfully evaded my attempts to teach her cross-chest rescue holds we towelled off and scrambled over the rocks. The blankets did come in useful, as some of the grasses on the Herra were uncomfortably prickly. The mixture of pink Thrift and the azure blue of Sheep's Bit poking through the Marram grass reminded me of those precious moments on our farm in Jersey when my brother and I had taken a break from the fields and sprawled on the cliff edge chewing our way through Mum's beef dripping sandwiches. The pain of his loss was still powerful as I visualised the scene and his grave mere yards from where we'd feasted and thrown vegetation at each other. I plucked some Sweet Vernal grass now, savouring its intense vanilla taste and offered a flowering spike to Molly.

She grabbed it and flung it over her shoulder. 'I thought you farming types had more sense. This vernal grass is a menace unless you're fond of diarrhoea, dizziness, headaches and liver problems.'

'What are you talking about? It's tasty and harmless.'

'Probably to a super human like you but to mere mortals like those I've attended to in St Vincent's Hospital it's a menace. There are patches of scrubland near Sandymount Beach in Dublin Bay infested with it. If you're that seduced by vanilla find an ice cream seller.' She laughed and poked her left index finger into my chest.

She was lying on her right side mirroring my position though she could see the creek over my shoulder while I was staring at a patch of sea spinach choking one of the smoother rocks over hers. We were about eighteen inches apart, close enough for me to shut her up with a kiss but that might pass on a whole host of germs which, with her medical training, she would doubtless identify as extremely dangerous. Given her previous reluctance to allow me to demonstrate some life-saving techniques on her in the water, I hesitated. She smiled, her green eyes, now flecked with amber, twinkled as if she'd read my thoughts. Despite my previous experiences with girls I was no seducer and was always a step behind and reacting rather than initiating. Now, I was frightened of embarrassing myself by inviting rejection so rolled onto my back and looked up at the almost cloudless sky which wasn't a good idea as some of the cider I'd consumed tried to escape up my gullet and I had to twist away from her to try, in a futile attempt, to control the inevitable burp.

She laughed again. 'See, I told you that chewing grass isn't good for you.'

Was she just teasing me for fun or trying to provoke me into action? I couldn't be sure. I sensed her moving and her left hand gripped my shoulder and rolled me onto my back. My face was in shadow now as she bent forward and brought her head close enough until our noses were almost touching.

'Tell me about Caroline...the truth please. I've heard Saul's and Willie's versions but they don't make much sense.'

I sighed. 'It's complicated—'

'What? Even more than Rachel and...Masha?'

So this would be the price of admission. The truth and nothing but the truth? I didn't really understand myself but I doubted she would accept that so the factual bare bones would have to do. 'I first met her in the water at the Jersey Swimming Club's pool when she jumped from the side onto my head. Normally, divers don't aim for moving targets but this wasn't an accident as the reaction from those watching confirmed. She was applauded for her effort and swam away too quickly for me to catch her and retaliate—'

'Would you have applied one of your life-saving techniques on her if you had?'

'No. There were so many people watching I was too surprised anyway. I'd been aware of her and seen her performing from the three metre and ten metre boards but we'd never spoken. She'd only been at the club for a few weeks and I was rather focused on Rachel that summer. I chose to swim away and ignore her. Later that day, when I was sunbathing on the top terrace, she sneaked up and chucked a bucket of seawater over me. I chased her along the upper row of changing cabins until I had her trapped. She stood her ground and I didn't know what to do so just glared at her. She smiled and advanced as I backed away until I felt a wooden door behind me. She placed both hands on my chest then shoved me against it. I fell inside and sprawled awkwardly onto the seat expecting her to run away laughing but she barged in, pinned me down, and kissed me on the lips—'

'Wow, how did you feel about that?'

'Surprised, confused but—'

'Delighted?'

'Yes. And that, I'm afraid, set the tone for our relationship.'

'She dominated you? When she called, you came running?'

'Sadly, yes.'

'But, if you'd known then what you know now, would it have been any different.'

'What do you mean?'

'About your father and her mother—'

'Who in the Hell told you about that?'

'You know who but Willie has an opinion as well.'

'Too many opinions and not enough facts. Caroline's mother, Isobelle, seduced my father in similar circumstances at the club in 1919 just after he'd married my mother.'

'Whoa. How do you know this?'

'My mother and her brother, Uncle Fred, told me and my father later confirmed it. He stopped the affair when he discovered that my mother was pregnant with me. Look, it's a long and complicated story. Back in 1911, Captain Hayden was serving with an English regiment in Jersey and, along with his wife and daughter, Isobelle, used to frequent the Swimming Club. From what I've been told she caused ructions with her flirting and singled my father out for her attentions. Fortunately for the local girls, her father was sent to Berlin as a military attaché at the British embassy and he took her and his wife with him. There, she met Captain Wilhelm Kempler. They were married in 1912 and had a son, Rudi who was born a respectable time afterwards. Wilhelm was killed in July 1917 and his family took Rudi away from her and kept him in Germany. She returned to England then Jersey and after the war, reacquainted herself with my father who was now married. He gave her up. She bounced back and married Wilbur Brown and they produced Caroline—'

'And she made him change his name to Hayden-Brown. She sounds a bit feisty. Where is she now?'

'In a sanatorium in Switzerland, apparently. I last saw Caroline in November, Hayden-Brown was with her—'

'Willie told me about that. He says he had to drag you away. Is that true?'

Truth? I stared into her eyes. 'Yes. I couldn't stay and

I couldn't take her away—'

'Why not? You brought Rachel and your daughter out?

'She wouldn't let me.'

'But she can't be happy under German occupation can she?'

'She doesn't have a choice!'

'Why ever not?'

'Because her half-brother, *SS-Standartenführer* Rudolph Kempler, hates me so much he has promised to have my entire family killed if she ever left the island!'

'Sweet Mary and Joseph.' She sat up and stared across the creek before turning back and taking both my hands in hers. 'What can you do?'

'Only one of two things, I'm afraid. Win the war or kill Kempler.'

CHAPTER 12

She hugged me. Her costume was still slightly damp and her breasts were soft against my chest, but it was a comforting rather than sensual embrace. I held her tight resisting my natural instincts though well aware that my little brain had ideas of its own. She must have felt the interest but chose to ignore it so I tried to relax and enjoy a closeness and intimacy I hadn't experienced since those last moments with Caroline over seven months before. Rachel and I had cuddled fully clothed on the hillside above the Royal Naval College at Greenwich in June, the day we passed out as sub-lieutenants in the RNVR but that was part of a teasing friendship which, despite having a daughter together, could never grow into anything else. My three offers of marriage had all been rejected. Whatever she really felt for me she seemed determined not to take advantage of our moment of madness underneath that raft at the swimming club. I loved her and always would but we both knew that we weren't right for each other though she seemed more convinced than I did. Did I love Caroline or was I merely, as Saul contended, in lust with her? I didn't know the answer to that either. If it was love why had I fallen under Masha's spell and why was I now fighting off the passion I felt for this gorgeous Irish girl?

I squeezed her and she kissed my forehead then struggled free. Her eyes were misty with tears. For me, for her, for us? I just didn't know. It was time to retreat from this so I asked the question which had been intriguing me since she returned with Saul. 'Do you really find Fleming charming?'

She adjusted the straps of her costume, shook out her hair, and grinned. 'Yes, he's fascinating and I'm sure he's a real love rat but he has something quite...magnetic. Oh, and I forgot to mention, he's my cousin[J1].'

'WHAT?' I sat up so quickly I felt the blood drain from my brain. 'You're not serious?'

She laughed so loudly that two seagulls, who had been eyeing the remnants of our picnic, screeched in panic and soared away. 'Look at your face. You'd think I'd stabbed you. No, of course he isn't — just kidding. I have met him before though. I was twelve at the time when he visited us at Horswood looking for help with his family tree in Ireland. His maternal grandmother was Beatrice Quain whose father, Sir Richard Quain, even though he was born in a poor village about twenty miles north of Cork became Queen Victoria's surgeon—
'

'Fleming would have loved that but I'm not so sure about the poor Irish background. What's his connection with your family though?

'His father, Valentine, was at Eton with my father. They served together in France—'

'But Valentine was killed in 1917. Ian keeps a framed copy of Churchill's obituary of him in his bedroom—'

'You've been in Ian's bedroom? Well, I would never have guessed that about either of you.'

'Stop it. Nothing like that. He was lending me his dinner suit but it's a story for another day.'

'So he took you out to dinner as well?'

'Not just me. Saul, Litzi, Masha and her two guards, and a taxi driver—'

'Who's Litzi?'

'She's married to Harold Philby known as "Kim", senior post in the Foreign Office. One of Fleming's friends – mad as a crapaud on heat—'

'What?'

'A little toad – jumps about a lot. What a Guernseyman calls a Jerseyman – the legs are quite tasty fried in butter—'

'I'm going to regret this but what do you call the Guernsey folk?'

'Donkeys.'

'Why?'

'Don't know and it doesn't matter. They—'

'I'm more interested in this Litzi. What's she like?'

'Frizzy hair, slender, Austrian, Jewish, communist, mid-thirties, husband's a creep and she's fond of young men.'

'Including you?'

'Naturally, but if you want to know more talk to Saul —he's slept with her.'

'Now, that does surprise me.'

'Not as much as it surprised him!'

She dug me in the ribs. 'Tell me about your dinner date.'

'Café de Paris—'

'Before the bombing obviously. That was so sad. Back in March wasn't it? More than thirty killed outright and loads more injured.'

'Yes, direct hit with a fifty kilo HE bomb I believe. So unlucky. Fleming thought it was the safest place to dine in London. I heard the bandleader, "Snakehips" Johnson, lost his head, literally. We were there last October dancing with him though we had to escape into the underground later that evening to avoid the bombs.'

We were both silent for a moment. Bombing was such a random thing. She'd lost her fiancé Eamon and I'd lost Alan to a bomber although that one had shot him with a heavy machine gun. Caroline and I had sheltered in a hole on a hillside overlooking St Helier when three German Heinkels had bombed and strafed Jersey on 28th June 1940. We'd survived that though others hadn't been so fortunate.

She broke into my thoughts. 'No Ian took me to lunch in one of his clubs, the United Service in Pall Mall. He called it "The Senior" as it used to be for officers above the rank of commander only.'

'Yes, one of his less charming attributes is an innate snobbishness. He'd love mixing with colonels and wing commanders but last time I saw him he was only a lieutenant commander. How did he get in?'

'Even you'd get in now. Much to Ian's disgust, the club opened its doors to all officers to balance its books some years ago. He did apologise but he was pressed for time otherwise he would have taken me to his main watering hole at St James.'

'You didn't get to see his apartment and his bedroom then?'

'Sadly not. Would I have been impressed?'

'Well I didn't spot any notches on his bedpost but those sheets could tell a tale if Saul's to be believed. It used to be owned by Oswald Mosley until Fleming bought it. I found it very creepy; black everywhere – like a crypt. Not to my taste but I think he has quite a dark side. If your lunch wasn't an attempted seduction, what did you discuss?'

'Well, don't feel flattered, but you were mentioned more than once. As was Churchill and someone called Mayskiy—'

'The Russian ambassador. We've met under the portrait of Stalin which hangs like the sword of Damocles over his head. He's Masha's uncle—'

'Yes, Ian did tell me about your little indiscretion—'

'I think I can guess who told him!'

'He's quite fond of his little "monkey".'

'Is there a Russian involvement in this latest plan then?'

'I'm only guessing because Ian isn't always transparent but I think, from what he didn't say, that Stalin wants some sort of show in the West to distract the Germans—'

'And retaking the Channel Islands would achieve that?'

'Listen, I'm a simple Irish girl. Any chance to upset the Germans suits me.'

'There are probably still nearly 50,000 civilians left on those islands. I don't know how many Germans but dislodging them is going to cost civilian lives. Unless the French coast is neutralised the islands can't be held. The supply route from the UK is over 100 miles long and evacuating that number of people by sea under enemy fire is impossible. I can't see the point unless this is just a planning operation to appease Stalin.'

'You could be right. Ian came up with the idea and passed it over to Saul to turn into a plan. I'm not sure he's entirely convinced himself yet.'

'Well, there's not much we can do about it from here. Fancy another swim before you teach me how to be an Irishman?'

'No to the swim and teaching you would be impossible. Saul tells me you are hopeless with accents. Apparently you played the Jew, Shylock, in a school play and sounded like a demented Welshman. No, you can pass as a Frenchman and a Breton on the Lisbon run wouldn't be out of place. I'm not sure about the disguise either. We need to work on Saul's plan a bit more. I don't—'

'Shush. Listen.' I pulled her back into the hollow. 'There, a boat — you can hear the water on its hull. Someone is sneaking up on us.'

'Ahoy the Herra.' It was Saul's voice — not quite English because of the Afrikaans undertone but certainly not Welsh. 'I hope I've disturbed you!'

I raised my head. I was tempted to berate him in my best gutter Breton but he had far more languages in which to retaliate so I just stood up, pointed, and shouted. 'Come here, you and I need to talk!'

'No, you need to come with me. We have some guests from London and we need to listen!'

CHAPTER 13

Ridifarne was a well-appointed property borrowed by the Royal Navy as headquarters for the commander of the Helford Flotilla. Appropriately, this was the summer retreat of the family who made the Bickford fuse used in Cornish mining – now an essential ingredient in S.O.E.'s demolition charges. It enjoyed amazing views over the Helford River and was a far better place for a meeting than the Ferry Boat Inn. Not everyone would agree with that, as tea was the only beverage on offer.

I'd overcome my initial surprise at one of the three "guests". Kurt Behring, abandoned by his German father and brought up by his Portuguese mother had helped us in Portugal and Spain even though I'd wanted to dispose of him as I was so incensed with the murderous activities of his comrades. Fortunately, Willie had restrained me and forced me to accept that, due to his language abilities, he might be very useful to us. What swung it was the revelation that he was half-Jewish and had been forced to work for the Germans. His English hadn't been very impressive but in the seven months since I'd last seen him boarding the SS *Cassequel* in Porto he must have worked hard because it now sounded almost perfect with only a slight Portuguese inflection so I'd welcomed him with a warm embrace. Lt Grady, on the other hand, I'd favoured only with a brief nod, as I'd never taken to his pompous manner even though Fleming seemed to believe, as he'd been reading physics at Cambridge, he had a useful set of skills. The final "guest" was a very different kettle of fish. Slightly built of an indeterminate age but with the extrovert persona of a typical theatrical, he was introduced as Bunny, the "makeup artist". There was something familiar about him but I couldn't remember it. He insisted on shaking all our hands, held on to mine rather too long, and treated me to a winsome smile with a lingering wink. I sensed Saul about to burst into giggles but Grady called us to order and made us sit at the long oak table in the gloomy drawing room. Beyond the mullioned windows, the sun was still sparkling off the flooding river and our group of disguised fishing boats moored in mid channel.

Dermot, Rory, and Liam, had joined us from the Ferry Boat and were now perched on stools they'd retrieved from the adjacent storeroom.

'Now, gentlemen and lady, I've been charged by *17F* —'

'Who's that?' Willie interrupted much to Grady's irritation.

'He means Commander Fleming – it's his code name.' Saul replied for the naval officer who was the same age as me but because he was full time RN and not a pesky RNVR volunteer like Saul and myself, always took on superior airs in our company.

'As I was about to explain, the Commander had instructed me to amend the provisional plan that Marcks produced. To this end I have brought Behring and um... Bunny to assist us. Behring will take on the role of a Portuguese sailor but, as you can see, he can also pass as one of Hitler's minions—'

'Blonde hair, lovely blue eyes, nice tan. Doesn't look

like Hitler at all, dear boy.' Bunny's voice suffered from a slight lisp or it might have been affected just to annoy Grady whom he'd been stuck with all day.

It succeeded. 'I've already made it clear that you are under naval discipline now so don't speak unless you are invited to and—'

'Ooh dear. I didn't mean to upset you young man – just trying to be helpful.' He pouted and batted his eyelids.

'Well don't. Now, where was I? Yes, the change of plan, well not really a change but an enhancement shall we say—'

'*Scheißkopf.* Just get on with it, will you!' Willie professed to hate Nazis and wished them all dead. He wasn't that enamoured with British or French officers either and had rejected Fleming's offer of a commission. He also had a very short fuse and was impossible to intimidate —especially up close when there were no weapons available.

Molly said something in Gaelic which probably trumped Willie's German expletive then banged the table. 'For God's sake, boys, and Bunny, behave, and let him explain!'

Grady stuttered, Dermot burped, Rory laughed, Willie grunted and Saul said, "Hear, Hear!"

The pucka RN man was no great communicator but he stumbled and mumbled his way through the "enhanced" plan. Gone was the necessity for blood and bandages, replaced by an attempt to disguise me more professionally, hence Bunny's presence. I queried this and Bunny assured me that, having worked on Charles

Laughton's *Hunchback of Notre Dame,* he had the skills to change my appearance completely. Saul found this amusing and started intoning, 'The Bell! The Bells!' before Molly kicked him under the table. I pointed out that whatever makeup he applied would have to survive a sea journey and the aggressive inspection of suspicious German officials. It might be fine for a film close up but from my own experience of stage makeup; it had a distinct smell which cued another Saul witticism: 'The roar of the greasepaint and the smell of the crowd.' Willie clipped his ear. Bunny sighed heavily then explained that modern rubber prosthetics didn't produce noticeable odours though there wasn't much he could do about my pronounced nose anyway.

We batted his ideas about for a while but when he confirmed that producing a live cast using plaster of Paris would need over twenty-four hours to dry before painting I sensed his enthusiasm draining away. Molly suggested that the only real risk to me was being recognised by a local and not a German. This was true and I wondered how many locals, if they identified me, would report me to the authorities. Centenier Phillips certainly and Surcouf and his family wouldn't hesitate. The chances of encountering Kempler were pretty slim as he was probably in Russia extracting payment from the grateful peasants as the SS liberated them from Stalin. According to Caroline, making Hitler's war pay was his principal concern especially as the director of the *Reichsbank* was his uncle. Though killing the bastard was *my* principal war aim, I wasn't planning on a suicide mission.

Grady decided to move on and return to disguises

later but, before he presented the revised operational plan, he asked Bunny and all non-naval personnel to leave the room. The makeup artist was relieved and asked for directions to the pub but the Irish contingent refused as did Willie. Dermot made it clear that his crew had every right to be involved as they were the ones taking the risks and not just pushing pens around desks. Willie was more direct and told Grady that if he didn't stop being an *arschloch* he'd bundle him into the Bedford, drive to Truro and dump him at the train station. Fuming, but realising he couldn't win, Grady relented and revealed the plan for getting to Jersey. It was certainly more promising than Saul's original and I looked at him to see his reaction but he was stony faced.

Fleming had arranged for a Royal Naval vessel to "intercept" *Irish Lass* in the Channel. Ironically, the vessel was named HMT *Macbeth*, one of the new Shakespearian-class of anti-submarine trawlers. At over 500 tons and nearly 170 feet in length she was much heavier and longer than the schooner. She was powered by a steam engine and produced nearly 900 horsepower. Well-armed but with that weight and displacement she could only manage about twelve knots. The scheme was for *Irish Lass* to take flight and keep out of range of their guns as though she had something to hide. If it was a real chase the schooner would have struggled unless the wind provided a boost. Unfortunately the forecast for the next few days was for a max force two from the southwest and only a slight sea. However, this deception would only work if the Luftwaffe or Kriegsmarine spotted the chase and frightened *Macbeth* away. Fleming had chosen an area centred around forty-nine degrees and fourteen minutes north and three degrees and thirteen minutes west which was a known flight patrol area for the Luftwaffe. Cloud was forecast as between three and five tenths with a base of 4,000 to 6,000 feet. This was an area regularly patrolled by Coastal Command Sunderlands to prevent U-boats slipping up channel to attack coast hugging convoys and Luftwaffe Dorniers looking for stray merchant shipping to bomb.

If we weren't spotted, *Irish Lass* would proceed up channel towards Jersey and *Macbeth* would return to her normal duties. Overnight, we would keep going until we were closer to Jersey than Guernsey as being taken to our sister island would destroy the plan completely. After dawn we should be between the Minquiers Reef and the south coast of Jersey. We'd fake engine breakdown and main mast failure and wait for an aircraft to fly over or a patrol vessel to spot us. Under the Neutrality Act we'd then seek help to repair our vessel in the nearest port which should be St Helier. Hopefully, the Kriegsmarine would take us in tow and deliver us to our destination. Our story of hot pursuit by the Royal Navy would stand either way, only we'd need some good reason for refusing to be boarded. Dermot had already suggested that the navicert which permitted safe passage could have been "mislaid" so that he was reluctant to explain to the Royal Navy. That might not be such a convincing reason which is why they'd flown in several unmarked cases from London. These items would not appear on the manifest but included some six cases of 1910 *Andresen Colheita* vintage port and four of *Fim de Século* 1898 brandy which Dermot would claim he was hoping to sell on the black market and which would get him arrested by the British if found. I wondered where Fleming had found those but then he had friends in high places with low cellars. We picked at the details but, as a Fleming plan went, it was more seaworthy than others to which we'd been subjected. Dermot pointed out that the navicert would only protect him if he was to the west of the twelve-degree line of Longitude anyway and the Germans would know that.

Grady confessed that he didn't know how to proceed on the disguise issue and suggested that I find Bunny and have a chat with him about possibilities which could survive the conditions and scrutiny I was likely to suffer.

I found him in the Ferry Boat and persuaded the landlord to provide us with one of the bottles of cognac I knew he had behind the bar. *Daisy May* had returned from Brittany recently and Daniel had sold him a case he'd liberated from the Germans.

Bunny examined the amber liquid and smiled before speaking in a completely different voice, a rich baritone devoid of any theatrical inflections. 'Thank you, Jack. Don't be surprised. My professional life demands a certain manner, if you understand but I'm quite normal really. By the way, your uncle sends his love and—'

'Uncle Fred? You're one of his comrades, aren't you?'

'Naturally, and from what he tells me you are almost a believer yourself.'

'Bollocks. I'm no Bolshevik but, as Churchill says, 'my enemy's enemy is my friend'.

He laughed. 'He warned me about your sense of humour. Anyway, as you might now have gathered there's more to this over-elaborate plan than poor Grady realises. As you probably know simultaneously with their surprise attack on the Soviet Union the Gestapo raided the embassies in Berlin, Rome, and Paris. Most of the diplomats escaped with the help of the Protecting Powers but were unable to dispose of their records. Since then we have received little information from the "Occupied" territories as our agents have been rounded up or are still in hiding. We—'

'Whose "we"? Does Fleming know about this?'

'Of course. You know about his and Churchill's relationship with Mayskiy. Your Prime Minister is very keen to offer Comrade Stalin all his support in these treacherous times and has charged *17F*', he laughed again, 'with discovering the level of fortification and preparedness of the Germans in the Channel Islands—'

'How well do you know my uncle?'

He sipped his drink slowly before answering. 'We were at school together along with your father—'

'They've never mentioned you.'

'Why would they? It was nearly forty years ago. My real name is Clifford Noel, my mother, Enid, is still in the island living in the family home in Byron Road, number 19a, just behind the church. I haven't seen her since May 1940. She refused to leave and I'm worried about her. Listen, you can ask me anything you want but at the moment we have to sort out this disguise as I suspect you are far better known in the island than I am. Especially as you have such a habit of stamping on other people's toes. You played *Shylock* in the College production of *The Merchant of Venice* in 1939. I watched you and, despite what Saul says, you were very convincing in the role of the old Jew. You're probably not aware, but there was an earlier production of that play in April 1907 in College Hall and guess who played *Shylock* then?'

'I suppose it was you though I've never heard of it.'

'That's because it was stopped after the dress rehearsal following complaints that our version was too sympathetic to *Shylock*. I made a bit too much of a fuss, was very rude to my betters and, to cut a long story short, was invited to terminate my education. So, at eighteen in a fit of pique, I took the "boat that leaves in the morning" and found work in London theatre land.'

'If that's true it does explain why my father didn't want me to play that role and hated my interpretation. So you did return. What did you think of Saul's interpretation of Gratiano?'

'Oh dear. Don't you think I wouldn't be better prepared if I was trying to fool you? He played *Antonio*, the Merchant, which caused almost as much offence as your performance. Anyway, as I was trying to explain, you looked effective as the long robes, beard and wig provided a good disguise. The greasepaint, though far from subtle and not really suitable for footlights, did age you but we both know that stage work is all about illusion and the suspension of disbelief.'

From my experience of German officials complete disbelief was their default position when questioning strangers. I didn't mention that and let him continue.

His film and stage work were based on characters so

he quizzed me on my role on the schooner. I told him that, even though I had to muck in with the sailing and rigging, I was the engine specialist and spent some time in the cramped space which housed the diesel. He thought for a while then suggested that we start with that. I would be a bit stooped after all the crouching so I should focus on hunching my shoulders. I might have injured myself in the past so a slight limp would help. A pencil rubber trapped in my sock under the ball of my foot should alter my gait without causing any pain. I could wear a cap or woollen hat appropriately soiled. My face could be smudged with oil and my fingernails coated in it. He'd already examined my farm boy's hands and noted that, unlike Grady, I was no pen pusher. He also suggested a pair of heavy framed spectacles with one arm repaired with tape. They'd have to have some magnification, as an interrogator might want to look through them. He could discolour my teeth but I would have to refrain from shaving. Dabbing my stubble with a black Leichner paint stick might help but it wouldn't pass close inspection — oil smears would be more effective. I told him that we'd given up on the Irish idea and that I'd pass myself off as a Breton fisherman instead as we knew of several on the Portugal run. In which case he suggested a smock and other French sourced clothing of which we had plenty in store — some as ripe as the mouldy Camembert the fishermen loved. He also suggested that I chew some garlic which should keep any interrogators at a reasonable distance from my face.

Molly approved and we went off to raid the stores though I'd leave the garlic until the last moment. I loved the smell of it in cooking but it didn't agree with my stomach and I was still hoping for that kiss.

CHAPTER 14

Tuesday 22nd July 23:05 49° 20' north 05° 55' west

Still no kiss but we'd been so busy preparing *Irish Lass* and then struggling to reach the rendezvous with *Macbeth* in time that our paths had barely crossed. Fleming had sent us some additions and replacements for our crew, as he had other plans for Saul and Willie. Tomas and Miguel, the two with Portuguese fathers and Irish mothers, were very experienced and known to Dermot but the Irishman, Quigley, soon succumbed to seasickness and was of little practical use. I suspected that he had his own mission and, when he wasn't vomiting over the side, was as tight lipped as the special agent he undoubtedly was.

Even with the moderate north-easterly and a slight sea, I'd had to boost our speed with the iron topsail, so we were still nearly an hour behind schedule when we arrived, using dead reckoning and star navigation, at the point the anti-submarine trawler was due to meet us. It was a fine night and Dermot was sure he was within a one nautical mile radius but there was no sign of the other player in Fleming's game. We'd waited for an hour.

'Well, Jack. Do we stick around or go ahead to Jersey and hope?'

Fleming had put me in charge again. 'There's little point in returning so let's press on. I didn't have much faith in this *Macbeth* pursuit charade anyway.'

'So, we'll head east until the Luftwaffe or the Royal

Airforce sinks us.' He pulled a coin from his pocket. 'Heads or tails?'

'OK, it's fifty-fifty at the moment but after a hundred miles the Luftwaffe will be odds on. If they get too excited we can always throw oranges at them!'

We had sailed under blackout conditions but now Dermot lit us up like a Christmas tree making sure that the large EIRE signs on both sides of the hull were illuminated and, for good measure, the Irish tricolour flag was picked out with a spotlight on the main mast. That would put some strain on the generator but submarines on both sides were active in this area.

We were roughly sixty-three nautical miles from Ushant, forty-five from the Lizard in Cornwall and 152 miles to the west of Jersey. If we could maintain twelve knots we should be in the known Luftwaffe patrol area by 06:00. We had planned to zig zag when *Macbeth* was pursuing us but now we headed straight for the island.

Quigley had brought a present with him — copies of letters from six of the Irish nationals trapped in Jersey. Apparently, the Germans had recently allowed censored mail to be sent from the island to the occupied territories and some neutral countries. These had been intercepted by the G2, the Irish Office of the Directorate of Intelligence, and had mysteriously found their way into British hands. They contained no information about the Germans or their fortifications and had eventually been released to the addressees, some of whom had been encouraged to write back. So far no replies had been received. These missives would have had a long circuitous journey which probably involved Sweden or Switzerland before crossing France and on to the islands.

However, they had been intercepted and Quigley's department had copied them and he now had the originals in his bag. As part of our deception these would be offered along with our cargo and an invitation to establish a regular trade link. Whether the Germans would fall for this was another matter on which Fleming and I didn't agree. Although he had vast experience of plotting and planning, he hadn't been up close and personal with the average Nazi bureaucrat. Willie had sneered at his scheme so hadn't been too disappointed to be left behind. Though Molly was fluent in German we wouldn't want to reveal that so Kurt would do the interpreting, as he was half-German and Portuguese with authentic documents to match. The pair of them seemed to be meeting far too often to practice their German for my liking as he seemed rather smitten and she did little to discourage him. The Irish and other Portuguese on board had their own ID which was also genuine. I was the only fake and now masquerading as Jacques Renault, born in Ireland of a French father, sadly deceased, and an Irish mother still living in Arklow. Jacques had spent much of his childhood in Brittany and was fluent in Breton but had an odd inflection in his English, not quite Irish; in fact oddly similar to the way a Jerseyman spoke when he was taking the micky of his own heritage.

During the cruise I did manage to spend some time with Molly but it was in the company of Liam and Quigley. All three interrogated me on my manufactured childhood. We weren't concerned about the Germans testing my background but there might be Quislings amongst the Irish who could trip me up. So I quickly learned the route from the Arklow Pottery, where my supposed mother had worked, back home, via Father Murphy's statue in the Parade Ground, to our flat above Condren's shop at 81 Lower Main Street. According to the legend provided by Quigley, I'd attended St Mary's and St Peter's infant school before moving to Concarneau in Brittany. It was unlikely there would be anyone on the island familiar with that port town and I'd visited it the previous year albeit at night with a Sykes knife in my hand. My genuine worry was that, despite my ragged and oily appearance, some local might recognise me but none of the others knew Jersey so, as far as Fleming was concerned, I had to go.

We called a halt at a quarter to four to watch the nautical twilight envelope us. We were heading towards it and soon we were bathed in violet light as we scythed our way eastwards towards the rising sun keeping alert for any patrolling aircraft.

'There, listen.' Molly tugged my arm and pointed high up above our port side.

It was faint but growing; the hum of a multi-engined aircraft. Soon the volume decreased and changed to signify a slow descent as the engines were throttled back. I was sure I could hear four engines as the pilot reduced the revs in two of them creating that strange "wum, wum, wum" gut wrenching sound. Apart from their Condor, the Luftwaffe's bombers were all two engined so it was almost certainly British. As it droned down I spotted streaks of brighter light bouncing off its fuselage.

Dermot stood next to me and lowered his binoculars. "Sunderland flying boat; anti-submarine. This should be interesting. Best get that code sheet."

We had a radio capable of communicating with the plane but the pilot wouldn't want to use it, as German listening stations would pick up the transmissions so I scurried off. The sheet held a series of Morse sequences and their meaning. These related to our operation which Fleming had cheerlessly named *"Lochaber"* after *Banquo, Macbeth's* best friend and his second victim in the play. Back on deck I waited with Dermot and Liam who grasped a small Aldis lamp in his hands. The Sunderland had throttled right back and circled us once. Its fuselage was painted white and as it banked revealed a mottled grey and blue camouflage on the wings and upper frame. The roar from its four massive radial engines was deafening and we could clearly see the racks of depth charges slung from their pylons.

We were expecting a string of meaningless Morse but it flashed at us in the clear demanding to know our name and destination. This wasn't one of Fleming's playthings then. I told Liam what to reply and he signalled back. "Irish Lass, Jersey. Neutral.". We waited for a response but it completed another turn before the pilot increased revs, resynchronised the engines and climbed away with a brief waggle of its wings.

'I don't think we'll be needing the codes then,' Dermot observed, 'better send them to *Bodmin*.'

If we did get to Jersey, the Germans would search the schooner thoroughly so I slipped below and stowed the sheet next to the Marconi radio in our little mad house. We were making a good twelve knots now and should soon be within the Luftwaffe's patrol area. Minutes

later we heard the "crump crump" of depth charges det-
onating off to the west and assumed that our friendly
Sunderland was delivering breakfast to a U-boat.

CHAPTER 15

Two hours later, one of Hitler's flying pencils, a Dornier Do 17, dropped in to say hello with a burst of machine gun fire from its cockpit. It was just a warning but I was trembling with the memory of the last time I'd encountered one of these. My brother, Alan, had been foolish enough to fire his rifle at it and it had casually raked our motor cruiser from stem to stern as it thundered over. The hull was steel but Alan was just flesh, bones and blood. He was ripped apart and I'd had to take him home and explain to my parents. That also happened on a Wednesday just thirteen months before about five miles off the east coast of Jersey. Two weeks later the Germans had invaded the island. I squeezed the stanchion until my knuckles were white. We had weapons aboard but even if I managed to load one of the MG-34s and aim a full belt at the Dornier there was little prospect of hitting a vulnerable part and it would rip our wooden hull apart and probably bomb us as well. So I steeled myself, removed my hand, waved in a friendly fashion, and pointed at the Irish tricolour streaming out from the yardarm.

Disappointed that we had no hostile intent and almost certainly aware that we were a neutral vessel protected by the rules of war, the pilot throttled back and began a slow circle. I knew that the Luftwaffe didn't have a marine channel on their radios and wasn't surprised to see the flicker of Morse code from a lantern in the cockpit. Liam was standing by with our Aldis lamp while Dermot wrote down the letters. Kurt was alongside him in case they were in German. However, the pilot must have accepted that we were Irish and would understand English better. It always amazed me that for every Englishman who spoke German there were at least ten Nazis who understood English. But then, the bloody Fuhrer was one of our great admirers!

Dermot interrupted my train of thought. 'He's asking the same questions as the Sunderland.'

'Give him the same answers then!'

Liam worked the trigger and we waited. The Dornier circled for several minutes obviously communicating with his base. What I would have given for one Spitfire at that moment but the sky belonged to the Nazis today. Eventually, he flashed back telling us to proceed at 90° due east until we met an escort.

Molly took my elbow and led me across to the starboard side. 'Are you alright? You're very pale.'

'It's OK.'

'No, it's not. Tell me.'

So I did. She listened and when I'd finished hugged me tight. I was aware now that the others were watching us so I fought back the tears and gave the horizon a thousand yard stare. It wasn't just Alan I was thinking about now. As we slipped closer to the island Caroline started to intrude and the notion of kissing Molly bled from my mind.

I disengaged and returned to the quarterdeck. We'd have an hour or more to prepare for the inevitable boarding and search so I sent everyone to ensure that were was nothing compromising to be found. That included English currency, magazines, newspapers and anything which might indicate we'd come from there. Rory had to dump some bottles of Cornish cider overboard but apart from that they'd all followed their orders to the letter and had even left Portuguese escudo notes and coins in their baggage. Once again I inspected the hidden hatch to our weapons store and convinced myself that it was invisible. We'd secured the vintage port in a more obvious place to give the Germans something to find and hope they'd appreciate the fine brandy and appropriate it for themselves rather than make a fuss.

Now, all we could do was wait and hope.

At 08:13 Rory who was up the mast called out that he'd spotted the bow wave of a vessel bearing down on us from 075°. Dermot and I went forward with binoculars. It was certainly travelling at speed bouncing over the slight sea.

'It's an E-boat.' Dermot decided.

I examined it a bit longer. 'Close but no cigar. It's not an S-boat or *schnellboote*. It's a bit smaller. Almost certainly an R-boat though. That's R for *Raumen* — the German for removing. A small but lethal minesweeper.' Those hours of vessel recognition and tests at the Royal Naval College in Greenwich had not been wasted. 'It's well armed with cannon and machine guns but max speed of no more than twenty knots. Fully crewed; probably thirty-five to forty. Not that we'd want to fight it!'

'To be sure, that's a blessing then!'

CHAPTER 16

But it wasn't. *Leutnant zur See* Schneider, who introduced himself with a click of the heels as the commander of *R-72*, was one of those Germans who deigned not to speak English or French and certainly not Portuguese. His face was heavily scarred on the left side and his reefer jacket displayed the distinctive Ritterkreuz ribbon attached to the top button. This was the highest award in the Iron Cross category and I'd given mine to my brother, Alan. It was in his pocket when he died. I hadn't won it but removed it from the body of the first German I'd shot and killed. After I'd vomited from the shock, Willie had explained what it signified and I'd retched again. I wouldn't mention this to Schneider but studied him now. He was one rank above and probably two years older than me but already a wounded veteran. Apart from the livid scar he was handsome in that blonde German way. His eyes flashed a light blue as he stomped about the deck and barked at us after we were assembled under the machine pistols of four of his crew. I'd asked Kurt and Molly not to reveal their fluency in the language just in case we had to fight but to warn me surreptitiously if it looked like we were about to be shot. Dermot took the lead and spoke softly in his best Irish brogue but his words were ignored by Schneider who sent for more sailors. I hoped one of them would understand English otherwise it was going to be a very long morning.

One of them, whose collar badges suggested he was a petty officer, listened to Dermot's explanation then whispered in Schneider's ear. He nodded but made no attempt to respond other than ushering us into the bows and forcing us into the foc'sle space. The petty officer explained that we would be confined until they had completed their search of the ship. We'd hauled in our sails before they'd boarded us and these were still sprawled untidily on the deck. I'd guessed they might do this and, as I didn't want to be cooped up when we approached the island, had taken a gamble and created a problem with the engine hoping they would call for the schooner's engineer to help to fix it. Having first of all secured a spare in a secret spot, I'd "accidently" loosened the special nut attached to the decompression lever to the point where any vibration would make it fall off into the confined space. In my "haste", I'd also dropped a cleaning rag over the air intake filter.

My clumsiness seemed to have worked for we'd been wallowing in the swell for nearly thirty minutes — five of which were spent listening to futile attempts to start the engine. I doubted they had the skills to sail the schooner so hoped they would soon come looking for the mechanic. It was stifling in the cramped space and I was jammed up against Dermot and out of reach of Molly. During their search, I was hoping they'd find the letters which Quigley had left in his cabin, as they would provide the Germans with some answers before they asked any more questions. That is if one of them could read English. At least the letters, although produced by different families, were all clearly handwritten. The benefits of a good Catholic education I assumed though Molly pointed out that they'd all been neatly written by women.

My gamble seemed to have failed as no one sought my expertise though, just after nine o'clock, we were escorted out blinking into the bright sunshine. I cast around but couldn't see any landmass to the east or south though there was a faint smudge to the north. That would be Guernsey so we were still at least twenty miles to the west of Jersey.

Schneider was holding what looked like our manifest and our falsified ship's log in his hand. There were four cases of port and six of brandy on the deck. Doubtless, the balance would be in his cabin on *R-72* by now. He smirked then waved the manifest and barked at us in German.

As soon as he had finished, the petty officer spoke in passable English. 'My officer has completed a search of your vessel.' He pronounced it "*wessel*" but I bit my lip to suppress a giggle. 'He has examined your manifest which does not appear to include these items.' He prodded one of the cases with his boot. 'He has also found some letters from Ireland addressed to Irish working for the Reich on Jersey. We are aware of these men and wish to know why you have these letters.'

This was Dermot's cue and he launched into a long-winded explanation during which he expressed his gratitude for the generosity of the Reich in allowing them to communicate with their families in Ireland. However, they were concerned that their return letters might not be delivered and, knowing *Irish Lass* was off to Portugal again, had asked if they could be handed in to the German Embassy in Lisbon for censorship if necessary and onward delivery. Sadly, the diplomat had declined and shown us the door and we still had them.

As the petty officer was translating I realised just how feeble this sounded. Schneider shrugged and indicated that Dermot should continue so he carried on with our confected story about escaping from the Royal Navy because of fears that our "special" supplies might be confiscated. During this Schneider seemed to be nodding as though he understood, which would give the lie to his lack of English, but he didn't interrupt so Dermot continued with the other confection that we'd decided to bring the cargo, especially the oranges, as a gift to the workers on the island. He wondered if the local authorities would be interested in purchasing any of the excellent coal and wheat as well. If so, he, as a neutral, would guarantee continuing supplies of similar items if required.

Schneider spat a stream of German. Molly gave me an anxious look. The interpreter focused on me. 'You,' he pointed, 'are the mechanic, no?'

I nodded and stared at the deck not wanting to risk my bastardised French/Irish accent in front of everyone.

'Your engine is not working. My officer wants to know if you have sabotaged it.'

I looked alarmed and stuttered. 'No, no. To be sure, she's an old temperamental bitch. She usually responds to some love and caressing.' Molly rolled her eyes. Perhaps I was overdoing it. 'Would you like me to fix her for you?'

Schneider marched over and looked me in the eyes. I wanted to stare him out but daren't. Instead, I lowered my gaze and almost giggled because there were food stains on his jacket just above his bravery award. His breath was a mixture of garlic, stale alcohol, and tobacco smoke. *'Papiere!'*

I reached into the inside pocket of my jacket and held out my forged ID. He examined it closely, especially the photograph. He handed it to the petty officer and muttered a few sentences.

The sailor handed it back to me. 'So Renault Jacques, my officer says that you are French/Irish. This is not a good combination. You are—'

'Irish/Breton. Begorrah, that's what I am and that's the right way round.' I snapped back. 'My father was a Breton fisherman and he drowned. My mother, God bless her, is alive and living in Arklow where I grew up. God save Ireland.'

He shrugged then returned to Schneider and muttered something. I glanced at Molly and she seemed alarmed. While Schneider's back was turned I glanced over the side and noted that the R-boat was holding station about 100 yards away. I could also see a painter tied to our taffrail and supposed it was securing a dinghy.

Schneider turned and stared at me. He barked a string of commands and two of his sailors slung their machine pistols and grabbed my arms while a third pointed a pistol at me. I didn't struggle but was perplexed. What had spooked him?

He strode back, fumbled in his pocket and pulled out a nut. He held it under my nose and spoke in lightly accented English. 'Recognise this? Your engine is well maintained but scruffy. I do not think you would allow this to fall off.' He placed it in my top pocket. 'My engineer is suspicious. We too have diesel engines and he tells me that no one would block the air intake with a rag unless he wished to sabotage it.'

Trapped by my own stupidity. I wasn't in the position to resist let alone fight. The best I could hope was I could persuade him it was an accident and apologise profusely. If that didn't work, Dermot would have to intervene and invent some excuse for my behaviour. Perhaps say that I hadn't wanted to take part in this, that I hated the Germans and didn't want to supply them with coal and food, that I didn't believe in this sort of black market trading. At least Scheider hadn't challenged my identity yet though if he was suspicious, he would have less polite colleagues back in the island who would.

These thoughts were tumbling through my head during his speech and I responded as soon as he finished. 'That's feckin' crazy, that's my engine, I've worked on her for months. Look at my hands.' My arms were held but I managed to twist my wrists to show my palms and the oil stained fingers. 'That nut is from the compression lever which I was fixing when you forced us to heave to.' He looked unimpressed and I was winding up for more blather when we all heard the growling from above.

CHAPTER 17

The noise was produced by four Hercules radial engines attached to two Coastal Command Bristol Beaufighters as they plunged from the sky. Schneider seemed frozen by indecision. His R-boat was minutes away by dinghy and he could be sure *Irish Lass* wasn't the fighters' target. I knew a lot about those lethal planes. A pair of them had scuppered Fleming's *Operation Ruthless* by accident in November and now were they about to rescue *Lochaber*? Our crew was quietly moving away from the port side towards some shelter though I was still held by the two seamen who were staring blankly upwards. They'd need to shift their gaze for those two planes would drop to sea level soon and snarl their way towards the R-boat.

Schneider was now shouting across to *R-72*. I guessed he was ordering it to close with us to confuse the two enemy planes but it was too late. Diesels are great for cruising but for instant acceleration you need big petrol engines. I spotted plumes of black smoke from the twin exhausts as the German craft tried to gain speed but, from the corner of my eye, I spotted the twinkling of tracer from the first Beaufighter's wings followed almost immediately by a stream of splashes as the machine gun bullets stitched their way to the wooden hulled boat. Most missed but as it turned, dozens rattled off its minesweeping gear. Its foredeck cannon was tracking into action but the first fighter had speared overhead and was already turning before it could fire off its first rounds. The R-boat was perilously close to us now. My two guards abandoned me and sought firing positions on the rail but the wash from the R-boat hit us and their MP40 rounds were wasted as we floundered helplessly.

I followed them to the rail and saw Schneider leap into the rubber dinghy with his petty officer. A sailor already had the outboard running as they cast off. Schneider was pointing towards his command and shouting. The R-72 slowed and a rope was thrown towards the dinghy. The petty officer grabbed it and hauled manically to close the distance. In seconds they were alongside and reaching for the hastily deployed scrambling net when the second Beaufighter's heavy 20 mm cannon rounds struck the R-boat's stern. Immediately, the boat lost way as the engines were hit and dense black smoke poured from aft. The dinghy bounced off the hull and the crew were catapulted into the water.

There were still four seamen blasting away from our port side to little effect as the smoke was now billowing over us. R-72 was drifting but still enveloped in the black cloud. Schneider was struggling in the water, clearly injured. I tried to picture the scene from the pilots' perspective and realised that, unless they were prepared to sink a neutral ship with the risk of killing its crew, they couldn't pursue their attack. It wouldn't have bothered Luftwaffe pilots so I wasn't surprised when their engine notes changed as they clawed for height. Perhaps they'd circle until the smoke cleared and then attack again. I looked for Schneider. He was alone, drifting away from us and not attempting to swim or even move at all. Call it natural instinct or years of training but I only stopped to kick off my boots and discard my jacket, before diving over the side and swimming towards him. I prayed his compatriots wouldn't interpret that as an attempt to attack him and shoot me in the back. I reached him and realised that he was only semi-conscious and bleeding heavily from a scalp wound. I got him in a cross-chest carry so scissor kicking my legs and, using my free arm in side-stroke, I hauled him back to *Irish Lass*. Liam jumped in to help me and soon with the strength of Dermot and the sailors who'd given up shooting he was lifted aboard.

By the time I'd clambered over the side, Molly was tending to his wounds on the deck. She fussed over him for a while then gave her diagnosis. 'Flesh wound and he hit his head on something solid. Probably concussion but he'll live. Well done, Jacques.'

Dermot handed towels to Liam and me as we surveyed the mess of the R-boat yards off our bow. Her crew were fighting the fire on the stern and shouting for help. Molly interpreted and told us they were asking for any medics and firefighters. Quigley grabbed an extinguisher while Rory ran out the hose. It would need the engine to be running to pump across to the burning boat so I retrieved the nut from my jacket pocket, hurried into the compartment, fixed the compressor lever and started the engine. Soon the hose was spurting a powerful stream of seawater towards the R-boat as Dermot manoeuvred us closer. With all hands helping, the fire was soon under control and Molly giving first aid to the casualties. None were serious and there'd been no fatalities.

Schneider was still only semi-conscious but the petty officer agreed to Dermot's suggestion that we take his boat in tow and head towards Jersey. Our two guardian angels were long gone and I looked forward to telling Fleming about their actions and how, inadvertently, they had saved his latest but not daftest scheme.

CHAPTER 18

An hour had passed and Schneider was still with us and dressed in grey leather working gear retrieved for him from R-72. Liam and I were wearing borrowed overalls and watching closely as Molly sat on the deck chatting with her patient. She'd told him that his wound would need several stitches and that, if he wished, she would insert those there and then or he could wait until he reached hospital. He'd chosen to wait but she took the opportunity to tell him about the Irish nurses who worked in the General in St Helier and revealed that she was a medical student herself.

Much to my amusement and slight tinge of jealousy they seemed to be getting on very well so I interrupted. 'How is he, Molly?'

'Ah, the Irish/Breton. I am in your debt and you seem to have sweet-talked your bitchy engine into life again. I understand that we will be able to relieve her of the strain very soon as a tug is on the way.' He scrambled up but had to steady himself on a stanchion. Once upright, he extended his right arm. 'Heil Hitler.' Then he offered me his hand which I shook. 'Thank you. Your help will not be forgotten.'

I was searching for any undertones in that statement when one of his sailors called out to him and he pulled himself along to the bow. I followed and watched as the States of Jersey tug, the *Duke of Normandy*, now wearing the designation *FK 01*, approached to take over the tow.

Once the handover was complete, Schneider transferred with some difficulty to *R-72* leaving four of his sailors with us. Before he departed he'd asked Molly if she'd pay him the honour of dining with him once she was ashore.

'Will you do that?' I asked.

She grinned. 'Why not? Perhaps we can make it a foursome. Your Caroline could join us with her Kriegsmarine officer.'

She'd stunned me again. 'How do you...of course Saul.'

'No, Willie this time. He doesn't like Caroline, does he?'

Of that, I wasn't entirely sure. I'd yet to meet a man who wasn't attracted to her and, yes, I had worried about Karl, the handsome *Korvettenkapitän* who'd been her father's houseguest before Willie knocked him out, rolled him up in a carpet, and chucked him into the cellar. She'd been dismissive when I asked if he was more than a guest and had shown little sympathy for him before we'd locked her up with him, her father, and his mistress. But that was many months ago. Anything could have happened since. Perhaps Rudi Kempler, Caroline's obsessive half-brother, might have moved her from the island and thus released my parents from a potential death sentence. Perhaps that was just my wishful thinking. There was only one way to find out

Molly touched my arm. 'I'm only kidding but don't you see this could be a perfect cover for getting the information Fleming needs.'

I shrugged. 'Yes, but do be careful. It could be a high price to pay.'

She laughed. 'Come on, Jack. Have some faith. I can look after myself—as you well know.'

I had to have the last word. 'Just make sure he brushes his teeth first.'

Before she could offer any retort I went in search of Dermot. He was talking with the harbour pilot who'd been dropped off by the tug. Our arrival had caused a stir and another, English speaking, Kriegsmarine officer had boarded with instructions that we should drape and secure our sails over the hull on both sides to obscure the EIRE sign. We also had to hide our name and port of registration, haul down our flag, and run up the Nazi one. These orders were clearly in breach of the Neutrality Act but Dermot only made a half-hearted protest. It was quite a small tide at just over thirty feet and would be low at 13:21 according to our tables and the Germans had decided that we should berth in the deep water at the end of the Victoria Pier. Our chronometer and watches were set on Daylight Saving Time so we were advised to adjust them forward by another hour to Central European Time, as Berlin was now the centre of the Nazi universe and everyone in the occupied territories worked to that clock.

The German sailors made no attempt to prevent us from looking at the coastline as we rounded Noirmont Point. I spotted gun emplacements and construction workers busying themselves above the cliffs. Transiting St Aubin's Bay, it seemed that the Germans were holding some sort of landing exercise, as there was a host of rubber boats being paddled towards the sand. Clearly, they hadn't yet mined that stretch of beach. Elizabeth Castle, isolated from the land, as the causeway was still underwater, loomed large as we slowed to pass the breakwater. There were anti-air craft guns in sandbagged emplacements along its length and evidence that more permanent housings were under construction. Because of his local knowledge, Saul could have navigated the final stretch avoiding the submerged Oyster Rocks and squeezing in between Platte Rock and the end of the breakwater but I would have struggled with such a large ship so having a pilot on board was a blessing.

Eventually, we slipped through the pier heads, both guarded by more anti-aircraft installations, before being helped to turn via a cable strung from the wall of the Old Harbour. This allowed us to tie up facing the sea with help from a team of dockers alongside the Victoria Pier. The *Duke of Normandy* had deposited the R-boat alongside the Albert Pier across the harbour and I saw Schneider raising his arm in our direction. Molly waved back.

It seemed the difficult bit was over but, now, we faced the twin challenges of German bureaucracy and local officialdom. We were in the same berth that the destroyer, HMS *Jersey,* had used when I'd had my second altercation with Rudi two years before. That had ended badly as I'd been arrested for a public order offence by the odorous Centenier Phillips. I wondered if he was still in office and cosying up to his Nazi friends. To protect us from uninvited visitors and discourage us from wandering about, the Kriegsmarine had provided armed guards at the end of a gangplank. Two of them were taking advantage of the shade under the large crane which towered over us on its rail tracks. I didn't blame them as the sun was high now and I could feel the heat bouncing off the granite flagstones. The Kriegs-marine had taken possession of the harbour complex and their battle ensigns, including the one hanging limply from our jack staff, dominated. A much larger administrative Nazi flag, just the blood red background with a white circle and central black *Hakenkreuz,* flut-tered intermittently from the weather station over Fort Regent while another slouched over the abattoir at the town end near the bus terminus. The Nazis loved their flags.

CHAPTER 19

None of these sensible precautions prevented our first visitor from chugging up in a battered old Morris J van and waltzing past the guards. He was sweating in an ill-fitting three-piece woollen suit and sported a greasy trilby on a head sprouting with unruly greying hair. His eyes were probing but held that infectious Irish twinkle.

He spoke softly with the cadence of Southern Ireland. 'Howsitgoin' boys'?

'Grand altogether', Dermot responded and offered his hand, 'and you are—'

'Molony —'

'Diarmuid, you old rogue.' Liam stepped forward and they embraced with much backslapping and would have continued reminiscing and catching up on family gossip if Dermot hadn't intervened.

As we planned to eat outside where it was marginally cooler than in the saloon, we'd set up an awning over the stern deck behind the wheelhouse and arranged some sacks of wheat as chairs. Dermot sat him down and placed Molly on one side and Liam on his other. Quigley joined them then I made myself useful by retrieving a bottle of Jameson's whiskey from our "medical" supplies and poured a tipple for everyone. I positioned myself out of Molony's eye line but with a good view of the approach from the town. Dermot toasted Ireland then gave a brief, for him, sanitised account of our journey to Jersey. Molony listened attentively while his eyes roamed the deck and he smiled in turn at each of us, though he had to twist his neck to see me.

During one of Dermot's longer pauses for breath Molony spoke up. "Well, well, this is fascinating and quite remarkable. I believe that you have some cargo you might wish to sell and something about oranges you plan to distribute. Is this correct or is my German not as good as I thought it was—'

Quigley interrupted. 'Do you understand German then?'

'To be sure, I do, if it's spoken in Irish.'

We all laughed and Quigley continued. 'There would appear to be nothing amiss with your German, Mr Molony. You seem to be well connected and have reached us first. We are carrying 508 sacks of the best Portuguese coal, about twenty-five tons in our measures, 500 sacks of Alentejo wheat — you're sitting on one — and 338 crates of Algarve oranges. Those 200,000 oranges won't keep so they are a gift but the coal and wheat would all fetch a very good price in Dublin. However, we also have something more precious for some members of your community.' He held up the unsealed envelopes. 'Letters from loved ones back home which we tried to deliver to the Germans in Lisbon. Lt Schneider has examined them and deemed them harmless but he's not a censor. Would you be kind enough to take them to the correct authority so that they can be checked and delivered?'

'Of course, to be sure, I will.' He reached out and Quigley handed them over. I wondered what postage he would charge the lucky members of his community. 'Now, you need to be careful with your produce. I can't buy it off you, much as I would like to, because the blessed busy body States has a purchasing commission —'

Quigley interjected. 'I thought the Germans were in charge.'

'And so they are. They govern from an ivory tower at the top of Mont Millais called College House. It used to be the boarding school for Victoria College.' I knew it well. Saul had lived in a dormitory there for nearly two years until his parents bought a block of flats at Havre-des-Pas. Molony sighed. 'Look, I've only been here since 1937 so I'll never be seen as a local and have often been told that if I don't like the way things are done I could always catch the morning mail boat.' He grinned. 'That option is no longer available so I have to put up with these pesky politicians.' He removed his fedora and scratched his damp hair. 'It might help if I give you a run down on how things work with the Germans. I'll try to keep it simple. The big cheese up at College House is Colonel Schumacher, the *Feldkommandantur*. There's a Senior War Administrator, Doctor Casper and more assistants and clerks than you could imagine — total waste of money but then the French are forced to pay for it! Rough justice because, before the Occupation, we hardly did any business with them. War reparations apparently and you wouldn't believe how many German mouths there are to feed here now. And they're increasing every day. From what I hear, Hitler has decided to replace the current division, the 216th which was raised in Hanover and most of them are very reasonable, with the much larger reinforced 319th from Berlin. At least the Hanoverians understand rural life. A bunch of city boys is going to be a real challenge. Besides, the 216th are green, have never fought but this new bunch have lots of veterans so God help us.' I wanted to ask some questions but sensed that Molony was best left to rant on and let slip some useful information. I could find out more later. 'It's bad enough that we have all these French and Spanish workers who seem to operate their own internal market but we have to put up with Poles and Czechs as well. I've also heard that because the box heads need more labour they'll be bringing Russian prisoners over soon. God help them. At least we don't have any Jews left, or so the Germans say, though I don't think they've been looking hard enough.'

Now, I wanted to do more than interrupt and chuck the bastard over the side into the harbour, just as I had two years before with Caroline after she'd behaved so badly but I bit my tongue. The others didn't seem too impressed with Molony's casual racism either but he didn't seem to notice their looks.

Before long, we had some understanding of the supply and demand structure currently operating in the island and Molony's role in it. He seemed inclined to swallow our story without question especially after he was shown the manifest and told about the remaining treasures in Dermot's cabin. It transpired that he'd been instrumental in recruiting the 500 or so Irishmen to work here in 1939. Since the Germans had arrived he'd been providing labour for their many projects as the locals were sometimes reluctant to work on war related construction. His little empire had expanded and he now owned two warehouses on the Esplanade and other storage areas in St Peter's near the airport. He was cheerful and obviously having a good war.

He warned us that the Germans were not as efficient as we might have been led to believe and that there were tensions among the Army, Luftwaffe and Kriegsmarine, all of whom were fighting their own battles with the *eejets*, as he put it, who were trying to run the island on behalf of the Reich. There were also conflicts between the Germans and the civil authority who were allowed to police the population. Wages were more or less fixed but prices kept doubling every year especially as virtually everything had to be purchased in France. Unsurprisingly, supplies were "lost" in transit through St Malo, Granville, and Cherbourg with a large percentage down to pilfering. The opportunity to purchase from a neutral country would be mana from heaven for the many crooks working within the island's supply chain. Without blushing he included himself in their number so he was most willing to advise us on the best deals available if he wasn't allowed to make the purchase himself. A ten per cent fee would be appropriate. I wanted to shove his percentage up his fat Irish arse but kept silent as the more hooks we were able to get into the prevailing graft mechanism the more we could learn about current and planned fortifications.

He was reluctant to provide details himself though he did hint that high-ranking engineers were in the island surveying and that very large quantities of building materials had been arriving on a regular basis. Out of curiosity I asked him about the troops we'd seen storming the beach at West Park that morning. He found this amusing as this regular exercise, or so his sources amongst the poor sods who had to cope with this soaking told him, was a deception to convince any photo reconnaissance planes that the Germans were still preparing for the invasion of Britain. Many of these troops were worried that they might be transferred to the East where real fighting was taking place. Artillery had certainly been arriving at an increasing rate and the Mayfair Hotel had been turned into a *Soldatenheim* for the pleasures and needs of the troops. Another was to open soon at the St Brelade's Bay Hotel. He'd had men working on both sites so knew of the comforts provided – especially for the officers.

Dermot asked him if there were any Irish who might wish to return to Eire. He said that several had evacuated before the Germans arrived but the majority had remained as the Germans treated them well and they received far better rations than the locals did and there was plenty of well-paid work even though they were remunerated in Occupation Reichsmarks. There was also no shortage of local or French girls who wanted a good time either. He didn't think Eire had as much to offer especially as they believed that most of the population were out of work, poverty-stricken and living on subsistence rations. Besides, they felt safer here, as the only bombing had been out at sea.

He told us he'd speak with the relevant authorities and arrange for us to attend a party he would throw in our honour and assured us it would be an excellent craic. He was elaborating on that when I spotted a Morris Ten approaching from the end of the pier. It looked official and I wondered if it would be full of German *eejets* from College House or members of the local purchasing commission. It was neither and my heart hammered in my chest as I watched our family's worst enemy, the odious, officious, lump of blubber, Centenier George Phillips hoist himself out of the front passenger seat. He rearranged his clothing before opening the rear door and helping out my Uncle Ralph. If there was one man I despised almost as much as Phillips it was Jurat Ralph Poingdestre, former president of the Finance Committee and as slimy as fish guts. He'd lost his presidency because of me but I doubted he'd lost any influence amongst the island's oligarchy. Phillips was a straightforward fascist with peculiar and disturbing tastes but Uncle Ralph, my mother's first cousin, was a scheming completely amoral bastard. As they both donned their hats and ambled towards our gangplank I realised that my flimsy disguise would fool neither of them. Fortunately, Molony chose that moment to take his leave. As Dermot helped him around the wheelhouse I beckoned Molly aside and explained that I'd need to retire to *Bodmin* until our new guests had left.

CHAPTER 20

At last, the kiss but it was only on my cheek to wake me up. I opened one eye, 'are you trying to take advantage of me?'

She giggled, 'Of course but not until you've had a good wash and brushed your teeth...and probably not then either...remember you have issues.'

I was tempted to try to resolve one of them without delay but she giggled again, 'You can't begin to imagine how difficult the last hour has been—'

'They didn't suspect anything, did they?'

'That pair of buffoons? No, they were so preoccupied with calculating their profit that they only focused on the goods. The problem we've all had is suppressing our laughter at their antics.'

'What do you mean?'

She lowered herself onto the bunk alongside me; distressingly close. 'It started with their arrival. Molony was so keen to depart that he was half way down the gangplank as they started up it. It was a standoff. They doffed their hats to each other then couldn't decide on the etiquette. Molony held the height advantage of the slope but their self-importance was more imposing. Pomposity won and your friend, Phillips barged upwards. Molony tried to give him space to squeeze past but they both have such big bellies that there was no room. Your uncle shook the hand rail—'

'You're not imagining that are you? He hates lifting

anything heavier than a pen. The only time—

'Shush. I'm telling the story. Anyway the gangplank wobbled and the pair of them were wrestling and hissing at each other. We thought at least one of them was going to fall off and land headfirst onto the quay but they carried on squabbling like a pair of toddlers. We were biting our lips, desperate not to laugh out loud, before the seagull swooped down and bombed Phillips's Panama hat. He must have felt it because he stopped grappling with Molony to remove and examine it. Bullseye; gull shit splattered all over the crown. He looked fit to burst but it gave him the impetus to grab Molony's shoulder and turn him as though they were dancing a quickstep spin turn and gained more space on the gangplank. Finally, his fat arse was higher up than Molony's. In triumph he smacked his Panama at the Irishman's Fedora dislodging it and, in the process, lost the grip on his own. Both hats sailed off; Phillips's landed on the German sentry and the other at your uncle's feet. Molony hurried down to retrieve it but your uncle stamped on it before he could reach. And thus, my dear Jacques ended the battle of the hats.'

It was the first time I'd seen her completely carefree in enjoying the retelling of a piece of slapstick worthy of Oliver and Hardy. Her eyes were shining as she burst into giggles again. I wanted to hug and kiss her but it might have ruined the moment. Instead, I asked her to repeat the battle on the gangplank which she did with relish. She also gave a blow-by-blow account of the collisions between Phillips's fat head, now hatless, and the low beams of the schooner as Dermot navigated them around. After all the huffing and puffing it transpired that they were only inspecting the ship before the official party arrived and weren't in a position to offer any deals. Dermot was disappointed, as he had wanted to play them off against Molony for the best price.

After she'd finished her description she sat up and stared at me for a while. 'What's the story with those two and you then?'

'As I was trying to tell you earlier, Uncle Ralph helped us bury my brother in an unmarked grave. The effort nearly finished him off and we thought he'd have to join Alan underground. Basically, he's a supercilious self-regarding bugger. Unfortunately, he's elected as a jurat for life and has considerable powers though I don't know if he has any role in the States at the moment. He's miserly and obsessed with screwing as much as he can out of his tenants and the fools who voted him into power. We've clashed in the past so there is no love lost but he's family and my mother's had to suffer diatribes about him from my father and Uncle Fred on a regular basis. I should imagine he's doing very nicely at the moment especially if he's teamed up with the butcher.'

'You think they're involved in the black market?'

'Running it probably which would explain the altercation with Molony who I suspect has more influence with the sort of Germans who actually carry out the transactions.'

'What about the "butcher"; why don't you get along?

I laughed at the thought, hesitated, and then told her. 'He was a friend of my parents and a stalwart of the swimming club. Charming when he wants to be and very helpful to young swimmers — the younger the better.'

She touched my arm, perhaps anticipating. 'You mean—'

'Yes, everyone knew about it but no one wanted to accuse. I've come across men like him before; fortunately there aren't many of them. Generally they're quite creepy but you learn to avoid them. Phillips was, probably still is, a senior honorary policeman in St Helier which includes the harbour. He has significant powers of arrest and is a member of a small group of fascists at the heart of policing in the island. He must love working with the Germans. He's probably settled many old scores. He still has several outstanding on me but I suppose the one that rankles the most is that I dealt with his wandering hands very directly—'

'Do tell. I imagine that you were a difficult boy.'

'Depends on whose hands are wandering. I wouldn't be difficult with you, for example.'

'Fortunately, you won't need to be either.'

'I suppose I didn't need to be with him — I could have swum away.'

'What happened?'

'I'd accepted his offer to teach me some water polo tricks. He's a very good swimmer and immensely strong in the water despite his shape and size. I've seen him swim four lengths of the 50-yard course underwater on one breath. However, that afternoon, there was no one in the water with us and he was demonstrating how best to mark an opposing centre forward from behind. It can be quite uncomfortable playing the game, as there's only a thin costume between you and the guy pressing against you. On this occasion, I felt the discomfort as he pressed his erection into me. I was only thirteen, used to showering naked at school after sports with loads of other boys. There were a couple of masters who used to enjoy showering with us so I'd seen mature cocks before but none as erect as this one felt. I suppose I could have coped with that but when he held me with one arm around my chest and used the spare hand to caress my tackle I wasn't aroused — just bloody angry. I slipped away from him and kicked his balls underwater. That's not unusual in a water polo game and you usually twist your hips to guard against it. He hadn't and I caught him square on. My God, it must have hurt but I swam away and left him to his misery. We never spoke about it but, since then, he's used every opportunity to attack my family and me. Mind you, we've beaten him at every turn so far.'

'It's your parents. You're worried that they're vulnerable now?'

'Yes. I almost feel the same way about the fat bastard as I do about Kempler.'

'You want to kill him?'

'No. But while I'm here I want to find out what he's up to, who he's been hurting and expose him if I can.'

'Jack, you are such a soppy romantic. You're not Don Quixote, you don't have a white charger, and I can't see any windmills for you to tilt at.'

CHAPTER 21

I couldn't see any windmills to tilt at either even from 100 feet up straddling the cross trees of the main mast. I knew there were still some standing in the island though none were operational. There was one high above Rozel which would make a good observation post over the north coast though the sails and mechanisms had been removed during the last war. There was one near the airport at St Peter's also without any sails or machinery. Another in Grouville but that was at sea level. They were all well out of sight though, from my perch, I could inspect the main and subsidiary harbours towards the town. The Pomme D'Or Hotel and the Weighbridge were clearly visible and if I looked towards St Aubin I could see the fort and, at West Park, the old swimming pool which was just being covered by the rising tide. The Jersey Swimming Club's pool at Havre-des-pas, though only about 1,000 yards to the east, was on the other side of Mount Bingham and blocked from view by the old Jersey Militia barracks. To the north was the mighty edifice of Fort Regent towering over the town. I spotted lots of construction work including the beginnings of a wooden trestle bridge spanning the English Harbour. It looked like the Germans might be preparing to install some railway track there.

My viewing platform was too good and I sensed many pairs of binoculars trained on me so I busied myself with the confected task of repairing a pulley and reeving a new sheet through it. Simple sailor's work which shouldn't arise too much suspicion if I was very careful but unnecessary if I could get up to Fort Regent which at another fifty feet of elevation would lay the whole harbour complex bare. I felt frustrated as we were confined to the ship and the contents of a harbour, while interesting, didn't reveal much about the overall defence of the island. I needed to get away from the sentries and explore but couldn't see a sensible way of achieving this. Along with the weapons secreted in *Bodmin* were two captured Italian rebreather aqualungs and the Pirelli frogmen suits Willie and I had used on our last insertion into the island. Though we hadn't utilised the aqualungs on that occasion because of the sea state we had trained with them in the Helford estuary. When it was dark, I could don one and slip over the side of *Irish Lass* then swim out through the pier heads and around La Collette and the Three Sisters to the pool at Havre-des-pas. I was sure it wouldn't be guarded and knew I could stash the diving equipment in a space behind the workshop. The pump in there serviced the sewer pipe which was accessed via an iron hatch and ran under the bridge and up to the road. I remembered it well because it often broke down during busy summer periods and the stench percolated onto the terraces. On one occasion I'd been asked to help rescue the plumber who found himself wedged tight in the cramped space. I was used to slurry and muck spreading on our farm but animal waste is so much more fragrant than the human equivalent. The diving suit was skin-tight and I'd had to use liberal amounts of French chalk to ease myself into it. The water temperature in the harbour wasn't a problem so I wouldn't need a suit as I'd only be immersed for about thirty minutes but it was black and would provide essential camouflage when I had to swim out through the pier heads. It was only a thirty-two foot tide and high at nine p.m. Sunset would be about 22:30 and the German imposed blackout would run from 23:00 to 05:30. The tide would be falling as I left which would help exiting the harbour. Fortunately, the moon was in its final waning crescent phase with a forecast for a cloudless sky — perfect for sneaking about. I could secure a weighted waterproof bag with my clothes to my waist, dry off in the workshop and change there. I'd creep across the beach to the Dicq Rock and follow the route of the old perquage or sanctuary path to the land locked Church in St Saviour's Parish. But then what? I was sure I could navigate across country to our farm in St Martin and find my father without alerting my mother. I was sure he would have updated his notebook on German defences. But that was one very risky way which endangered them even more. Alternatively, I could probably travel in daylight and make some observations of my own. The whole island had a circumference of only forty-three miles and most defences would be on the coast. However, Grady had indicated that RAF photo reconnaissance had spotted some activity in several of the valleys and it was felt the Germans were probably preparing underground shelters for personnel and munitions. Coastal defence with anti-tank walls, barbed wire, and mines would be a first line of defence but there would be a second ring and almost certainly heavy artillery away from the coast camouflaged in some way. With luck I could discover some of this but I really needed inside information. There had to be a safer more indirect method. Cultivating Molony was the most sensible option and I knew there were a few trusted people I could approach who would have access to military information. Subtlety was the key, though not my natural inclination.

I'd seen all I could reasonably expect from the main mast and committed it to memory so I finished off the shackle and block work and was clambering down to the deck when I spotted a deep maroon Alvis cabriolet turn off onto the quay. Its registration was J111 but was driven by someone in a Kriegsmarine uniform so it must have been requisitioned. The passenger was also in naval uniform. I stopped my descent and carried out some unnecessary maintenance on one of the ratlines while I watched. The Alvis bumped over the crane rails then glided to a halt, gave a throaty roar from its six-cylinder engine then shut off. Schneider was driving and I spotted a bandage poking out from under his cap. He clambered out and opened the passenger door for someone wearing the uniform of a *Korvettenkapitän*. As he straightened his jacket he looked up and caught my eye. I almost lost my grip on the shroud. The last time I'd seen him was when Willie had rolled him up in a rug and dumped him in the wine cellar at Caroline's father's house the previous November. We'd thrown Caroline in there as well as part of our deception for a burglary as we'd removed some very useful documents from Hayden-Brown's safe. These were now with Fleming along with my father's coded analysis of the German establishment though these were now more than eight months out of date. Luckily, the sailor, who according to Caroline, was billeted with them had never seen my face. Willie and I had explored his room and discovered his name was Karl Hemming and we'd borrowed two of his uniforms for our escape. Caroline had sworn he was just a friend but she was trapped and, because of her half-brother and father, locked into the German social circle. I was trembling as I remembered the hour or so Willie had allowed me to spend with her that night and how I'd tried to persuade her to leave with me but she'd refused before I forced her to tell me why. Later, Rachel had confirmed this before Willie and I had escaped with her and my daughter but I still yearned for the woman from whom I couldn't escape.

Yes, I'd made a fool of myself over Masha and was in danger of doing the same with Molly. Rachel had rejected me but was Caroline still here? If so, I knew I would have to find a way of seeing her, if only from a distance. She wasn't an imaginary windmill and I didn't have a lance but I knew I had no alternative but to confront the 'giant' who had stolen my heart.

CHAPTER 22

Molly greeted the two officers both of whom surprised me by kissing her on both cheeks. I kept by the corner of the wheelhouse but Schneider spotted me and called over. 'There he is, my rescuer. Come forward, my Celtic friend.'

I could hardly refuse so I shuffled over. Dermot was lining up the crew for a formal presentation as though they were honoured guests rather than the enemy. Molly was all smiles. I tried not to scowl. Schneider grinned, 'those lovely Irish nurses in the hospital have repaired my head.' He removed his cap to show the extent of the bandages. 'So, I've come to thank Molly for her first aid and to introduce my superior, *Korvettenkapitän* Hemming who is most interested in your ship and cargo.'

Hemming stepped forward, removed his cap, and offered his hand to Dermot who shook it enthusiastically. 'Thank you Anton. My colleague is most grateful and has spoken warmly about your hospitality. We are very fond of our Irish cousins and are familiar with Mr Molony and his associates.' A grin cracked his serious face and, although I had seen parts of it before Willie had rolled him up in the carpet, hadn't appreciated how handsome he was. The bastard's English was perfect without the slightest trace of an accent. He was probably very cultured and an expert on classical piano music as well. Was that a surge of jealousy warming my cheeks? If so, no one noticed as the two Germans were focused on Molly and the crew members were trying their best smile at them. Molly might have sensed my discomfort as she volunteered to show them around the ship. To my horror Schneider, who seemed to have been christened Anton, insisted I join them and show him how I'd repaired my "bitchy" engine. I let Molly lead sure that they would be too focused on her derriere to take much notice of me.

They were both amiable without any trace of the earlier arrogance Schneider had displayed. I couldn't warm to them though as they reminded me too much of Rudi Kempler and his unwholesome charm. We poked about in all the usual places and Molly rewarded their interest with a couple of bottles of *Fim de Século* brandy though I suspected the opportunity to be so close to her had been a prize in itself. I wondered if it was residual jealousy over Caroline and Karl or was my protectiveness for Molly progressing into possessiveness. When Hemming saw the cramped space which housed our temperamental engine he changed his mind about inspecting the oily confines and we moved slowly up and down companionways while Molly chatted about the cargo and asked questions about the hospital.

Back on deck, Dermot offered them a tipple but they declined as they had to return to their HQ in the Pomme D'Or hotel for a meeting. Before they left, Hemming took Dermot aside for a whispered conference while Schneider and Molly engaged in an intimate conversation. I couldn't eavesdrop on either but felt sure both would reveal the contents later. As I leant on the rail, I noticed a dark green Humber Snipe approach. The driver stopped short of the cranes and a tall man wearing a rumpled suit eased himself out of the near-side rear seat, plonked a Panama hat, untainted as yet by seagull poo, on his balding head and strode towards the gangplank.

'Ahoy, I wish to speak with a gentleman by the name of O'Connor. Would he be so kind as to meet me down here?' He certainly wasn't German and though I didn't recognise him I suspected he was a civil servant working for what remained of the Island's government. Most Jerseyman have an accent, even those educated at Victoria College but this one sounded like a BBC announcer.

Liam answered. '*Fáilte*, but there are no poxy O'Connors here. Sure, you must mean Captain O'Connell. He's busy with the Germans at the moment but if you stay there he'll be with you shortly.'

The civilian didn't look impressed. 'Tell him I am here to convey him to the offices of the Purchasing Commission and that we require him to present his manifest as soon as is convenient. I will wait...oh, and if you have someone on board who understands German it would be helpful if they were to accompany Mr O'Connor.' He smiled at the Kriegsmarine sentry and looked uncertainly about, gazing at the crane, the bollards, the quay, and eventually looked up and caught my eye. He gave a nervous wave. 'Are you Irish as well?'

I couldn't resist and sent him a mouthful of Breton then relented and added, in my best brogue, 'sure, but only some of the time.'

The two officers were on the move and I watched as both kissed Molly's hand then shook Dermot's. In passing, Anton patted me on the shoulder and said, 'perhaps we will see you later.' I must have looked puzzled as he added, 'Molly will explain.' They clattered down the gangplank and were quickly away in a cloud of exhaust. That would be another engine which needed a mechanic soon.

Dermot invited the civil servant on board but he tapped his pocket watch and declined insisting that the captain go with him. Dermot grabbed my elbow beckoned Molly to follow and dragged me into the wheelhouse. 'What does he want?'

'The cargo I suppose, says he's with the Purchasing Commission.'

'Bugger. Now we have four of them after it. Your sailor pals want me to meet with their port quartermaster. Your uncle, and your friendly butcher, both mentioned that the head of the local unit of the *Geheime Feldpolizei* is a friend of theirs and is very interested. Molony thinks he's got a deal already and now your government has come calling. Someone's going to be disappointed so how do I cope with this — who's the biggest threat?'

Molly answered first, 'sadly we can't ask Fleming. They're all dangerous but the only ones with the power to scupper us are the navy boys. Uncle Dermot, I have complete faith in your ability to play them off against each other.'

'Yes, Dermot play your Irish tinker card but remember the sentry with the bayonet down there is under Hemming's orders. I'm more interested in what Schneider was cooking up with Molly.'

'And so you should be. He's invited me to dinner this evening with Karl and his girlfriend. That should be fun...' She looked at me, 'my God, you've gone white. What is it?'

'Nothing much, only I suspect that Karl's girlfriend is my Caroline. Looks like you're going to be meeting her before me!'

'Oh dear, he's also invited you.'

'Why? Did you encourage him?'

'Why not — I didn't know about Caroline, if it is her. It might not be. Even if it was, she wouldn't let on would she?'

'No, she's too clever for that but I can't go. There might be others there who know me.'

'What, at a German officers' dinner, surely not?'

'Her bloody father gets everywhere. If he's heard about *Irish Lass*, he'll want part of any deal. Besides, I can't go. I haven't got anything suitable to wear.'

She laughed. 'That was the excuse I first used but Anton assured me that he would find something suitable so I've given him my measurements. And Karl reckons you and he are about the same size so he can lend you one of his civilian suits.'

Dermot broke in. 'I don't really understand what you two are talking about but I have to go. Mr Impatient will be chewing his watch if you don't get a hurry on. I'd better take Fergus with me. You two have a nice cosy chat and tell me all about it later.' He hurried off.

It wasn't "cosy" she persuaded me after she revealed

that she'd also negotiated with Anton to let her off the ship to visit the hospital and she could take some-one with her. She'd volunteered me and he was going to send us a couple of bicycles and passes so that we could explore instead of being cooped up on board. He would send a car to collect both of us at seven o'clock for dinner at the Grand Hotel where we could change into borrowed clothes. Anton had promised to bring a selection for Molly after she warned him that she wouldn't be seen in public in something that didn't suit her. She saw additional benefits as Molony had men-tioned that a team of construction engineers had ar-rived from France and were staying there and thought we might pick up something about their plans. The hospital would also provide some interesting gossip as well. I was more dubious as though the freedom to ride around would provide opportunity to collect informa-tion the risk that I might be recognised would pose a considerable danger.

She pointed out that I would know where to look, it was less fraught than fighting a motor torpedo boat or the IRA, and that I needed to be more optimistic. Her primary concern was would any of the dresses fit and would there be someone there to adjust them if they didn't. I knew the perfect person but Rachel, who was a dressmaker by profession, was now somewhere in France probably stitching up the German's communi-cations rather than their uniforms.

CHAPTER 23

Dermot hurried back on board with Quigley in tow. Even though it was nearly evening, both were sweating heavily. He grabbed my arm. 'Jack, the whiskey now!' Molly overheard and scurried off. Quigley mopped his brow with what once would have passed as a handkerchief.

'What's happened?' I asked, 'you look like you've been having tea with the Gestapo!'

'Close, but the Krauts we met didn't touch us. All very civilised in that polite German way. Oily tongues, slippery words, which would impress the most devious politician, but no overt threats—'

I interrupted. 'I thought you were meeting the local purchasing commission not the German bureaucrats.'

'We did meet them but they have an impossible job as everything has to be rubber stamped by Colonel Schumacher, the *Feldkommandantur*, though even he seemed cowed by the other civilian in the room. They all spoke excellent English so I wasn't really needed—'

'Oh, I think you were, Quigley.' Dermot's hand shook as he tipped the bottle into a glass and flung the liquid down his throat before spluttering, 'I think you and he have a lot in common.'

I was sure that Quigley had his own agenda which Grady and Fleming had omitted to brief us on and our captain had now issued an open challenge. Saul had hinted that he might not be all he seemed and that Fleming might not have the full story. If Willie had been here, poor Quigley would be eating his own socks. I had a rough idea how he extracted information though I could never convey his level of menace but I could make a start. I waited until Quigley was sitting comfortably on a stack of sacks with a full glass of whiskey then placed my hands on his shoulders and gave them a gentle shake. As he stiffened in protest I pressed my thumb hard into the vagus nerve behind his right ear. We'd learnt this during our commando training and I knew that too much pressure could be fatal but we'd also discovered how to moderate this technique to produce dizziness to the point of fainting.

'So, Quigley, what is your mission?'

'What the feck are you doing?'

He tried to rise up so I bore down on him but relaxed my thumb pressure. 'Let's keep it polite unless you wish to take this below decks.'

'For feck's sake, Renouf, there's no need for this. My mission is the same as yours...but I'm looking at it from a different angle. You're meant to be examining the defences, I'm supposed to analyse the Germans' attitude to how far they'll go to secure the islands. Fleming needs to know if they're prepared to sacrifice the civilian population—'

'He already knows that! Of course, they will. Hitler isn't going to surrender the islands. Fleming is just covering his own arse.' I removed my hands. 'I suppose he's asked for a written assessment?'

'Yes. OK, we both know how this works. The request has come from much higher up than Deputy Director Naval Intelligence—'

I shook my head. 'It's the Russians. Now that Stalin has woken up, he's looking for us to distract Hitler with an invasion which will be utterly futile and catastrophic for the population. Not that Stalin would care about the loss of life.' I grabbed the bottle, poured a huge tot, sat down next to Quigley, and patted his knee. 'Sorry, but you've confirmed what I suspected. Not that any of us can do much about it. Even if I reported that Hitler was making the islands impregnable fortresses it wouldn't deter Churchill if he felt it would help the war effort. Look what he did to the French fleet. We're not even really British. Ten miles from France and over one hundred from England. Within range of heavy artillery from Normandy. It would be slaughter—'

'And the English have never been sly of the odd slaughter to prove a political point.' Dermot shrugged. 'But, you're correct, there's bugger all we can do about it. The Germans would defend to the last Englishman but we already knew that. You need to hear what that other German had to say.'

'Did he have a name,' I asked.

'Of course but it wasn't mentioned though he was wearing a Nazi Party badge and, from his bearing, I would guess he's a relatively senior officer — probably in the Abwehr or SS.'

'Describe him.' I was dreading his response.

'Six foot two, athletic, light blonde cropped hair, tanned face, ah... grey eyes, scar on his forehead; women would find him attractive, early to mid-twenties, thin lips, and broad shoulders like yours. Stand up a minute.' I stood. 'Very similar in body shape to you but probably more heavily muscled, perfect English, but a superior and patronising tone. The perfect Aryan — probably, Hitler's ideal superman.'

'Any rings?'

'There was one on his right hand ring finger; silver, heavily engraved...bugger —'

'What?'

'I've seen one before. I think it's an *SS* honour ring. In fact, I think I've seen him before.'

'Where?'

'On the dockside in Lisbon, the day before you and Willie were brought from your embassy to board *Cymric*.'

'Oh God!'

'What?' Molly stared at me.

'I think it's Kempler — *SS-Standartenführer* Rudolph, bloody, Kempler, Caroline's bastard half-brother, one of Himmler's favourites and the man I have to kill.'

They were all staring at me now. 'So what the fuck is he doing here?' I asked.

Molly spoke first. 'From what you've told me you can't let him see you. You'll have to stay hidden until this is over. We can't—'

Dermot interrupted. 'No, don't worry about that. He left for the airport and France after the meeting. It seemed like a coincidence that he was here and merely curious about *Irish Lass*. He did ask about our next port of call once we left Jersey though. I told him, if we managed to sell our cargo here, then we would sail empty back to Dublin. If the island authorities wanted any more produce we'd purchase it and try to evade the British and return here. He quizzed me on Irish customs checks and seemed satisfied that we could get through without too much trouble. He seemed more confident than I feel—'

'Was he interested in the cargo we have now?' Molly asked.

Quigley shook his head. 'Not really but, and this is the worry. He's asked Schumacher to keep us here until he returns later this week. I suspect that he might ask us to smuggle something or someone into Ireland but I could be wrong.'

'He can smuggle a whole bloody infantry division into Ireland for all I care. All I want is five minutes alone with the bastard.'

'Careful what you wish for, Jack.' Dermot raised his glass. 'God save Ireland.'

CHAPTER 24

Quigley followed me below and demanded I join him in *Bodmin*. I had no concern that he would seek to retaliate for my earlier assault, as though he was quick and wiry, I didn't sense that he'd had any serious combat training. He was probably what he claimed to be — an analyst. As I activated the hidden lever, I recalled what Saul had revealed in his usual whispered conspiratorial manner, about inter-agency tensions and that S.O.E. wasn't just Fleming's plaything. Menzies, commonly known as "C", was the head of the Secret Intelligence Service and a co-sponsor of the Special Operations Executive. He also controlled all the government's secret communications and had Churchill's ear. I suspected that Quigley was his creature so, after securing the entrance and blocking off the ventilation opening to keep our conversation private, I sat on a bunk and waited for him to reveal whatever story he had confected to placate me. Instead he surprised the Hell out of me.

After fiddling about in one of the crates he produced a suitcase which I knew held one of the experimental field radios S.O.E. had been working on. I'd used one in Portugal and was aware of its strengths and weaknesses but I hadn't realised there was a false panel in the lid. He extracted a handful of photographs and placed them face down on the mattress. 'This is between the two of us, no mention to Dermot or Molly. I want you to look at these. Tell me if you recognise any of them.' The first was of an officer in German dress uniform. It was a posed studio photograph with sympathetic lighting. Prominent was the Iron Cross and, from the style of his jacket, I thought it was probably taken during the Great War. There was something familiar about his face but I was sure I'd never seen him.

The next picture brought back some unpleasant memories. I pointed at him. 'That's Ferdinand Kempler, Rudi's uncle. He was counsellor to the Director of the Reichsbank and involved in that attempt to smuggle industrial diamonds to Germany. That bastard Wilbur Hayden-Brown, Caroline's father, was the instigator.'

Quigley nodded. 'He's still there but now has a leading role in the *SS* acquiring assets from the countries the Nazis have invaded and squeezing every morsel of wealth from the individuals who have displeased Hitler — even their gold fillings.' He waved my question away and held up the first photograph. 'That's Captain Wilhelm Tobias Kempler, Rudi's father—'

'Ah, that's him. I've never seen a picture. Caroline told me that he was killed by a British sniper on 21st July 1917. My father and my mother's brother, Fred, were a sniping team. I've often wondered that, if by the weirdest coincidence, he was the one who'd pulled the trigger. I did ask him once but as I didn't have any details of place and time, he couldn't recall. He wasn't disconcerted by the possibility though he claimed that he wiped his memory after each kill. Fred had told me that my father was so ruthless and cold blooded about it he'd always volunteered to stick to the spotting. It's not something I've ever mentioned to Caroline though I am tempted to tell Rudi if I ever get the chance.'

Quigley sighed, shook his head, and turned over another photograph.

This one stunned me. 'That's Isobelle, Caroline's mother. I've only seen her once but, given the chance, I think my mother would kill her. She's also Rudi's mother though he was taken away from her when his father was killed in 1917. I believe that she's now in a sanatorium in Switzerland—'

'I understand that your father could provide more intimate details about her, couldn't he?

I froze, clenched my fists, and sucked in a deep breath. Of course, Saul knew the whole story about my father's infidelity with Isobelle and the impact it had caused. He would have confided it to Fleming and, doubtless, it was attached to my file...unless Molly had been indiscreet. I stood but Quigley held his hands up in a surrender gesture. 'Don't shoot the messenger. There's more.'

I sat down. 'Go on.'

I'd anticipated this one. It was Rudi in his full *SS-Standartenführer's* dress uniform — a rank equivalent to Colonel Menzies himself. Rather high considering that he was only five years older than me. The next showed Rudi and his uncle, Ferdinand, with Himmler.

I sensed Quigley studying my face as these thoughts whirled around in my head. 'And now, the last two.' The first showed an ornate building though I had no idea where it was. 'That's our embassy in Bern, Switzerland'. He turned over the last. It was of Isobelle posed sitting on a sofa with a distinguished looking middle-aged man. 'That's Sir David Kelly, our Minister to Switzerland, with Rudi and Caroline's mother. She's living in the embassy having sought sanctuary there.' He handed me the photograph. 'This is why you cannot be allowed to kill Rudi Kempler. We have uses for him ourselves.'

'How?'

He held up the photo of my nemesis. 'We know he's tough, ruthless, and very intelligent but he has a weakness—'

'In unarmed combat and underwater wrestling—'

'Yes, Willie has told us about your little fight in Portugal and Saul remembers you knocking him out twice —'

'Three times. The last, I foolishly rescued and resuscitated him before he tried to knife me and—'

'We know all that but, to be truthful, Renouf, he's probably more use to us than you could ever be. Now, shut up and listen. Fleming may have put you in charge of the ship but now our intelligence has been confirmed, you will obey my orders for the mission.'

'What intelligence?'

'Don't ask me how because, even if I knew, I wouldn't tell you but we received information that Kempler would be in the island this week.'

'Are you planning to kidnap him?'

'Don't be daft. He's no use in captivity.'

'You're planning to turn him then?'

'Stop guessing and listen. We know that he and his uncle have been transferring large quantities of sequestered property, paintings, furniture, jewellery and other works of art to Switzerland and not for the benefit of the Reich.'

'Wow, I thought he was a fanatic.'

'Like his uncle, he is greedy but he's also realistic. Now that Russia is in the war, the pair of them have sniffed the wind and don't like the smell.'

'But Russia's collapsing. Hitler will be able to add Moscow to his travel plans soon.'

'Possibly, but Moscow is only 500 miles from the Polish border. There's another 850 miles to the Ural mountains and then nearly another 4,000 or more to the east. It crosses seven time zones. Stalin has vast reserves of manpower and materials beyond the Urals. Napoleon failed and Hitler will as well especially as this invasion was postponed for five weeks while he saved Mussolini from the Greeks and that's before General Winter intervenes. It's going to be a long war though and we'll still have to liberate Western Europe.

'*Otkuda ty eto znayesh*?' I wondered how much he really knew about Russia.

'*Potomu chto ya zhil i rabotal tam*!' He responded immediately.

So, he'd lived and worked there just like Fleming. 'I thought I was going to be sent there—'

'But you aren't. We have something more important for you after this.'

'What the Hell is that and who the buggery are "we"?'

He smiled. 'You'll just have to wait and see unless you cock this up. Your job is simple. Come back with a convincing report on the German defences and preparations so that Churchill can explain to Stalin that an invasion is neither realistic nor of any strategic value.'

'I understand that so what's the plan for Kempler?'

He picked up the photograph of Isobelle and Sir David again and held it out. 'This is his surprising weakness. Even though he's hardly spent much time with her, he loves his mother and will do almost anything to keep her safe.'

I shook my head. 'I find that hard to believe but, even if it's true, you're not stupid enough to think that, if you hold her hostage, you can force him to work for you.'

'No, of course not. It's leverage, but not enough to terrify him.'

'For Christ's sake, Quigley. What is the plan?'

'It's Major Quigley, Sub Lieutenant Renouf, and my boss and your boss are agreed in this matter.' He sighed heavily. 'Look we have to work together whether we like it or not. There's a large element of improvisation in this but we want Kempler to think we're working for him so that we can collect enough evidence to compromise him with his masters. Sure, he'd be devastated if anything happened to his mother but rather more distressed, don't you think, if the Gestapo hauled him into the dungeons in Prinz-Albrecht-Strasse to discuss the evidence we slip to them of his treachery?'

I wouldn't have any complaints about that so long as my family weren't involved but I suspected that Major Fergus Quigley and his boss might have underestimated Rudi Kempler. He had some very powerful friends including Himmler and he might even be working on their behalf. 'Is Hayden-Brown involved in this?' I asked.

'Of course; that note book you smuggled out during your last excursion here was most revealing. We suspect that Kempler would like to shift some of their acquisitions to Eire. You know Hayden-Brown already has business interests there, one of which includes a large warehouse. But, we think there might be more and that Kempler could see *Irish Lass* as an excellent means of smuggling agents into Ireland and on to England—'

'So, you're planning to use *Irish Lass* as a sprat to catch some mackerel?'

'We already have a little shoal of fish we've turned inside out and are working for us. The Nazi's aren't very good as this spying game.'

I didn't say anything but thought the pompous twit had probably spent too much time in esoteric planning instead of applying common sense but, as he had dictated, it was his mission and I should just shut up and listen. So, I did for another ten minutes while he outlined the sequence of events he expected to unfold while we sat in our neutral schooner in a captured port.

CHAPTER 25

After he'd left, I spent some time checking the diving apparatus almost convinced now that I would have to use it before Kempler returned to the island. I also took the opportunity to double check the weapons but mostly I just sat and pondered the bizarre situation and my place in it. If we really could exert influence over Kempler then perhaps I would be able to extract Caroline without plunging my family into extreme danger. However, if Rudi was as sharp as I knew him to be, he couldn't really fall for Quigley's plan. Would he really ship the precious items to Ireland on a ship over which he had no control? Why take the risk? Admittedly, with Hayden-Brown's connections in the Emerald Isle it would probably be safer than any other neutral country. Quigley had told me about the Swiss Army's preparations to defend their country, how they'd mobilised over 800,000 men and women, and how unlikely it was felt that Hitler would risk invading. After all, neutral countries have their uses. It struck me that a safer place should Hitler come unstuck would be South America where Argentina could provide a safe bolthole.

Of more pressing concern was the biggest neutral of them all — America. The day after Hitler had launched Operation Barbarossa I'd been meant to meet Brian "Buster" Avery at their embassy. He'd been very helpful in Portugal but Fleming had changed my orders at the last moment and I'd been diverted to the Russian embassy instead and met, once again, with Ambassador Mayskiy. His primary concern was the whereabouts of his niece, Mrs Mariya Dobruskina. I knew her as Masha and we'd become rather too close during our time together in Portugal and Spain. He was also worried about Comintern's principal organiser in Normandy and Brittany, Hélène Guzman, now that Hitler had invaded not only Mother Russia, but her embassy in France as well. As always, he seemed to know more than our security services about Resistance efforts in Occupied France. He felt that Masha and Hélène might try to set up new operations in the un-occupied zone and hoped that I might be able to supply information on the safe house Hélène had taken me to in a farm a few kilometres from Quimper. Fleming had already ordered me to cooperate so I'd told him what I knew. He'd thanked me and hoped that, if asked through the appropriate channels, I'd be able to help again.

He'd also enquired after Rachel and hinted that he knew where she'd been deployed by S.O.E. Whether this was offered as a reward for past services or an implied threat I was unable to decide, as he was as inscrutable as ever. This conversation had taken place outside near the memorial to fallen Heroes of the Soviet Union at 13A Kensington Palace Gardens probably to avoid the paranoid eavesdropping of the NKVD who Fleming had informed me had the whole place bugged. On this occasion I suspected that Stalin would be too preoccupied to concern himself with his ambassador's private conversations. When I mentioned this to Fleming later, he'd laughed at my naivety and told me a little about Lavrentiy Beria, the head of the Soviet State Security and his daily execution lists.

Fleming had also assured me that soviet agents and

their helpers would have to look after themselves for the time being as S.O.E. had no resources to spare. I assumed this included Rachel. We'd both been taught some fluency in Russian during our RNVR officer training in Greenwich. I suspected that had been something agreed with Mayskiy on Hélène's recommendation. She'd looked after Rachel and my daughter, Taynia, during the German invasion of France even though the Soviet Union and Germany were nominally allies at the time. Later, their cell had been compromised and Rachel had fled to Jersey while Hélène and Masha had tried to rescue their husbands, Doctor Juan Guzman and Captain Anatoliy Dobruskina from one of Franco's work camps in Spain. Juan had been captured during the Spanish Civil War and Anatoliy shot down while fighting in a Russian plane against the German's Condor Legion. Both had been believed to be dead but Hélène had been contacted with a ransom demand which involved the industrial diamonds she'd hidden. Fleming had sanctioned the operation though I was still unsure about his real motives and it had been overseen by Kim Philby who, at that time, ran MI6's Iberian desk. At some cost to the Spanish fascists we'd recovered both of them but Anatoliy had died from the inhuman treatment he'd received at the hands of his guards. Juan had barely survived but we got him and Anatoliy's body out through Porto. Then, Willie and I had driven back to Lisbon, smuggled aboard the schooner *Cymric*, captained by Dermot, and sailed back to Liverpool Later, I'd been invited to Anatoliy's funeral and burial in the embassy's garden.

It was this episode which I was running through my memory again. Kempler had been in Lisbon and he'd clashed with Willie and me. He'd sent scores of German agents after us, but fortune and Willie's expertise, had favoured us. The Germans enjoyed a cosy relationship with the Portuguese secret service and Captain Menendez of their PVDE had followed our antics closely so Kempler would surely have been aware of our escape on an Irish schooner. So, would he really not suspect another Irish schooner conveniently turning up in my island and risk any of his purloined fortune or agents on it? Was there something I was missing here? Quigley wasn't a fool and would have connected the dots and realise that at best Kempler would be suspicious and at worst would have us all arrested and sent to France for a less than cosy chat. Was I the sacrificial pawn in this game? If so, I had better stay out of sight and certainly not attend a dinner with Schneider where I would be unarmed and highly vulnerable.

I picked up the latest of S.O.E.'s toys. This was still experimental and had been produced by BSA, though there were no manufacturer's markings on it, for Station IX which was based in Welwyn. I'd tested it and it was as near silent as possible for a pistol. It was single shot with a bolt action and a foot long suppressor which was filled with self-sealing oiled leather washers. Though it weighed a couple of pounds, it was perfect for silent killing if the target was within fifty feet as it only fired a subsonic 32 calibre ACP round. Despite Quigley's diktat, I had the motivation and the means to put it to good use. I just needed the opportunity. The stubby magazine which doubled as a pistol grip held eight rounds but I loaded only five, as the spring could be a bit tricky. I clipped it back in and replaced the pistol in its protective box. There were far more effective weapons within reach should someone breach the entrance. At least down here I could make my own sacrifice expensive. I glanced at the two crates of plastic explosive and box of detonators — very expensive.

I was still musing over my bleak future when someone rapped on the hidden door. It was Molly and she wanted to talk. I let her in.

'It's a bit smelly in here, Jack—'

'Let's go topsides then—'

'No, this needs to stay between the two of us.'

Before I could provide an unsuitable retort she handed me a copy of "The Evening Post" my father's favourite read and a staple in most island households.

This was from Tuesday 22nd July 1941, yesterday's edition, and a much reduced version on thin paper but the front page with its boxed adverts seemed little changed. I scanned it and chortled on the main story by Keith Baal under "Rabbit Corner" about dealing with a new epidemic amongst the local furry population. It included a number of letters from readers giving tips about preserving them as food stock. I realised that she was giggling as well.

'Molony brought this aboard just now with a warning that it might not be all that it seems. Apparently the Germans oversee the work of the newspaper's sub-editors to ensure that all output is corrected to protect the local population from British propaganda.'

'He's right. I know Mr Baal and most islanders will remember the disparaging description applied to those "rabbits and rats" who fled the island before the Germans invaded. It would seem that these highly intelligent German censors lack a full understanding of the British sense of humour—'

'Or it could just be that you have a rabbit problem.'

'Let's hope that the real 'pests' to which Keith is referring catch a dose of myxomatosis then. Look at this. They've taken over the cinemas as well. You have a choice of "the amusing German comedy – What Do you Want Brigette?" with English subtitles at the Opera House, or "The Moving Mountain – a German Masterpiece" with subtitles at The Forum.' I flipped over the page. 'Oh joy, West's Cinema is showing "The Earl of Chicago" starring Robert Montgomery with German subtitles. It's reassuring to see Hollywood supporting the German war effort!'

'Life seems quite normal then.'

'Yes, it's the perfect model occupation — until you read about the "Severe R.A.F losses over France" and the "Shrinkage of British Ship Tonnage" and the ease with which the glorious German Army is conquering Russia. I doubt anyone is fooled as I'm sure there will be many still listening to radios or crystal sets and spreading the British "propaganda" around the island.' I turned over another page which was full of small advertisements; several for sales of standing wheat and oats which tied in with the "Situations Vacant" column which indicated that farmers were struggling to find labour. I knew from experience that townies weren't much use in the fields and, from what Molony had said earlier, this reinforced the notion that the Germans were using the local labour force to construct their fortifications.

I put the sheets down for a closer perusal later. 'But you didn't come down here to discuss the newspaper did you?'

She sat down on a crate alongside mine. 'No, I'm worried about this evening. I don't think it would be wise for you to come out with Schneider and me to this dinner at the Grand Hotel. There are bound to be local girls there and you could easily be recognised.'

'You're right but it's not the girls who could be a problem. There'll be collaborators and hangers-on like Phillips there. It's too risky but how best to explain this to your new best friend?'

'That's not a problem. I'm sure he'll be only too pleased to have me all to himself!'

CHAPTER 26

'For fecks sake, Renouf, that's even crazier than a Fleming scheme devised after he's spent a night on the town.' Quigley shook his head in despair. 'Molly's right about you staying away from the Grand Hotel but, swimming underwater out of the harbour and around the rocks to this swimming club of yours at night on a falling tide. Really? No! I can't sanction that. You'd be—'

'Invisible, that's what he'd be and it's no more crazy than sailing here in the first place,' Molly continued, 'besides, now that Molony's got permission to take the crew to this "craic" he's organised in that town pub, it could be perfect. The guards will count the crew off and back again. If Jack and Kurt stay on board and show themselves occasionally, they won't be suspicious—'

'What about tomorrow? He can't swim back in daylight. What if your "friends" come looking for him; how will you explain his absence. You can hardly say he's popped out for a pint of milk can you?'

'We could pretend he's ill and confined to his cabin.' Dermot suggested.

'Why would they want to see him anyway?' Molly asked.

Quigley shrugged. 'To award him the Iron Cross for rescuing Schneider, probably.'

'The worst that could happen is that you apologise and explain that I've gone AWOL because I met some tart in this pub—'

'But the guards would have counted you back on board—'

'Not if you confuse them when you return with a little drunken acting—'

'That's an idea. I'm sure Rory would like to practise his diving. He could trip over one of the mooring ropes and make a big splash. He'd love that.' Dermot smiled. 'Well, that's fixed. But how can Jack keep in touch with us? What happens if he doesn't return tomorrow night? How long do we wait for him. Molony thinks they're going to unload the cargo in the afternoon. Does someone else have to fall in to create another diversion?'

'Listen, if I'm not back tomorrow night then I'll either be dead or in custody. Then it's my problem. You leave with the tide on Monday as planned. But, don't worry. If I'm still operational, I'll find a way back. Just make sure someone is listening during the night for my rapping on the hull to drop a rope and haul me up.'

'I still don't understand what you hope to achieve, blundering about in the dark.'

'Information, Quigley, information and the instructors at Achnacarry would be insulted if you suggested that I didn't know how to ghost around at night after all the time they've invested in my training...anyway it's best if I don't explain my plans just in case you're asked difficult questions later.'

'Very well but if it goes belly up it will be reflected in my report.'

The three of us laughed at him and he had to smile at the ridiculous statement he'd just made.

Schneider didn't seem in the slightest interested when he and Molly drove off without me, didn't even enquire about my excuse of an upset stomach which actually had started performing somersaults when she donned the beautiful and rather slinky dress he'd brought for her.

Thirty minutes after Schneider had goosed another burst of unburned oil out of the exhaust, Molony arrived with a covered Bedford and the guards escorted Liam, Rory, Miguel, Tomas, and Dermot aboard leaving Kurt and Quigley to help prepare me. Molony had explained that the curfew didn't apply to neutrals so he didn't expect to return until the wee small hours. We waited until the blackout had been in force for half an hour before Kurt helped me into my skin tight diving suit and harnessed the rebreathing kit. The two guards had changed just before blackout and the new ones settled in for a dull shift, one seated in the deck chair and the other ambling up and down between the crane, and the port side bow and stern lines. As we were still fully loaded the midship freeboard was only seven feet. While Kurt wandered down the gang plank to offer the two guards cigarettes I slipped down the rope and into the sea. A watertight weighted bag containing clothes, shoes and a towel was secured to my hips. I'd eschewed weapons other than a sheaved diving knife and my little burglar's pouch.

I'd swum between the Pool and La Collette many times as the Club maintained a diving board on the rocks below the promenade but had never attempted to swim into the harbour apart from during the Elizabeth Castle to harbour race once a year. It was going to be tricky because of the currents around the Point De Pas and the shrinking tide but once I was through the pier heads I could stay on the surface and use the luminous wrist compass, which we'd captured from the Italian frogmen, to keep on course.

Anything less than a twenty-six foot tide would not cover the pool so I only had about forty minutes before I'd be stranded on the wrong side of the seawall. I lost some time navigating the rocks but had been able to keep up a good pace with my fins and there was less than a foot of water covering the wall as I slithered over near the sluice gates and powered across to the lookout steps. As hoped, the pool was deserted and I ascended the worn granite steps praying that the door to the workshop alongside the café wasn't locked. It was but it was a simple padlock which I unpicked easily. After changing and stowing my kit beyond the hatchway which wasn't secured by anything other than a smell barrier, I checked my pockets for anything incriminating. Just before midnight, I set off across the beach keeping to the sand and avoiding the noisy shingle below the promenade and houses along the road until I reached the Dicq Rock where Victor Hugo had spent precious time in 1853 bemoaning his exile from France before he was expelled, under pressure from the British authorities, for peddling his political views. His revolutionary ideas wouldn't have appealed to the Germans either.

Once in the lanes I could almost have managed blindfolded and it took me only forty minutes cross country to reach my farm above St Catherine's breakwater. It was deserted and there was no sign of Victor, the mad bull, though I could hear some cattle in the fields. This time of the year they stayed pegged outside to confine them to a small area and stop them eating too much of the rich grass rather than snuggled up in the milking parlour but I didn't want to disturb them so crept into the yard and up to the back door. The house was silent but the door was unlocked. I eased in and, avoiding the creaky step, crept up the stairs and listened for my father's snores. There were none which was worrying but I could sense a human presence. I paused outside my parents' bedroom and bent my ear to the door. I could hear regular breathing and the occasional snuffle so I opened it slowly and tip toed over to the bed. The curtain was partially drawn and the window was open. It was still very warm. My mother would usually be awake well before dawn and out ready to milk the cows before breakfast. My heart was pounding but it wasn't from exertion. I didn't know if what I felt for Caroline was really love but I knew beyond doubt that my mother was the most important person in the world to me and I would give my life for her. Some faint moonlight struggled into the room and now I could see she was alone in the bed and lying on her side in an almost foetal position. I wanted to reach out but couldn't. I would have to though as it would now be well after midnight and there was much to do. I eased towards her but she stirred, raised her head, then screamed. 'No, No, leave me alone. Get out. Go, Go!'

Stunned, I stepped back as she catapulted out of the bed, scurried into the corner and grabbed a pole capped with a vicious looking spike. She was trembling with fear and on the edge of reason. What had happened to her?

'Mum, mum, it's me —Jack!'

'Keep away, you bastard!' She shuffled to the side and dragged the curtain open as she moved into the corner.

More moonlight filtered into the room and I held up my hands in surrender, praying that she would recognise me and that she wasn't locked into a nightmare. As my eyes adjusted I could see that her wrists were badly bruised and one of her eyes was swollen. Where was my father? Had he done this? Was she defending herself against him? That was an impossible thought — he'd risk everything to protect her.

I spoke softly. 'Where's Dad?'

She advanced, spike first, towards me — five feet two and seven stone of confused anger driving her to some sort of vengeance. I retreated until my back was against the wall and she was only the length of the improvised spear away. Her eyes scanned me like a snake building up for a strike but she was awake and this wasn't a dream. I could disarm her in a trice but in her crazed state might damage her frail body beyond repair.

I started to speak but she cut me off. 'Shut up, for God's sake, Jack what are you doing sneaking up on an old lady in the middle of the night.' She dropped the pole and threw herself into my arms. 'Thank the Lord you're here.'

She was like a terrified bird, trembling in my arms, sobbing and gasping for breath. When she regained her composure, she insisted that I go down to the kitchen, make us a pot of tea, and wait while she made herself presentable. She was a proud woman and would have found it unseemly to be in such close contact with a young man, even her own son, while in a state of undress. She was no prude and in her youth had enjoyed the attentions of many young men at the Swimming Pool while wearing very little but now she had a station as the wife of a well-known local farmer and pillar of the community and her best friend was the Rector's wife. As schoolboys Alan and I had never been invited into our parents' bedroom and, though she had always been loving and tactile with us, she had an innate reserve which added to her considerable inner strength.

I watched by candle light as she sat opposite me at the scarred table and cradled the cup of tea in her bony hands. I'd missed her fiftieth birthday in January but the last time I'd seen her, over eight months before, her wavy hair had still been a natural chestnut brown. Now it was almost completely grey and her face was lined with worry. Her eyes were watery from crying and dark bags marred her cheeks. I waited for her to sip a few mouthfuls. The tea was stronger than she liked and she pulled a face but declined my offer of lightening it up with a drop of medicinal brandy.

There was so much I wanted to ask but I knew better than to interrogate her. She would tell me what

I needed to know if I was patient. She knew me better than anyone else and before I could prompt her she swallowed and sighed sadly. 'Before you ask, Dad isn't here…he's in prison.'

That wasn't what I was going to ask but…'Where? Why?'

'Newgate and it's not the first time. As for why? Because he doesn't know when to keep quiet and avoid trouble.'

'Well, that's not new. At least he's not in a padded cell in St Saviour's again; or has he been there as well?'

She smiled weakly. 'No, but I fear he's been somewhere worse.'

'Where?'

'Ben Rhydding, at the top of Mont Millais, near College House from where our new masters rule. It's a large house, requisitioned by the *Geheime Feldpolizei* for—'

'Gestapo?' I tried to keep the alarm out of my question.

'In a way, but they're military and not part of the *SS*; or so Aubin tells me. They're busybodies, policemen who try to catch islanders breaking petty laws. It's also where collaborators send anonymous letters about their neighbours. George Phillips spends a lot of time there.'

There was something about the way she said his name which answered the question I hadn't asked. But, I sensed she wasn't ready for that yet so…'What did he say or do the first time?'

'Tried to stop the orders of *Reichleader* Rosenberg

from being carried out.'

'He's Hitler's Jew hater in chief isn't he? Was Dad trying to protect someone?'

'Not someone, but something — his temple.'

'The Masonic Temple?'

'It's a horrible story but after your visit in November he did try so hard to keep his nose out of the Germans' affairs. Our telephone still worked back then and he was called by George Knocker, one of the Worshipful Brothers early in the morning, January 27th I think — it was a Monday and we were about to start the milking...we still had the lorry before it was confiscated so he drove off muttering something about Nazi bastards. He didn't return that day, so I called Ken to find out if he knew anything. He didn't want to speak on the phone so rode over on his bicycle...'

Ken Gallichan was the Constable of St Martin, similar to an English mayor but also head of the honorary parish police force. He was a solid Jersey farmer who could be trusted and close friends with my parents. If my mother hadn't been here, he was my next port of call. I listened intently as she explained that Aubin had arrived in time to see a squad of SA Brownshirts break into the Temple in Stopford Road. They were accompanied by armed guards who set up a perimeter cordon. My father parked the lorry in Springfield and entered the back garden of Knocker's house which was across the road from the overbearing façade of the massive Temple which was almost as large as the Forum cinema. Through the net curtains they watched in horror as the Germans carried out the Masonic treasures from the museum inside. These included the Vonberg collection of silver and gold jewels. Mother explained that, while it wasn't obvious at the time, he discovered later that everything of value, including all the portraits and the embroidered banners of the many local lodges had been stolen. My father was the Master of one of those lodges and when he saw those precious items being thrown carelessly into the waiting lorries, he lost his temper and stormed out to protest with the officer directing the troops. General von Schmettow, the overall commander, was there observing but Colonel Schumacher, who runs the administration wasn't. My father was surprised because the General was a known Freemason and also believed to interpret Berlin's demands liberally rather than literally. However, Major Dimmler, the adjutant and also "on the square", was present and knew my father who thought him a reasonable man. However, that day he had his Nazi face on and ordered Aubin to leave. Unfortunately, he refused and tried to grab his lodge's banner from one of the Brownshirts' hands. He was clubbed to the ground and it took half a dozen soldiers of Hitler's paramilitary bastards to restrain him before he was handcuffed and dragged off.

Mother learned from George Knocker that even more Germans had then arrived and all the furniture, carpets, and curtains were dragged out and thrown into lorries. These were observed travelling to the harbour where they were unloaded and the contents craned onto the SS *Holland*. From other accounts it seemed that some of the trucks went in a different direction and, at least two, were seen entering the drive to La Hogue farm near Five Oaks in the parish of St Saviour.

'Who owns the farm?'

'Well, it's scandalous. Ken found out from Etienne, you know, the Constable of St Saviour but I can't remember his surname—'

'Le Gallais; he's a sensible sort—'

'Yes, charming man. Anyway, where was I? Oh yes, the farm had been confiscated by the Germans after they had found the owner, Ted Brouard, who's always been a few pence short of the full shilling, guilty of storing explosives. Apparently, someone —probably Phillips — had informed the "not so secret police" and they found some gunpowder and shotgun cartridges in his workshop. Just as well your father buried all of Alan's stores and shell-making equipment before the Jerries started nosing around here. Ted ran the farm by himself as Mildred had evacuated herself on the first free boat to leave and their two sons are both in the navy. I can't say I blame her—

I interrupted her story. 'What happened to him?'

'Oh, it's a serious offence, normally punishable by death so they tried him in the *Feldkommandant's* court and he was given a twenty year sentence to be served in France. No one has heard about him since but the story is that the Germans ordered St Saviour's Parish to take responsibility for the farm and that Phillips is now renting it.'

With my father out of the way, Phillips would almost certainly have designs on our farm as well. From what my uncle had told me, the bugger had been rather keen on my mother as well when they'd all been members of the Swimming Club. 'Was Dad tried in Schumacher's court?'

She clenched her fists. 'No. He should have been tried in the Police Court. He wasn't the first to get into an argument with the Jerries but his trial was held in secret and he was sent to Newgate prison for three months hard labour with a threat of deportation if he misbehaved again.'

'So, if he's there now, he's ignored them?'

'No! After his release he realised the risks and kept away from the Germans. They'd declared that the Masons, the Salvation Army, the Boy Scouts, the Girl Guides, the Rotarians, all the service clubs, the Buffaloes and...I can't remember the rest...were subversive organisations and had to be closed down. They only sacked the Temple, as we learned later, so that Hitler could put on an exhibition in Berlin of their treasures. This was the centrepiece of another of his lies that the Masonic Brotherhood were in league with World Jewry and enemies of his Master Race. Such nonsense. I know you've never been sympathetic to your father's beliefs and found his involvement with Masonry amusing but it's not as bad as my brother's obsession with communism is it?'

It was silly though but I'd always avoided clashing with my father about it. He was a good Christian and great supporter of the Church though, rather like my uncle, I'd lost any faith I might have had in that institution. I didn't believe in communism either but realised that, if we were ever to defeat fascism, we would need Russia's help. 'No, but the Nazis feel threatened by any organised dissent and are ruthless in suppressing it which is why we have to fight them without mercy.'

She stared at me — a look somewhere between horror and fear. 'Is that why you're here now? To sabotage and vandalise?'

I shook my head. 'For obvious reasons, I can't tell you but I'm not here to cause trouble, just to gather as much information as I can which is why I wanted to talk to Dad. Do you know if he's been keeping notes as he did last year?'

'If he has, he's hidden them well. We were visited soon after he finished his sentence — unbelievably it was reduced by two weeks for good behaviour.' She smiled. 'I think he was more worried about his new reputation for cooperation than early freedom. Perhaps, they needed the space. Anyway, about a week later, one of those German pests who claims to know everything about farming turned up with a representative from the Jersey Herd Book to examine Victor—'

'I thought they'd given up on him since that episode with one of Snowdon Huelin's cows. Didn't he try to sue us for that?'

'He tried but was persuaded to drop the case after we paid him off but Huelin is now a Herd Book judge and seems to be well in with the Jerries. Victor's still got one of the best pedigrees in the island but it's not his fault that he's a bit too eager with the cows.'

'Well that's a polite way of putting it but surely they weren't considering letting him loose again?'

'The German explained that their experts have been carrying out some research into artificial insemination and would like to borrow Victor for tests. It seems the Americans have been perfecting this technique. Huelin gave him the usual examination and admitted that, if it wasn't for his aggressive nature, he would have received the white card and qualified for the Book. We wondered what this was all about then the penny dropped. The German, who had been making notes on a clipboard, scribbled something on a form then handed it to your father. It was in German but he explained that it was a requisition order for Victor to be transported to France for tests. Well, you know your father's always thought that his only value lies in his stored meat and has been saving him for when we really need the food but he wasn't going to let him go for nothing. The German refused any payment but wrote out a receipt and told us he would be collected the following day.

'You know how fond I am of the poor dumb animal but, despite everything that's happened between us, I still love your father so I persuaded him to keep his snout out of it.'

'I sense a "but" coming, Mum.'

'I know it's a small thing given what's happened to all of us here but we still believe in fairness and the rule of law so, against my wishes, Aubin went to see Uncle Ralph to ask for his help.'

'I can imagine how well that went. Dealing with Jurat Poingdestre is like trying to clean a spark plug while wearing boilermaker's gloves.'

'And, now he is so accommodating to the Jerries, more than a little dangerous. But he was sweetness itself with your father and promised to exercise his best efforts on our behalf—'

'And?'

'The next day six soldiers, an army vet, the German expert, Huelin and, you'll never guess who—'

'Phillips. I bet he was behind the whole business. He'd love to butcher Victor.'

She looked down, seemed to be considering then shook her head. 'Well, you're right about Phillips but wrong about the butchering. It took them considerable effort, at least one broken leg and arm, and multiple bruises to get Victor into their van as he didn't seem to want to leave but he's still alive and we hear Phillips has been giving him the opportunity to practise his particular skills on some of Percy Le Gresley's cows at La Hogue Farm.'

I shook my head in disbelief. On the breeding market, Victor our nickname for *Marcus Piavonius Victorinus* was, in theory, worth far more than our entire farm. *Sybil's Gamboge*, a bull bred on a farm in our neighbouring parish had been exported to Ohio in America a few years back and then sold at auction for a world record sum of over thirteen thousand pounds. A group of financiers had invested in him and, so pleased with their purchase, had paraded him down Wall Street. I knew that, despite my father's anger and disappointment with Victor, he'd always hoped for a similar outcome and now, Phillips had stolen him to make money for himself. I knew about artificial insemination and if that could really work, Victor would be worth his weight in gold.

'So there's nothing he can do to get him back?'

'He did try. He went to see Phillips, who's got some

other business going at La Hogue Farm, and…that's why he's back in prison.' She sighed. 'And it gets worse. Phillips turned up here two days ago with your friend, Rudi Kempler, along with a squad of soldiers. They searched —'

'Kempler, Caroline's bloody bastard of a brother?'

'Mind your language. And, before you ask, I haven't seen or heard from Caroline since before Christmas.'

'Is she still here?'

She hesitated and looked down again. 'I don't know and don't care. You're best shot of that one — nothing but trouble. Have you any news of Rachel?'

My mother was a very good whist player but would be hopeless at poker though now wasn't the time to question her about the Hayden-Browns and the heartache they had caused her. She almost certainly didn't know about Kempler's threat to kill my parents if Caroline tried to leave the island and discussing it wouldn't help. Despite Quigley's orders there was only one solution to that as there was an obvious one to Phillips. So, finally, I asked, 'has Phillips been back to see you… alone, since?'

She hesitated, fumbled with her cup then looked straight at me. 'Yes, he has.'

'And?'

'Nothing…nothing that I can't handle.'

'Even without that homemade spear?'

'Yes, love. For your father's sake there's nothing and he knows it.' She got up and refilled the kettle then set in on the range. 'Anyway, enough about me. What news about Rachel and Taynia?'

I watched closely as she settled down again, stared at her wrists and her black eye then lifted her right hand to inspect the three broken nails. We stared into each other's eyes for a long moment during which a sentence was passed and an obligation accepted.

Then I told her about Rachel and our time together at the Royal Naval College in Greenwich training as officers in the RNVR. I didn't mention her new role but reassured her about her granddaughter, Taynia, and how Malita and Fred were looking after her. Then I spent some time extracting information from her about Phillips and Kempler's visit to our farm and the location of Ben Rhydding. There were only a few hours left before dawn and I had work to do under the faint illumination of a waning moon.

CHAPTER 28

La Grande Route De St Martin, which ran from the Parish Church all the way to Five Oaks, would be the quickest but, even though I'd encountered no traffic on the way to our farm, it was probably an unnecessary risk. I'd removed some tools from our workshop and, after passing our slurry pit formulated an interesting idea so returned to borrow one of the gas masks we'd been given before the Germans arrived. I knew that over forty million had been issued in the UK but, though no gas attacks had been reported, everyone was still required to carry them. It was also true that millions of cardboard coffins had been produced for the expected casualties from German bombing. If one believed the BBC news then less than five percent of those had been required so far. I remembered my old headmaster, trying to explain conscientious objectors to us by quoting a French diplomat, "The death of one man: that is a catastrophe. One hundred thousand deaths: that is a statistic!" With the Russians and Germans now fighting a war without rules I suspected that even larger numbers would be assigned to that clinical way of counting. However, as I paused to consider the slender crescent on the left hand side of the moon hanging high in the western sky I was planning to inflict only one small catastrophe and hoped that it's faint light would guide my path. I'd left home just after 01:30 and should reach La Hogue farm in less than thirty minutes. I didn't know what or whom I'd find there but was sure it wouldn't be the end of my journey that night. Mother had told me where Phillips now lived in a villa in Val-lee Des Vaux called Rossmore which he'd acquired for a pittance. That would be a more difficult journey as I wasn't as familiar with that part of St Helier. I did have one landmark I could aim for but wasn't ready for a potential confrontation with Caroline at her father's house above Grands Vaux especially at that time of the morning. I might visit on the way back if I had to snare Phillips at home.

I'd heard a motor cycle engine travelling towards St Martin's Church along the main road which was almost parallel to my cross-country route but, apart from that echoing exhaust, all was quiet. I heard the cows first but it wasn't me who had disturbed them. Away to the west was the growing growl of aircraft engines seemingly heading towards me. It sounded like a large formation of multi-engined planes probably on their way to bomb France. Our German troops must have thought otherwise as searchlights began to probe the sky, thin pencil beams which had no clouds to reflect off and added little illumination. I stepped into cover anyway but was startled by the sudden cacophony of anti-aircraft fire apparently directed aimlessly into the heavens. This futile barrage obscured the thundering engines and went on for nearly twenty minutes. Had the Germans panicked or just taken the opportunity to practise and deprive the entire population of their sleep?

One small calibre battery had been chattering away behind me and I guessed it was mounted high on one of the medieval chapels above the ancient burial chamber at La Hogue Bie. Even 20 mm shell fragments can make a mess of a human body when they tumble to the ground so I stayed under a large oak tree until the anti-aircraft fire stopped. However, the muzzle flashes had illuminated the farmhouse with pulses of bright light and revealed a portly figure standing outside looking up at the sky. I was pretty certain it was Phillips and felt a great relief which turned to an excitement quickly harnessed into purpose by my training. But was he alone?

I waited until, in the new silence, I heard the door close as he went back inside. I slithered under the double barred gate before running at a crouch to the building. It was a typical, if substantial, granite-faced two storied Jersey farmhouse entered through a central arched front doorway with two windows either side and another two directly above. There were three chimneystacks on the tiled roof. It seemed to be south facing but on the eastern side closest to me was an additional lean to with a sloped roof. Phillips, if it was him, had entered through a side door. I crept along the south side, past the window which was shuttered for the blackout though chinks of yellow candle light leaked out. I couldn't see into the room but could hear some strange whimpering sounds. These were human and made my skin crawl. I also heard laughter which convinced me that it was Phillips as his high-pitched voice was almost girl like when he was amused. The whimpering turned into muffled screams. I was now dreading what I might find but I could no longer listen without attempting to stop whatever was happening in there. Training took over. If there was a witness, however unwilling, I couldn't let my face be seen so I pulled on the gas mask, unsheathed the knife, then slowly turned the handle, and eased the door open.

I'd seen too many sickening sights in the past year, had witnessed Willie extracting information from recalcitrant Germans but, even through the misted glass eyepieces, this turned my stomach. Phillips had his back to me and was bent over a young boy whose legs were spread and rhythmically thrusting himself into him. He had his butcher's hands on the boy's shoulders and was giggling as he pleasured himself. His trousers were around his ankles and he seemed unaware of my intrusion. My urge was to stick the knife where it would give him no pleasure or just step in silently and slit his throat. But I needed him alive and unmarked. We had matters to discuss so I sheathed the knife and crept up behind and to the side of him pinched his vagus nerve until he collapsed in a heap at my feet. I noticed that the boy's wrists were tied to the table so stepped back and closed the door. The young lad was trying to turn his head to see what had happened. His buttocks were streaked with blood and I noticed a slim cane on the table. All my human instincts wanted me to cover and comfort him but I couldn't, even after I'd finished with Phillips. Instead I found his vagus nerve and sent him to sleep as well. Once I had Phillips awake and cooperative I would find out more about this boy and how he had got there, before deciding how best to have him found. I forced myself to inspect the damage the pederast had caused but it wasn't life threatening so with a heavy heart I dragged Phillips out of the door careful not to leave any obvious marks on him. I closed it on the sickening scene then sat Phillips up against the cider press in the yard, removed his shoes and stuffed his socks into his mouth noted the claw marks on his left cheek then waited until he came round.

It was only a matter of minutes before his dull eyes fluttered open and he saw the tip of my knife under his left nostril then flooded with alarm as they focused on my mask. I explained in muffled French, as I knew he was fluent, then made him pull his trousers up, and prodded him towards the stone barn. With some more gentle encouragement he produced the key to the heavy-duty padlock and I ushered him inside then switched on the torch I'd taken from our farm. It was a large space but almost completely filled with crates and furniture. The two windows had been bordered up from inside and iron bars fixed over them. I spotted a light switch and to my surprise it worked and a row of hanging lamps shone down on us. He was trying to remove the socks when I shoved him against the wall and pressed the knife into his larynx careful not to draw blood. His eyes were protruding with fear but I spoke calmly in heavily accented English.

'We need to talk so I will remove the gag. If you wish to leave here with all your fingers and that filthy thing between your legs then you will listen and answer my questions. Nod if you agree.'

He nodded but I could see from his eyes that he was beginning to recover from the shock and trying to plan an escape so I squeezed his nerve again this time to send pain through his body, spun him around and made him spread his arms and legs so that all his weight was balanced on his fat hands against the cold stone wall. I yanked his trousers down again and touched his balls with the flat of my knife before stepping to the side and pulling the socks from his mouth.

'What do you want?'

My torch was a similar size and shape to the object he had been using on the boy so I rammed it into him in the same area and hissed. 'We can be civilised about this or not. It's your choice.'

He whimpered then nodded his head. I had to be careful not to leave any marks so removed the torch and wiped it on his shirt.

'Tell me about the boy, his name and how he got here.'

'I don't know his name—'. He screeched in pain. This was going to be difficult but I couldn't leave any visible bruising on him.

'Last chance!'

'OK, OK. I don't know his name but he was brought here by a friend.'

'His name?'

'Marcel.'

'Family name?'

'I don't know, he works at Haut de la Garenne. He drove him here.'

I knew about the children's' home and had heard rumours so wasn't too surprised. 'When is he collecting him?'

'Before dawn.'

'How many others has he brought to you?'

'Please, I can't help myself. Some of them don't seem to mind, some enjoy my attention. I'm kind to them and give them little presents—'

'That's not what I saw!' God, I wanted to hurt him but I had to convince him this was my main concern before tricking him into revealing more about his operations in the barn.

'He was being difficult, needed a bit of discipline.'

'His first time with you was it?'

He hesitated which was answer enough. 'What do you want from me, an apology?'

'That will be a start. A short note listing the others you have entertained here, along with a promise not to do this again. You must sign this note.'

'Do you know who I am?'

'Yes, I do so do not make up a false name or you'll never write again.'

'Is that all?'

'No, I'm curious about this barn. What are these goods? Who owns them, where are they going? Once you've satisfied my curiosity then we can talk some more about the boy and Marcel.'

'Can I sit down? This is most uncomfortable.'

Without a word my mother had passed the sentence and I was going to execute it and with every word he uttered any regret I might have felt was draining away. I lifted up the mask for a moment to let in some fresh air and escape the rubber suction then steeled myself for the next actions.

At the far end of the barn was a wooden enclosure with a door, probably a small office. I replaced the mask, made him pull up his trousers and buckle his belt. He didn't seem to have a coat, perhaps it was in the house. With me prodding from behind he waddled towards the office and I offered him a seat at the ornate oak desk which seemed completely out of place. I stood behind him while he followed my instructions to write the note I'd demanded. He listed five names which I suspected was too few so I made him rethink and add rough dates to their visits. Of course he would deny everything and claim it was forced out of him but that didn't matter. Even if the authorities did discover this confession, it would be suppressed.

He baulked when I made him print his name and add Centenier as a title but as soon as he felt my thumb touching his neck he complied. I checked his signature. I'd seen it several times before and remembered it on the letter he'd written to my headmaster in an attempt to get me expelled. Fortunately, Dr Grumbridge and I had shared the same opinion of him so I made him get up and leave the letter on the desk then pushed him out into the barn.

He didn't have the wit to invent fictitious items so I soon discovered that most of these treasures were from looted properties in France. There was a section with items from the Masonic Temple in Stopford Road but little from the island. I sensed that he was convincing himself that I was merely a thief working out what to steal and planning to use his written confession for blackmail. The fact that I hadn't attempted to help the tortured boy would have reinforced that hope. To establish his authority and connection with the occupying powers he mentioned that he was merely a guardian for these items and that I would be foolish to take too much as they would hunt me down and he wouldn't be able to save my skin. He'd always been a patronising, pompous prick but now he seemed to have gained delusions of grandeur and invincibility. All the information I needed for Quigley would be in the filing cabinets in that office as I knew the Germans were punctilious in keeping records of their larceny. I would examine those later but for now I was satisfied that I understood when and how these goods were processed. I was curious about his interest in my farm though and asked about shipments through the main harbour. He was gaining in confidence and explained that he and his associates were planning to move everything to a new location closer to a jetty which wasn't so tidal and under such intense scrutiny. That would be the breakwater at St Catherine's which extended over half a mile out to sea and probably suitable for a submarine if needed. If this was the case and people like Kempler were thinking that far ahead it could only mean that the belief held in London that Hitler's excursion into Russia would end in the same way as Napoleon's before was shared by the real gangsters in the Fuhrer's entourage. If there was this canker at the heart of the Reich then that would be far more valuable than all the loot in this and all the barns and storehouses in the occupied territories.

I invited him to tell me about his other enterprises and how successful he'd been. He was very proud of the fact that he now owned five shops and the main meat wholesaler and was spreading into other retail opportunities. He even told me about his bold plan to make money from a bull he'd stolen from some stupid farmers with the help of a German friend.

After we agreed my price of half a dozen crates of mixed jewellery and gold and silver ornaments to be collected and shipped to my associate's fishing boat later that day at La Rocque he offered to show me this bull. I didn't think Victor would recognise me in the mask so agreed. I was still undecided whether to stage Phillips's tragic accident in Victor's pen or in the slurry pit. The only problem with a one sided bullfight was that Victor might get bored as he bored and leave the bastard alive to tell his tale. I'd never liked Victor and the feeling was mutual but even a dumb animal deserved some consideration.

I declined the offer and suggested that he show me the cows instead. We'd have to pass the slurry pit to reach them. It was more of a lake than a pit and contained by a low concrete wall. A tarpaulin was stretched over it and well tied down to hooks along the wall. I'd donned the gas mask earlier when I'd loosened one section. Phillips was a townie and I was counting on his ignorance of the toxic dangers of the gases produced when slurry decomposes. After I'd loosened the cover I'd broken the crust with a stick and agitated it for a few moments. Though the rotten eggs smell of hydrogen sulphide is immediately noticeable higher concentrations off ammonia, methane, and carbon dioxide released at ground level can't be smelled. I may have slept through some chemistry lessons but I'd learned at an early age that this mixture is poisonous to humans and animals, is fatal in seconds and just one breath is enough. I stopped him near the gap I'd created.

'What a stink. Bloody animals.'

Much as I wanted him to know who had helped him

to a better place, I daren't remove the mask. One shove and he tumbled forward, overbalanced, and landed face down next to the gap. The breath he took to complain was his last. After confirming death I left him there and returned to the barn to examine the contents of the filing cabinets and make some notes for Quigley. I was feeling quite light headed. It could have been because of the restrictions imposed by the mask filter or some fumes from the slurry pit or just relief from the burden I had now removed from my parents. If only the Kempler issue could be resolved so easily. Though tempted to wait for Marcel to return to collect the poor boy there was no way I could extract any retribution on his behalf without incurring unnecessary risk. Phillips' letter should be sufficient if found by the right people first. I could make an anonymous call from one of the public telephone boxes in Five Oaks but to whom? The duty centenier for St Saviour's Parish? The Germans in College House? The *Feldpolizei* in Ben Rhydding? That would raise suspicions of foul play rather than an unfortunate accident or suicide. I also considered letting Victor loose to hump whatever took his fancy but he might be clever enough to find his way home and our poor cows were still pegged out. My mind was buzzing but I realised that what I really needed to do was find somewhere safe to grab some sleep.

CHAPTER 29

Mum was still up when I returned and fussing about with chores before starting the milking. She didn't ask any questions but led me to the barn and suggested I settle down amongst the hay bales in the loft. She promised to wake me after she'd finished the milking but I told her I wanted to help and insisted she give me two hours then we could work together. The previous November, Franz, a[J2][J3] young German soldier stationed in the guard post at Verclut, had visited the farm every morning to help out and receive milk in exchange then try to engage Rachel in conversation. As soon as he discovered that she and Taynia had disappeared, he never returned and while Dad was incarcerated she had to manage by herself though Ken Gallichan occasionally sent one of his farm hands to help.

While I was teasing the milk out of my group of cows I rehearsed my next moves and tried to assess the risks involved in each one. I'd remembered that we were in the middle of the *Visite du Branchage* season and had asked Mum if the Parish's roads inspectors had been round yet. During my night time journey I'd stumbled across some pretty unkempt vegetation overhanging the lanes. These were more than just traditional checks as the Parish officials were quite ruthless in imposing fines. Ken had told her that, due to staffing issues and very limited motorised transport, St Martins and other parishes were a couple of weeks behind schedule but hoped to start soon. When I'd worked for Ken as a constable's officer between the evacuation and the German bombing in June 1940, I'd been authorised to visit all abandoned property. Armed with a clipboard and overalls no one had challenged me and I wondered if I could hide in plain sight again and wander around the countryside. My fake ID would be of no use if stopped by the Germans though my old parish police warrant card was still in my bedroom. Apparently Ken's men were having to use bicycles and we still had one in the barn. The tyres were worn but sound and once I'd patched the inner tubes the bike was serviceable. Dad's brown overalls were a good fit so I secured one of the clipboards he used for recording the milk yield to the handlebars and strapped my old canvas haversack with some snacks from the kitchen and other essentials to the carrier. Armed now with some paper, a couple of pencils, one of my father's old caps and his reading glasses and heeding Mum's warning that the Jerries had changed the rule of the road from left to right the previous month, I set off for the one high risk destination I should have avoided at all costs. Before leaving, I begged Mum to take a few days break and go and stay at the Rectory with the Cabots. If she was curious about my request she didn't show it, merely sighed, shook her head and agreed before hugging me and whispering. 'À la préchaine,' in my ear. Who could possibly know when the "next time" would arrive?

I stuck to the lanes and by 09:30 I was coasting down Les Ruettes towards Paul Mill on the east side at the head of Grand Vaux valley. The stream bed was almost dry and further down the valley a gang of workmen was digging away under German supervision. From the noise and banter I guessed these were some of the Irish contingent. I pushed the bike around them and noted that they seemed to be diverting the stream. One of the German soldiers spotted me and started to approach when one of the well-dressed civilians supervising the digging called him over and pointed to a mechanical shovel grinding its way towards them. I carried on slowly up Les Ruisseaux until I reached the bend which led to Les Routeurs, Hayden-Brown's converted farmhouse. It was two years almost to the day that I had spied on her flirting there with Rudi Kempler who I then believed to be a Dutchman. I'd borrowed my father's binoculars on that occasion and sneaked into a field of high grass overlooking the courtyard. The grass had been damp then from overnight rain but now the island was experiencing a drought. Fortunately, I wasn't allergic to the clouds of pollen I released when I crawled forward for a better view. I'd taken a risk in bringing his binoculars again and, as I wriggled into a comfortable position, some vernal grass tickled my nose. I suppressed a sneeze then, in a moment of inspiration, broke off a stalk of Molly's least favourite plant extracted one of Mum's envelopes from my pocket, slipped the grass inside, licked the flap and sealed it. The gum left a bitter taste in my mouth so I pulled my sack to me, pulled out the canteen and swallowed some welcome if rather warm water. I'd write her name on it later and find a way of delivering it to her on Irish Lass.

It was heating up in my little nest but there was no activity outside the house. Could I risk getting closer and looking through the windows? There were two cars parked outside the main entrance – one was Caroline's red Bugatti and the other the Alvis used by Schneider so perhaps I should wait a bit longer. Apart from the occasional clanking from the shovel's tracks and revving of its diesel engine from the valley below, it was very quiet. Caroline... why was I here? What would I do if I did see her? It was hopeless. Even if I could persuade her to leave and smuggle her aboard *Irish Lass,* as long was her half-brother was alive, I would forfeit my parents' lives. The equation hadn't changed so I was wasting my time but my pulse was racing in anticipation of even a brief glance. But why was I torturing myself? It was passed ten o'clock now and there was important work to do. I had to leave. But, as I eased up onto my knees the conservatory door opened and piano music flew out. It was her though I couldn't be sure of the composer. Chopin, Beethoven? It didn't matter because it was her playing without doubt. Abruptly, mid phrase, it stopped and there was a brief silence before her voice carried out. She was calling for someone. Then, there, blinking into the sunlight was the woman who'd burnt herself into my soul, whose spell I couldn't break however hard I tried. She'd trimmed her hair short though it was still golden. Her strapless summer dress snagged on the patio door as she brushed through and she lifted the hem revealing her bronzed legs. I held my breath as she walked thoughtfully to the garden bench then slumped into it as though exhausted. She looked back to the house and called out again in German. She sounded impatient and imperious and seconds later was rewarded when Karl, in open necked shirt and uniform trousers with dangling braces, trotted out holding a bundle wrapped in a blanket. He hurried towards her and deposited it in her lap. She sighed and examined it, rapped out some more exasperated German then shrugged the top of her dress off her left shoulder and revealed a breast. My heart was pounding now — a frantic drumbeat thumping in my ears. It couldn't be. But it was. Caroline — the only woman I had ever truly loved, was breast feeding a baby while its father leant over and kissed the mother's head. I dropped the glasses and buried my head in the rough grass. Now, I finally knew what despair felt like. I could use fear, harness its energy and release it violently but this was something new, an impossible weight which sucked the life out of me. I needed to escape its clutches so could no longer face the reality of the betrayal playing out only yards from my pit of misery in the vernal grass. Slowly, using every ounce of my dwindling strength I retreated, crawling backwards until I was on the roadside verge.

I couldn't afford to dwell on the anger and hurt and had to focus on the task I'd been given. Riding down the hill might cause problems with the guard who had spotted me earlier so I pedalled up Oaklands lane then down Mont Neron until I emerged further down the valley. There were more teams of men at work under German supervision clearing brush from between the road and the steep hillside. They ignored me so, still in a daze, I rode on into Val Plaisant and dismounted outside St Mark's church where Joe had retrieved a mysterious package just over a year before. It had been dropped by parachute and was dangling from the railings when he'd spotted its trailing red ribbon and had taken it to the Town Hall. No one there could translate the missive and Joe had remembered that Caroline was fluent in German and had been authorised to call her. We'd been in bed when he telephoned and twenty minutes later we were in the inspector's office and Caroline was trying to make sense of the ultimatum. The Bailiff had started an all island search to find others who might be able to translate but she was the first with the worrying news that the island would be bombarded until we surrendered. It brought back bitter memories but they were beginning to freeze over so I decided to do something useful and kind. I pushed the bike into the church yard and wheeled it along the passageway which I knew led into Byron Road.

Bunny had entrusted me with his mother's address and asked, if I had the opportunity, to deliver a message to her. He wasn't foolish enough to endanger me with anything in writing but had given me his St Christopher on a chain. I still wore the one I'd given Rachel the night she told me about her discovery that she had been adopted and her mother was a Jewess. She'd returned it to me after spurning my third offer of marriage and I supposed that if I was hauled in for questioning my interrogator might find it unusual that I wore two of the traveller's charms but I could explain that one was for Ireland and the other for Brittany. He'd told me that I shouldn't risk speaking with her as she might say something to a neighbour and it would be sufficient to post the cross through her letterbox as it had an inscription on the back which would reassure her that he was alive.

It might also frighten her so I decided to try a different approach. No 19a was a terraced house which looked well maintained with window boxes on the sills outside the dark green front door. I tried to peer through the windows but the net curtains defeated my attempt so I wandered along the lane until I saw a narrow passage which should lead around the back. There were half a dozen properties and 19a was two from the far end. Each house seemed to have a courtyard and backdoor where dustbins were placed for the weekly collection. I rested the bike against the wall and tested the door. It was unlocked so I let myself in, clipboard in hand, and listened. The outside toilet door was ajar and smelt like it had just been disinfected. The door into the kitchen was wide open letting in some fresh air and expelling the steam from a pot boiling on the range. It reminded me of the fish stew my mother sometimes brewed from crab shells. I was also aware of a kettle beginning to whistle and waited until it was stopped by someone lifting it from the hearth before knocking and entering.

'Mrs Noel?'

She looked startled, noticed my clipboard, then my smile. 'The meter's under the stairs if you've come to read it. Would you like a cup of tea?'

'That's very kind of you — yes please.' It would be most welcome though I doubted it would be the cure all in which most of the English believed. While she busied herself with the ritual of warming the teapot before carefully inserting two spoons of tea into its warm interior, I examined her surreptitiously. She was wearing a pinny and looked healthy enough for someone probably in their late sixties. A pair of wire-framed spectacles dangled from a chain around her neck and I spotted yesterday's *Evening Post* on the table alongside a copy of Shakespeare's complete works. Reading upside down it looked like it was open on a page from the *Merchant of Venice*. After she'd placed the tea, "sorry no sugar", on the table she sat down and placed her spectacles on her nose then studied me.

'Is that the new Gas Company uniform? Looks a bit dusty?' Her voice was strong and tinged with that faint Jersey accent of someone who was used to talking in polite company and had probably enjoyed an extended education.

'Yes, I'm new to this job though I don't think the Gas Company would be happy with this uniform. I'm not here to read your meter, Mrs Noel. In fact, I shouldn't be here at all and you must swear to keep my visit secret—'

'Who are you then?' She sounded alarmed and confused.

I reached under the collar of my overalls and undid the St Christopher, hoping I'd selected the correct one and placed it on the table.

She reached over to touch it then gasped. 'Is he alright?'

'Yes, he's in rude good health. I last saw him two days ago and he asked me to find you to tell you how much he loves and misses you. I hope to see him again soon so is there anything you would like me to say to him?'

Her hands were trembling as she held the cross and rubbed her finger over the inscription. She sighed deeply then reached over to hold my hand. 'Thank you. I realise that you've taken a great risk but please...don't worry...it'll be our secret. Tell Clifford that I love him and understand. I'm fine. It's not perfect here but the Jerries leave us alone and life goes on. I miss him terribly. I pray for him every day when I'm cleaning the church so tell him not to worry about me. Just be careful and don't take risks.' She smiled, 'but if he's a friend of yours then I suppose he has little choice.' She picked up the book and opened it at the fly leaf. 'Remind him that he left this behind and tell him that I'm still trying to work my way through it. He was playing a big part in that play when he was at Victoria College...before his father died...I didn't really understand it when they stopped the production. He did try to explain — something about being too kind to the Jews.' She handed me the book and I read the inscription "For Clifford, from Mum and Dad, Christmas 1905". As I returned it she looked at me shrewdly. 'We will win, won't we, now that the Russians are on our side? He believes in them, you know, this communism. My late husband would turn in his grave if he knew. He wouldn't be too happy with this mess we're in here either but,' she shrugged, 'what can you do — just live the best life you can, I suppose.'

'Mrs Noel, you're a brave woman. Have faith. We will win but it is going to take time so keep out of trouble with the Germans and their sympathisers and, if you think it helps, pray for all of us fighting their evil.'

She laughed, 'Mr not the gasman, I hope you're a better fighter than a preacher! Now you had better be off... but wait.' She reached back, undid a clasp behind her neck and produced a locket on a gold chain. 'Give this to him with my love and you take care of yourself...is your mother still with us?'

I nodded while gulping down a final mouthful of tea to hide the emotion her question had prompted.

'Well, think of her and, if you have the chance, tell her how much you love her as well because you can be sure she's thinking of you.' I got up from the table blinking back the sudden tears and hugged her until she extracted herself, stood on tiptoe and planted a kiss on my cheek. 'Thank you...you have no idea how much this has meant to me. Now, Godspeed.'

How safe was it to continue riding around the town? I suppose my light brown overalls bore some resemblance to those worn by Gas Company workers but would any busybodies especially Germans stop me for ID? If so should I play the local going about his lawful business or play the confused Jacques Renault and babble at them in a mixture of French and Irish English? Too many questions, so I retrieved the bike and pedalled off towards the junction with St Mark's Road.

There were several pedestrians walking towards the town centre as well as a few on bicycles but very little motorised traffic so I crossed over and carried on for fifty yards or so then turned left into Bryon Lane. I knew this area very well as Springfield sports ground was around the corner as was my father's masonic temple. He'd shown me around the interior on a couple of occasions but I found it overbearing and much preferred watching Jersey and Guernsey football teams battling it out in the annual Murratti Vase match on the pitch. I turned right into Oxford Road and stopped at the junction with Stopford Road to look at the massive temple which dominated the skyline with its bleak and somewhat sooty Victorian interpretation of Greek classical architecture. It was intended to impress and with a splash of paint it might very well stand as a monument to the Masons but now it looked unloved and almost as forbidding as some of the Methodist chapels scattered around the island. As I watched a relatively new Bedford lorry pulled onto the pavement and two German soldiers jumped out. They left the engine running as they unloaded a stack of what looked like domestic radios then one unlocked the main door and they carried them inside. I was tempted to take a closer look but I doubted there would be anything of military value to see so I rode over and continued down Oxford Road until I emerged into Gas Place under the shadow of the enormous gasometer. No one had shown the slightest interest in me so I decided to head for the centre of the town. David Place led into Bath Street and the Jersey Evening Post building which dominated the corner with Charles Street. It was heating up now and I could see the first floor windows above the main entrance were open. A German officer, tunic unbuttoned, was leaning out of one of them and looking up to the granite edifice of Fort Regent which commanded all approaches to the town and its harbour.

I heard a string of German shouted at him from inside and a passing workman looked up then spat into the gutter. Also visible just a few yards further down the road was the magnificent art deco Wests Cinema with its twin pillars. I'd spent many happy hours there watching the latest American films and even more enjoyable time in the Plaza Ballroom above, where Saul and I had learned to dance. That Hollywood film, *The Earl of Chicago* was indeed showing at 7.30 with matinees of Thursdays and Saturdays. I was surprised that the Germans would allow such decadence but after I read the poster and advertising material and realised that it was about bootlegging and a gangster discovering that he'd inherited an English earldom I could see their perverted reasoning[J4]. From the black and white photos I surmised that it was taking a poke at the British aristocracy and the way they treated the ordinary people. Straight out of Goebbels's propaganda machine. At least the locals had a choice as there were two other cinemas but I imagined that one, probably the massive Forum, would be mainly used by the occupying troops.

I remounted and rode along Beresford Street past the covered market and turned into Waterloo Street. Most of the roads had patriotic names, many after former governors and the fort was named after George III and constructed when he was Prince Regent. Though so close to France, the island was fundamentally English therefore it was no surprise that Hitler seemed keen to hold on to it. There was a long queue outside Le Riches Stores and the market seemed crowded as well. I remembered it was Thursday so half day closing which would explain the press of people. Perhaps they were shopping before the matinee in Wests and a dose of anti-British sentiment. There were very few local men and most shoppers seemed to be middle-aged women who appeared to be avoiding any contact with the many off duty German soldiers and sailors wandering about aimlessly. As I was debating which route to take next, I saw an elderly lady accompanied by a very attractive younger woman walking along Don Street towards the side entrance to Voisins department store. They were arm in arm but a gust of wind funnelling down the narrow thoroughfare caught the brim of her summer hat and blew it along until it ended up at the feet of a German army officer. He bent down to retrieve it and looked around for its owner. Recognising the bareheaded lady, he bowed and moved towards her. She was frozen for a moment then turned tail and, dragging her companion with her, dashed off in the opposite direction. I stifled a laugh recognising that the price of a hat was insignificant compared to the reputational cost should she be seen conversing with the enemy. As they hurried past me the young woman, who must have been my age, smiled at me and rolled her eyes. Fortunately, I didn't recognise her and she didn't pay me any further attention. I carried on towards King Street and past the small group of officers who were examining the old lady's hat while laughing at their comrade who had suffered her disdain for his moment of nobility. They were still teasing him as I dismounted and pushed the bike up the island's main street and turned off into the Royal Square where we'd been forced under threat of further bombing to display a massive white cross on the flagstones before the Germans invaded. They'd gone beyond invading now and I couldn't believe my eyes when I saw a group of them netting pigeons much to the amusement of the locals sitting on the benches outside the States Building and some waiters sweeping up in front of the Peirson Hotel where the Irish had gone to celebrate the previous night. They swept on the bemused pigeons like birds of prey and emptied their nets into a Morris van they'd purloined from Orviss grocery store. Perhaps they were hungry. I circled back to King Street and turned into New Street and the rear entrance to de Gruchy's where Rachel had worked as a seamstress before she abandoned her adoptive parents to find her real ones in France in 1939.

My route had been rather random so far but now I decided I wanted to get closer to the harbour and see what I could discover. I rode into Union Street and stopped outside the terraced house where Uncle Fred and

Malita had lived. The door had been blood red but now it was a dusty black and the windows were boarded up. In the distance I could hear the strains of a band playing so, like I'd always done when visiting bands turned up for our annual Battle of Flowers, I followed the music. I cut into Old Street and headed towards the Town Hall which had been the scene of several adventures and humiliations. Phillips had been a senior centenier there and thrown his weight about with such arrogance and disdain for others that I doubted very many would turn up for his funeral. The sounds of the brass and a steady bass drum beat were growing in volume so I stopped and watched as a quite large German Army band trooped past and marched towards the Parade gardens. Some locals followed them and I supposed that if school had been out there would have been a gang of children in their wake. The Germans were very good at some things — armoured warfare, dive-bombing, sinking unarmed merchantmen, goose-stepping, and playing martial music but I did find it amusing to watch them blowing trombones as they stretched their legs out almost horizontally before slamming their feet down onto the tarmac in time to the beat.

Once they'd passed I rode along Seale Street and made for the warehouses behind the Esplanade. If I was going to discover any really useful information I would have to take a great risk. The reward was enticing and as I had to find a way of getting my message to *Irish Lass,* I didn't really have many options. Hedley Pallot, known to all as Nutty because his obsession with sunbathing in the nude in the members "open air" enclosure at the Swimming Club made him look like a pickled walnut, was a family friend. If he couldn't be trusted then we were probably fighting this war in vain anyway. On a glorious July day like this he would almost certainly have been topping up his tan at the Club but now it had probably been commandeered as a German lido I was hoping he'd be at work in his office. It was only a year since he'd helped us and my father had told me during my brief visit in November that, though there was no organised resistance, there were several key figures who could be relied upon. Nutty, because of his shipping and warehousing business was always in the know from his conversations with visiting crews about conditions in France and Guernsey. He also had useful contacts with the German authorities and was far more reliable a source I felt than Molony who would always guild the lily to his own advantage. Uncle Fred had also suggested in his usual mysterious way that should I ever find myself back in the island I should contact Hedley. As many of my uncle's friends were connected to the shadowy underground network run on behalf of Comintern that did give me pause as I had yet to convince myself that our new allies weren't engaged in their own separate war.

So, it was with some trepidation that I rested the bike in the yard alongside what I hoped was still his main warehouse and tried the side door. It was locked but gave way to my pick in a matter of seconds. Inside was lit from dusty windows in the corrugated iron ceiling which arched over a concrete floor about 150 feet long by eighty wide. Spread on this space was an organised chaos of crates, barrels, and canvas wrapped bundles. Sacks of cement competed with packs of fertiliser all bearing French names. There were two Bedford three tonners parked against the far wall, one of which had been converted to gas. A Brandt gazogene charcoal burner had been welded onto the load bay and the pipe work ran over the cab's roof and into the bonnet. It looked a bit of a lash up but probably a reasonable means of transport with rationed access to petrol or diesel. The main doors which opened onto the Esplanade were closed and locked. It was cool and shadowy inside and the mix of fertiliser and seed along with residual fumes and oil from the vehicles reminded me of the heady days of queuing for the potato boats. I padded across the floor until I could peer through the filthy panes of his office which was inside a timber partition in the corner. It was empty but the smell of real coffee from a percolator in the corner was enticing and suggested that he wasn't too far away. I knew he lived with his widowed mother in a substantial house at Westmount overlooking St Aubin's Bay but wasn't sure which one. It looked like I wasn't even going to get the chance to gamble then I noticed sunlight beaming through a glazed panel in a door at the top of steps which led off the office. I let myself in and checked the paperwork on the desk. From the invoices it was clear that this was still a Pallot operation so I crept up the steps and listened at the door. I could still hear faint echoes of the band and the clatter of machinery and heavy lorries from the harbour area but the most obvious sound was rather strenuous snoring from the space outside. I peeked through the dusty glass onto a rectangular space which had been turned into a roof garden complete with furniture and cushions. On an inflatable air mattress angled towards the south and lying on his side was Hedley Pallot naked as the day he was born.

CHAPTER 30

But he wasn't alone and he wasn't snoring. Hanging over the back of a cushioned chair were the elements of a German Army uniform. Its owner was also on his side and wasn't snoring either. I'd never been a prude and, having heard many jokes about such activities in my time in the army, knew how seriously the authorities took such behaviour but that paled into insignificance where the Royal Navy was concerned. It had been made clear to us during our officer training that such criminal behaviour had to be reported and acted upon immediately. The culprits would be severely treated with long terms of imprisonment which was some improvement on their fate in the age of sail. I suspected that the Nazis were even less tolerant. I wasn't outraged, but worried for Hedley that he'd taken such a grave risk but felt sad for the German for sharing "the love that dare not speak its name". At Oxford such love hadn't been quite as hidden as in normal society so, as a student of English Literature, I was aware of that last line of "Two Loves", the poem by Lord Alfred Douglas allegedly written for his own lover, Oscar Wilde. Though I was in no position to judge, their actions could now solve two of my immediate problems.

I doubted that Hedley was fluent in German or that the young man spoke English and suspected that they communicated, verbally at least, in French. I needed to speak to Hedley directly so chose Jèrriais, the language of the farming community with which I knew he was familiar. I knocked on the door.

Charlie Chaplin couldn't have been more entertaining as the young man scrambled up, looked over to the door, and saw my face in the window. He scarpered like a rabbit being chased out of his hole by a ferret, scooped up his clothing and disappeared out of my line of sight. Hedley was slower but rolled over onto his knees, glanced up at the door, peered almost in resignation at the interloper then shook his head in puzzlement. I smiled at him then eased the door open and said, in Jersey French, that I needed to speak with Mr Pallot urgently and, using a farm hand's slang, added that, now he had finished mounting his cow, he should come down to the warehouse where I would be working on the Bedford.

While I examined the pipework and connections under the bonnet I watched as Hedley ushered the young German down the stairs and out through the door. I was too far away to see his rank but was sure he wasn't an officer.

Hedley called over to me as though I'd just arrived with a load of Jersey Royals. 'Cup of tea, Jack?'

'Coffee, if you have it.' I closed the bonnet and strolled over to his office.

He was dressed in his usual khaki shorts with a crisp white shirt which made his rich tan stand out though it emphasised his wrinkles as well. I noted that he still dyed his hair which actually made him look much older than his fifty-one years. He'd been in the same year at college as Uncle Fred and my father and two years ahead of Bunny Noel. As far as I knew he wasn't a Freemason and probably not a churchgoer.

'Well, young Jack, you can wipe that smile off your face though it is a pleasure to see you.' He didn't seem in the slightest embarrassed by being caught in flagrante and appeared amused by the whole episode.

'Don't worry Mr Pallot; your secret is safe with me.'

He laughed. 'I wasn't worried but my little friend's had the fright of his young life!'

'Who is he?'

'A useful idiot but very sweet. No names, you understand but he has unwittingly been very helpful—'

'To which cause, Mr Pallot?'

'There's only one cause, Jack and that's the defeat of the Nazis, which is why you're here risking your neck, isn't it? I was expecting you—'

'How did you—'

'Know about *Irish Lass*? Your uncle has a long reach and messages reach here all the time through France. Most of our labour comes from there and, as you already know, we have many friends. We also have the Irish who are a trial at the best of times. I have some in my employ but when I discovered they were celebrating the arrival of your schooner with a craic at the Peirson Hotel last night I gave them the morning off. It's half-day closing anyway and trying to get even a few hours useful work out of hungover paddies is as futile as trying to mark you in a game of water polo.' He poured some of the rich brew into a tin mug and brought it over. 'Now let me look at you more closely.' He handed it over with a ready smile, his cologne competing with but losing out to the aroma of the coffee. 'You've filled out somewhat and look rather careworn but I suppose you've been up to no good since you arrived.'

I almost spilled the coffee. Did he know about Phillips already? 'What do you mean?'

'Well, I haven't heard about any dead Germans yet but you've only been here a few hours. Visited your mum, I suppose. So you will have heard about your father and his temper. My little friend works for the *Kommandantur* and it's not too difficult to tease information out of him...you can stop smirking. There are more subtle ways of obtaining information than truncheons and hot irons you know. Speaking of the Gestapo, don't worry too much about Aubin, he's in no real danger unless he lashes out—'

'The secret army police have him though don't they?'

'They find that a bit embarrassing. They're really here to police the troops but some of our citizens insist on sending them anonymous letters about their neighbours. The latest craze is informing on some of our young hot heads who've been painting "V" signs on walls. There is a wonderful combination of naivety and subtlety in the German mind so that their immediate response is to claim that the signs are there to celebrate their success in Russia and are now painting some themselves.'

'Which is very real isn't it. They're almost at the gates of Moscow.'

He laughed, 'which is almost 800 miles from their starting point in West Poland. You know your geography; they've got another 3,000 miles to go before they can say they've slain the Red beast. You're a military man now, Jack. Three million Germans and allies trying to maintain a supply route while the enemy falls back and destroys every village, every field of crops, and every well, on the way. The mighty German war machine might be mechanised but it needs fuel and there aren't any petrol stations like there were in France. Besides, most of their transport is horse based and those beasts need a lot of fodder; all of which will need to be ferried to the front.'

'Sounds like you believe your own propaganda, Mr Pallot.'

He laughed again. 'Even your uncle doesn't believe everything the Russians tell him. No, it's common sense and fortunately Hitler doesn't have much of that. If he'd studied Napoleon's campaign he'd realise it. Did you know that I was in Russia with your father and Fred after we'd settled for a draw with the Germans?'

'So you were indoctrinated by the Commies?'

'Hardly. It was the unbelievable cruelty of the Whites that affected both of us and we were fighting on their side but don't get me started on the evils of capitalism I've got a business to run! Come on, it is what it is and you've got work to do.'

'Work?'

'Yes, you're here to evaluate the German defences aren't you?'

I nodded.

'Of course Moscow already has a very good idea of what the Nazis are doing but your Prime Minister isn't foolish enough to trust their reports which is why your boss, Fleming has sent you to find out.'

'How the hell—'

'It doesn't matter. Look, I'm sorry you had to witness that earlier. Christian is a gentle soul and most unhappy with his lot and needs lots of sympathy. He's learned how to disguise his inclinations but like most of his comrades he's not really sure where he is or why he's here. Most of the division is leaving and a new bunch of conscripts are taking over. Because of the Russian adventure, there's precious little transport available in France so home leave has been virtually non-existent. Now the 216th Division is going to the East and God knows what. He's staying and has told me about his less than exciting new role.' He held up his hand to pre-empt my interruption. 'Hitler has taken time off from attack to focus on defence and has decreed that these islands will be turned into fortresses and never surrendered to the British so what little transport is still available has been dedicated to importing cement, steel reinforcing bars, builder's sand, along with rail tracks, and much else. You've probably spotted some heavy artillery being unloaded, well that's just the beginning. I've heard that the Jerries are planning to dig deep into the hillsides to store munitions and supplies sufficient to withstand a siege. There's a team of engineers staying at the Grand at the moment and from what Christian has let slip they're going to construct impregnable bunkers to defend the coast line. A shipment of thousands of personnel and land mines is on its way as well. Of course Moscow is aware of this but—'

'They won't have told Churchill as they want him to start a second front and draw off German—'

'Precisely, so you understand what you have to do. I'm going to fire up that gas contraption over there; that'll take twenty minutes to produce something for the carburettor to feed on so, while we're waiting, you're going to help me load some of those cement sacks then an island tour beckons.'

While he supervised my heavy lifting I asked him about something which had puzzled me earlier. 'Are the Germans short of rations?'

'Not at all. What made you think that?'

'Well, I saw them netting pigeons in the Royal Square earlier and wondered if—'

He laughed. 'They're not hungry just paranoid. They seem to think that the non-existent resistance will use the pigeons to send messages to England so they've been ordered to round them up. Silly things like that make us realise that Aryan supremacy is a bit of a myth but there's no doubt their scientists and engineers are very clever.'

As we drove around he pointed out how these engineers had already improved the fortifications the British garrisons had built over the centuries to keep the French out but this wasn't the age of sail any longer and bombers would reduce granite castles like Elizabeth and Gorey very easily. Hedley explained the German thinking based on his chats with Christian about in-depth defence which started with steel reinforced concrete anti-tank walls on the exposed western beaches covered through enfiladed fire from protected casements to destroy infantry if the mines hadn't already done their ghastly work. The second line would be a few hundred yards back with concealed resistance nests spouting machine guns and anti-tank weapons. On the heights in the centre of the island would be batteries of medium and heavy artillery zeroed in on the beaches and interconnected with Guernsey and Alderney to offer mutual protection. All of these would be disguised and serviced by a network of tunnels and bunkers. It was impressive though the work had hardly begun. If we had to invade to assist Stalin it would have to be very soon before the construction work was complete and the new troops bedded in. There was no escaping the reality that it would be a suicidal gesture resulting in massive civilian casualties. I had to get back and make sure this information was relayed with urgency as Churchill had a history of high risk military adventures which he believed could surprise the enemy and bring rich political rewards but usually involved significant human loss. To defeat Germany we'd have to return to Europe but we were nowhere near ready for that yet.

We stopped for coffee from a flask at the top of L'Etacq and left the engine running as according to Hedley the beast was a bugger to start again. It had been more than a handful already as the driver had to manage four levers and a pull knob to keep the limited power flowing. Climbing this winding hill had been a real challenge. Now, looking back over the length of the Five Mile Road and the majestic sweep of St Ouen's Bay, it was obvious that this was the only landing beach which could support a large scale invasion. The north coast was largely composed of 400 foot high rugged cliffs with a handful of small harbours which could be mined and commanded by fixed gun emplacements.

The south coast was shallow but navigation through the rocky outcrops very difficult. The east, apart from St Catherine's, was also composed of small bays and within visual range of artillery on the French coast. It would have to be St Ouen's and any invasion fleet would be under the guns of Guernsey as it approached. In truth, Hitler was probably right and the island could be made virtually impregnable other than through a long blockade and siege.

Hedley felt it would be too risky to explore the valleys as the German police had been restricting access in all of them for groundworks to be carried out. I knew how narrow they were and could see the potential for tunnelling though I wondered how they could hide the massive spoils from excavations which would surely show up on reconnaissance flights. After three hours we returned to the warehouse via the back door of a friendly baker who didn't require ration cards.

'Now, you realise that someone the British trust has to relay this information so we've got to get you back to your ship. By the way, how did you get off it?'

He was amused by my circuitous route and suggested that I'd over engineered the escapade when I could just have joined the Irish lads the night before when they were ferried to the Peirson. I explained the difficulties involved in getting past the guards but refrained from mentioning Quigley or his other plans. He shrugged and offered me a much simpler return route.

As we parked up at the top of the bridge linking the road to the Swimming Club, I noticed two things; first the Club flag which normally flew alongside the Jersey flag was at half-mast and second, the Nazis seemed to have missed an opportunity to fly the *Hakenkreuz* in its place. A crocodile of school boys were leaving clutching towels and wet costumes ushered by Harold Le Druillenec who I knew taught at St Helier Boy's School. Hedley explained that they had been holding their end of term swimming gala. As it was a half-day and, as the tide was a long way out, locals would soon be flooding there for a swim and fighting for deck chair spaces with off duty Germans. That was where he'd met Christian who was a good diver. It was difficult for the young ladies who found it challenging to keep a modest distance from all those handsome young Aryans sunbathing in their skimpy costumes. I suspected that, given his own preferences, he was probably just as intrigued by them as the girls.

His plan was simple enough though he had taken the precaution of telephoning the secretary's office first. Since Commander Brewster had been recalled in 1940, Mr Killminster had been managing the club and Fred Cooper, who I knew very well as he'd clipped my ear for misbehaviour more than a few times, was still in charge of maintenance. Fortuitously, the sewage pump had been playing up again and Hedley had already promised to source a replacement from France. One had been sitting in his warehouse in anticipation of installation for a couple of weeks so now he agreed to deliver it this afternoon and promised to arrange for a plumber the following day. Both Killy and Fred would recognise me but Hedley persuaded me to take the risk as they were both highly trustworthy. As he expected both of them to be busy hauling in the swimming lanes we probably wouldn't bump into them anyway. We had the replacement pump in a large canvas sack and leaving the boiler steaming away, I laboured along the bridge with it and queued up behind a group of German soldiers. Muriel was in the entrance kiosk as always and waved us through the delivery gate while she was munching on a sandwich and too distracted by something she was reading, probably a Mills and Boon romance, to look up. As predicted, the management were poolside and the workshop was empty. The swap took moments and, relieved, we carried the sack with my diving equipment out into the sunshine and straight into Fred Cooper.

CHAPTER 31

Fred was dressed as usual in a smart blazer, pockets bulging with various tools and a whistle, and his top pocket crammed with a range of pens. His black shoes had their usual mirrored shine and his outfit was completed by light grey slacks and wide collared white shirt. Black hair was well brylcreemed to his high forehead but the thin roll-up cigarette normally stuck to his lip was now on the floor where it had dropped when he recognised me.

'Renouf, what the—'

'Fred, you remember the three wise monkeys,' Hedley interrupted

'See no evil, hear no evil, and speak no evil. Yes but—'

'No "buts" Fred! What do you see?'

'Why, you, Mr Pallot and—'

'Nothing else. We'll talk later. You'll find the replacement pump at the end of the workshop. Have a good day...One thing though, why is the flag at half-mast?'

'You haven't heard? Obviously not. George Phillips had an accident last night and he's dead.'

Hedley sucked in a deep breath but avoided looking at me. 'I see. What happened?'

'We don't know. Something on a farm but we're all very sad.' His wry smile belied that statement as Phillips had been as patronising and bullying to the staff as he had to the members. 'The flag's for Doris —'

'To celebrate the removal of that great burden of a husband, I assume.' Hedley mimicked the tones of a vicar and I fully expected the pair of them to break into giggles so I tugged his arm, reached out and shook Fred's hand then suggested we get a move on.

Fred retrieved his fallen fag, drew on it then stood watching as we trundled off with the bag towards the kiosk. I could sense Hedley bursting with curiosity alongside but resolved to follow his advice to Fred and say nothing about Phillips' accident.

At the top of the bridge Hedley tapped my arm and pulled me to the railing as a group of German soldiers barged past. He pointed towards the Dicq rock, 'Look, you can see the garden of Silvertide from here.'

'So? What's important about that?'

'Apparently, the *Geheime Feldpolizei* are moving there. Christian told me they're not happy being so close to the *Kommandantur's* office. They have a new chief who's arriving soon, he's only a sergeant but he calls himself "Wolf of the Gestapo"'.

'Bit of a comedian then?'

'No, but he's been living in Canada for years and returned home to assist the Reich in its hour of need. Reputation precedes him — a nasty piece of work by all accounts.'

'OK, so what's your point?'

'They keep "persons of interest" at Ben Rhydding but there's more room in this villa...and it's close to the sea which Wölfle likes so—'

'They might move my father there?'

'Yes, more convenient if you wanted to extract him but it probably won't happen for a few more weeks.'

'He wouldn't leave my mother or the farm so it's not worth thinking about.'

'Everything is worth some thought, Jack, but you're right and I can't imagine your mother donning one of your frogman's suits for a swim to freedom.'

Back in the warehouse Hedley ushered me into his office and brewed some fresh coffee. 'That was the easy bit, now getting you back aboard...I've an idea. From what I've heard the Purchasing Commission will be taking some of the produce from your schooner. I'll give them a call as they'll need transport. If that doesn't work I've got Molony up my sleeve. He dropped by yesterday afternoon. He's acquired some merchandise from France...we have an arrangement and I'm storing some of it for him. Should fetch a very good price in Ireland or even more in England. He might want me to deliver it along with the fresh goods your captain wants.'

'That could work but if I carry stuff aboard the guards will count me on and want to count me off.'

He stroked his chin. 'We'll just have to confuse them or—'

'Pretend that I'm an engineer called aboard to replace one of the bilge pumps.'

'Brilliant. I've got another of those we took to the club...that should work especially if I explain that you will have to stay until it's fixed.'

He made a couple of telephone calls while I waited

nervously, my stomach still churning with a mixture of jealousy and anger with Caroline but a phrase about spilt milk kept blocking any serious contemplation of her betrayal.

His contact had agreed and offered to arrange a petrol voucher for the journey which pleased Hedley no end. By now, I was fairly sure that he was heavily involved in the Black Market along with Molony and almost certainly a small group of Germans in the supply system. I wondered if he'd had any dealings with Phillips but didn't want to raise that as an issue as he hadn't probed any further about the sad news of his demise. We pushed the Gazogene monster back into the warehouse and readied the other Bedford. Its tank was already full and he showed me his stash of jerrycans of petrol hidden behind some hay bales in the corner.

I made myself scarce when the man from the Purchasing Commission turned up with the voucher and authorisation which was just as well as Molony arrived while they were sipping yet more coffee and enjoying the celebratory chat business men who've just negotiated a good deal enjoy. As I'd propped the door open, I could hear snatches of their talk from my perch on the balcony. Molony seemed to believe that *Irish Lass* would be a regular visitor and was already counting on making a handsome profit. It was clear this bureaucrat was part of their racket and after fortifying their coffee with some medicinal brandy they debated which currency they wanted to ask for from Dermot. Fleming had provided American dollars which could have been acquired in Portugal and, as a joke, he would have offered Irish punts or even Sterling but I knew he had teased them with the only currency which was universal – gold. Saul had told me of Fleming's undercover excursion to Madrid in February with a substantial amount of the yellow metal in the diplomatic bag to try to bribe Franco to remain neutral and how well that had been received. Every one of the Helford Flotilla boats now carried gold coins for oiling the machinery of corruption in Occupied Europe. The Purchasing Commission would pay in Francs or Occupation Marks or might even have some proper German currency all of which might just as well be tossed overboard but Dermot was shrewd enough to strike a good deal over anything which came on board otherwise they might be suspicious. The negotiations would be lubricated by more alcohol. However bad it might be on the fighting fronts there were always those who enjoyed a good war from behind the scenes. I watched in distaste feeling more censorious about the financial corruption than the moral depredations I'd witnessed earlier though those were perhaps justified by the demands of the underground war.

Eventually Molony and his corrupt friend traipsed off and Hedley called me down. We had to move his desk to reveal a trapdoor under the carpet. It was padlocked with something more sophisticated than his warehouse door and he invited me to try picking it. Willie would have managed it but I'd not encountered one of these number combination locks before and after five minutes I gave in and let him enter the code. Steps led down to a basement which was packed with crates and cases. It was well illuminated and he showed me around. It was all high value wine and spirits. Caroline had educated me in perfume and tried the same with her father's stock of vintage wines but my palate lacked the necessary sophistication, she declared, to appreciate the finer aspects of the carefully selected wines. We still got drunk though and to my mind that was all alcohol was useful for. Now, Hedley waxed lyrical about the 1900 Bordeaux growing season and showed me cases of Medoc, Graves, St. Emilion and Pomerol, though the pièce de résistance was a half-dozen beautifully crafted wooden boxes containing1899 Chateau Margaux.

When I asked him if that was a white or red wine, he accused me of being a total philistine and explained that this was for trade and not consumption. As were the crates of Armagnac, Cognac, Calvados and at least fifty cases of Pol Roger Champagne from the 1890s. There were foodstuffs as well, including cans of foie gras. I asked him if he had any caviar as I was hungry. Caroline had fed me that as well on very expensive biscuits but it seemed no more attractive than the mouthfuls of kelp I encountered while swimming in rough seas. Fortunately, as Hedley explained with some exasperation Caviar had to be refrigerated and didn't keep for very long. If I was desperate he had a contact in the kitchen of the Grand Hotel only a hundred yards or so away and could acquire some with a quick call. I thanked him for his kindness but declined. However, Fleming would probably have an orgasm if we delivered even a small fraction of this cave of delight to him especially as he wouldn't have to pay for it. No doubt, he'd pass some on to Churchill and his friend Mayskiy, the Russian ambassador. Mine not to reason why but I was sure Dermot would loosen his money belt. I told Hedley as much and he selected a variety of boxes and had me carry them up to the office while he made a note of the contents for Molony. Really! So there was honour amongst thieves.

Once we'd inserted them into old potato sacks and crated up the rebreather, fins and Pirelli suit, we packed the Bedford, and, as a last minute thought, Hedley had me empty the large tool chest which was welded to the rear of the cab and occupied the whole width of the load bed. Finally, we removed one of the pumps from its crate and stuffed it into a canvas holdall to show the guards if they were curious. What could possibly go wrong?

CHAPTER 32

The guard. It had changed and was no longer mounted by slightly bemused Kriegsmarine ratings, but two NCOs in army uniform. Hedley grimaced and whispered. 'Bugger. GFP. What are they doing here?'

'GFP?'

'*Geheime Feldpolizei* the higher ups wear suits but the foot soldiers are normally in army uniform but look at their shoulder tabs. They're mainly ex-police and not very friendly. Be careful as most of them speak English.'

The one by the gangplank, doubtless relieved at the opportunity for a break in his dull routine, took an immediate and unwelcome interest in our lorry as it pulled up alongside the crane. He straightened his uniform, puffed out his not inconsiderable chest, stuck out his jaw, and marched towards us. Hedley was quickly out of the cab and moved to greet him but the policeman held out his palm and barked '*Halte! Zeigen sie mir ihre papiere.*'

Hedley handed over his ID and the guard scrutinised it looking from photo to face repeatedly. Dermot and Molly were on deck observing and I could sense their concern as the guard turned to me and held out his hand. While my forged ID would pass muster he'd want to know why I was working for Mr Pallot when I didn't have local papers. As I fumbled in my pocket I caught a movement on deck out of the corner of my eye as Molly threw something overboard. As it fell it spilled pieces of bread all over the dock and we were mobbed by a screaming flock of seagulls fighting each other for the morsels. It distracted the guard who didn't seem too keen on collecting bird shit on his smart uniform so darted back under cover of the crane and motioned us forward. Hedley grabbed the sack with the diving kit, handed it to me and told me to get the "bilge pump" aboard quickly. I hurried up the gangplank, explained in my imitation of an Irish accent what it was and asked if they could spare some crew to unload the supplies from Mr Molony. I added that we'd be relieving the ship of as many sacks of coal as they could fit onto the lorry for the Purchasing Commission. Dermot sent Rory and Liam down to help Hedley while I nipped below with the pump — the sound of shrieking seagulls was music in my ears.

Molly followed me down to the mess room and flung her arms around me. I didn't resist and pressed into her slim body as she kissed me on both cheeks in the French manner. I was hoping for more but she pushed away, tweaked my nose, and then slapped my face. 'Calm down. You can't turn a welcome hug into—'

'Sorry, but I'm very pleased to see you.'

'I can tell but we were *all* worried about you.'

'Well, Renouf, clearly some of us more than others.' Quigley shook my hand. 'Now, down to business. We haven't much time. Apparently, the passengers Kempler has wished upon us are due in short order. Let's go to *Bodmin* and start with what's in that bag that isn't a bilge pump.'

I told them everything they needed to know apart from my visit home and the episode with Phillips. I also edited my initial meeting with Hedley and his Russian connections but mentioned everything I could remember from our island tour. Quigley made notes and interrogated me on some of the details. He seemed particularly interested in the works I'd seen in Grand Vaux and Hedley's comments about excavations in the other valleys. After he'd satisfied his curiosity he tapped his watch and explained that he had to be up on deck to keep an eye on Dermot and investigate these new supplies which he assumed were contraband and would need to be hidden. The noise of the crane lifting the coal sacks on their pallets filtered through from the forward hold as he slipped out and left the two of us alone.

'Wow, you've had an interesting time. Bunny will be very pleased. I won't probe but I suspect that you've had a few little adventures you didn't mention so do you want to know about my night out with the boys?'

I didn't really. Would have preferred to sleep but she seemed somewhat excited. 'Do you mean your two admirers in their purloined car?'

She laughed. 'One admirer at a time is enough and cars can be very uncomfortable. No, they were real gentlemen and looked after me as if I was royalty even though I was in the presence of someone far more attractive and regal than a mere Irish lass.' She paused trying to gauge my level of interest as I yawned. 'Well, if you'd rather sleep I'll go and find something more useful to do.'

'Sorry, again. I am tired but carry on, I'm all ears. Who's this queenly figure?'

'Well, Anton drove us to the Grand Hotel which

wasn't very far and we waited in the bar for Karl to arrive with his date—'

'A local tart, I suppose.'

She grinned. 'Local resident, but certainly not a tart. In fact she turned out to be quite a celebrity as the officers all stood and clapped when she entered. Mind you she is a dazzling blonde with an imperious manner and an amazing performer on the piano—'

'No!'

'I'm afraid so. I've now met the woman who's had you in her thrall for so long and I can see why. She is stunning and surprisingly charming. But also bohemian and outrageous and...I'm sorry to have to tell you this but—'

'She has a baby.'

'How the Hell did you know?'

'I saw her this morning, from a distance mind, with *Korvettenkapitän* Karl Hemming, the bastard's father; all very happy families etc.'

Molly sighed. 'So you've been torturing yourself haven't you?'

I nodded.

'Well, you've got it wrong. Caroline brought the baby with her and I joined her in the ladies rest room when it needed a feed—'

'It?'

'It's a little girl and she's only just over two weeks old and wasn't very well. During our chatter over dinner, Caroline had learned that I was a medical student specialising in obstetrics and wanted me to have a look. I think she also saw it as an opportunity to escape from the men. She confided that the baby had been born prematurely by about three weeks and the post-natal care had been rudimentary. It had left her depressed. After I examined the baby I felt that she was underweight and probably born even further away from full term — probably six weeks but I didn't press her. I did ask about the father but all she would say was it wasn't Karl and certainly not Anton who she finds far too Germanic. I discovered some more about the child and its putative father later from the two men when she went off to entertain the troops with some amazing Beethoven and Chopin having left me literally holding the baby. Not that I minded. I must be more maternal than I thought. She wasn't unwell just a bit of colic. I should probably be thrown out of the medical profession but I introduced her to her thumb and she was fine. It's lovely—'

'Spare me the mother's delight. What do you know about the father?'

'OK, do keep calm. Typical man. Well, she won't say. Karl has seen the birth certificate and under "father" is just a blank. As you can imagine it's caused more than a little gossip in the officers' mess. Before Karl was billeted at her father's house the slot was occupied by another Kriegsmarine officer, Dieter Wirz but he was killed when his boat was attacked by British aeroplanes near the end of last October. They'd been quite friendly and there'd been gossip at the time. Caroline's father believes it was him and your great friend Rudi Kempler was so angry that, when he returned to the island for the anniversary of the Occupation two weeks later he frightened her so much that her waters burst and she had to be rushed to the hospital. Well, that's what I pieced together from their conversation. It seems everyone is terrified of him. He's acting more like an enraged husband than a concerned brother.'

'I'm not surprised. He's always been desperate to keep her for himself. Not that she'd ever agree to something so incestuous but I suspect he lives in hope. But what about this Dieter's family? Do they know?'

'No. For the simple reason that Dieter leaves a widow and two young children. Even your brutish Kempler decided that his half-sister would have to bear the shame and responsibility alone though, from what I could gather, he even offered to adopt the child himself but she refused and would not confirm that Dieter is the father.' She paused and studied my face. 'You're looking very pale.'

Of course I was. It had taken me a little while but I'd done the maths. If it was Dieter Wirz, the baby couldn't have been born more than three weeks premature if he was killed before November. If it wasn't any of these Kriegsmarine officers and it was a premature birth there was one other suspect. 'Does the child have a name?'

'Yes, I believe it's Mary.'

'Oh my God.' I was shivering with relief, elation, but most of all a depth of despair for the woman I loved and what was almost certainly my second daughter.

'What's so special about the name?'

'Everything. It's my mother's.'

Molly gasped. 'Oh, Jack. Are you sure?'

'Yes, the dates fit. I have to see her, both of them—'

'You can't. It's too dangerous.'

'I've brought back the diving kit. I could go again to-night—'

'To do what?'

'Tell her that—'

'You love her; will look after both of them?'

'Yes, of course.'

'Think, Jack. Think. You've already told me that Kempler will kill your family if she leaves the island. And how will it help if you get caught and Kempler finds out Mary is your daughter? How will that help?'

'But, I can't just ignore this and leave her all alone—'

'She's not alone. Her father is wealthy, her half-brother is all powerful and she's safe here. After what you've told Quigley there's no way the British will risk an invasion. The war won't last for ever. I believe that she'll wait for you...if you survive. In fact if I was a bookie, given your past form, I'd say it was odds on that you wouldn't, but even well fancied favourites don't always win. But, you go back now and get caught, it's a racing certainty that little Mary will never meet her father.'

'You're right but if I follow your betting logic there's still a good chance that I won't get caught so thanks for the advice but I'm going tonight and you know that's the right decision.'

But Quigley and the others didn't agree and that

evening while I was sleeping in the safety of *Bodmin*, someone had secured the door from the outside.

CHAPTER 33

When I woke it was early Friday morning. I tried the door again but it was still locked from the outside. It could also be barred from the inside which could be useful if they really annoyed me but then they could retaliate by shutting the air vents. Stalemate, and while it was tempting to hammer out my frustration on the bulkhead, I had no idea of who might be on board. As the voice pipe was covered at both ends the electrician had installed a small light to indicate that a communication was imminent. I flicked the switch but there was no answering light. So now I was imprisoned by my own crew. I could hardly describe it as a mutiny though it was frustrating especially as I could understand their concerns. Perhaps they were right and there would be other opportunities to visit the island though that would depend on whether the War Office needed more information and if Fleming could spare me to collect it. There was little I could do apart from answer the call of nature. After availing myself of the primitive facilities I used one of the large containers of seawater kept in the compartment to flush the results down a soil pipe to a tank in the bilges, I broke open a ration pack and drew some fresh water from the cylinder attached to the bulkhead. At least the buggers had unstopped the vent on the deck so I wouldn't suffocate. There were noises above but I couldn't make out any individual voices. Perhaps they were drawing lots to decide who should be the first to risk my anger and open the door.

There wasn't much in the way of entertainment in *Bodmin* and I couldn't see any attraction in playing chess against myself and card patience held little appeal. If only we'd thought of providing some reading material, like the complete works of Shakespeare, the Bible or even *Mein Kampf,* it would have passed the time. Instead, I fumed quietly, stripped and cleaned some of the weapons again, mused about using some of the PE and detonators to get their attention then resorted to the old soldier's trick of grabbing more sleep.

Molly had drawn the short straw and she woke me by pinching my nostrils. I looked at my watch before glaring at her.

She waved her hand about trying to shift the air. 'It stinks in here. You'd better come up on deck but I suggest you freshen up and change your clothing first.'

She turned to leave but I grabbed her arm and tugged her down onto the bunk. 'You smell very nice. What's that scent?'

She wriggled away but I had her trapped against the bulkhead. 'I believe it's *Shocking* by Schiaparelli. There was a case in that hoard your friend brought on board along with a suitcase full of silk stockings.'

'And the dress?'

'Anton brought it for me this morning. He's taking me out for lunch at Caroline's house which is just as well as Uncle Dermot has just been told that Kempler is to inspect the ship later this morning. Best that Anton is out of the way lest he wants to introduce you as his saviour to the man you've apparently tried to drown more than once—'

'Kempler's coming here? Bugger. He's bound to poke his nose into everything, especially the ship's log. Don't try to hide the contraband from him as he probably liberated most of it himself.' I grabbed both her hands and forced her to look at me. 'Promise me that you'll try to find a way of telling Caroline I know and that I will do everything I can to see her and Mary soon. Suggest, if you get the chance, that she visit my mother though...' and then it struck me —my mother already knew; had tried to warn me off...God, why hadn't I listened? '...belay that. I think she already has. What a mess. Just be careful and let's hope that you don't bump into Kempler or, if he's joining you to eat, try to divert Anton so that he doesn't talk about the action.'

'You don't expect much do you?'

I released her hands. 'From you, I expect...I don't know what...' Small mouth and big foot hovering too close now. '...but, if one of those Germans had been the father, my expectations would have been much easier to manage.'

She shook her head. 'You really don't know the difference between lust and love, do you? I'll be honest with you, Jack. From what I've seen and heard, I'm not sure you deserve the love of any woman...but I suppose that could be said about most immature men.'

Although metaphorical, it was another slap in the face which left me speechless.

She pushed herself up, patted her dress down and smiled. "Do what you're good at and leave this "love" stuff to those more in control of their emotions. This is not the time for complex relationships so—'

'How about simple physical ones stripped of emotion? Would you like to try one of those?'

This time the slap was physical and well deserved.

She didn't close the door so I followed her meekly up the companionway trying, not very hard; to keep my eyes off her stockinged thighs as she wiggled her bottom either provocatively, or in anger. If only I could tell the difference.

CHAPTER 34

Quigley and Dermot stood on either side of me at the rail as we watched Molly descend the gangplank to meet the man I'd saved from drowning. He waved graciously then helped her into the Alvis glancing appreciatively at her stockinged legs as she manoeuvred her derriere onto the leather seat.

Quigley gave me a sly nudge as he licked his lips. 'Women!'

'So, what's been happening since I've been in prison?'

Quigley responded. 'For your own good, Jack, I'm sure you realise we can't have you charging around the island even though we understand why. You've been lucky so far and now we're on the cusp of a real breakthrough—'

'Why not go the whole hog and capture Kempler as well. I'm sure Fleming would find him an interesting dinner companion.'

'Undoubtedly, but rather self-defeating don't you think?'

I shrugged. 'Depends on your overall objective, I suppose.'

'Precisely, so you stick to tactics and leave strategy to those with a broader perspective.' He turned and took my elbow. 'Time for you to have a shave and clean your teeth; perhaps a good wash as well?'

Dermot spoke softly. 'He's right. We're sorry but the mission must come first. Kempler should be here soon so you'd better hurry up before we incarcerate you again. He shouldn't be here too long then we can have a pleasant lunch while we work out how to get his agents to a safe place. Molony's sent us some seafood and more wine and hopes to join us to seal the deal.'

'How much did you offload?' I asked.

'All the coal and wheat and got paid the market rate in a mixture of Sterling and Francs; none of their Occupation currency. We donated the oranges to the island's children but I doubt they'll see many of them.'

'What about the black market stuff?'

'That was a more delicate negotiation as some of the items were not for sale. They wanted ridiculous amounts for the booze but we settled on a figure which still leaves a margin for Fleming to replenish his pot of gold though I suspect he'll distribute them for influence rather than cash in. The paintings—'

'What? Where did they come from?'

'That wouldn't have been a sensible question but along with several crates of silverware and some furniture they're for storage in Dublin in a warehouse owned by a Mr Hayden-Brown. We've been told to prepare some space for a consignment from Kempler as well and we definitely won't ask for the provenance of those goods!'

'What's our sailing plan?'

'We can leave on this evening's tide or early tomorrow morning. The sooner the better I think but we can't appear to be in too much of a hurry — after all we have an Irish image to live up to. We'll also have to wait for Molly, and Molony has invited the crew to another session in that pub this evening. I still can't get over the fact that our Republican lads have the freedom of the Germans while you poor British are confined to your homes under curfew. Great to be neutral, so it is.'

There was no polite answer to that so I went off to inspect the stolen goods bound for neutral Ireland then a good wash and brush up.

I was in the middle of soaping some intimate bits when Liam burst into my cabin. 'Quick, the Nazi's arrived. Grab what you can and get back in the hole!'

I remembered the *Complete Works of Shakespeare* this time and scurried along the passage and back into my prison. The vents were still open and I heard muffled exchanges as Kempler landed on deck. I thought the most appropriate play to read in the circumstances would be the blood, guts, torture, rape, cannibalism, and general mayhem of *Titus Andronicus*. So many met grisly ends that if was difficult to decide how to cast Kempler. Perhaps Aaron, who is buried up to his neck in the ground and starved to death, would be the most appropriate.

By the time I'd reached Act 5 Scene 3, Kempler was still alive and neither buried nor eviscerated. He had finished his inspection and I was released for a lunch which I hoped didn't include any of my relatives in a pie.

I didn't spot any blood on the decks either but Dermot looked a bit shaken. 'God save Ireland, but that Nazi is sinister. He doesn't raise his voice which makes you listen more attentively but he just oozes menace.

He interrogated me over the log book and poked his Aryan nose into every nook and cranny. At one point, I thought he might even start tapping the walls looking for hidden empty spaces. He even inspected the bilges. But he seemed satisfied though I've had to release Molly's cabin for his passengers so you had better move what she needs into *Bodmin*.' He glanced at his watch. 'They're due here at 16:00 precisely though he won't be with them. He's attending a lunch then flying back to France. In the interim we're to receive two more lorry loads for storage in Cork. He's given me the name of the company I have to contact—'

'Let me guess, it's Mermaid Trading.'

'How did you—'

'No real surprise – it's one of Hayden-Brown's. I'm still bemused by the risk he's taking though. Surely, his trophies would be safer in France or even Germany or—'

Quigley interrupted me. 'Perhaps he's more worried about other Nazis higher up the food chain requisitioning his prizes. I hear that Goering has special teams scouring the occupied territories looking for loot.'

'It still seems a risk for him.'

Dermot looked at Quigley who nodded.

'Well, he's decided to reduce his risk.'

'How?'

'He demands that we return from Ireland for more cargo and to ensure that we do he's...'

He seemed too pained to continue and stared at the floor.

I looked at Quigley and he sighed. 'He wants a hostage from the crew.'

I felt sick. 'Who?'

'We explained that we needed a full crew for the rigging and he accepted that so he's going to keep—'

'Oh God no, not—'

'Molly, I'm afraid. But don't worry. She can work in the hospital.'

'Does she know?'

'We haven't been able to tell her but we believe that she's in German hands at the moment, staying with Caroline in—'

'We can't allow this. Didn't you remind him that we're neutrals and don't have to take his bloody cargo or his orders?'

They looked at each other before Dermot replied. 'No. There is little point. We cannot leave without their permission and I'm sure even you will realise that we couldn't fight our way out.'

'Besides, you have to consider the bigger picture, Renouf. We have a great opportunity here and must get back with this information. Molly...well we know you're very fond of her but it's a small price to—'

Then there was blood on the deck and a body as, forgetting all my training and the importance of not using bare fists, I punched Quigley so hard on his unsympathetic nose that he collapsed in a heap. This didn't solve the problem but made me feel a whole lot better about it. I walked off. I needed time now to try to devise some plan to save Molly.

CHAPTER 35

Where was Saul when I needed him? With his mathematical brain and logical approach he would have offered some elegant if impractical solution. At school, he'd been bullied because he was different and not just because he was the only Jew. Anti-Semitism wasn't overt but there was a social undercurrent even though there were probably fewer than a couple of dozen Jews in the island. Perhaps this was triggered by inherent jealousy because of their financial skills rather than religious beliefs because they didn't flaunt their wealth and integrated well. Saul and I had competed to see who had the most sangfroid often laying traps, mainly verbal, for each other. I felt on balance that we were about even but had to concede that he was pretty unflappable especially as he'd suffered so much petty injustices at the hands and sometimes fists of a few of the other less intelligent boys. I'd rescued him with mine a few times as some of our class mates were too stupid for their own good. Now, he had the perfect job and, despite Fleming's casual racism and gratuitous insults, I knew he was valued for his analytical approach and surprising inventiveness. But he wasn't here and neither was Willie who was infinitely more direct and almost completely devoid of subtlety. Only half-Jewish, and a master of many languages, he was driven by a visceral hatred of the Nazis and inevitably approached planning through a prism which displayed only black and white. Though, to be fair, he was enticed by a good splash of red blood whenever possible. They would have come up with entirely different but equally hazardous plans and looked to me to make the final decision.

So what did we know? Kempler was a dangerous combination of Saul and Willie; sophisticated, charming and utterly ruthless. He wasn't a thug and didn't offer blind obedience to the Nazi creed. However, he had no time for Jews though he would use them to his own advantage. In the context of the German occupation of Jersey he was very powerful. Neither the bureaucrats nor the military authorities would dare challenge him directly. It was clear to me that he was working towards a single goal of making himself as wealthy as he could during the chaos of war and fighting internal battles with similar minded opportunists. From what I'd heard from Saul, reinforced by both Hedley and Quigley, Hitler's invasion of Russia was probably a gamble too far now as it had been delayed long enough to give the Soviet's General "Winter" the chance to defeat it. Churchill wasn't banking on it and currently diverting resources in material that we could ill afford to Stalin while plotting to drag America into the war as his primary aim. Kempler would be aware of Hitler's gamble especially as he would have inside information. He would be hedging his bets though but keeping his hands as clean as possible. Everything would be channelled through Hayden-Brown who really did hate the Jews and believed in Aryan superiority. Part of his inferiority complex I suspected, as he'd married the widow of a German war hero who, had he not been killed in 1917, would be one of Hitler's key advisers along with his brother who was now running the Reichsbank.

My brain was fizzing, trying to find a path through this elaborate game of chess. Unlike Saul, I'd never been able to plan more than four moves ahead and, while I could now see the pieces and their positions more clearly, I was struggling with a strategy. So back to basics: I couldn't let Molly remain captive — she knew too much about Fleming, the Helford Flotilla and, having been privy to discussions about the secret war, had knowledge which the Nazis would love to acquire. Should she fall into the hands of the real Gestapo I doubted she would remain silent for long. She would also know that there was no real plan for *Irish Lass* to return and that Fleming wouldn't lose any sleep over her fate and almost certainly had other schemes for the vessel. If Quigley was correct, and the two agents we were conveying to Ireland were turned by our own secret service, then the fiction could be preserved by making *Irish Lass* disappear either with a new identity or sinking her in a way which could be conveyed to the Germans to allay any suspicions and her real role. Despite what Quigley and Dermot might believe Molly's fate was not negotiable.

How to achieve this and escape in one piece? I would need help from within the island and the only one I could rely on was Hedley Pallot. It hadn't struck me as strange then but, in all the time we'd spent together, he'd not mentioned Caroline though, as he had been working with her father he must have been aware of her pregnancy and the birth. I'd been relieved that the subject hadn't been raised but now realised that he'd been saving me from difficult news. Caroline was well known in the island, especially at the Swimming

Club and most of the members had been surprised at my relationship with her as she was perceived, like her mother before her, as a danger to red blooded men and best avoided. She didn't help herself as her imperious behaviour from the diving boards was carried over into her social interaction. I knew that she was almost universally hated by the females while every man, despite what he might say to his friends, would not have turned down the opportunities afforded to me. She was beautiful in a glamourous Hollywood way, exceptionally talented musically and a right pain in the arse but I loved her and now I was convinced she had given birth to my daughter, was desperate to see her again. Knowing all this, Saul would have counselled me not to visit her as he was desperate for me to evade her spell. Willie's solution would have been more robust. In these circumstances he would have regarded Molly as a severe security risk and Caroline a traitor so disposing of both of them would have been his priority.

I examined the mental chess board again and now I could see a path through the defences. The opponent's weakness was clear — the king was in love with his sister, the queen, and that I could exploit. If Molly had reported the gossip accurately, he'd already forgiven her indiscretion and even offered to adopt the child. He would protect her at all costs which was his real blind spot. If I could nip in and remove the captive pawn, which represented Molly, even with the queen's assistance he wouldn't wipe her from the board. Silly analogy perhaps but I could now start planning the details of the raid. It was all about timing but depended on Molony turning up as promised. If he didn't then plan B would have to be implemented.

CHAPTER 36

He did and Dermot, who had been as concerned about his niece as me agreed with my plan and together, after I'd apologised for his bloody nose, we persuaded Quigley to give it a try. Molony was brought down to the engine space where I demonstrated that the pump Hedley had delivered was malfunctioning and needed some replacement parts. I gave him a list and he agreed to deliver it to Hedley and ask him to bring the parts himself to the ship. Shortly afterwards, Kempler's lorry arrived and more crates were deposited in the hold. If we hadn't had protection from the Royal Navy I don't know how we could have explained this cargo but Dermot believed that, as this was destined for a neutral country and wasn't arms related, we should be safe and Kempler clearly felt the same. We were now due to leave at 08:00 on Saturday and Dermot had cancelled the party in the Peirson on the basis that he needed the crew sober for the morning. As he now had sailing orders he expected the harbour pilot to join us as navigating through the rocks, even in broad daylight under power, was fraught with difficulty as it was only a thirty-three foot tide and not high until 09:45.

It was after six o'clock before Hedley arrived. I took him below and explained what I needed. He didn't seem too disturbed and agreed to help. Dermot was still waiting for the two passengers as I carried the perfectly serviceable pump in the canvas sack down the gangplank and past the guards. That was the easy bit. Now I had to enter the lioness's den and it wasn't just hunger torturing my belly as we bumped along the cobbled dock and Hedley aimed the Bedford towards Grand Vaux.

The driveway was empty and the garage door open displaying only Caroline's distinctive red Bugatti. A black Morris Ten with German number plates was parked outside the gate and two *Feldpolizei* were chatting but stopped to wave us down. Hedley stepped out and, to my surprise, spoke with them in German. They shrugged and returned to their conversation over the requisitioned car's bonnet but one of them noted our registration number.

'We hadn't thought of that. Of course there'll be a record of all visitors, time in time out etc. That will make it difficult for you if—'

'Relax, Jack. I'd anticipated this and it's not going to be a problem. Just keep calm and bugger on.'

So we buggered on, crunched through the gravel and pulled up outside the front door of the converted farmhouse.

'Best stay here while I have a recce, Jack.' Hedley jumped down and headed for the doorway.

I watched in trepidation. My pulse was hammering and I felt bilious with nerves. But there was little point in torturing myself, so I listened to the engine ticking down like a doomsday clock while pricking my ears to focus on any sound from within the house. As hard as I strained, there was nothing other than the background noises of the machinery still at work in the valley and the occasional snorting from the two horses tethered in the adjacent field.

After what seemed like an eternity, Hedley returned and motioned me to dismount and follow him. I scanned his face for clues but it was expressionless. 'Well?'

'She's there with Molly but her father has gone with Kempler; to Paris apparently. They're not expected back until Monday.'

'Is Christine there?'

'Who's that?'

'Hayden-Brown's housekeeper and bedroom assistant.'

He laughed. 'No, but come to think of it, I have heard about her. She was arrested and deported back in November. There was a rumour about a robbery she might have been involved in.'

So Caroline had exacted her revenge on her father's mistress. Now as I entered the hallway the memories flooded back and I shivered with insecurity. He stopped, looked at me, and then nodded his head in the direction of the lounge. I rubbed my hands against the dusty overalls, hesitated again, and then trudged towards the large room with expansive views over the rear garden. I could hear female voices speaking softly and wondered how much Hedley had told them. Molly wouldn't be too surprised but Caroline...I daren't think how she might react. So, like someone facing his first jump from the ten-metre diving board I crept forward to confront my fate, praying that the guards were too far away to hear any screams — hers or mine.

Caroline turned towards the door, took in my overalls then turned back to Molly whose face was frozen in surprise. 'Not in here. In the conservatory go on, shoo.'

I was so weighted down with confused emotions that I couldn't move. She looked so beautiful, so vibrant and as haughty as ever. I was desperate to take her in my arms but, like Molly's face, I was immobile. She was staring at Molly now clearly puzzled by her expression then she swivelled sharply and stared at me. Recognition dawned and she bounded up from the armchair, rushed forwards then stopped abruptly. We were a yard apart but both frozen in time. Our eyes locked but we couldn't speak.

It was Molly who broke the silence by giggling then spurting out. 'A picture's worth a thousand words but this is a whole novel in front of me.' Caroline and I turned our heads to look at her. 'Yes, I can understand now.'

'Understand what precisely? What's the bastard told you?'

'Enough to understand. Now, why don't you two find somewhere private to talk or just stare while I go and make a pot of tea for Mr Pallot and myself.' She got up, and struggling to keep the smile off her face, left the room.

I didn't really want to move, as having this beautiful woman within touching distance was something I'd been dreaming about for so many months. Her perfume, the sheen of her skin, her eyes, her luxurious hair but no smile. I was expecting to be in heaven but now felt like I was trapped in purgatory.

'What the fuck are you doing here? Have you lost

your mind? Don't you realise how dangerous this is... and not just for you?' She clenched her fists, looked around wildly, hurried to the hallway then returned with some relief though I could see she was struggling to breathe. 'The guards are still there. But this is crazy. Why? Why?'

My heart was pounding. I wanted to explain but all that came out was a question of my own. 'Where's Mary?'

'How did...,' she sighed, '...it doesn't matter. Come on, I'll show you. She's asleep so please don't wake her up.'

Mary was indeed fast asleep in a cot in Christine's old bedroom now converted into a nursery. This was my second daughter and another that I hadn't seen until sometime after her birth. Taynia had been born full term in St Lo and little Mary had arrived before she was ready. She looked like all babies I suppose, beautiful, peaceful in her sleep and a wonder to behold. Caroline held my hand while I bent over our little surprise then pulled me away gently. 'If she wakes before you have to leave we can cuddle her together. Now, let's go to my room and have a cuddle by ourselves — if that's OK with you.'

It was more than OK and, following her along the corridor, I was on fire with expectation. She closed the door hurried across the room and slumped onto her bed. I rushed towards her but she held up her hand in a stop sign. 'No, Jack. I'm not ready for that. We can hug but you must promise me to keep yourself under control. Pregnancy is not a condition I wish to experience again...for a very long time. Do you promise?'

I nodded meekly trying to control the blood surging through my intimate parts.

'Good,' she patted the counterpane beside her, 'sit down with me. I'm sorry, but I wasn't expecting this. I'm not ready physically or emotionally. You have no idea how difficult this has been...no I don't blame you. I could have taken care of it, you must know that—'

'So why didn't you?' I put my arm around her shoulder and she rested her head against my neck.

'I didn't discover it until the end of January and kept it secret until March. Believe me, I didn't want to keep it but I just couldn't kill our child.' She pulled away and then took my face in her hands and kissed me gently on the lips. 'I hope you understand. I love little Mary but this bloody war, this fucking island. I hate it, hate them, and hate my bastard brother. I'm so trapped but I have to put on this brave face and let them believe that our little girl is the result of a casual affair with someone else who's now dead and whose grieving wife and children are living a life of misery in Germany. He was kind and wanted me, as many of these lonely Germans do, and he'd showed enough interest for his friends to believe it though I never have and never will condemn him by admitting it—' I tried to interrupt but she carried on. 'You must realise the consequences if Rudi thought for one second that you were Mary's father. It's bad enough that he believes I've been fucking a lowly Kriegsmarine officer—'

'When he'd like to do that himself?'

She flopped back on to a pillow, sighed in exasperation. 'No, you bastard. He's just overprotective, suffocating at times.' She laughed until the tears were rolling down her cheeks. 'You really don't know do you?'

'Know what?'

'Rudi, the Aryan model Nazi, the poster boy for the *Schutzstaffel*, isn't interested in his sister in that way or in any woman in that way. He can only be aroused by... pretty boys like you.'

Everything that had happened between Rudi and me suddenly took on a totally different meaning; from our first meeting in a water polo match when he fondled me where he shouldn't and I'd retaliated so viciously that he had to be rescued from the pool and taken to hospital. Later I'd punched him on the nose when I was jealously drunk because he refused to let me cut in when he was dancing with Caroline. The fight in the hotel when he'd insulted Rachel. The struggle in the sea when I'd knocked him out and dragged him back to the breakwater and resuscitated him. My wrestling a knife away from him as he was about to stab me in the throat and reversing the position until I had it inches from his. Caroline had stopped me then. The meeting in this house after the German invasion when he'd instructed his aide to shoot me and Caroline had saved me. The fight in the hotel in Portugal. All those episodes had now to be viewed from an entirely different perspective. It was too much. I could understand Hedley and others I'd met at Oxford but this was unbelievable. I wanted to ask her if she was sure but that would make me seem even more naïve. She didn't know about Portugal but had been involved in all the others and the most significant when he'd dragged her from my grasp as we were being towed away from the island under the guns of his troops. I'd believed his actions were driven by jealousy because he wanted her for himself but was all that because I'd spurned him?

She'd watched my face as I'd tried to process this then it struck me that perhaps Quigley knew as well and this was why Kempler had been selected because this was perfect for blackmail and probably why he was so busy hoarding stolen goods and sending them to a place of safety. Which led to one question.

'Does your father know?'

She laughed again. 'Of course not. Rudi is too clever, too experienced in disguise. I know you hate him and I despise him at times but I also understand how difficult it must be to have that burden in a social order where such behaviour leads to immediate imprisonment or worse.'

'Is he aware that you know?'

'It's not a subject that we'd ever discussed but I'm sure he is aware. You might find this strange, but I believe he does love me, as a sister. Our mother is in a sanatorium in Switzerland, his father is dead, his uncle and aunt are cold and remote so I'm the only blood relative he can talk to. You probably don't realise it but men like Rudi make excellent companions for lonely women like me who aren't looking for love.' She rolled onto her elbow and stretched her other hand to my hair. She ruffled it. 'What have you done to your curls? Now, come here, silly, we can cuddle — but no more.'

And she meant it. Which probably as well because I was so confused, even in her warm arms, drinking in her scent, kissing her softly, that anything further would have been a leap in the dark. So we cuddled, talked about how she would cope. She claimed it wasn't a big problem as throughout Europe there were millions of women and children separated from the husbands and partners perhaps for years and in some cases forever. She was in a very comfortable position compared to many and Mary would not want for anything. She did her best to reassure me about our daughter but then, as I was becoming reconciled to the inevitable, she inserted a stiletto and twisted it.

'You must promise me never to return here until the war is over, one way or another. It's not only Mary who's at risk if you are caught but your parents and other relatives. Rudi is ruthless and will have them deported to a camp in Germany if he believes that you have been here. Promise me.'

I couldn't as I might be ordered to return so I lied and offered her the reassurance she needed.

'There's something else. I believe we do love each other but...we both know that we are not best suited. No, let me finish. You love this island and your farm and that is where you want to be. Even in peace time I felt trapped here which is why I travelled so much. I don't want to settle here. There's so much I want to see and do and not just because of my music. We might be the same age in years and now share a child but you also share a daughter with Rachel who also has very wide horizons. I will always love you, Jack but I cannot see any sort of future which would make both of us happy.'

'But—'

'There are no "buts". I've thought this through so

many times and I will bring up Mary and she will one day know who her real father is and you will always be able to see her and celebrate as she grows into a beautiful woman...but you will have to share her with the right man when I find him.'

Anger, dismay, disappointment, anguish all competed with a strange emotion which I suspected was a sickening sense of relief. One I'd felt before with Rachel though my intensity of feeling for her had never matched what I felt for Caroline. On the bright side, Saul and Willie, my parents and all my friends would be pleased as none of them had ever believed that this gorgeous woman lying in my arms was the right one for me. There was no point in bickering so I hugged her tightly while the tears of laughter she had shed earlier morphed into sadness and mingled with mine until we were both strong enough to leave the room and spend some time with our daughter whether she was awake or not.

CHAPTER 37

She was still asleep so we stood over her in silence in our private world where time had frozen though, in reality, it was now more than thirty minutes since we'd been let through by the guards. We eased back out of the room and closed the door softly.

'Does my mother know?'

'Yes—'

'Does she know I'm the father?'

'No. Of course not. I wouldn't tell anyone—'

'Not even Molly?'

'I didn't tell her but she seems to have worked it out. She never mentioned you before you barged in this afternoon. But I'm sure you've told her about me, haven't you?'

'Not much but I know someone who might have.'

'Blabber mouth himself, I suppose, Saul?'

'He's told her about Rachel as well. He can't seem to help interfering.'

'Well, you know why he disapproves of you and Rachel, don't you?'

'I'm not Jewish.'

She smiled. 'That as well but I've always believed that he is in love with her himself. It must have been so difficult for him given your relationship especially when Taynia, that's her name isn't it?' I nodded, 'was born—'

'It won't come as any surprise to you then that she's rejected me as well.'

'That's for the best for the same reasons I've given you for us.' She touched my cheek with her hand. 'Poor Jack, we women are difficult to understand aren't we? I bet you're having trouble with Molly as well. She's lovely but not for you either, I suspect. But what is it you men say? There are plenty more fish in the sea?' She touched my lips with her finger. 'I shouldn't tease you.'

'Why did you call her Mary?' Two could wield the knife.

She removed her hand and looked away. 'I don't know, I just did. Don't imagine there was any other reason.'

But I did and her carefully constructed disdain seemed very flimsy and brought back the memories of her intense jealousy over my friendship with Rachel and the barbed comment about Molly was revealing. Perhaps I was fooling myself but something beneath the level of logic suggested that our relationship wasn't as dead as she maintained. There was nothing further to be said about it now but I vowed to myself that whatever relationships either of us entered into before this war was over I would find her and, however painful it might be, I would risk further rejection because, despite what she had said, we were in so many ways an excellent match. Yes, I was a farm boy and while you could take the man out of Jersey but not take Jersey out of the man, I would follow her anywhere, join her exploring the world and arts. I'd never be able to play the piano at her level nor manage high tariff dives from any height but there was so much we could do together. I might even persuade her to read Shakespeare but I would draw the line at learning German. I turned her back to face me and smiled then kissed her on the lips. She let me and responded tenderly. A picture might be worth a whole host of words but that sweet sensuous touch sealed an understanding that language had been unable to convey. As we released our lips, I just managed to stop myself from whispering Juliet's line *"parting is such sweet sorrow"* as I didn't want to invite a slap on the face. Instead, as the scholar I'd almost become, I fretted over the inherent contradiction in that line as I followed her down the staircase because there was such a lot to do in a shortening space of time.

We found Molly and Hedley in the kitchen chatting over a pot of tea. They greeted us with knowing smiles on their faces then offered to make some more tea. We declined. A nice cuppa could cure many ills but I suspected we would need something stronger to get us through the next few moments.

Caroline started. 'To misquote Oliver Hardy: "Well, here's another nice mess you've gotten us into". Do you have a plan to extract us from the manure, Jack?'

'I did have but the guards have put the kybosh on it but, never fear, there is an alternative—'

Molly interrupted. 'Before you start a new flight of fancy, Jack, I am aware of what Caroline's bloody brother has arranged and we've been discussing it. Whatever scheme you come up with I'm afraid there is no way I can escape—'

'There is, but—'

'Listen to me! I will not imperil your parents or Caroline and you know that *Irish Lass* has to get back. The truth is...I am expendable, yet safe here. It's not the holiday I would have chosen but I'm in no immediate danger. There's plenty of work for me in the hospital and the Irish community will look after me—'

'No, they won't especially when Kempler discovers that the schooner isn't coming back. I don't want to say too much as the less Caroline hears the better for her... and us. Dermot and Quigley have agreed that you cannot be left behind so shut up now and focus on how we are going to do this.'

'Yes, I'd be interested to know that.' Caroline removed a bottle of scotch from a cupboard and waved it at us. First problem is the guards. If Molly disappears they will report that Mr Pallot was here with an assistant who they will describe—'

'They didn't get a good look at me and they won't discover that she's gone until you tell them which you won't do until well after the ship has left. Your father is away and won't be back until Sunday with your bloody brother. Is there anyone else who might come here before tomorrow lunchtime?'

'Yes, the nanny. Rudi supplied her. She's a humourless Bavarian, looks like a milk maid and acts like one of those deluded souls from Himmler's *Lebensborn* programme—'

'Where is she now?'

'In town. She has her eye on a Luftwaffe pilot and I let her have the evening off. She won't be back until the morning.'

'Does she know about Molly?'

Caroline shook her head as she poured herself a slug of the whisky. 'No, she left before lunch.' She smiled. 'But, how can I explain Mr Pallot's visit when Rudi starts screaming?'

'The piano,' Hedley suggested.

'What? I'm not playing the piano now...wait a minute, of course. Rudi and my bastard father know about it. They pissed me off so much with their dithering and I told them I'd been looking for someone to help. I'm sure I mentioned that I'd discussed it with you—'

'What about the piano?' I asked.

'You might even remember the bloody thing. An old Bechstein D that my father paid a fortune for because it had Cortot's signature on the plate—'

'Yes, I do remember you ranting and raving about it — something to do with a split in the soundboard.'

'That's right though that's not got any worse. The pinblock has and my piano tuner is fed up with trying to get the right tension in the strings. He advises a new block or replacing the pins. Mr Pallot offered to get it fixed but needs to inspect it so that he can send the details to his suppliers—'

Hedley interrupted. 'And that's what I've been doing while you were—'

I sighed. 'Was that what you told the guards; that you'd come to work on the piano?'

'I mentioned it but told them we'd been sent to collect some furniture... I did tell you not to worry.'

'How can you explain my presence though?'

'Well, I haven't got that far yet but I'm sure I'll come up with something.'

'Under the sort of interrogation that Kempler will arrange you can be sure of that! I can't let you take that risk.'

'I have friends in the right places and let's be honest, even if they can't help, it's something I've had to face for a long time now...as you know. Anyway, it's not material as you will both be long gone before Kempler's friends can discover anything useful from me so let's end that discussion and focus on getting you both back on the ship.'

The silence was fraught and broken only by the clink of bottle on crystal glass as Caroline poured us all a drink. The tumblers were particularly chunky which gave me an idea.

'How heavy is the Bechstein?'

'Well, it won't fit on the kitchen scales so I have no idea.' Caroline offered me a peculiar look. 'I know you farm boys love lifting things. Hang on, I remember now. I think it came up when you were moaning about that crazy bull of yours. When I gave you a number you said it was about the same.'

'I don't remember that but Victor was one hundred stone at the last weigh in which is 1,400 lbs or about 630 kilos. Get your kitchen scales, we'll go and weigh.'

They followed me into the conservatory and watched as I attempted to lift one side. It was impossible. 'How long has it been on this piece of carpet?'

'Three years at least and, according to my father, this is a very valuable Ghiordes rug and the castors have damaged it. It's not in the best position for me...and I'd rather it was on the parquet floor. I've asked him to move it several times but he's just a man — so promises the earth but delivers nothing. He says it would take at least four men to lift it off a corner at a time.'

'I do remember you persuaded me to get the lid off so you could make an even louder noise and that alone weighs at least one hundred pounds. Even off the carpet and on the parquet, overcoming the inertia of that bulk must be very difficult—'

'Yes. A theatre always lays on a team to move a concert grand even on castors—'

'What's the point of this?' Molly interrupted.

'I think we might involve the guards, make them complicit. Caroline, can ask the two Germans if they could come inside to help us move the piano off the rug —'

'You're not planning to try to get it onto your lorry are you?'

'Of course not. We'd need a crane but I want them to able to report what we were doing here so you will need to stand around so they can testify you were here when we left.'

'You do realise that you have to dismantle it before it can be moved don't you? It took four men from Donaldson's music shop and a special cradle to deliver it and they really struggled to get it on the rug.'

'That's the point. You'll tell them that you only want it moved across the room into the light but, despite its weight, it is rather delicate and we don't want to shove it lest we break the castors so four pairs of hands will be best.'

'Then, I suppose you want me to thank them with some coffee and perhaps whisky and play them a tune?'

'Now, you've got it. Show them the problem with the soundboard and pinblock. It's a distraction while Molly prepares to slip away over the field and waits for us at the head of the valley near Paul Mill. I see she's wearing a watch so we'll synchronise and meet up in thirty minutes. You OK with that, doctor?'

'Not really and what if I'm observed?'

'The two guards won't see you. I've been listening and I'm sure the working parties have finished in the valley now. Before Caroline goes outside, I'll show you the way. What do you think, Hedley?'

'They'll get a good look at you,' he responded.

'All they're going to remember is Caroline's legs, beautiful smile, magical playing and Molly serving them refreshments. I'll just be a scowling, bored look-ing Frenchman who you'll drag away while they're sip-ping their drinks and being entertained.'

Molly only had her dress and formal shoes so Caro-line found some slacks, blouse, cardigan, pumps, and a cardigan then I took her up to the attic and pointed out the route through the corn field and down to the val-ley floor. We could just see Paul Mill on the other side of the dry stream. The mill wasn't in use and she could wait out of sight there until we arrived in the lorry. I explained the second half of the plan while she changed then we went back to say goodbye to Caroline.

The only flaw in this improvised concoction was the possibility that Mary might wake up and start bawling for her mother and her milk.

CHAPTER 38

One day, I felt sure a plan I had devised would actually work without last minute improvisation but not today. No sooner were the guards seduced into assisting the local concert pianist when Mary woke up and realised she was hungry. She might have been born prematurely but from the level of sound she was producing she would probably develop lungs to rival mine. The four of us paused in our efforts having so far only released one corner of the rug which did reveal a pot hole under the castor. It's difficult to ignore a crying baby and as men we tend to turn immediately to find the nearest woman to deal with this intractable problem. Caroline was nearest but she was also supervising. Molly, however, seized the initiative and hurried up to the bedroom.

She returned almost immediately with a purple faced bundle hitting high notes almost out of the Bechstein's range. 'Is there a bottle ready in the fridge?' Molly inquired.

Caroline snorted. 'Can't be bothered with that nonsense while I've got these. Bring her here.'

I'd seen it all before but to the Germans and, a lesser extent, Hedley, it was the height of embarrassment as she dropped her dress off one shoulder and hauled out a breast heavy with milk. It stopped Mary and flummoxed the workers. 'Carry on. Don't mind Mary. She has to eat you know.'

As a distraction it was perfect as the two guards kept

flicking surreptitious looks at Caroline's breasts while bending to the task. Fortunately, they were strong and within minutes we'd released the rug which Hedley dragged aside to inspect. He offered the opinion that it would need some expert repair and he knew just the man to carry out that task for a small consideration. He caught my eye and I wondered if, like me, he'd had to study *Anthony and Cleopatra* in his English lessons.

After we'd manoeuvred the piano to a position which satisfied her, Caroline was most gracious in thanking the Germans and chatted to them while holding Mary to her exposed breast and showed them to the door. Molly had hurried upstairs to change but called out to me within moments. I joined her and she took me to the window overlooking the fields and pointed out something which really shot my latest plan down in flames. Two other guards were patrolling the perimeter of the field. She changed anyway as I concocted then explained yet another tweak to my design.

'Let's hope their knowledge of Egyptian and Roman intercourse is limited and they haven't read much Shakespeare,' she intoned.

I was tempted to suggest to Caroline that she ask the two Germans to assist in the removal but Hedley thought that might be pushing our luck too far. A rolled up antique Persian carpet wouldn't need four men to lift it even with *Cleopatra* inside. I paced it out – probably just under seventeen feet long by ten feet wide. With Hedley's help I rolled it up from the short end then hoisted it on to my shoulder. This was dense material and I guessed it weighed between five to six stone. Add in our little Egyptian beauty and it would total close to 200 pounds. It would be a bit floppy in the middle though so Hedley suggested we utilise one of the curtain poles to keep it more rigid.

Given the choice of being carried out like a pharaoh or running like a fugitive through a corn field, Molly decided that the royal approach would be more in keeping. Caroline thought we were mad but refrained from trying to change our minds. Hedley then suggested that we revert to our original idea of using an empty crate, several of which were in his warehouse, and have it craned aboard along with other treasures and supplies. It would certainly be more comfortable for Molly unless it slipped off the crane. We discussed this with Caroline and she reminded me of the escapologist who staged a show at the Pool in 1938 which involved a crate with a secret hatch. This had supposedly been constructed for him by a local builder and, in front of nearly one thousand spectators, he had been secured inside with chains and padlocks before the crate was lowered into the sea. Unfortunately, the tide was coming in and there was a small swell. The crate didn't sink as planned and he must have been disorientated inside as, to the great amusement of the paying customers, he emerged above the water level through his concealed opening. To add to the fun, he was overcome with motion sickness and puked all over the crate.

Caroline retold this with some skill so we were giggling with a mixture of mirth and horror which released some of the tension. Molly lay down on the rug, shut her eyes, folded her arms across her chest and nodded that she was ready. We placed the pole over her body before she wrapped her arms and legs around it, then we tucked one side over her body and rolled her up. If she was frightened of confined spaces and having her arms and legs pinned in layers of carpet she didn't show it but I knew that, once on the road, we'd have to stop as soon as possible and transfer her to the empty tool chest until we could reach the warehouse. I took the heavier head end on my shoulder and forced my face into an effortless expression as Hedley lifted the largely empty section and took the strain of the curtain pole on his. We couldn't give the appearance of struggling lest the Germans offered to help. Caroline checked that Molly's torso wasn't bulging then came out with us, nursing Mary in her arms though her breasts were now under the flimsy cotton of her dress. She wandered over to the two policemen by the gate to engage them in conversation and let them coo over the baby. While this pantomime was playing out, we manoeuvred *Cleopatra's* rug onto the load bed with as few bumps as possible. When she saw that we had accomplished our task, Caroline said goodbye to our helpers and walked back to us. She shook hands with Hedley and then, hidden from the Germans by the cab, handed him the baby while she hugged and kissed me. It had to be brief but that delicious and now forbidden taste would linger for a long, long time. I couldn't push her away and she had to extract herself before retrieving Mary and holding her out to me. I kissed her forehead fighting back tears now before Caroline tugged her away, turned her back, and retreated into that sad and lonely house as Hedley turned over the engine.

The guards stopped the truck and one mounted the running board to exchange some sentences in German which made the three of them laugh. From the gestures the one standing by the bonnet made with his hands I assumed they were discussing Caroline's magnificent breasts and bravely laughed with them fighting down the despair that it might be the last time I ever saw them.

We daren't stop within earshot of the guards so had to turn in to the shadows of Les Grands Vaux before finding a scrubby area under some oak trees to pull up. Hedley kept watch while I unrolled Molly, for which service I received another slap and a string of invective which would have outdone Caroline at her very worst. She claimed that I had taken advantage of her helplessness and enjoyed manhandling her too much. Perhaps there was a spot of guilt under the red blotch on my cheek so I kept my distance while she climbed into the chest then wedged the heavy lid open a couple of inches to provide some air to cool her down. At least she could escape from this temporary prison.

When we were finally safe inside the warehouse I set to work on turning a suitable crate into an escapologists prop. It wouldn't survive a close inspection but it should be robust enough to be craned aboard and, if it did end up in the harbour, at least she could slide the panel aside and swim out. That information merited another slap and a few sentences in what I took to be Gaelic and of which, fortunately, I understood nothing at all. To keep Molly's crate company we then loaded four others containing a range of not particularly useful items and our much travelled pump.

To test its resilience we packed four fifty pound sacks of cement into Molly's crate and used the wheeled hoist to lift it onto the load bed. Even she seemed impressed as she scanned its surfaces for signs of the escape hatch. Once on board I removed the cement and helped her into it, careful to avoid her hands as she settled on to the sacking and curled up into a foetal ball. I'd already drilled some air holes under the top lid so, unless we were unduly delayed, she should still be breathing when we unpacked her in the hold. As soon as Hedley was ready I completed the deception by screwing the lid down before joining him in the cab.

When we reached *Irish Lass*, the sun was dipping over Noirmont Point in the west and it was quite peaceful in the shadows of Victoria Pier. The crane driver had long since gone so Dermot had to use the schooner's derrick to swing the cargo aboard. The guards didn't interfere though I did spot one making a note on a clipboard. Once inside the hold, I stood well back while Molly was extracted from her temporary tomb, fearing another wild cat strike, and let Dermot take her into our special compartment. There was still no sign of Kempler's passengers but a message had been delivered to order us to stay moored until they arrived. Molly could have moved about below decks freely but Quigley wanted to talk to her in private so we left them alone.

After a suitable interval, Hedley disembarked. We had discussed whether he should explain to the guards that I would work on the pump through the night until it was installed and then make my own way home, as being Irish, I wasn't subject to curfew but thought it better to say nothing and hope that in the confusion of Kempler's human cargo arriving later, head counts might be overlooked.

CHAPTER 39

While Liam kept lookout topsides, Quigley, Dermot and I examined the chart of the English Channel. We were a neutral vessel and if we kept to the international portion of the seaway theoretically we should be safe from English or German interference. A simple plot running at an average speed of twelve knots showed that it would take us at least twenty-four hours to reach Cork. Doubtless, we would be observed until dusk when we should be about twenty nautical miles due south of the Isles of Scilly. To continue to Cork we should run north-west for another two hours then directly north for the run in to Ireland — another eleven hours away. Five of those would be in darkness which would give us the opportunity to disappear. Though our new destination would provide considerable navigational challenges it did seem to be a move any shadowers would not expect. We'd been ordered to file our plan with the harbour authorities before the pilots came to assist us through the pier heads and the rocks around Elizabeth Castle's breakwater.

By half-past ten, there'd been no further activity on the dock and we now wondered if the passengers wouldn't arrive until the morning. We were about to stand everyone down when there was a burst of noise from the harbour control point and search lights started probing the entrance. I scrambled up the mast and watched as a *raumboot* lumbered through against the falling tide. It seemed to be towing another boat which looked a bit ragged. These two had shallow draughts though the one under tow was listing heavily. The RAF must have been enjoying some more target practice.

I expected the boats to process down to the much longer Albert Pier but, instead, they manoeuvred to the short berth between us and the pier heads. Even in the bright coned lights it was difficult to pick out detail but I was sure that Hemming was on the bridge of the first boat. Sailors on the listing one cast off the tow and let the first nudge them into the side on the lower level of the recessed landing stage. Our bow was now obscuring the activity so I shimmied down and scrambled over the chains to the foremast deck. Shadowy figures moved about but, on the damaged boat, it seemed that a couple of stretchers were being passed across. I was aware of a vehicle rumbling over the cobbles now and realised that it was an ambulance. Our two guards hurried over to assist and eventually the stretchers were carried up the granite steps and lifted into the ambulance. Shortly after, a mixed group of sailors and civilians appeared and walked towards us. Three of them were carrying suitcases but leading was Anton Schneider minus his cap but with a bloodied ribbon of bandage around his head. By now the whole crew, minus Molly, were on deck and watching this curious parade.

A bullish individual clad in a worn leather overcoat arrived first. He handed a suitcase to Dermot and ordered him to put it in a safe place before standing aside and helping a middle-aged couple onto the deck with their large cases. Schneider brought up the rear and offered his hand to Dermot. 'Allow me to introduce *Hauptwachtmeister* Wölfle who will complete the formalities with your two passengers. I must apologise to them and to you for the lateness but we had an unexpected encounter with the Royal Airforce who can't seem to accept that they have lost this war.'

I bit my tongue as he looked around at us. 'Ah, my friend, Jacques. You see, it is impossible to finish me off so perhaps you could persuade the Irish to join us and give Mr Churchill a good kick up his bum.'

I joined the others in appreciative laughter but before I could find a humorous retort Schneider's eyes lost focus and he staggered, slipped, and then collapsed against the wheelhouse. In his fall he banged his head and the bandage slipped off exposing a long gash in his scalp. Blood was streaming out now so I called out to Liam and Rory to assist and we carried him into the cabin and lay him down on the chart table. He was fading from consciousness which, though I bore him no particular malice, was fortunate as the last thing we needed was him searching for Molly at Caroline's house. Dermot extracted the first aid kit from a bulkhead locker and shone a torch on the wound. Though it had been dressed and smeared with some Vaseline like substance it needed stitches and a doctor to examine him for concussion. The ambulance had left and there wasn't any transport close by. I asked Kurt to go and tell the guards that he needed to get to hospital immediately.

Wölfle stepped in and brushed me aside. 'I'll deal with this.' He spoke English with an American accent which confused me until he unleashed a string of German at the two guards who had now appeared. They scuttled off. 'Who's in charge here?'

Dermot stepped forward. 'I'm the captain.'

'Good. Lt Schneider is very brave but quite fool-hardy. This will be mentioned in my report.' He motioned the two civilians forward. 'This is Mr and Mrs MacBride. I have escorted them here on behalf of *SS-Standartenführer* Kempler and now hand them into your care. I understand that you will be returning here in the near future when I will have further conversations with you as I will soon be assuming my post with the *Geheime Feldpolizei* on this benighted rock. If you need any assistance or guidance then please ask for "Wolf of the Gestapo". He chuckled to himself. 'You'd be amazed at how many doors that opens without having to use my boot.' He turned to the bewildered looking couple and launched a string of German. They responded with nods but didn't speak. 'Good. That's done. If my breakfast is promptly served I will attend before you sail in the morning. An ambulance should be here shortly if those two wooden tops have done my bidding. I won't wait.'

He stalked off whistling as he went and hurried down the gangplank while one of the guards picked up his bags and struggled after him. Within minutes a staff car had arrived and he clambered in. Shortly after, Hemming returned up in his sports car and hurried aboard. I showed him to Schneider and he examined his friend closely.

'Bloody idiot; literally. His old wound hadn't healed properly yet he insisted on carrying out this mission. He was lucky that I chose to join him as he'd be crab bait by now. Those Beaufighters are a real menace.' He shook his head. 'I think it looks worse than it is, so rather than wait for the ambulance, I'll take him to the hospital if you'll give me a hand getting him to my car.'

He supervised while Dermot and I carried him down the gangplank and lowered him into the sports seat. I'm sure a doctor wouldn't have approved but he did seem to be coming round. He tried to speak and Hemming bent over to listen. He laughed then swung himself into the car. 'He wants to thank you for letting Molly stay with us for a while and is angry that he won't be able to see her until he is patched up. I'll give him to the medics to play with then I'm back on duty for another convoy in the morning. Bon voyage.'

Dermot looked at me and winked. 'For a Jersey *crapaud*, you certainly have the luck of the Irish. Come on *Jacques* we have some guests to make comfortable.'

The MacBrides were not very prepossessing and appeared somewhat bemused by the activity around them. For some reason, I'd imagined that Kempler's agents would be more Nazi like but these two looked like shopkeepers, in their fifties and worn down with their daily drudge. On reflection that would make them perfect as agents. We'd find out more later but Dermot offered them a hot drink and some food. The man who introduced himself as Henry and his wife as Theresa had a pronounced Ulster accent though it might have been Scottish as my ear wasn't finely tuned to those northern regions. He had a muttered conversation with his wife before she declined and explained that they were exhausted and would like to retire to their cabin. She was polite but insistent so Liam took them below while Rory followed up with their cases.

Once they were out of earshot Dermot ushered Quigley and me into the cockpit. 'Peculiar. He's from Donegal but she's from the South, Cork maybe. Not quite what we were expecting. I can't—'

'But you should, Dermot. Most of the German agents we've discovered are rather non-descript and seem harmless. Once you dig a bit deeper you discover that they're motivated more by a hatred for the British than any love for Hitler. They generally respond to kindness and aren't too difficult to turn if we don't meet their expectation of being brutal bullies.'

'You must find that rather challenging, Quigley—'

Dermot grabbed my arm. 'Enough. Don't start that again. Fergus, go and make sure our guests are comfortable and you and I will do the same for Molly and, if you don't behave, Jack, I'll leave you alone with her!'

She'd calmed down and after we'd brought her up to date with events topside we went over the plans. I checked the Marconi set and we agreed the protocols we'd need if we had to make an emergency transmission. During our abortive *Operation Ruthless* escapade we'd used the Cornish language for key words and Molly and Dermot had learned some key phrases before leaving Helford this time. Hope for the best but plan for the worst had been hammered into us during our training so we rehearsed the likely outcomes should it be discovered that Molly was missing after we sailed. If it happened while we were still docked then we had to trust that any search would not reveal her hiding place. In one way it would be better if they did search and find nothing but it would probably mean *Irish Lass* would be detained until Molly was discovered. In any event there was nothing we could do about that so we focused on how we might best save ourselves should the Luftwaffe and Kriegsmarine chase us down at sea. We would never be more than 100 miles from a listening station in the UK so we determined to transmit a short burst of Morse with a Cornish code word and a rough latitude and longitude position using numbers in that language. From the chart we calculated that if we left at 08:00 we should be in position forty-nine degrees eighteen minutes north and three degrees fifteen west by 12:00. *Tri* was three and *pymthek* was fifteen. In a Morse message a dash was three times as long as a dot. A pause between each letter should be three dots long and between words seven dots. Though it was laborious to code even a semi-skilled operator like Rory could be understood at least eighty percent of the time. We tested Molly and, using the crib sheet, she produced an accurate note for the operator which should confuse any German but make sense to our listening base in Helford when the message was relayed. It would start with the name of our operation and most urgent code word for a header of "Lochaber". Though not Cornish this would be the same for any message and would indicate that we needed immediate assistance. We had other less urgent codes with estimated time of arrivals but that word followed by an approximate navigational fix should be sufficient. We would then maintain a listening watch for acknowledgement and any coded instructions.

Rory and Molly spent another hour practising until they felt comfortable that a position relayed from the cockpit could be transcribed and transmitted in under a minute. While they were working I opened a case of a dozen Mills bombs and unscrewed their base caps. The fused detonators were kept in a separate box so I inserted them carefully into the narrow chamber hole next to the Baratol high explosive filling. While holding the safety lever they wouldn't explode but as soon as I pulled the pin and threw the pineapple shaped grenade I'd have four seconds to take cover as these had a lethal explosive range for the iron shrapnel of up to forty yards. I placed them in four pouches attached to an adapted commando cross-braced webbing belt and hung it from a hook on the bulkhead. They could be defused if not needed but it would be easier and more fun to chuck them overboard and stun a few fish though the shrapnel might shred them into bite sized morsels. Finally, I cleaned three of the .45 cal. Thompson sub machine guns and loaded six of the twenty-round magazines with special 300 grain cartridges and taped them together so that they could be reversed when empty. This had been a favourite man stopper of our instructors even though it lacked accuracy and was a heavy beast. Before leaving Helford I'd taken Molly to our improvised shooting range at Trewothack, a local farm, and tested her weapons handling. She was an excellent shot with our .303 Enfield sniper rifle from a prone position but found it too heavy when standing. She struggled with the weight of a Colt .45 automatic pistol and had to fight the muzzle drift of the Thompson. It was a powerful weapon so I persisted until she could manage single shots with good accuracy and short bursts with some control. I handed one to her and asked her to strip and reassemble it then select single shot. It was obvious that she'd been practising and seemed very confident. But could she pull the trigger and send one or more of those devastating rounds into a human being? I hoped neither of us would ever have to find out. While she practised stripping a Colt .45 I had another check of our Bren gun and Boys anti-tank rifle but soon realised that we were just making work now so with little else productive to be done so I suggested to Rory that we leave her to sleep and returned to my cabin to await my stint on lookout duty.

Dawn wasn't at all spectacular as there was a low cloud base but as the light crept over the harbour from Mount Bingham I had a chance for a closer look at R-72. From the visible damage topsides it was obvious that the *raumen* boat had been lucky to survive. No wonder, the MacBrides had looked to be in shock. Wölfle had either been putting on a very brave face or had anti-freeze running through his veins. As the harbour came to life a tug secured the stricken boat and towed it across and into the English Harbour where I assumed it would be beached for repairs. I scrambled up the main mast to check on other vessels still in the harbour. Hemming's departed before 06:00 along with another of his flotilla. There were two *schnellbootes* moored further up the Albert Pier though there was no activity on their decks. One cargo ship, SS *Diament*, was getting steam up and preparing to leave. After 07:00, two more were craning on loads of what looked like tomatoes. I guessed they would be going to France and returning with more military supplies and equipment. The *Duke of Normandy* tug was busying itself and two pilot boats were fussing about. I counted five fishing boats as they transited the pier heads. From their size and equipment they looked like crabbers and were probably off to pull up their pots around the south coast. One converted cabin cruiser which looked incongruous with a heavy machine gun installed on its foredeck followed them out like a sheepdog. At 07:30 Dermot descended the gangplank and was escorted to pier head control. He returned fairly soon and nodded to me to join him in the chart room.

All seemed to be well and he said that a sailing time of 08:30 had been agreed and that we would be fourth in the queue behind the cargo ships. The weather forecast in the Channel was for a force two NNW wind with a nine tenths cloud base at 500 metres and surface visibility at eight plus. This might help us with the Luftwaffe but there'd be no hiding from the Kriegsmarine until full darkness which wouldn't be until after 23:00. This was going to be a very long day.

CHAPTER 40

German efficiency dictated that we pass through the pierheads at 08:30 on the dot following close behind the *Holland*, and the *Normand*, which were both stacked with boxes of tomatoes, and flying the Jersey flag with larger versions draped over their sterns as well — probably hoping the RAF wouldn't attack them. As those two steamed due south to France we closed up with the *Diament* which was crossing the flat sea towards Noirmont Point and the western approaches. She had now been joined by the two steam trawlers both heavily armed with anti-aircraft guns which had left the harbour earlier. As the other two ships hadn't picked up an escort I assumed that this one was carrying military supplies north to Guernsey and needed protection.

We motored until well clear of Elizabeth Castle's breakwater. Behind us, there were still several vessels preparing to exit the harbour though none seemed to be naval. I'd trained the binoculars on the two *schnellbootes* before we'd untied confirming their 20 mm cannon and torpedo tubes. I knew they could cruise at over thirty-five knots with short bursts up to forty-five in the right conditions which meant they could overhaul us very rapidly. If they left one hour after us we would be in their sights within fifteen miles and we had over 250 to travel. The Luftwaffe would find us first even with the low cloud though I doubted that Kempler would authorise an attack given the nature of our cargo but there was nothing we could do to fight off two fast torpedo boats. A two hour delay would only give us a maximum of forty-miles of grace but, to escape them in the dark, we'd need at least an eight hour delay and lots of luck. We had to slow for the boat to collect the pilot before I joined the other crew in the rigging and unfurled enough sail to achieve a steady fifteen knots then we settled into a straight westerly course in the middle of the channel equidistant from France and England.

As we were on a straight course and the little wind had already shifted to the north east there was nothing to occupy us other than our thoughts. Perhaps we'd been overthinking this and the Germans wouldn't discover Molly's absence. If not, Quigley would want us to proceed to Cork and deposit our passengers and cargo so that whoever had added this element to Fleming's plan could turn them into double agents. My preference would be to forget Ireland and land them in England and create a new deception that *Irish Lass* had been lost. If the MacBrides were to be turned then they could be schooled in that new narrative. It was very risky docking in Cork and I couldn't see any real benefit. Needless to say, Quigley disagreed though I suspected Dermot was on my side. If we were intercepted then the game was up and fleeing to England would be the best option. The optimal point for making a decision would occur when we reached the location I'd used as an example in Molly's Morse code test and that was at least another six hours away.

Time dragged so much that I was happy to be relieved and as there was little pleasure in lying on deck without the sun I retreated to my cabin and my copy of Shakespeare and thinking of my own circumstances turned to *Love's Labour's Lost* and joined the King of Navarre in swearing an oath to avoid, amongst other things, all contact with women for three years. After a few scenes I realised I would probably be just as unsuccessful but the comedy did lift my spirits somewhat and I was still engrossed when Dermot knocked on the door to invite me to join him and the MacBrides for lunch in the mess.

Apart from the heeling over and trying to eat on a tilted deck the couple seemed comfortable enough though they were very circumspect in conversation. We did learn that they'd been living in Germany for several years having left Ireland when their two sons were killed by the Black and Tans during the uprising back in 1920. I supposed that was motivation enough as the brutality of those paramilitary thugs employed by the British made most civilised people recoil. However, there were two sides though, as the MacBrides would expect a southern Irish crew to be sympathetic, no one mentioned the actions of the IRA. I had no idea what they had been told about *Irish Lass* but they seemed comfortable enough to mention that they'd been asked to return to Cork to look after some property for an unspecified person who was hoping to live there once the inconvenience of this "horrid" war was over. With the sort of wealth Kempler was accruing I could see how it would make a more attractive bolt hole than somewhere like Argentina. But, to neutral observers — especially the Americans — the Germans were winning the war on all fronts so why prepare to abandon ship so soon unless he really believed that his secret predilection was on the verge of being discovered? I wasn't sure if I shared Saul's belief that if the Soviets held out long enough and the Americans were persuaded to join us Germany couldn't win. It was still going to be a long war and refraining from involvement with women for the duration was an attractive idea—in theory at least.

I was back on duty in the wheelhouse digesting the less than wholesome meal that Rory had served when Liam called down from his perch up the main mast that he could hear aero engines. My watch was still set on Berlin time and read 14:20 so nearly six hours and eighty-five nautical miles since departure. We were entering the golden circle time when I might be able to impose my plan on Quigley even if this was a false alarm. I stepped outside and scanned the cloud base in the direction that Liam suggested. He was right, it was a twin engined plane but it could be one of ours though in this area it seemed unlikely. All the crew were on deck now several with binoculars. Dermot spotted it first as it dipped out of the cloud. It was several miles away and just a black dot but it seemed to be growing larger by the second. Certainly the engine sounds were increasing in volume and I imagined the throttles being pushed forwards as the pilot was alerted to our presence. It was diving now, the engines thrumming a new urgent note as the high octane fuel was flooding into the carburettors to increase revolutions and speed. We couldn't hide and, in keeping with our neutral status, already had the Irish tricolour flying from the three masts and streaming from the staff on our stern. EIRE was on both sides of the hull but that wouldn't be visible until the aircraft was much lower and circling us. We'd rehearsed this but couldn't be sure what action the Luftwaffe would take. As expected it was a reconnaissance Dornier, the flying pencil, and soon it was crabbing up on our stern dropping now to under a hundred feet and slowing to provide an observational platform.

Rory called from below. 'They're trying to raise us on the radio.'

We'd been through this before. Without a prior agreement they couldn't be sure we would be listening on their particular channel so I was tempted to shout to him to ignore them but I'd spotted Henry MacBride was approaching the cockpit. It was still possible that the mission could be preserved so I called back an imaginary channel to try.

The sleek fuselage was very close now as the pilot throttled right back until I guessed he was close to stalling speed but the plane was still travelling five times faster than us so it was only a brief glimpse of the detail of the decks before he shot past and banked for another run in on the port side this time. As he approached an Aldis lamp was flickering in Morse. Quigley was alongside me noting it down. 'It's in English. Simple enough. "Heave to and await instructions".'

'Bollocks.' Dermot had our lamp in his hands. 'I'll send them the usual. We're a neutral ship in international waters.'

While he clicked away I noticed that the lower rear facing gunner had his weapon trained on us. I was sure he wouldn't shoot at us but perhaps a stream of tracer over our bow might be sufficient to indicate he meant business. I cast around. Nothing had changed; the wind, sea state, cloud cover, visibility were all against us. There was no sign of fog. We were trapped. Time to send for help. I called Rory down, gave him our approximate position and sent him to *Bodmin* with instructions to give Molly the location to code and prepare the Marconi for transmission. He was to press the button to flash the red light in the wheelhouse when everything was ready then wait for a return flash before he sent the message with the urgent heading and wait for an acknowledgement. I then walked calmly down to the radio room and told Liam to wait for my signal then transmit our neutrality message endlessly on the frequency the aircraft was using. I hoped that both messages would go at the same time with the one on the aircraft's frequency preventing the operator hearing the second in case he was scanning a broader spectrum.

On deck the aircraft was approaching again with more flashing Morse. Dermot shrugged and looked at me. 'He's losing patience. Claims that he will start shooting if we don't stop and hold position.'

'We need time. Keep sending the same message. Liam will do the same on the radio as soon as Rory is ready to key in our distress signal. I'll wait with Tomas at the wheel.'

Within a minute the red light flashed and I clambered down to Liam. 'Give me time to get back to the wheelhouse then send it and keep transmitting.' Ten seconds later I was ready but hesitated. My action now would create a change of events over which I would have no control. There'd be fatalities. I just prayed they wouldn't be on my island. I wasn't worried about Caroline but my mother and father were hostages to a violent and evil man whose plans I was about to destroy. I pressed it and in that instant felt a new calm descend on me.

Back on deck, Dermot was still busy with the lamp though the Dornier had crabbed away and was now flying perpendicular to our course. He shrugged. 'I tried but he must have robust orders. Time for our tin hats.'

We didn't have any so there was nothing we could do as the black beast with its sneering swastikas dropped even lower and spewed a dazzling display of green tracer less than twenty yards short of our bow.

'What's happening? Why are they shooting at us?' Henry MacBride was screeching now and tugging at Dermot's arm.

'They want us to heave to but we don't know why.' He removed MacBride's hand. 'We'll just have to be patient. We've experienced this before. I don't want to alarm you but we know that the Luftwaffe have sunk several neutral Irish ships recently. It's best if you return to your cabin and stay there until it is safe.' He turned to me and whispered. 'Have Kurt escort them below and lock them in.' Then he shouted to the crew. 'Come about. Haul in the sails. Reduce speed to steerage way and maintain course.'

Quigley nudged Dermot. 'As soon as they see us stopping, ask them why and for how long we have to wait.'

I doubted the pilot would authorise a true answer so returned to *Bodmin* to find out if we'd received an acknowledgment yet. On the way, I told Rory to keep sending messages to the Dornier to keep their radio operator busy. Kurt passed me with a huge smile on his face. It seemed that the MacBrides were so upset after he locked them in Molly's cabin that they were now shouting at each other — in German.

From Molly and Liam's glum expressions, I guessed that we were still waiting for an acknowledgement. I asked him to try again while Rory was also busy on his key above. I pictured the chart. We were within a sixty mile radius of several airfields in the South West of England, and St Ival, from where we'd flown our Heinkel for *Operation Ruthless*, was less than twenty minutes away for a fast fighter though endurance would be a problem for a Spitfire or Hurricane. The twin engine Beaufighter wouldn't be much slower and could loiter for longer and some were based at the new Predannack airfield on the Lizard Peninsular which was thirty miles closer. One would soon scare away the Dornier unless it called for support which would be subject to the same distance calculations for fighters. I knew there were Messerschmitt Me 109s and twin-engined BF110s based on Jersey and Guernsey though the airfields around Brest were half the distance way. It was really down to how seriously either side was prepared to treat this and how quickly they could provide support.

It was out of our hands so all I could do was run various scenarios through my overworked brain and try to match them in our favour with time and distance calculations. Best case, if our message was acted upon and Fleming could persuade the RAF to sortie their fighters, help could arrive within the hour. Worst case, our message wouldn't be received. Between those two extremes there was a whole range of possibilities though, without knowing how far away the Kriegsmarine boats were, perhaps it was futile to torment myself. However, the thought of a pitched aerial battle in the airspace above *Irish Lass* didn't hold much comfort either.

Molly interrupted my thoughts and pointed at Liam. He had one thumb in the air and had lifted his left headphone. 'Acknowledged. More to follow.'

The real living breathing Irish lass threw her arms around me and kissed my cheek. Perhaps love's labours weren't entirely lost after all.

CHAPTER 41

I was still absorbed in time and distance calculations interspersed with day dreams of that Sunderland or even the anti-submarine trawler *Macbeth* hurrying to our rescue when a call from Kurt, who was now in the lookout position on the main mast, kicked me out of my reverie. 'Ninety degrees – two fast bow waves.' Those of us with binoculars rushed to the nearest vantage point and trained them to the east. The Dornier had been circulating without further communication for over an hour now but it banked out of its holding pattern and fired a green flare in our direction. The calmness I'd felt after sending the message had been replaced by an anxiety that I'd acted in haste instead of assessing the options in more detail. We would be boarded and searched. I was confident that they wouldn't find Molly or much else so what would they do? Make us return to Jersey until she was found? Take someone else hostage? They might have discovered from the GFP guards that we might have an extra person on board. They wouldn't find him either though I could pretend to be him. That might work but they would take me with them and, depending who was on those rapidly approaching boats, they might be surprised to find that "Jacques" was missing. We couldn't see them yet but unless the RAF suddenly dropped out of the sky they'd be alongside in less than five minutes.

From any angle these two *schnellbootes* were a frightening sight. They looked like torpedoes with their curved sinuous low slung hulls. As they closed and throttled back the red noses of their very real torpedoes were visible in the open tubes. One sped up again and circled us while the other approached slowly until it was alongside our starboard side and pointing in the same direction. Our rail was about five feet higher than its deck though the top of the cockpit was almost level. There were half a dozen armed sailors on its well deck between two spare torpedoes and three officers standing in the cockpit alongside the helmsman. One officer stood on a high step inside the cockpit and looked across. His eye level was just above my stomach which was creating as much acid as if I'd just drunk a whole bottle of Coke. Underneath his peaked cap was a bandage wrapped around his forehead. It was Schneider and he seemed to have recovered far more quickly than I had hoped. Two ratings shouldered their machine pistols and slung mooring ropes over to us. The sleek, submarine like vessel, was almost as long as *Irish Lass* though its beam was narrower and, with our masts and rigging, we seemed to dwarf it.

Rory had left Molly closed up in *Bodmin* though the vents were still open. He and Liam now split and grabbed a rope each before securing them to fore and aft capstans with, what I hoped, were disguised slip knots. There was so little sea movement that the Germans were able to fix a plank across from the raised platform behind their cockpit and run it between our rails' stanchions to provide more dignified access than a rope ladder.

Schneider was first across and made a bee line for me. 'Where is she, Renault?'

'Who?'

The slap was vicious and I wasn't in a position to respond now there were two gun barrels aimed at me. 'Don't waste my time. This is not one of your jokes. Get Molly from wherever she is hiding and bring her here immediately.'

Dermot moved between us. 'If you are looking for my niece I believe you have travelled eighty-five miles for nothing. She is in Jersey where you "invited" her to remain, or don't you remember?'

He ignored him and counted the crew members who were now all on deck. 'Good. You will all stay here while I conduct a thorough search.' His eyes were wild and I wondered if he was still suffering from concussion. My cheek was stinging but I kept my mouth shut. He threw a string of German towards the S-boat and an officer with three more men strode up the gangplank with pistols in their hands. The officer didn't look very happy and barked at us in German. No one reacted.

'My officer orders that you sit on hands on deck and speak nothing!' The rating who had spoken waved his pistol over us and pointed down. There was little point in resisting though Dermot spoke softly to Schneider and offered him the key to Molly's cabin explaining that the *Standartenführer's* special passengers were locked in for their own safety.

Sitting on my hands wasn't a comfortable position especially as I wanted to scratch the irritation on my cheek but Germans are a bit intolerant of those who don't obey them immediately, something I believed extended all the way up the chain of command to the house painter himself. We waited. There were plenty of cubby holes on board and lots of crates to be examined in the hold. I couldn't see my watch but I was sure we'd been sitting here for at least twenty minutes which meant that my signal for help was now at least ninety minutes old.

It was nearly two hours old before Schneider appeared on deck again. His face was pallid and it wasn't due to lack of daylight in the hold. He approached me again and motioned me to stand then sat down on a bollard, looked up and me and shook his head. 'I have spoken with the strange Irish couple and they haven't seen her so where is she?' His voice was almost pleading. He would have a lot of explaining to do when Kempler returned to the island.

'We don't know. None of us has seen her since you took her to dinner.' Dermot answered.

Schneider removed his cap and ran his fingers over the bandage which seemed to be stained with fresh blood. He handed the key to Dermot. 'Here, keep those two rats locked up. I hate spies.' He turned back to me and spoke quietly. 'Two men delivered a crate to the house where Molly was staying. They invited the two police guards in to help them move a piano and extract a rug. Molly was there with *Standartenführer* Kempler's sister and still there when the men left with this rug. One of those men was a Mr Pallot who is well known to the *Feldkommanteur's* office. Mr Pallot claims the other one was an Irish engineer who had been working on this ship and who helped him with this task at the house before he returned him here with a replacement pump and other items which were loaded. The GFP guards on the harbour confirm this and that Mr Pallot left by himself having told them that the engineer would make his own way home when the pump was installed. They don't have a record of him leaving. Do you recall when he left?'

I shrugged. 'There was a lot of disturbance if I remember correctly and you, amongst others, were taken to hospital after your battered boat returned. I didn't see him leave but, as you've discovered, he's not here so he must still be on the island.'

'Some might be convinced by that, Renault, but these aren't ordinary guards. They are highly trained and disciplined policemen and they haven't recorded his exit. *Hauptwachtmeister* Wölfle is continuing to interview them to see if their memories can be refreshed...' he shook his head sadly, 'the *Standartenführer* is returning to the island to oversee this process. Now, for the final time, did anyone here see this engineer leave?'

Dermot shook his head. Rory, Liam, Miguel and Tomas did the same. Quigley kept a blank expression but Kurt spoke up. 'I did. This man, who calls himself "Wolf of the Gestapo", made him carry his bags off the ship and to the car that picked him up. He didn't offer him a lift and he didn't return.'

Before Schneider could question him I asked. 'When did you discover that Molly was missing?'

'I called to see her at 09:30 after those fussy nurses let me discharge myself. Caroline, that's the *Standartenführer's* sister, told me that both of them had been up until the early hours of the morning as the baby was distressed so she'd let Molly sleep in. I persuaded her to let me wake her up but instead of Molly there was only a bolster and a cushion under the covers in the blacked out room. I called in the four guards and we searched the house and the grounds thoroughly but without result. Caroline was most concerned and insisted that we call her brother which we did just before 11:00. He's in Paris so it took some time to locate him. Shall we say he was displeased and demanded that we find Wölfle and put him in charge of an island-wide search. He asked about your ship and then demanded that I find your sailing course and set off in pursuit with the fastest vessels I could find. He told me that he was going to contact the Luftwaffe to arrange a search and here we are.' He stood up. 'This is most unsatisfactory and I remain unconvinced. She is not on this ship but perhaps there is someone who shouldn't be.' He shook his head and focused on me again. 'And what happened to this "someone"? Did he swim ashore? Because the guards saw him board the ship but not leave.' He sighed, '...or so they think. This is a puzzle and look at the cost of trying to solve it.' He waved his arm towards the boat tied up alongside and the one further out which was still circling slowly. 'Sadly, it's not within my power to solve it, or ignore it. I have my orders from *SS-Standartenführer* Kempler. If Molly cannot be found, he still wishes you to continue with your journey but I must return with another "volunteer" to enjoy our hospitality until your schooner returns.' He stood up and replaced his cap. 'Now, which of you will be so kind as to accept this generous invitation?'

No one spoke or moved.

'Very well, I shall have to choose but be warned that

should that person resist I have been authorised to shoot him and make another selection.'

A collective hiss of anger made him reach for his holstered pistol. He withdrew it and pointed it at Kurt. 'You are selected.'

I couldn't let him take Kurt as he was half Jewish but, before I could object, Dermot stepped forward and said. 'Take me.'

Rory and Liam spoke in unison 'Take me.'

Then Tomas and Miguel joined them; which left Quigley and me. I'd learned a trick once during an acting class about focus. If you concentrate on your heart beat until it is all you can hear it is possible to extend the range and shift the focus to the blood flowing through your limbs then your breathing. The next stage is easier as you include everything in your immediate vicinity then within visual range and finally at the limits of your audio perception. It's very calming. I needed to be calm and it was so effective that what I heard at the very limits was so soothing that I stepped forward until I was almost in Schneider's face. 'Forget them. I'm the only one with a real reason to help you find Molly.'

'And what's that?'

'I'm in love with her!'

From the look in his eyes that was as effective as a slap to his face. He glared at me for a long moment. '*Arschloch*. We will discuss this on the journey back. Now, get your baggage before I change my mind.' He motioned to one of the guards to follow me.

I called out. 'Talk amongst yourselves, why don't you? Ask Quigley.' I needed some distracting noise and hoped they'd discuss my revelation. I slid down the companionway which gave the guard a problem but he hurried along and caught up with me and my elbow in the middle hold. There wasn't time for niceties so I used the butt of his machine pistol to deliver a message to his skull and he collapsed in a heap. I shoved him between two crates and rushed to the compartment and Molly. She was surprised to see me but didn't pull the trigger on her levelled pistol as I barged in. 'Quick, grab two of those Thompsons, insert the double magazines and cock them.' She didn't ask why but started work. While she busied herself I shrugged into the webbing harness and buckled up the belt with the Mills bombs in their pouches, picked up my Thompson, and slotted a magazine. As soon as she was ready I told her to follow with the guns. On the way out I pressed the button which should produce a red light topsides then hurried to the engine compartment, opened the throttles, engaged the screws, and scuttled out.

I stopped at the foot of the starboard companionway to the aft deck and explained what I'd heard and needed her to do. If she was frightened she didn't show it and crept up the steps behind and listened with me at the top. The faint sound I'd detected had now resolved itself into the thunderous roar of four rotary engines as a Sunderland flying boat dived from the clouds. There would be consternation on deck — particularly on the *schnellboote* tied up to our hull.

The last position of the other boat had been some points off our starboard bow and, if it had continued to circle in a one hundred yard radius, it should now be half way down our port side. As I emerged from the hatch, Schneider was running towards the port scuppers, screaming at the other boat, and gesturing for it to come into *Irish Lass* probably for the protection a neutral vessel might afford from a devil with depth charges. I didn't wait to see if he was successful but hurried to the starboard side where I could see the panic on the deck of the sleek hull below. I grabbed a Mills bomb from its pouch, yanked out the safety pin, and lobbed it into the cockpit. Before it landed I threw a second one while screaming for everyone to lie flat then raced over to Schneider and kicked him over the side. Molly was crouched behind the wheel house sheltered from what I had warned her what was about to happen.

The twin explosions erupted with such force that *Irish Lass* might have shaken her ballast loose. I had convinced myself that the grenades wouldn't set off the torpedoes as they had precise guidance systems and special fuses so rushed back and aimed my gun at the devastation below. Before the dazed sailors on our deck realised what had happened Molly had passed a Thompson to Quigley and they were pointed at the poor sods who dropped their own weapons and fell to their knees following her barked command in German. I called out to Rory and Liam to cast off the mooring lines while I looked more closely for life on the stricken *schnellboote*. Behind me, I was aware of the giant shadow as the lethal whale shot over. I followed it and spotted four large drums falling from its wings to straddle the other boat. The sea erupted and where, seconds before, there'd been a sleek elegant triumph of German engineering, now there was only two halves of a broken hull.

Irish Lass was gaining speed and slipping away from the previously attached *schnellboote* which was wallowing in the swell caused by the concussive effect of the depth charges. We'd been struck as well but our deep keel gave us more stability than the shallow draft of the German boat. The Sunderland was circling back for a new attack on our victim but banked away when it realised that it was still too close to us. It looked as though it didn't need a coup de gras and would sink of its own accord. At least one of those grenades had fallen into its interior and it was on fire. It still had a 20 mm cannon but, if there were survivors, none seemed keen to use it. At last a plan which seemed to have worked.

I rushed to the port side for another look at the wreckage and right into Molly but she wasn't alone. Schneider had his arm around her chest and a luger pistol pressed into her skull. There wasn't time to work out how he'd scrambled back onto the ship but he was dripping seawater, was wild eyed, and looked desperate. Molly grimaced as he pushed her forwards. Her Thompson was on the deck, mine was slung over my shoulder. I had two grenades on my belt but no other weapons other than my training. 'Don't be silly, Schneider. This battle is over. Put down your gun and surrender like your men have already done.'

He shook his head which splattered some blood onto Molly's face. 'No, Renault. This is not over. The Luftwaffe will return and blow you all out of the water. You must surrender to me.' He backed away dragging Molly with him so that he couldn't be outflanked. 'You say you're in love with her. Let us see if that is true. If you attempt to capture me she will die first. You might kill me but what satisfaction will that give you with the woman you love dead at your feet.'

She hadn't heard my declaration of love and stared incredulously at me. 'Is this true?'

I sensed movement behind me but couldn't see who was risking Molly's life. I barked out. 'Stand down. I'll handle this. Schneider, don't you want to live?'

'After you've massacred my men? Why would I. The only pleasure left is to take some of you with me. Starting with this bitch!' He jerked his arm into her neck and lifted her off her feet.

Someone shot past me and Schneider moved his gun from Molly's temple and fired two shots. It was Kurt. He stumbled and fell at the German's feet. Schneider snarled and fired another shot into his face. Molly struggled and as the German tried to reposition his grip and re-aim his pistol at her head, she sank her teeth into his wrist. He screamed, confused now and lost balance as she twisted her body, arching her back and kicking at his legs. He let her fall and turned to me the Luger steady in his hand. "Say goodbye, Renault.' His finger tightened on the trigger. He couldn't miss at this range. I wouldn't shut my eyes and stared into his, hoping to anticipate the shot and throw myself sideways before the bullet reached. It was a futile plan. I couldn't react faster than a bullet. Yet I sensed that he was waiting for me to blink. I did and the bullet flew. But it wasn't his. Molly had fired the Thompson on single shot and the heavy slug smashed into his head undoing all the remedial work and shattering his skull in one a lethal blow.

The gunshot echoed into a silence suddenly shattered by a flock of seagulls diving on the fish blasted to the surface by the depth charges. Molly dropped the gun and vomited over the side before rushing to Kurt to see if he could be saved. But it was futile as the head-shot had shattered his skull and his brains were leaking onto the deck. The butcher's bill was severe for the Germans and heart breaking for us. Kurt had been brave but reckless. Schneider had lost his mind and I could understand why though I would shed no tears for him. But it wasn't over.

A new sound penetrated my thoughts. As Schneider had predicted, the Dornier was back. It was faster and more manoeuvrable than the Sunderland but only had machine guns. If it were to engage I would put my money on the great white whale. But it held back. It would be transmitting but what had it seen? Two boats destroyed by a rampant flying machine adapted specially for that task? Or had it seen my attack?

There wasn't an answer but the Sunderland returned to pose its own questions with its nose mounted heavy duty machine gun whose red tracer now arced towards the Dornier which dived away. The Sunderland had a powerful sting in its tail with a quad turret of machine guns and, as it banked to bring them into action, they ripped a fusillade of bullets and tracer towards the German plane. But there was no way it could catch the German. If only...and another prayer was answered as two Beaufighters swept in from opposite sides for an acute angled attack on each of the Dornier's engines. One pass was sufficient before the crippled plane crumpled, split at the seams, and splattered into the sea. Not a good afternoon for the Reich. And to make it better for Britannia, Rory called out that the Royal Navy was in sight. A heavily armed trawler powered towards us. *Macbeth* had arrived though the witches were already dead.

It wasn't just the witches. After the trawler had sunk the mortally wounded *schnellboote* with its three inch anti-aircraft cannon we lowered our gig and between us, we hauled thirteen survivors from the wreckage and collected seventeen corpses, some barely recognisable as humans. They would be afforded a burial at sea later According to the list, compiled by the one remaining officer, of the combined crews' total complement of fifty-one, only eighteen had survived and four of those were on *Irish Lass*. The one in the hold was badly concussed and needed immediate treatment. *Macbeth* had a medic on board but even with Molly's help there was little he could do. We searched for the wreckage of the Dornier but apart from a few pieces of fuselage found nothing.

The captain of *Macbeth* was disappointed because

he'd missed the "party" but confided that he'd seen worse, especially when he'd come across survivors from U-boat attacks. There was no remorse. It was total war now — kill, or be killed and, if I'd been taken back to Jersey and the tender mercies of Kempler, perhaps a quick death would have been, in the words of *Hamlet, "Devoutly to be wish'd"*.

CHAPTER 43

The sea was still calm and there was no sight or sound of the Luftwaffe though that could only be temporary. *Macbeth's* captain had received a terse message from the Admiralty which ordered *Irish Lass* to continue on its planned route to Ireland until nightfall then await further instructions. He was instructed to return to Falmouth with any survivors and await their collection. From previous experience I knew they would be detained in a special facility which MI6 and S.O.E. had established where those captured during sensitive missions could be isolated from ordinary POWs and their fate kept from the protecting power of the supervising Swiss. Their families would only learn from the German authorities that they were missing in action.

We had to move quickly to preserve our neutrality and, after an inspection of our hull revealed no shifting of the ballast, flooding in the bilges, superstructure damage, and only some superficially scarring from shrapnel to the starboard side from the grenade blasts, we set sail. It was 16:20 and we had another six hours before sunset. The chart showed that if we maintained twelve knots we would be in a position approximately thirty-three nautical miles south west of the Isles of Scilly at that time. The Sunderland would shadow us from a distance while the two Beaufighters kept overwatch on the *Macbeth*.

The aftershock of the engagement had created a febrile atmosphere where we were all trying to appear calm. I could almost hear the pounding hearts of the crew as the realisation of how close we had been to disaster sunk in. No one seemed ready to discuss it though I caught strange glances from each of them as we went about the business of keeping *Irish Lass* on course and up to speed. Kurt's body had been sown into a hammock and at some point after dusk we would slow right down and hold a short ceremony and commit it to the deep. After a navigational correction which involved some trimming of the sails we were less busy and Dermot took me aside. 'I don't know whether to congratulate or kick you overboard but I suppose fortune favours the eejit. Shame about Kurt. What would you have done if he hadn't rushed in?'

I looked him in the eye. 'Taken his bullets while you all saved Molly, what else.'

He clapped his hand on my shoulder. 'You've been very rash this afternoon but perhaps the most irresponsible thing was declaring your love for Molly. You'll recover from the fight but that might haunt you for some time. Anyway, it can't be unsaid so back to business. I'm surprised that Fleming didn't order our return to Helford—'

'He would have but I suspect that whoever is really in charge here,' I nodded towards Quigley, 'and his boss would want to preserve their core mission which was to compromise Kempler and the bonus of two agents to turn wasn't going to be rejected easily.'

'You don't really think that we'll sail all the way to Cork, do you?'

'Probably not. Kempler will have a way of communicating with the German legation in Dublin and *Irish*

Lass turning up would create even more problems if you remember the watchers watching the watchers before we left. No, I might be wrong, but I expect there's an argument going on between Naval Intelligence, S.O.E. and MI6 at the moment. If he was here Saul would be able to explain the intricacies but, in terms of levels of influence, I think MI6 will have the final say. We'll just have to wait but, if you want a bet, I'll wager that Fleming wants this schooner but he also needs the Germans to believe it's sunk.'

'What about the MacBrides? They can't be used if they're presumed lost can they?'

'Fortunately, that's not our problem though I'm sure Quigley is giving it some thought.'

And he had been. But I didn't like his thoughts and told him that our prime mission was to deliver the intelligence on the German defensive preparations and that I didn't want to risk any further delay by sailing to Ireland and confronting any challenges there. Dermot kept a straight face when I said that *we* had decided to change course for Tresco on the Scillies where S.O.E. had started to establish a base and wait for further instructions in the hope that Fleming might send a seaplane to extract Molly and me. He was so angry that I thought he might decide to punch my fist with his nose again but he just threatened me with the wrath of "C", the head of MI6, and the real prospect that my commission would be revoked and I would be busted back to the ranks and returned to my foot sloggers' regiment.

I recalled Saul's information about the Secret Intelligence Service's chief, Major General Menzies, another old Etonian, and his rivalry with Fleming so I was aware that I would be merely an easily sacrificed pawn in their constant manoeuvrings for Churchill's ear. Not wanting any more blood on my knuckles I told Quigley, if that was the outcome, it was perfectly acceptable if the information I provided prevented a massacre on my home island. Short of staging a one man mutiny there was nothing he could do. He stormed off to his cabin to write a report while we took a closer look at the chart and realised that we might have made a serious mistake.

Though there had been a seaplane base at New Grimsby for anti-submarine patrols it had shut down soon after I was born, but navigation through the rocks at any state of the tide looked hazardous. From our Admiralty charts it was clear that, even down the more open North Channel between Bryher on the west and Tresco on the east, steering a ship of this length and draught was going to be a serious challenge and, to do so at dusk was possibly suicidal. Molly intruded on our musings so I asked for her opinion. She studied the chart grabbed a tide table and made some calculations on a sheet of paper.

'Look, this is not as difficult as you might think. If we time it right we can catch the tide on the flood and instead of taking the obvious route around the north-west we can slip up the channel towards the Seven Stones and come in from the east. If my arithmetic is correct then we can catch the flow and get to New Grimsby Sound before dark. I know there are overfalls and eddies and probably sea monsters as well but the tide will be with us and the alternative is much longer and slower against the flow. But, I'm a medic and not a navigator, Sub Lieutenant Renouf, so it's your call. One thing though, which I'm almost sure, you will have considered, is that you're going to have to cram on full sail and crank up your engine. Eighteen knots should do it.'

Dermot and I looked at each other in amazement. Perhaps what I'd said to Schneider hadn't been too far from the truth. She smiled at us and laughed. 'By the way, Jack. Well done before and... I take back what I said yesterday. A daft boy couldn't have managed that – only a completely mad...man.'

The wind had picked up and come around to the east a few points so we managed to reach over twenty knots at times which was fortunate because, as we sped past uninhabited St Helen's, there was just enough light left for me to realise that Dermot was changing course too soon and turning us into Old Grimsby Sound which had hardly any manoeuvring room and might leave us grounded at low tide. Fortunately, I'd visited the proposed S.O.E. base on a recce mission with Saul and Daniel previously and remembered in time. I knew the plan was to keep some of our disguised Helford Flotilla boats there eventually and took a sighting from Cromwell's Castle which marked the northern entrance to the secluded mooring area. Not wanting to draw attention to ourselves we'd turned off all the illumination as we rounded St Martins. The risk now was that we'd be challenged by the small garrisons on Tresco or Bryher though it was more likely some Home Guard sentry would panic and start shooting first. However, they must have all been looking the wrong way or asleep as, after turning to face up the channel, we managed to drop anchor in the middle of the deserted sound about 120 yards from either shore. We were equidistant from the uninhabited rock of Plum Island, off our port quarter and Cromwell's edifice off our starboard bow. From the chart it looked as though we were about 1,200 yards from the slipway to the old seaplane base. I spent a torturous thirty minutes drafting a message in S.O.E.s' variation on the standard naval cypher code for the attention of *17F'*, briefly explaining our situation and asking for his orders.

We'd consumed one of Rory's special concoctions which he passed off this time as depth charge stew complete with dumplings and washed it down with some of the ridiculously expensive vintage wines from the hold. Quigley had stopped sulking and joined us revealing a connoisseur's appreciation of the apparently excellent Margaux though my taste buds still refused to recognise the floral notes and spicy red fruits let alone the cherry core he described after sniffing, inhaling, sipping and swallowing.

We rotated lookouts each hour so that everyone had the pleasure of enjoying Rory's glutinous mix and imbibed more than we should have. Quigley had told to us that the ageing process had increased the alcohol content of these vintage wines though Dermot whispered to me that he was talking through his arse as that was fixed during fermentation. Perhaps he was right but I certainly felt more tipsy than usual after a few glasses and decided to relieve Tomas on lookout early.

It was almost silent on deck; just the gentle swish of the falling tide as it sucked in and out of the rocks and the occasional sound of laughter which I assumed emanated from the pub half a mile away. It was a warm night and I was preparing to strip off and have a swim when I felt a presence behind me. It was Molly and she was tipsier than me. Whether it was deliberate or the effect of the alcohol she stumbled into me and wrapped an arm around my shoulder to steady herself. I couldn't appreciate the aroma of wine but I recognised the perfume immediately. 'That's *Joy* isn't it?'

'Clever you. Do you like it? I'll take it off if you insist.' She burped and my nose did at last register the aroma of the wine... and the dumplings.

'Where did you get it?'

She hesitated. 'Caroline gave it to me...do you mind?'

Of course I did but that would have been churlish especially as that particular perfume had always had an immediate effect on a certain part of my anatomy. 'No, it's lovely and it really suits you.'

'You charmer. Just because I called you a man earlier doesn't mean you have license to act like—'

I cut off her sentence with a kiss which she didn't resist and then returned with a passion which surprised and delighted to the extent that a hot flush surged through me. Sensing her guard was well and truly down I pulled her into me feeding now on a desire I had suppressed for so long. Yet my conscience was trying to make a coward of me. Should I take advantage of this beautiful creature or should I be the real man and stop it now before we moved into territory we could only but regret?

She must have sensed my confusion and ran her hands down my back then slipped them under my shirt and caressed my spine. All thoughts of cowardice, conscience and restraint dissolved as she pulled me down onto the deck then onto her warm and lithe body.

I woke up in *Bodmin* wrapped in her arms without regret or shame or clothes, and little memory of the night's activities other than a nagging belief that at one stage she had chided me by saying that, as she wasn't ovulating, I could try a little harder. Could it all be explained by the eternal truth that war replaces fear with love? I was about to test that again when there was a discrete knock on the bulkhead. 'Sorry to disturb you two but there's a message from Fleming which needs an immediate response.' Dermot couldn't hide the amusement in his voice.

CHAPTER 44

It was a short message which didn't take long to decode. Typical Fleming. Do this. Do that. Wear this. Now. I sent an acknowledgement then returned to *Bodmin* while Molly went to her old cabin to collect her few belongings. For reasons unspecified Fleming had ordered me to wear my dress uniform which I now donned though I was buggered if I was going to shine my scuffed and dusty shoes. While we were getting ready, Dermot covered the EIRE signs on the hull, obscured the vessel's name and port of registration and removed all the Irish flags. Instead he hoisted the merchant marine red duster on the stern jack staff. The message said that further instructions for the schooner would follow. So far it didn't seem as though we'd been noticed which was surprising as, even though our hull was hidden, our masts towering over one hundred feet above should have been spotted. There could be some red faces in the local garrison unless Fleming had already contacted them.

We listened intently for the first sounds of our transport which I suspected would be one of the high speed RAF rescue launches from St Mary's barrelling in from the south but apart from a distant outboard engine droning across from Bryher to Tresco and the usual squabbling gulls, all was quiet. Molly heard it first and pointed to the north. Gradually the faint growl of rotary engines grew into a roaring wine as the largest seagull I had ever seen swept in towards us. It was very low, too low to clear our masts. Had the Luftwaffe

found us? It was a seaplane with a long parasol wing
and sculpted hull which matched the description of a
Dornier Do 24; a long range reconnaissance flying boat.
I knew there was a squadron of Hurricanes on the main
island of St Mary's so it was taking a crazy risk. I
grabbed the binoculars and as soon as it was in focus I
realised that instead of the German plane's three engines there were only two. We didn't need to break out
the machine guns as this was one of the amphibious
PBY Catalinas the RAF had acquired from Canada. Head
on it did look like a predatory seagull but as it pulled up
over our masts I could see the landing wheels folded up
into the fuselage. As it passed, an Aldis lamp started to
flicker. It was in plain English and I managed to interpret the message which was a request for us to move
240 degrees west by south 100 yards. I shouted the
message out to Dermot but he'd already understood
and someone had started our engine. Rory and Liam
hurried forward to haul up the anchor and within two
minutes we were in position. The aircraft was circling
over Tresco Abbey in the distance then it swooped
down for a long run in. Floats had appeared out of its
wingtips and I could see the first splashes as it bumped
onto the sheltered waters near the old slipway. It
bounced more and at one point disappeared into the
spray before settling. It was still travelling as fast as a
schnellboote as it entered the narrowest part of the
channel and snarled towards us. Then the engine note
changed as the pilot altered the pitch of the propellers.
Of course, a flying boat had no brakes but as the sea
clutched at its hull and the spray dissipated, it slowed
until it was in the spot we had been occupying earlier.
It wasn't a large plane though its wingspan occupied

about half of the channel as it passed Plum Island. I recalled that it had a crew of up to ten and wondered if two had been left behind to accommodate us as it was going to be a very tight squeeze — not that I minded sharing a seat with Molly

Molly squeezed my arm. 'Good God, have we got to fly in that thing?'

'Looks like it. You're not scared are you?'

She thumped me. 'Of course I am. I've never been in something so flimsy...or any sort of plane so you had better look after me.'

We'd not known what to expect but Dermot had launched the gig and he and Liam were at the oars now as we prepared to board. Everyone apart from Quigley was on deck to wave us off and Molly hugged them all. I handed Molly and our bags down to Dermot then slid into the gig and pushed off. The Catalina was a curious object with its bug like side blisters but we received a friendly wave from an airman in the bow gun turret as Liam paddled us along its hull. The starboard side bug eye was opened from inside but it was a tight fit especially as two of the crew were competing with each other to help Molly aboard. It was a bit of a muddle but she managed to squeeze between them. One of them, noticing me for the first time, attempted a salute before retreating into the interior and leaving me to clamber inside alone. It was more spacious than I'd expected but I couldn't see all the way into the cockpit as an airman was occupying a seat suspended in the space between the wings. The two blisters had machine guns and I could see a very narrow passage leading to the rear gun position. Fortunately, there was a compartment behind the blisters which had two metal bunks, one of which was hinged up and secured to the fuselage. I followed as Molly was led towards them. One of her assistants gave me a headphone set and rotated a switch.

'I don't know who you are sailor boy but someone seems to be in a rush to see you.' The voice was transatlantic, probably Canadian. 'We're taking off immediately so you and your pretty friend strap in—'

'Where are we going?'

'I'm not sure I'm cleared to tell you that but it's only a short hop…onto dry land. Here, settle down on those seats under Shirley and Greta but don't feed them.'

Hanging from a rail across the fuselage were two cages, each containing a pigeon. Molly asked the obvious question though I already had an inkling of the answer.

'No they're not for lunch but…I shouldn't really tell you this either but it's not really a secret. We are airborne for a long time on patrol and if we have to ditch we release these homing pigeons with our position and hope for the best.' He smiled. 'Our captain thinks we should cross breed them with woodpeckers.'

She fell for it. 'Why?'

'So they can knock on the door before they deliver their messages. Now, hand me your headphones and buckle in.'

We sat on the metal fold down seats facing each other across the fuselage. I'd been a pampered passenger in a luxury flying boat all the way from Poole Harbour to Lisbon in Portugal. There'd also been a couple of less than luxurious transport planes and I'd been pushed out of Whitley bomber at 2,000 feet as part of my commando training but this was brutal. Molly's eyes were wide with terror as the Catalina wound up and headed out to sea. Slowly at first like a fast motor boat rising onto the plane and then bouncing and thumping clawing for enough speed to escape from the clutching sea. The engines screamed and as we passed the rocky outcrops guarding the sound and reached the open sea we hit a cross current and started to squirm to escape Neptune's jaws. I couldn't reach across to her and daren't unbuckle as this was like trying to ride Victor in one of his foulest moods but all good things come to an end and suddenly we were free and climbing away through the low cloud base and into blinding sunlight. Molly's eyes were shut tight and her knuckles were white where she was clenching the base of her seat. As soon as we were in level flight I unbuckled and crossed over to her. Conversation was impossible as the two engines, even throttled back for cruising were unbelievable loud so I gave her a hug and tried to release her safety belt but she smacked my hand away. I tried to read her lips but decided whatever she was mouthing probably wasn't going to brighten my day.

A short flight could have meant Land's End airfield but we passed that fairly quickly and as the cloud thinned I watched as we continued along the north Cornwall coast. I recognised St Ives, then Newquay and when we started to lose altitude I realised that we were aiming for St Ival. I wondered if the station commander was still that grumpy old sod, Pascoe, who'd been in charge when we'd flown off in a captured Heinkel to implement Fleming's *Operation Ruth-*

less and pinch a code book, after we'd ditched, from a German rescue craft which would have to be at least of *schnellboote* size. The ditching went well but the Germans had only sent a converted fishing boat which didn't have the requisite codes so another of his schemes disappeared without trace and he was left to explain the failure to Alan Turing who was desperate for the information and who'd forced it on him in the first place. I was musing on what new adventure *17F* had cooked up and was awaiting me on the ground when Molly suddenly shouted. 'Are we there yet?'

Her eyes were still closed so I shouted back. 'Open your eyes and prepare for a few bumps.' I was going to add something amusing but she was probably storing up a series of slaps to indicate her displeasure with her first flight experience so held my tongue.

The landing, even though we seemed to crab in, was relatively smooth and despite a few bone shaking bumps, successful. After the pilot had taxied to the apron we were bundled out without ceremony along with our bags and left while the Catalina powered up and hurried off to do something more useful than cart passengers about.

Group Captain Pascoe it was and his mood hadn't improved since the previous Autumn. He looked Molly up and down from behind a desk even larger than the one from which he'd exerted his authority before.

He fiddled with a moustache which had grown in proportion to the size of his desk and sniffed. 'I see you have found yourself another floosy, Renouf and become an officer of sorts.' He shook his head. 'I just don't know how we're going to win this war but it won't be through irregulars like you masquerading as officers in the wavy navy. No child in tow this time, I see. I suppose that must be an improvement.'

'Thank you for your interest, sir but, with respect, my extended family is none of your bloody business. We have our orders so unless you have some amendments to give us, perhaps you'd be kind enough to provide us with some refreshments and a place to wait.'

I could sense Molly just about containing herself but Pascoe laughed. 'Quite incorrigible. Are they all like you in this creature Fleming's organisation?'

'No sir, I'm probably one of the most charming and polite...unless you're a German, sir, in which case you'd be—'

'That's enough.' He picked up a sheet of paper from his otherwise empty desk. 'I've received this telex from the Admiralty which advises me that transport will be arriving for you and er...'

'Molly, sir. She's a German agent.'

'What—'

But my little "agent" had launched into a stream of German which I assumed was aimed at me. Fortunately, neither Pascoe nor myself, understood though I had heard the words *trottel* and *bumsen* before.

After she'd spluttered into silence and offered him her most winning smile he pushed away from his desk, stood up, stalked towards the door, retrieved his cap, placed it on his head and stood at attention glaring at us. 'You will stay here but do not touch anything.' He seemed to be waiting for something then it dawned on me that he was expecting a salute from a much junior officer. It was tempting but I obliged with a regulation, if brief, naval gesture. He snorted and exited without a formal return.

'Well, that's one way of asking for a cup of tea but I don't think it's going to be successful. It would seem that you two know each other. Want to tell me about it?'

'Not now.' I stepped towards her and reached out for a hug but she wriggled away.

'Not until you have a lot more stripes on your sleeves. I suppose we'd better make ourselves comfortable. I'll sit in his chair and you can stand in front of me like the naughty boy you are while I consider an appropriate punishment.'

CHAPTER 45

I was still savouring the range of possibilities when Pascoe returned and ushered her out of his chair. 'Your transport is on finals so on your way with you and please don't return.' He indicated a sergeant standing rigidly at attention in the doorway. 'Flight will take you to departure and has instructions to hand you over to the RMP Redcaps if you annoy him in any way. Understood?'

'Roger that, sir. All clear. Over and out.' I saluted in the regulation manner, picked up our bags, then followed Molly out of his office. The airman marched along the corridor and down the stairs without a word as we tramped after him. An Airspeed Envoy was waiting, engines still turning as he escorted us over the apron. It was a low wing monoplane with twin radial engines and looked as though it was made of wood. The sergeant led us around the wing and folded down a short ladder then assisted Molly up it with rather too much of a personal touch for my liking. Once she was aboard he stood back and let me make my own way. Inside, separated by a narrow aisle, were three rows of two passenger seats, four of which were already occupied by RAF personnel. It was a tight squeeze and would have meant disembarking to change places so Molly had to sit next to a sour looking squadron leader which left me with the remaining space alongside a wing commander who seemed to be asleep. Our bags were passed in and shoved along to the rear. Up front was a single pilot with white hair poking out from his regulation cap. I couldn't see his rank and as Molly was one row behind and across the aisle couldn't make contact with her either. I hoped she wouldn't be so scared this time as her companion didn't look as though he was equipped to deal with female vapours over flying.

As soon as the door was secured the pilot spun us around and taxied to the main grass runway and wound up the engines to full revs. This wasn't a commercial flight so he wasn't constrained by passenger comfort and we climbed very steeply before banking sharply and swinging round to the east. There was little point in trying to strike up a conversation with my sleepy companion especially as the growling engines would have made it extremely difficult. The lightweight plane had excellent all round visibility with its deep and wide windows so I contented myself with peering out and watching our green and pleasant land from a couple of thousand feet as it sped along below. I guessed we were flying to London though, judging by the seniority of some of the passengers, we might be stopping enroute. The last time I had made this journey it was in an Albemarle with Fleming on board. On that occasion he had monopolised Rachel and been quite bad tempered with me. We'd landed at Hendon and been picked up by Russian agents and taken to Kinsale House where our daughter was being cared for by Uncle Fred and Malita. It had been a difficult time especially as Masha was there as well. The memories were not enjoyable but they passed the time as the little transport droned on without any stops. In a little over ninety minutes we literally fell out of the sky and bumped to earth at Hendon in North London. I wondered who'd be meeting us this time and hoped it wasn't the Russians.

It was worse than I'd imagined. Saul was there and spirited Molly away before I could say goodbye properly and left me to the tender mercies of Lt Grady who led me, protesting all the way, to a Morris Ten in RN colours chauffeured by an inscrutable WREN. Before he opened the rear door for me I spotted Molly driving off with Saul in what looked like Fleming's battle grey Bentley convertible. This really could be the last time I saw her as Saul's driving skills were only matched by his inability to catch or throw a water polo ball. I was back in the jaws of the machine and had learnt from bitter experience that kicking against the pricks which inhabited it was as futile as trying to squeeze blood from a turnip.

Grady had decided to sit up front and left me alone in the rear having refused to answer any questions. Had Quigley managed to file a report already? I'd just have to wait. We were soon whizzing through Finchley where Saul lived in one of his parents' houses, past Lord's Cricket Ground now requisitioned by the RAF and what looked like a barrage balloon squadron, around Marble Arch, then Hyde Park, and Buckingham Palace. We got stuck in traffic for a while but Grady still wouldn't respond to my questions so I sat back and watched as we crawled along Petty France then into Broadway before pulling up outside No 54. So it wasn't the Soviet Embassy this time. Grady let me out and wordlessly escorted me to the doorway of an ugly building which towered at least ten stories above. On the right of the entrance was a brass plaque with the words "Minimax Fire Extinguisher Company". I'd never been here before but knew very well who inhabited this pile. It was the London HQ of the Secret Intelligence Service.

I had to wait while Grady registered us then, as the lift was out of order, we trudged up several flights of stairs until we were high enough to see over the roof tops of the surrounding buildings. We had left the ornate sandstone façade and were on the final level of a three storey warren comprising dormer rooms built into the roof space. We hadn't met anyone on the stairs but there was a hum about the building and, as we passed a series of cheap doors in the narrow dingy corridors, I was aware of voices inside. Finally we stopped at the end of a corridor with a hand written sign which read Section VX. Grady opened the door. So, I wasn't going to a dungeon and, if I was to endure some interrogation, at least it would be in a room with a view. I walked in and dropped my bag. In the distance I caught a glimpse of Westminster Abbey and in the corner there was someone whose face I wouldn't forget.

Grady spoke to him. 'Good afternoon, Kim. Here's the package, as promised by Fleming.' He smiled at me. 'Renouf, this is Mr Philby. He has some questions for you.'

Philby stood up and offered his hand. 'Good to see you again, Jack.' He turned to Grady, 'Thank you Bernard but Renouf and I have met before. I'm sure he remembers. He taught my shoes how to dance.'

I had danced in Philby's shoes, after he was bullied into swapping them by Litzi, his estranged and flamboyant wife, who'd taken a shine to me but didn't want the Soviet Embassy's floor scarred by my army boots. Later, I'd been forced to wear a pair of Fleming's shoes and one of his dress suits during an evening which would live long in my memory. Saul and I had been ordered to meet Fleming at the Soviet Embassy in Kensington, ostensibly to celebrate the anniversary of their October Revolution but, on the way, our taxi had crashed into an Elephant on holiday from the zoo. I'd been introduced to Mayskiy, the ambassador, an old acquaintance of Uncle Fred, who seemed to know rather too much about my family and our affairs. I'd met, his niece, the widow Masha, danced with her at the Café de Paris while avoiding the clutches of Litzi and escaped from a Russian limousine, outside Madame Tussauds waxworks just before it was bombed by the Luftwaffe. I'd met Philby since then at S.O.E. headquarters in Baker Street where he was running the Iberian desk and in charge of our venture into Portugal and Spain.

Grady's face was a picture of confusion so I couldn't resist adding some more. 'How's Litzi, Mr Philby? I hope she's still living life to the full.'

He laughed. 'She's fine, Jack. I'll give her your regards next time I see her. Now sit down both of you. We've a lot to get through but first some coffee.'

He picked up his telephone and ordered some. While we waited I rehearsed again the elements of my story which I didn't want recorded. Philby handed Grady a clipboard and some pens. It was the sort of coffee that Willie would have spat out or emptied into the nearest pot plant but there weren't any in this bare utilitarian space. At least it was warm and slaked my thirst. I studied Philby while sipping it as he was reading some notes on his desk. I knew he was friendly with Fleming and, though a few years younger, shared his enjoyment of the unrationed things in life, especially women. He was also friendly with Uncle Fred and the Soviets were our allies, for the moment. Here we were at the heart of MI6 and this suave gentleman, another product of the English public school system, was about to extract as much information out of me as he could but for whom? If it was to persuade the War Office that invading the Channel Islands would be a costly error or to convince Stalin that it would be useful for the Soviet Union, then my answers would be the same. Perhaps there would be no harm in slanting my report to convey that message and suggest that the islands were sufficiently secure not to cause Hitler any concerns or force him to weaken his forces on the Russian Front.

Philby looked up from his notes and smiled. 'Right, let me make it clear that whatever you have discovered about German fortifications, plans and general preparations there is no conceivable need to attempt an invasion. Even if there was only a platoon of geriatric Germans on each island and we could capture them with a troop of boy scouts it would be pointless because of their proximity to artillery on the French coast. So, let's set that aside. Of course, Winston will continue with his S.O.E. pinpricks in France but I want to look at the bigger picture. Tell me everything you know about *Standartenführer* Rudi Kempler and his half-sister; Caroline isn't it?'

I hoped I had better control of my face than Grady and nodded.

'Fergus will be submitting his report though I understand that he isn't entirely happy with the outcome of *Lochaber* though I'm sure he'll find a use for his two Irish agents. Far more important is the information you obtained about Kempler's business activities but, for now, we will leave those on file.' He sat back in his chair and fiddled with a pen for a few moments. 'How would you feel about reacquainting yourself with Kempler in the future when the time is right for us to exert the right level of pressure?'

I considered my response for rather too long.

'Well? What's your answer?'

I shrugged. 'I'll follow orders but I must be honest and tell you that my preference would be to kill him rather than play games.'

He nodded, sighed heavily. 'Thanks for your honesty and while I would agree with your sentiment and have no doubt, given your record, that you could eliminate him, we would be foolish to shut off the route he could provide to the heart of the Nazi machine.' He got up and walked to the window, turning his back on us. The silence was unnerving though I could hear Grady breathing next to me. After what seemed like an eternity, he turned around silhouetted now by the brightness outside. 'Lieutenant Grady, please leave us for a moment. I will call when I need you again.'

Grady seemed about to protest but there was something in Philby's tone which suggested it would be futile so he uncrossed his legs, placed the clipboard and pens on the desk and left the room. Philby sat down in the chair Grady had vacated and pulled himself closer to me. He was a handsome brute, his hands were carefully manicured and his curly hair free of Brylcreem. His mouth was generous and he exuded a patrician confidence that even Fleming would struggle to match. His eyes were deep-set and, in the light from the window, a sparkling blue. He searched mine with them then, without breaking contact, pulled a pipe from his jacket pocket and went through the pantomime of filling and lighting it without speaking. After the first deep inhalation he smiled and nodded. 'I have heard much about you from your uncle and he believes that, even though you do not share his understanding of the world, you have an innate humanity and sense of fairness. You think for yourself and, despite what you said earlier, will not blindly follow orders. You have had a very difficult war so far and all I can promise is that it is not going to get any easier. We know about Caroline and the child which is almost certainly yours and...' He waved away my attempted interruption, 'understand the threat Kempler poses to your family. Yes, killing him would protect them and a month ago we might have encouraged you to do so but everything has changed. Jack, this war can't be won on the battlefield alone. Hitler's made a big mistake but the Russians will need a lot of luck to stop him. What I'm about to tell you must not be repeated though your friend, Saul, knows some of it. Can I trust you with this information?'

I waved away a cloud of his rich tobacco smoke

which at least mitigated his rather potent cologne before I responded, trying to sound more in control that I felt. 'You have a choice, Mr Philby. If you don't believe you can trust me, then bring Grady back in. There's nothing I can sign which will guarantee it and swearing on a bible is pointless. All I can give you is my word that beating Germany and freeing my island is my prime concern. I'm not really interested in politics but I do believe in democracy. I'm no socialist and certainly no *communist* but I will fight alongside anyone who wants to see fascism destroyed. I hope that doesn't sound too naïve.'

He laughed and spluttered as he swallowed smoke he was trying to exhale. 'Innocent yes; but not naïve. You're a farmer's son from an isolated island. You led a protected life until Hitler arrived. You've examined the intellectual arguments and concluded that the "people" can be trusted to vote sensibly. I understand but don't agree. What was it that Churchill said? "The best argument against democracy is a five minute conversation with the average voter."'

I remembered the school debate in which I'd argued and won against communism and fascism. It seemed years ago now but I'd seen or heard nothing which had changed my mind in the interval so I stared into his mocking eyes. "Yes, he did say that, "democracy was the worst form of government..." but concluded that sentence with "...except all the others that have been tried."'

'Touché and I suppose you have a view on dialectical materialism as well. Amusing though it might be to discuss these weighty matters, at present, our views are irrelevant; but answer this. Would you actively work to subvert democracy?'

Where was this going? 'What do you mean?'

He got up, returned to his desk, and fished some papers out of a drawer. He slid a sheet across to me. 'This is an extract from the latest Gallup Poll from America. These take place every month and the same questions are asked.' He waved a sheaf of papers at me. 'This is the important one though.'

I scanned the document:

"NINETEEN HUNDRED AND FORTY-ONE 289

JULY 20: EUROPEAN WAR

Interviewing Date 6/26-7/1/41

Survey #240-K Question #2

If you were asked to vote today on the question of the United States entering the war now against Germany and Italy, how would you vote—to go into the war now or to stay out of the war?

Go in.............................. 21%

Stay out.......................... 79'

'What do you think?'

'That's disturbing. I thought that Churchill and Roosevelt were working closely together.'

'They are but the great American *democracy* seems unconvinced but that's the current position.' He handed over another sheet. 'This is a summary of recent polls. There are lots of questions and the responses are analysed by region and other demographics but just focus on the main question about going in or staying out.'

The first was from July 1940 and the number for "staying out" was 88%. This gradually reduced until the current figure of 79% which still meant that only one fifth of Americans wanted to fight fascism with us. It was disappointing and this must have shown on my face.

'It is an improvement but you're right, it will take a long time to swing public opinion behind Roosevelt. Quite frankly, without America, there is a very good chance that Hitler will finish off the Soviet Union then crush us.' He let that sink in before continuing in almost a whisper. 'Now, this is what I shouldn't be telling you. Fleming has been over to New York recently and will be going again soon. We have nearly one thousand agents operating illegally over there to fight off about the same number of Germans who are desperate to keep America out. Russia is not popular in the USA so the burden is being shouldered by us. You bumped into Kempler in Portugal so you must be aware that there is an undercover war being fought in most of the neutral countries; principally in Europe to keep them out of Germany's hands — especially in Turkey. None of them are real democracies so, in a way, using bribery is far simpler than persuading public opinion and—'

'This is fascinating but why are you telling me if it is such a secret?'

He laid down his pipe, put his elbows on his desk, and rested his chin in his hands. 'Because we want you and Saul to go to America and help our effort.'

'How? What can the two of us do?'

'Saul has many connections in California through his family. He may even have told you. He's certainly shared some of the Hollywood jokes with me...no I didn't find them particularly amusing either but that region has the least favourable response to the important poll question.'

'I still don't see how I could be of use.'

'I'm not going to explain that now. We have experts who will brief you and make the arrangements. If you agree then, when we've finished here, you will be taken to the American Embassy in Grosvenor Square to meet with Brian Avery where we had planned to send you before Fleming was seduced into *Operation Ruthless*.' He sat back and picked up his still smouldering pipe. 'What do you say?'

'What will happen if I don't agree?'

He shrugged and shook his head. 'I suppose you will continue to "set Europe ablaze", kill Germans and collaborators, try to get back to your bloody island, get caught, and spill your guts to the Gestapo. All very worthwhile I suppose but...' he shuffled the papers together then laid them out like playing cards on his desk then pointed to one, 'there's one piece of information I have omitted which you might find of value.'

'That is?'

He held up the sheet so that I could see it. Underneath the "Secret" red stamp was an individual's biography which was difficult to read from this distance but the photograph was clear. 'Of course you recognise him. He's going to America as well but not on our side. Does that help?'

I stood up, took the sheet and stared at the image. 'Can I kill him?'

'Only if your life is in immediate danger. *Standarten-führer* Kempler could be of great help if you manage him correctly.'

'Will he try to kill me?'

'Undoubtedly, but this mission is of paramount importance — if you truly do believe in democracy.'

He moved around the desk and, as I handed the sheet back, I looked down at his beautifully crafted footwear, polished to a shine which would pass any regimental sergeant major's inspection. I offered my right hand and, as we shook, I said. 'I'll need a new pair of shoes.'

He glanced at mine and chortled. 'You're not wrong but you can't have these. He reached into his pocket, extracted a card and scribbled something on it. 'Here, take this to Hawes and Curtis in Jermyn Street tomorrow. Speak to Mr Collins. Tell him it's a rush job.'

'Where am I going and when?'

'Avery will give you that information but I believe you have to be in Scapa Flow by next Saturday and the real Royal Navy will expect you to look like an officer so, until then, spend your time wisely but remember, Sub-lieutenant Renouf, it's America first.'

Operation Ruthless (October 1940)

The plan was that the German bomber would follow on behind aircraft returning from a night bombing raid. When crossing the middle of the English Channel, it would cut one engine and lose height with smoke pouring from a 'candle' in the tail, send out a SOS distress signal and then ditch in the sea. The crew would then take to a rubber dinghy, having ensured that the bomber sank before the Germans could identify it, and wait to be rescued by a German naval vessel. When on board the 'survivors' would then kill the German crew, and hijack the ship, thus obtaining the new month's codes to help Alan Turing with Enigma decryption at Bletchley Park

A Heinkel 111 was available for this operation. The aircraft, Werk Nr. 6853, had been captured in airworthy condition after being operated by the German bomber unit, Kampfgeschwader 26. On 9th February 1940, it had made a forced landing after being damaged by a Spitfire over the Firth of Forth. It was subsequently assigned the Royal Air Force serial number AW177 and flown by the RAF's Air Fighting Development Unit and 1426 Flight.

Fleming had proposed himself as one of the crew but, as someone who knew about Bletchley Park, he could not be placed at risk of being captured. The aircraft was prepared with an aircrew of German-speaking Englishmen.

Fleming took his team to Dover to await the next suitable bombing raid, but aerial reconnaissance and wireless telegraphy monitoring failed to find any suitable German vessels. Wiser heads also decided that it would take the bomber too long to sink thus exposing its crew to discovery so the operation was called off. Alan Turing was very unhappy at this outcome and challenged the decision.

Lieutenant-Commander RNVR (SB) Ian Lancaster Fleming (1908-1964)

Details of his activities at the heart of the British war effort only started to emerge in the late 1990s long after he had become famous as the author of the James Bond series. There is no doubt that he played a significant role in clandestine operations throughout the war and many of his plans, such as *Ruthless*, *Goldeneye*, and *Mincemeat* were as imaginative as those he concocted for Mr Bond. Along with Alan Turing, whose decoding exploits helped win the war, he was also a supreme athlete though neither were team players.

Ian was very close to his elder brother, Peter, also a successful author, who enjoyed almost as interesting a war, and some feel provided much of the grit for the fictional James Bond. Ian's youngest brother, Captain Michael Fleming, was an early casualty. Captured while fighting a rear guard action to protect the Dunkirk perimeter he died on 1st October and is buried in Lille cemetery. Ian's younger brother, Richard, was also a captain and was recruited into the Lovat scouts, a commando unit, by brother Peter. The boys' father, Major Valentine Fleming, a personal friend of Winston Churchill, was an MP and had been killed in action during World War One.

Soviet Embassy in London

Like many of his colleagues Ambassador Mayskiy was stunned by Stalin's pact with Hitler but they all knew better than to challenge it! Stalin and Molotov, his Foreign Minister, had spent considerable time and effort trying to persuade Britain and France to join them in a pact but the Western Democracies dragged their feet to such an extent that he turned instead to Hitler to guarantee his borders while he continued to terrorise his own people.

Mayskiy and Churchill met on several occasions in the embassy in Kensington Palace Gardens before Hitler reneged on his pact. The British had acquired highly detailed plans of Hitler's planned invasion (Operation Barbarossa) but Stalin refused to believe they were genuine and he was still authorising rail shipments of strategic materials to Germany one hour before the surprise attack began at 03:15 on 22nd June 1941.

After this the Germans sacked the Soviet Embassies in Berlin and Paris and discovered a veritable theatre of horrors in the basements. Sound-proofed rooms had been set up by the Soviets as torture chambers along with acid baths and incinerators for the disposal of those they had interrogated. Even the Gestapo were surprised at the efficiency of their Russian counterparts in dealing with dissidents. As Britain never had cause to break into the Embassy we'll never know what "facilities" had been constructed in its basement in the heart of Kensington.

Harold (Kim) Philby (1912-1988)

English public school educated, he was recruited as a communist spy by the Austrian Litzi Friedmann who became his first wife. A friend of Fleming's he moved with ease in the social circles from which the establishment sourced their trusted civil servants. For years before and during the war he passed highly secret information to his handlers. Ironically, during the period of this novel he was in charge of Section VX of the British Secret Intelligence Service responsible for counter espionage! He continued to spy after hostilities were over and was responsible for exposing many Allied agents to his Soviet spymasters. Many of these were captured and tortured in other basements before being executed. After his defection to Russia in 1963 he was granted political asylum, Soviet citizenship, a pension and several medals for his services to the Revolution.

S.O.E. & Setting Europe Ablaze

Churchill set up the Special Operations Executive in July 1940 to strike back at the German occupiers in Europe. Fleming, in his role as Deputy Director of the Naval Intelligence Division, was closely involved. S.O.E. was also known as: "Churchill's Secret Army" or the "Ministry of Ungentlemanly Warfare". By 1945 the organisation directly employed or controlled more than 13,000 people, about 3,200 of whom were women. Of these only about 600 or so had served as field agents in Europe facing imprisonment, torture, and execution if caught. Twenty-five survived prison, 117 died in action, twelve were executed, and three died of natural causes. As S.O.E. was seen as a bastard child by MI6 there were inevitable tensions between the two organisations which did cause complications in some operations.

Helford Inshore Patrol Flotilla

The Helford River had been a smuggler's haven in the past and was perfect for the task of inserting agents into France. At its height the Flotilla employed more than a dozen vessels, mainly adapted French fishing boats. As it grew in size the splendid three-masted schooner *Sunbeam II* was moored up Port Navas creek and provided a floating base and accommodation for other ranks. Ridifarne continued to be used as the officer's HQ. S.O.E. had a separate base close by at Pedn-Billy in Bar Road. A second base was set up between Tresco and Bryher in the Isles of Scilly and a special high powered disguised fishing boat was built for the run to France. The fifty-five foot M.F.V 2023 a.k.a. *L'Angele-Rouge*, had a high speed shallow draught hull and a French fishing-boat superstructure. It was powered by two 500 hp Hall Scott engines and could run at 28 knots! This base was kept secret after the war and only revealed under the fifty year rule in 1995. Details of the Helford base were also suppressed but, as it was more obvious to the locals, rumours about it were in circulation long before it was officially recognised.

Occupation of the Channel Islands

After bombing Jersey and Guernsey on 28th June 1940, the Germans occupied the islands from 1st July 1940 until 9th May 1945. Prior to their invasion over 6,000 residents had evacuated from Jersey to the UK leaving a serious shortage of labour. Seasonal workers from Brittany and Normandy were no longer available so the island authorities imported 500 volunteers from Eire who were only too pleased to find employment. These neutral Irish were trapped during the occupation but were not subject to the same curfew or rationing restrictions as the locals. The Germans found them rather a handful, as they tended to enjoy a craic as often as possible and were frequently in trouble for fighting and drunkenness. However, they would work on fortifications which, under the Geneva Convention, the islanders could not be forced to undertake. Many did though and the Germans paid tradesmen well above the going rate.

There were many attempts, mostly unsuccessful, to insert commandos and other raiding parties onto Jersey. After the D-Day landings the islands were cut off from France and their populations, including the occupiers, suffered considerable deprivation until they were liberated nearly one year later. During the period of this novel, the Germans are consolidating their positions and building serious fortifications as, after the invasion of Russia, Hitler decided that he would never surrender the only British possessions he ever managed to conquer. Stalin did put pressure on Churchill to attempt to recover the islands and it was seriously considered. Later in the war *Operation Constellation* was devised for a combined American and British assault which would have caused substantial civilian casualties but more of that in a later novel!

In reality, Hitler was so obsessed that he diverted massive military resources to defend his island fortresses so that on Jersey alone by 1945 there were over 10,000 troops to guard a population of 30,000 in an area of only forty-five square miles encased in more reinforced concrete than the whole Atlantic Wall in France! The final commander he installed was Vice Admiral Friedrich Hüffmeier, an ardent Nazi, who was instructed to fight to the last man. Fortunately, Hitler committed suicide and, instead of going down with his ship, the admiral surrendered to Force 135 without a shot being fired.

Portugal & Spain

The continued neutrality of the two fascist dictatorships of Spain and Portugal was essential to Britain as there weren't the resources to counter any German invasion should Hitler decide Salazar and Franco were not being sufficiently helpful. Consequently there was much secret movement of gold from Britain and Germany to bribe both dictators. In one attempt to persuade the Spanish to resist Hitler's attempts to move German troops through their country to seize Gibraltar and effectively seal off the Mediterranean, Fleming even made the journey to Madrid himself. Travelling as a civilian wearing a dark-blue suit and Old Etonian tie, he carried a commando fighting-knife and a fountain pen with a cyanide cartridge. He christened this operation "Goldeneye"!

Wolfram & Industrial Diamonds

Those of you who have read **Against The Tide** will be familiar with the role industrial diamonds played in the war and the exorbitant price the Germans were prepared to pay for them. The same applies to **wolframite** which was so named by German miners in the Eighteenth Century as, in its natural form, it is black and hairy like a wolf. Contemporary accounts are quite descriptive with one claiming it "tears away the tin and devours it like a wolf devours a sheep". It was so important to the Germans that its price soared from just over $1,100 in 1940 to over $20,000 per ton by late 1941. Portugal, under the fascist dictatorship of Dr. Antonio Salazar, reaped enormous profit from this even though much of it was creamed off through corruption before it reached his coffers.

Neutral trade

Sweden, Switzerland, Eire, Portugal and Spain remained neutral throughout the war and continued to supply strategic materials to the combatants. Ships were brightly painted and well lit at night.

There were a total of fifty-six Irish ships in September 1939. Fifteen more were purchased or leased in the conflict, and sixteen were lost. The Arklow schooner *Cymric,* which featured in **Diamonds For The Wolf,** was real and had been converted to a Q ship by the Royal Navy during World War One. Her task was to lure a U-boat to the surface run out her concealed guns and sink it. Despite exaggerated claims, she had no success in this role though she did mistake J6, a surfaced British submarine, for the Kriegsmarine's U6 outside of Blythe. She fired at her killing the sailor who had been signalling about the mistake then pursued her until she was sunk with the loss of fourteen lives. An order under the Official Secrets Act prohibited mention of this incident until 1969.

During WW2 *Cymric* was charted to travel to Portugal to collect imported agricultural equipment and fertilisers from America. In November 1939, Roosevelt sig ed the Fourth Neutrality Act forbidding American ships from entering the 'war zone' which was defined as a line drawn from Spain to Iceland. Cargoes intended for Ireland were shipped to Portugal. Setting sail from Ireland, *Cymric* would carry food to the United Kingdom. There she would collect British coal and carry it to

Lisbon, load the awaiting American cargo, and bring it back to Ireland with any other suitable trade goods or contraband to be found.

On 23 February 1944, she left Ardrossan in Scotland where she loaded a cargo of coal for Lisbon. She was sighted off Dublin on the following day – that was her last sighting. No wreckage was ever found. She might have hit a mine, been sunk by a U-Boat, or been driven by a gale into the 'prohibited area' of Bay of Biscay and been attacked and sunk by Allied aircraft enforcing the blockade.

The Arklow schooner, *Irish Lass,* is fictitious but based on *Sunbeam II* which was employed as the H.Q. ship for S.O.E. in Helford and moored up in the creek between the Ferry Boat Inn and Port Navas.

Apart from the Clippers and other flying boats, normal land-based aircraft kept regular services going throughout the war. Initially, the Germans respected the flights from Whitchurch in England to Lisbon in Portugal but as the war progressed there were several attacks. B.O.A.C. flight 777, a Douglas DC-3, was shot down over the Bay of Biscay by eight Luftwaffe fighters on 1st June 1943. All seventeen passengers and crew were killed. Among them was the famous film actor, Leslie Howard. It is believed the Germans suspected that Winston Churchill might have been on-board.

***

If you would like to read more about the background to the novels in the Jack Renouf series please visit my website www.johnfhanley.co.uk

It's July 1939
you're 18 and in love
your father hates you
your uncle is a Communist
your best friend is Jewish
now a Dutchman is
drowning you
in front of 500 witnesses
you're Jack Renouf and
it's time to start swimming

against

the

tide

John F. Hanley

**It's June 1940
you're 19 and still in love
your father still hates you
your uncle is still a Communist
your best friend is still Jewish
Caroline and Rachel are ignoring you
now a German is
dropping bombs on you
you're Jack Renouf
and you're aboard**

It's October 1940
you're 20 and still in love
your home is occupied by the Germans
Caroline is in their hands and
Rachel is trapped in France
your best friend works for Naval Intelligence
his boss is Lieutenant-Commander Ian Fleming
his job is to set Europe ablaze
you've been training as a commando
you know how to start fires
you're Jack Renouf and
you're being sent to rescue the

ABOUT THE AUTHOR

Born in Jersey in 1946, John Hanley trained at the Guildhall School of Music and Drama before teaching in London, Jersey and Cornwall. After a master's degree at Bath University, he returned to Jersey as deputy head of his old school. His first novel, Against The Tide, was published in 2012 and since then The Last Boat, Diamonds For The Wolf, and Irish Lass. He now lives with his wife and family in Cornwall.

In a BBC radio interview he explained why he wrote **Against The Tide** and **The Last Boat.**

'I grew up in Jersey surrounded by the artefacts of the German Occupation. My mother lived through it and every adult I knew had a story to tell. Through extreme good fortune my mother avoided the fate of several islanders when the Germans bombed and strafed the harbour on Friday 28th June 1940.

During the summer evenings she always walked with her mother and a married couple from across the road to the harbour after their tea. That evening she had a stomach ache and only the married couple went. The husband was killed and, as the four of them usually kept together, it is more than possible that my mother and grandmother might not have survived.

Because of this I've always had a strong affinity with that period and an urge to relive it through the eyes of a young man who would have been my mother's age at the time. I wanted to experience what it must have been like to cope with all that was thrown at the hapless islanders after the British government abandoned them to the less than tender mercies of the Germans.

I'd already written **The Last Boat** before **Against The Tide** was published and have planned a series which follows the main characters through the war years. It took somewhat longer than planned to write the third, **Diamonds For The Wolf** and now Jack and company have dragged me through another adventure, **Irish Lass** which I hope you will enjoy.

Printed in Great Britain
by Amazon

42317571R00212